THE LOST KING

By Daniel Fansler

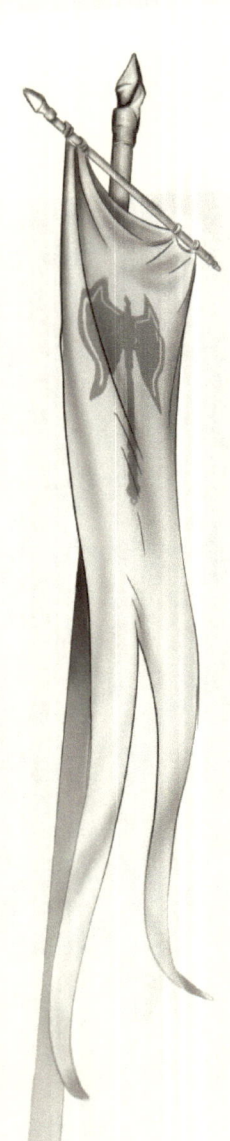
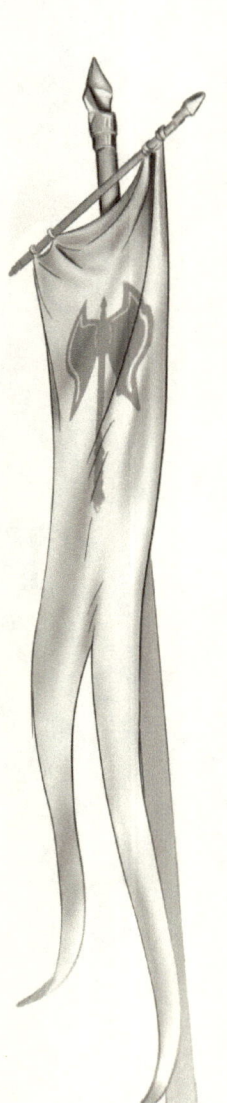

THE

LOST

KING

First Paperback Edition, October 2019

ISBN 978-1-7341325-0-2

Map by Daniel Fansler

Title Page illustration by k_olser

Book Design by Bobooks

Visit www.danielfansler.com

Follow me on Instagram and Tiktok
Instagram: @danielfansler.writer
TikTok: @daniel_saurus_rex

For Pap.

Thank you for buying this book, dear reader! As an indie author, I appreciate each and every one of you for supporting me. The best way to support an indie author, aside from buying and reading their book, is by leaving a review on Amazon and/or Goodreads! If you like this book, I would appreciate it so much if you took the time to do so. Thanks!

TABLE OF CONTENTS

ACKNOWLEDGEMENTS

I want to thank everyone who made this book possible. Thank you to my beta readers, Kelley Schorn, Andrea Sanchez, and Anthony Nguyen who have read this book since its initial drafts back in 2014 when we were back in high school and to Lauren Reagan for giving it a final proofread. Thank you to my mom for always encouraging me to follow my dream of being a writer. Thank you to my beautiful wife, Ellen, who supports me in everything I do and encouraged me to follow through with self-publication. And finally, thank you especially to my dad, Darin Fansler, without whom this book would not be possible (most likely, it would still be drifting away in the lonely abyss that is the query whirlpool authors have to typically get through when they're looking for an agent).

Without my dad, the idea for self-publication, the investment, as well as the encouragement that what I have written is something people might actually come to enjoy would not have existed. I will forever be grateful to him for helping my dreams come true.

The Lost King has been a work in the making since 2013. It's been six long years of revisions, re-readings, rewritings, concept planning, map drawings, etc. It's been a lot of work. Aside from *The Lord of the Rings* and *The Hobbit*, I've never encountered any novel that has had a focused story with dwarves as the main protagonists. Dwarves are underappreciated, I thought. So I created one. This is the result. I hope you enjoy this world, its characters, its adventures, its battles, its triumphs as well as its tragedies. Now, without further ado, I welcome you to the world of Azar.

READ WHAT PEOPLE HAVE BEEN SAYING ABOUT *THE LOST KING*

"Daniel Fansler's debut novel is a sprawling adventure in the Tolkien tradition with satisfying new twists to keep the journey fresh. It starts with palace intrigue and then tosses readers into an underground world of sword and sorcery sure to keep them hooked . . . readers will want to follow this band of warriors for pages to come."

- John McDermott, Author of *The Idea of God in Tennessee*

"Thuradin's journey to find his king explores the ideas of courage, loyalty, and what it truly means to be a leader."

--Kelley Schorn, Author of *Year 01*

"In *The Lost King*, Fansler takes the trope of the hero's journey and turns it on its head . . . every adversary is humanized . . . Fans of worldbuilding will delight as he makes the everyday new and puts the fantastic within reach."

--Lauren Jeter, author of "Lizard Light," *2020 Crab Creek Review Poetry Prize* semifinalist

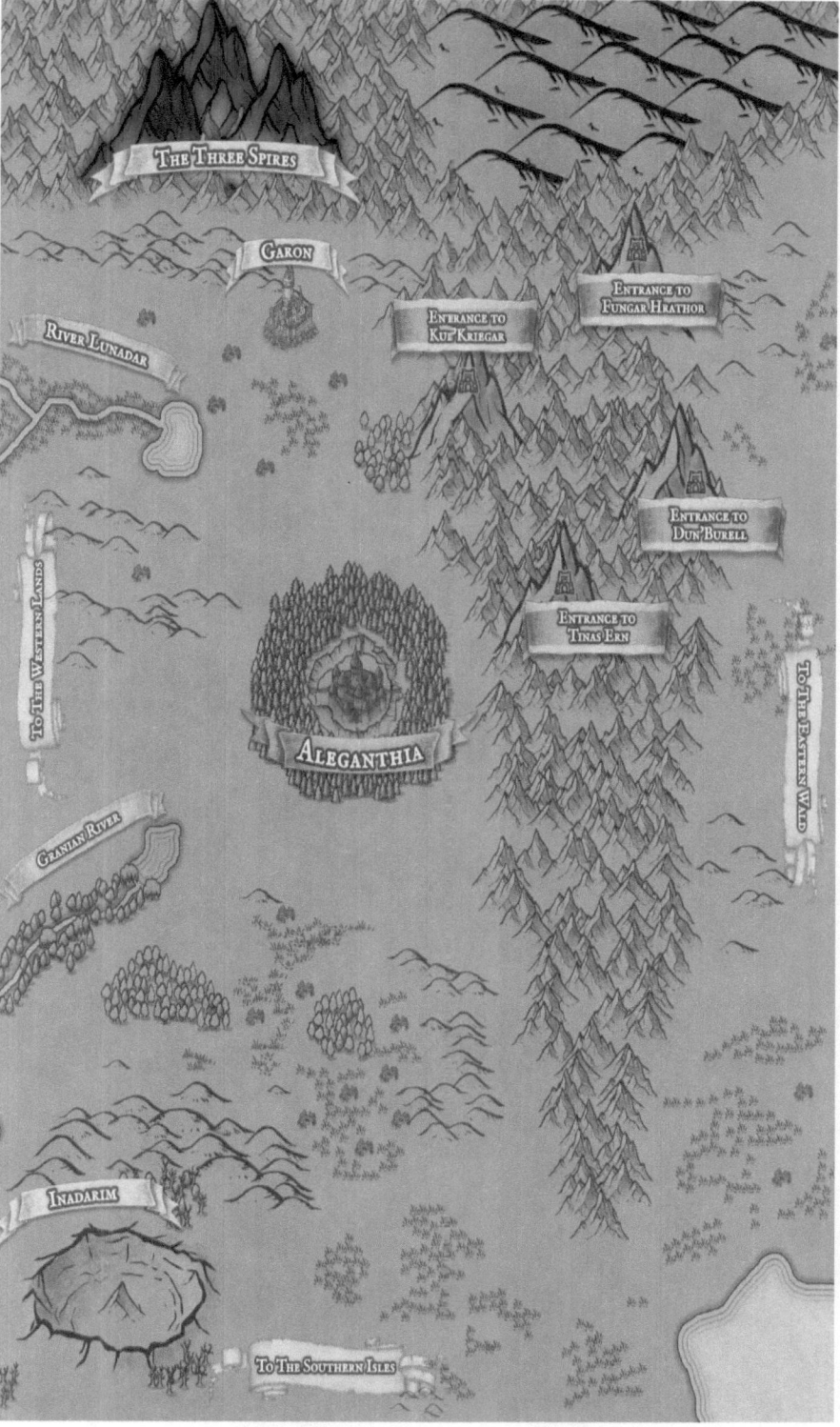

CHAPTER ONE

A dark figure darted between thick, stone pillars and large, beautifully carved statues, moving from one shadow to the next as he made his way through the halls of the dwarven King's palace. The torches fixed to the thick walls and the braziers scattered throughout presented little challenge for him as he continued moving past patrolling guards without being seen. And he would remain unseen. Morteth Shadowmeld was the best and most notorious assassin in the Dwarven Kingdom, after all. He had a reputation to uphold.

The mission he had was simple enough. He was to poison the personal drinking flask of Thelm Ironaxe—King of the dwarves—as well as his heir, Ronorim Ironaxe, with the ground remains of the lethal bitterskin root stored within one of the vials in his possession.

It was nothing personal. Morteth had no quarrel with the King or his son. His employer, however, did.

It was only a few weeks ago that Thelm had announced he would begin preparations for a campaign against the burrowers—an ancient enemy of the dwarves—to end the war that had been taking place between the two races for as long as anyone could remember. Thelm had always been a popular King, but his recent announcement had infuriated the opposition—those few who sought to bring about a lasting peace between the dwarves and the burrowers without any further bloodshed. The idea of actively campaigning against them now proved too much for these dwarves to remain silent.

As for Ronorim, everyone in the Kingdom knew the heir to the throne possessed a hatred even more intense than his father's for the burrowers. Morteth personally didn't care, but his strategic mind understood assassinating the King only to have him be replaced by his firstborn son would do no good for the opposition. In fact, it might do worse harm than if Thelm were to remain alive. Thelm, at least, knew when to show mercy.

Morteth stopped for a moment and sunk into the shadows as two heavily-armored royal guards marched past, their iron shields slung across their backs and their square-faced hammers resting comfortably over their shoulders. The assassin grimaced as he watched them round the next corner of the hall and disappear.

His chances of success were slim, especially with two high-profile targets. Morteth might be the best assassin in the Dwarven Kingdom, but those of the royal family were the most heavily guarded dwarves. This made them a rather difficult target. Despite this complication, the plan for the assassination was surprisingly simple. But the more he thought about it, the more he disliked it. It wasn't the simplicity that he had a problem with, though. It was the fact that his employer had a role.

He was in charge of giving the signal, which was necessary for Morteth to know when it was clear for him to sneak into the King's quarters and plant the poison, and then from there he would have to judge on his own when to move on to Ronorim's room.

Having to rely on an inside man always made Morteth nervous. Inside men had a tendency to get cold feet—which usually meant the job ended with the assassin's capture. He had seen many of his colleagues get thrown into inescapable prisons or exiled because of this. He hoped his employer wasn't this type of inside man, because he most certainly wasn't the type of dwarf who thought imprisonment would be a perfect, tidy end for his career.

Without hesitation, Morteth crept out of the shadows and ran lightly down the hall until the wall to his left turned into a balcony. He leaped over the stone railing and landed right into the shadowy corner recommended to him by his employer.

They had gone over the plan several days ago. His employer had brought a map of the palace, pointing out several locations that would give good cover while he waited for the signal. Morteth had also been told where the guards patrolled, how many there were, and everything else that had to do with the palace's security.

With a wall to his left and rear, and a tall staircase to his right, the location was more-or-less secure. Morteth crept forward carefully until he was at the very edge of the wall to his left. He was more exposed here. All it would take was a guard on patrol to look down from the balcony he had just jumped from and he would be discovered; but the risk was necessary in order to see the signal.

Morteth peeked around the corner and quickly took in the details.

The room the signal would come from was diagonally across from him and close enough to see inside. Light blazed from within, illuminating the features of the royal Ironaxe family. There was Thelm with his snow-white beard and rugged face. Ronorim Ironaxe stood next to him. His light brown beard hung all the way down to his waist, and he glared with eyes full of distaste at the other royal in the room, who Morteth recognized to be Ronorim's younger brother, Dunkell, despite the young prince's back facing him. He recognized his dark hair and the two braids that protruded to the side from his short beard.

Along with the royal family stood many more royal guards—Morteth counted seven—as armored and ready to fight as the royals themselves. Two more guards stood outside in front of the doorway. Had they been more attentive, they might have noticed the nearby assassin peeking around the corner. However, never speculating an attack could ever occur within the palace, the guards instead stared at the wall in front of them with dazed expressions.

Inside the room an argument was taking place, and Morteth was close enough to hear it.

"We cannae just go around killing all the burrowers we encounter," Dunkell's voice echoed through the stone halls. "They're barbaric now, but they can become civilized. All they need is a wee push from us."

"Aye, but we can," Ronorim's clear voice drowned out any surviving echoes from Dunkell's statement. "For far too long we've been troubled by those barbarians. Every time we encounter them it turns inta a bloodfest. What we cannae do, brother, is allow the dwarves in Dun'Burell, our borderlands, ta suffer from these burrowers any longer!"

Morteth chanced another peek and saw Dunkell standing nose to nose with his brother. It looked as if the two princes were ready to throw punches when a deep, gruff voice spoke.

"Stop it, boys. Ye both have some truths in yer arguments."

Thelm gripped both of his sons by their shoulders and forced them apart. He walked between them and turned to address Dunkell, who Morteth could now see fully.

"Dunkell, whether ye like it or nae, I'm pushing forward with this campaign. Ronorim is right. The dwarves of Dun'Burell live right next to the burrower caverns. They have to deal with their constant raids. They suffer every day at the hands of those savages and I will nae allow it any longer, so long as I am King."

Morteth thought he could see Dunkell frown disapprovingly. "Father, we cannae exterminate an entire race because of the paranoid idea that they might one day do that ta us. If we do this, we're no better than what we think they are!"

"Now, now, ye know I don't intend ta drive the burrowers ta extinction. Yer brother knows this as well, despite how much he fantasizes me doing otherwise. I only wish ta kill enough of them so that they no longer have the will ta fight against us." Thelm sighed and stroked his beard slowly, thinking. "I am the King, however. It is my responsibility ta protect and ensure the safety and happiness of our people. And if, in the end, that means I must completely wipe them out, then so be it."

"But Father—" now Ronorim was speaking, "—if we are ta campaign against them, then we might as well finish the job and not leave it only half complete. The burrowers breed like rats. If we leave only a handful alive, then they'll multiply and we'll have ta do this again and again until everyone grows tired of it. All the soldiers we'll lose on this campaign will have died for nothing."

Dunkell's fist flew through the air, knocking Ronorim to

the ground. The brothers clawed at each other's beards and the fight quickly turned into an all-out brawl.

From the narrow view Morteth held, he could see that many of the royal guards inside the room had accidentally joined in the fighting in their attempts to separate the brothers. The two guards standing outside glanced at each other, then went inside. He could only assume that they, too, would be sucked into the fighting.

For a moment, Morteth thought he spotted the King cursing and yanking on the beards of two of his royal guards as they kicked and flailed at his exposed torso. Morteth's gaze shifted over to where Dunkell and Ronorim were fighting. The two princes traded punches, oblivious to the damage they were dealing and receiving. Dunkell dodged a massive swipe from Ronorim and tackled him across the room. They rolled again on the ground, each one trying to gain the upper hand.

The signal.

Immediately, Morteth slid out of his shadowy corner and began walking casually through the hall. His stride didn't falter as he passed the room where the brawl was taking place, and no one inside noticed him.

He walked past several doors down the length of the hall before coming upon the King's room. Inside was an assortment of rich furs, beautifully carved stone furniture, and stacks upon stacks of gold, iron, and silver bars. Tempting as these riches were, Morteth took none of it—he was no petty thief. Plus, they would only slow him down during his escape.

The flask wasn't in plain view, much to his disappointment. If what his informant had told him was true, he had about ten minutes before a guard came in to check the room. He had to find and poison the flask and leave before then. He searched through drawers but only found stacks of paper, piles of clothing, and an assortment of strange looking trinkets whose purpose he couldn't comprehend.

Next was the wardrobe. In it, he found more clothes and the King's armor stand, which was currently just a thin wooden cross. The King had the habit of wearing his armor every waking moment of the day—a large reason why he was such a difficult target for assassination.

Morteth was running out of options and time. He turned to the bed and, careful not to misplace anything, searched through it. There was nothing under the covers, nothing under the mattress, nothing hidden in the overhanging curtains.

Frustrated, he jumped on the bed, trying to think of where the King might hide his flask. Several of the pillows fell to the floor as he jumped, revealing more of the King's personal treasures. Excited by this discovery, Morteth looked through the items with hungry eyes, and he soon found what he was looking for. Along with several more gold bars was a small tin flask—a drinking flask. He picked it up and stared at it thoughtfully. It was a simple design as far as he could tell, with only a few engravings circling the middle area. Based on what he could hear when he sloshed it around, it was half empty. Perfect.

He opened the flask, careful not to spill. The opening was barely big enough for him to fit his stubby pinky inside. He grabbed the vial containing the ground bitterskin root and dropped the contents inside.

A soft sizzling sound came from the flask as the poisonous herb corrupted the alcohol. The change would not be discovered until it was too late. The King would never believe someone could have the audacity to poison his personal drinking flask, and because of that, he would never properly check. The King was as good as dead.

Feeling satisfied, Morteth placed everything back where he found it until the room looked like no one had set foot in it in the first place. He turned to the door, but instead of opening it right away, he put his large, hairy ear against the wooden beams.

The sound of footsteps was coming his way. There was no telling if they would continue on or if the dwarves on the other side would enter the room. Either way, he was not going to risk being caught in the open like this.

Calmly, he placed himself against the wall next to the door and wrapped his gray cloak around his body. The cloak was woven to provide light camouflage in dark areas like the one he was in now, but it would be useless if someone were to look directly at him. He could only hope that, should anyone enter, they wouldn't look around too thoroughly.

Only seconds after Morteth finished situating himself, the door burst open and two dwarves entered. The assassin parted his cloak just enough to see who it was and was surprised to see Thelm and Ronorim Ironaxe. Of all the dwarves who could have stepped into the room, they were the ones he least wished for.

Ronorim had bruises forming on several parts of his face, and Thelm had a small cut on his forehead that was bleeding substantially. Despite this, the two were discussing the brawl that had happened in the other room quite cheerfully.

"—Aye, it was fun, but ye cannae go around striking yer brother every time he hits ye first," Thelm admonished with a chuckle.

"That's nae entirely fair, ye know," Ronorim grumbled.

Morteth watched Thelm dig around under his pillows and pull out the poisoned flask. His eyes widened. If he drank from it now, the King would die, and the commotion his death would cause would make escape for Morteth difficult and Ronorim's assassination impossible. The palace would be swarming with royal guards within minutes. Even if he chose to continue with his mission, there was no guarantee now that his efforts could bring about Ronorim's death, and he would be captured for nothing. No, there was nothing else he could do. He had to leave now, before Thelm consumed the fatal drink.

The door had been left slightly ajar. As stealthily as he could, Morteth opened it as wide as he dared without being noticed. He swiftly pulled himself outside into the hall and jumped into the nearest shadow. There he waited for several minutes to see if either of the two dwarves inside had noticed his exit.

Convinced he had gone unnoticed, Morteth lifted himself from his crouched position and prepared to make his escape. He had only taken a few steps, however, when a loud wail came from inside the King's room.

Morteth cursed softly.

He was too close to the scene. Escaping through the halls as he had been about to do would be impossible; the guards would suspect him right away.

Instinct took over.

Quickly, he undid the ties of his cloak and threw it into one of the shadows. Now he was fully exposed. His black and gray leather armor might look suspicious, but he hoped it would go unnoticed for what he was about to do.

Without giving himself time to think or realize how bad

of an idea this was, Morteth rushed back into the King's room with a look of bewilderment. He saw the King lying in Ronorim's arms, a sickly yellow foam escaping his mouth. His eyes bulged. His body shook and convulsed as he tried to fight the poison. Ronorim, holding his dying father close to him, looked up at Morteth, his eyes wide with fury.

"Get an *Enurg'en!* Now!" he yelled as he struggled to keep his elderly father from moving too much.

Morteth nodded and ran out of the room and down the hall he had come from. Guards streamed from everywhere as they noticed the loud cries coming from the King's room. A few cast a suspicious glance his way but otherwise left him alone.

Morteth allowed himself a small smile. His desperate plan had worked. Ronorim, distraught by what was happening to his father, hadn't even thought to suspect him as the assassin and had sent him to get a healer—a healer who would never come. The guards, seeing him come from the King's room, might have suspected him, but they would check to see what the problem was first before they put the pieces together and chased after him, and by then, he would be long gone.

Thankfully, his employer had gone over how he should escape if something were to go wrong. Secret passages ran underneath the King's palace which led to the outskirts of the city of Tinas Gran. He would have to take these passages and then, once he was out of the palace, he would make his way out of the city. But first he had to reach the entrance to one of these passages without being seen. He had no doubt that if he were caught, he would be executed.

He ran through the stone halls and bounded up the stairways without any care for caution. Time was the enemy now.

Morteth found the specific hall his employer had shown him and began looking for the two dwarven statues that marked the entrance. Luckily, they weren't too difficult to find.

The two carved dwarves gazed straight ahead, double-bladed axes held high into the air, as if cheering. Morteth began pushing one of them to the side. Behind it would be a narrow stairway that would take him down into the underground passages. But he had only begun to push the statue when he heard heavy footsteps coming from nearby.

He cursed. Without his cloak, Morteth was more exposed and couldn't hide as easily. But he still had to try. Anything would be better than simply standing there.

He made his way to one of the burning braziers set against the wall and hid behind it, doing his best to ignore the immense heat that now threatened to burn his bushy eyebrows. The light would illuminate him, but the glare from the fire contrasting with the naturally dark halls of the palace might be enough to keep him out of the dwarves' peripherals should they pass him.

The footsteps grew louder as the dwarves who owned them drew nearer. Morteth watched the first two pass by. They glanced around swiftly but the glare from the brazier seemed to be doing the trick.

They moved on into the next hallway but Morteth stayed where he was. He sensed someone else nearby, and any movement now would give away his position. He watched as the dwarf he hoped was the last guard passed.

His body tensed as he recognized who this particular guard was: Thuradin Stonebeard, commander of the royal guard.

There was no mistaking the long beard—separated into three individual braids with three golden rings encircling each one in different sections—that nearly touched his booted feet. The famous saphyrium helm covered his entire face except for the Y-shaped slit that allowed his eyes, nose, and mouth to be seen. Near the top, two separate wing-like growths sprouted on either side of the helmet, and, in between those wings, at the center, a light-blue sapphire glinted under the nearby brazier's light.

Thuradin appeared elderly—his beard was graying—but that didn't encourage Morteth in the slightest. Thuradin wasn't commander of the royal guard for nothing. This particular warrior had pushed through hundreds of battles, several of which had started out as lost causes, and had managed to turn most of them into decisive victories. There was a rumor that none within the Dwarven Kingdom matched his prowess in battle, not even the King who Morteth had just assassinated.

He watched as Thuradin stopped in his tracks, his gaze fixed on the slightly out-of-place statue and the half-revealed entrance.

"Orm! Garoth! Come back. I need ye both ta go and stand guard somewhere else."

Thuradin ran down the hall and turned the corner. Warrior that he was, he, too, failed to notice the assassin hiding behind the brazier next to him.

Morteth let out the shaky breath he'd been holding as he watched Thuradin disappear and returned to pushing the dwarven statue aside. Eventually, he pushed it far enough to slide through the entrance without difficulty.

There were no lights as he descended into the underground passages, but Morteth had memorized which routes to take and the distances of each. He would have no difficulties navigating his way through the dark.

Keeping one hand on the wall and the other outstretched, he walked forward with care as he counted his steps. He didn't know how long he traveled like this, but he was glad when he saw the small circular light ahead that marked the exit. He abandoned his reliance on the wall and walked freely toward it with a quickened pace.

It was lucky that Morteth was naturally light on his feet, or the two guards outside would have heard him approaching before he saw them.

Morteth immediately stopped moving and assessed the situation. They were the two guards who had passed him earlier. Did that mean Thuradin was nearby? Probably not. This wasn't the only exit from the underground passages. Based on what he knew about the commander, Thuradin would have set up guards on every exit as soon as he could, riding his mount from exit to exit to make sure everything was in order. Chances were good that the commander was on the other side of the cavern, checking on an exit Morteth would never emerge from.

Grinning, the assassin took out the two daggers he kept sheathed in his boots and crept slowly and carefully to where the dwarves stood guard. They were a few paces away from the mouth of the exit. He would have to be quick if he wanted to take them both out.

They were deep in conversation as Morteth snuck in from the side. Simultaneously, they turned when they noticed something moving in their peripherals, but it was already too late.

The first guard slumped to the ground as Morteth slid his dagger across his throat. The second managed to parry

Morteth's first attack with his axe but fell as the assassin ducked down and dealt a blow from below.

Morteth breathed deeply as he surveyed the scene. The first guard lay with blood streaming from his open wound, his gurgling growing weaker with each passing second. The second lay still, already stiffening.

He stayed until the first guard died, making sure no others were in the area waiting for him. Satisfied, he turned to leave. After one last glance back at the dwarves he had just slain, he ran from the royal palace, disappearing into the shadows. His work was done.

CHAPTER TWO

"After today, I will resign from my position," Thuradin Stonebeard, commander of the royal guard said, his saphyrium helm resting against his hip.

Ronorim finished putting on a silky purple cloak before answering, his voice gruff, "Ye'll do no such thing. And ye know I don't blame ye for my father's death."

"He died under my watch," the commander said through gritted teeth. "And worse, the assassin slipped away. I'm responsible for the deaths of nae only Thelm but Orm and Garoth as well. I have no right ta lead the most elite group of dwarves in the Kingdom."

Ronorim donned the royal crown—two strands of gold which crossed paths with each other, back and forth like waves, branching out in the front to surround a large red ruby—and turned to look at the seasoned warrior.

"Thuradin," he said. "As the new King, I order ye ta keep yer position as commander of the royal guard. I know how much it means ta ye, how much ye've sacrificed for it. Ye've served the royal family and the Dwarven Kingdom well for the past four hundred years as its commander. And I know ye will continue ta serve us well."

Ronorim walked over and gripped Thuradin's shoulders

reassuringly. "Now, enough talk. Today is for my father."

It had been three days since the assassination of Thelm Ironaxe. The death of the King had been a shocking blow to most in the Dwarven Kingdom, especially those in the capital city of Tinas Gran. But the dwarves were a resilient people. They recovered from their shock quickly and, within hours, were making preparations for the King's traditional burial ceremony.

There were three days of mourning in this tradition.

The first day had been Ronorim's coronation. It was a continuous practice for kings to be crowned by an Enurg'en of their choice. The Enurg'en, dwarves capable of manipulating the energy around them in order to carry out tasks that might otherwise be impossible, were necessary for blessing the crown to ensure a long and successful reign.

For his coronation, Ronorim had chosen Stürn Forcewielder, a childhood friend who could almost always be seen standing next to the prince for as long as anyone could remember. The two were vastly different, the King being brash and loud and the Enurg'en being the quiet, solemn type, but that hadn't stopped them from being friends. Indeed, their friendship had been encouraged publicly by Thelm, who had made Stürn the personal Enurg'en for the royal family.

On the day of the coronation, Thuradin had tripled the guard in order to thwart any more potential assassinations. But no attempt was made, and the ceremony proceeded without a problem. Stürn said the blessings in Ancient Dwarvish and placed the golden crown on Ronorim's head. The enormous crowd in the plaza below cheered in approval, and huge city-wide feasts were held throughout the day.

The second day had been the Vigil. A tall pyre was built

in Tinas Gran's main plaza and the body of Thelm Ironaxe was placed upon it for all to see. Dwarves came from different parts of the Kingdom in order to pay their respects. Businesses closed for the day. The forges were dark and empty. It was a time for everyone to remember their lost King.

A ring of kneeling Enurg'en surrounded the pyre, their hands lifted high over their heads. Their sole purpose was to channel the energy around them into Thelm's body in order to keep it from undergoing the *entombment* process too early.

Entombment happened to all dwarves when they died. It was a process whereby the skin of a deceased dwarf turned to stone. How fast it happened varied with each one, but the average time was a day. The dwarves had been created from stone by the elemental god of earth, Nythirim. It was only natural for them to return, once dead, to their original form.

Once a dwarf was entombed, they were virtually immovable. It was tradition, however, for dwarven kings to be buried under the city of Tinas Gran in the Hall of Kings. And it was for this that the Enurg'en constantly bent the energies to their will to preserve the late King's body, an honor not every dwarf could have.

On the third day Thelm was to be buried. The entire city would be included in the procession which carried the late King's body down into the Hall of Kings. The body was carried on a stretcher by royal guards, led by Thuradin, but at the front of it all were the late King's two sons, Ronorim and Dunkell.

It was a grim day in the cavern of Dun'Aldor. The royals and royal guards, as well as every soldier in Tinas Gran donned their ceremonial armor. Bright hues of white, gray, and green glinted under the city's braziers.

Thuradin followed the princes as they led everyone through the entire city. He noticed Dun'Aldor, normally dimly lit by the braziers, was unusually bright. Those in charge of working them had set them to full luminosity. The city's towering buildings, many acting as support pillars for the cavern, reflected the light and seemed to glow on their own. Red flags with a black, double-bladed iron axe in the middle hung from every tower and building. The city seemed empty as they walked through it, and yet, everyone was here.

It took the better part of an hour for the procession to reach the Hall of Kings. The spacious, sacred halls contained several altars, each one with an entombed dwarf lying on top. Gargantuan statues of dwarves in full armor with gigantic axes and hammers, impressively carved out of the hall's stone walls, stood guard over each altar.

The dwarves made their way down the hall, passing altar after altar. Once they found an unused one, Thelm's limp body was placed on top by his sons.

The burial ceremony began.

Ronorim approached his father's body with a double-bladed iron axe, his father's weapon, clutched in his folded hands. Gently, he placed it into Thelm's hands, guiding the stiff fingers around the handle. Dunkell then approached with three empty, golden goblets. He placed two next to Thelm's ears and then one above the head so that they formed a triangle. Then the prince took a small flask and poured a frothy pale ale into each goblet. His lips moved inaudibly as he said the prayers necessary for the ritual. Once this was finished, he stepped back to stand next to Ronorim.

With a signal from Thuradin the Enurg'en formed a

semi-circle around the altar. They knelt once more and raised their arms skyward. Their chanting intensified with each word, then ceased.

Thelm's body slowly lost its color. The soft, smooth texture of skin turned into hard rock. Within seconds the entombment process was complete. Before them now lay a stone dwarf in the perfect image of Thelm.

With the burial over, the dwarves of Tinas Gran made their way back to their city for another celebration—there was little point in dwelling on death when there was ale to drink. For Ronorim and Thuradin, however, the end of the burial meant it was time to work. It was time for the yearly meeting.

Representatives had come from the four other major cities in the Dwarven Kingdom: Kul'Kriegar, Tinas Ern, Kul'Burell, and Fungar Hrathor. They were here to give their monthly reports.

"I tell ye," Ronorim muttered as he and Thuradin walked through the halls of the royal palace toward the commons. "These blasted representatives always give the same damned reports only to request more money. I'd much rather be with the people."

They entered the commons, a large and spacious room, normally empty except for the long, oval-shaped stone table in the center and the chairs surrounding it. Now, however, it was filled with representatives from all five major cities. Royal guards stood against the wall and kept watch over the proceedings. They all stood at attention and beat their fists over their chests in salute as Ronorim and Thuradin entered.

Thuradin took his place with his royal guards against the wall and watched the meeting unfold.

The representatives took their seats, with Ronorim at the

head of the table. The meeting began with a series of reports from the different clans. The representatives of the Guardian Clan from Kul'Kriegar reported an all-time low in recruitment, which, Thuradin thought, was strange considering they were the most militaristic out of all the clans. They provided most of the soldiers for the Dwarven Kingdom.

The Oredweller Clan reported a good year for mining. The harvesting of important ores such as iron, mithril, gold, and silver had been so good this year that they predicted a surplus of raw ore. The final decision on what to do with it, however, was up to the King, and, after they finished their report, the representatives from Tinas Ern looked at Ronorim expectantly.

Thuradin saw the King's brow furrow, but, in the end, he pushed the issue to the side. The dwarves from Tinas Ern grumbled and muttered to each other under their breath.

The speakers of the Tiller Clan from Fungar Hrathor reported problems with the growing of new agricultural produce.

"It isn't that the conditions under the mountain make it impossible for these plants ta grow—we've copied the outside world's environment almost perfectly," one representative said. "But for whatever reason, the seeds our harvesters bring from the outside all die before reaching maturity."

Ronorim grunted.

Thuradin remembered how Thelm, years ago, had told the Tiller Clan that he wanted them to experiment with new farming methods in an effort to increase the variety of food the Kingdom had. Over many years, progress had been made, but no actual results ever came in. Because of that, the dwarves to this day were still forced to stick with their staple foods of potatoes, mushrooms, and ram meat.

"Do ye think it's possible ta start small farms on the outside of the mountain?" Ronorim suggested.

The Tiller representative shook his head sadly. "Ye know as well as all of us here what the sun can do ta our kind when its light touches our skin. It would be a hazardous profession and I don't think many would be willing ta risk their life for it. We hardly ever have any volunteers ta harvest seeds from the outside, despite the briefness of the job and the protective gear we give them—and the extra pay."

True, Thuradin thought. Having their entire Kingdom underground, the dwarves had no resistance against the sunlight and so never ventured to the outside world when they could help it. It was written in several historical texts that a dwarf's skin would melt right off if they were ever touched by the sun's light.

Ronorim shrugged. "Keep trying and find a way. I'll give ye all the resources ye require."

The Tiller representative bowed, clearly pleased with the response.

Finally the dwarves from Dun'Burell, the Border Clan, made their report. It was the same as always. Incessant attacks by the burrowers, dwarves dying daily in battle, insufficient food, insufficient building materials, insufficient dwarves, insufficient everything.

The representatives unfurled a large map of the Dwarven Kingdom and pointed out locations in their cavern that had seen the most action in the past year. Even from the edge of the room, Thuradin could see the map clearly.

There were five main caverns that the dwarves had occupied within the mountains, all of which were connected by a series of tunnels they had dug early in their history. The uncharted areas were the unused body of the mountain range they lived in.

Kul'Kriegar and its domain was marked at the top, around the same altitude as the mountain's middle area. It was the highest city and the closest one to the outside. Below, deep under the mountain, was Dun'Aldor, The Old Land. It was here that the dwarven capital of Tinas Gran was located. It was the second largest and the oldest area on the map. To the right of Dun'Aldor, at the same depth, was Tinas Ern and its domain. To the left, Fungar Hrathor. Both were smaller caverns compared to the others, occupied during the early years of the Dwarven Expansion.

Below Dun'Aldor was another charted area full of scribbles, scratch-outs, and all sorts of other changes. This was Dun'Burell, the largest cavern in the Dwarven Kingdom. It was also the only one that bordered burrower lands. There was a small circle to the right of Dun'Burell with a question mark in it, presumed to be the burrower capital. It was unknown where exactly they originated from. No one had ever ventured within their caverns and lived to tell the tale. To attempt it was suicide. All anyone knew was that swarms of them came from Dun'Burell's eastern tunnel. It was assumed their home was on the other side.

The poor location of Dun'Burell was an unfortunate accident, due to a lack of scouting runs during an era of expansion the dwarves had had many centuries ago. During the construction of the first tunnel that would lead to Dun'Burell, the scouts had returned with promising news of an enormous, empty cavern. But they hadn't scouted the entire region. They hadn't seen what was on the other side. Everyone had been surprised when news came that a horde of burrowers had surrounded the then-under-construction city of Kul'Burell. It had taken a huge dwarven army to lift the siege.

Victory went to the dwarves but at the cost of several thousand lives. The construction of Kul'Burell was completed, as well as a series of forts and towers scattered throughout the cavern, but the dwarves of Dun'Burell had been under attack by the burrowers ever since.

Thuradin was brought back from his thoughts by Ronorim's sharp voice.

"Ye'll get yer normal supply train of weapons, soldiers, and everything else ye need," he heard the King say. "And now that I'm King, I can give ye some good news as well. I intend ta march on the burrower caverns and secure the safety of our border clans. We will raise a mighty army and destroy these pests once and for all."

The dwarves from Dun'Burell looked at the King in shock. Several faces broke out in relieved smiles. This was better news than any of them could have imagined. Thuradin himself had difficulty believing what he heard.

"And what of my own cavern?" Ronorim turned and looked at Thuradin.

Thuradin stepped forward and took off his saphyrium helm, resting it on his hip. He knew he had a revered reputation in the Dwarven Kingdom because of his position and the battles he had been a part of. He also knew that many were now discussing his failure to protect Thelm from a single assassin. He noticed some of the representatives glance at each other at his introduction.

"My King," Thuradin said. "All is well within the city, but there are reports from the tunnel wall that you may want ta hear."

The dwarven tunnel system gave each city access to all the others as well as one that led to the outside—except for

Tinas Gran. For millennia, the tunnels stood as they had been dug, with no means for protection. However, centuries ago, walls had been erected at every tunnel entrance and exit after the burrowers had proven themselves to be a capable enemy. The walls of the upper cities served no real purpose, since the burrowers never made it past Dun'Burell, but they were kept as a precaution anyway and a small dispatch of soldiers always manned them.

"Word has reached my ears from Borim Tomestone, captain of the wall guard, that strange sounds have been heard coming from farther inside the tunnel. The guards have reported seeing strange figures crawling along the tunnel walls as well."

This report seemed to grab everyone's attention. The side-conversations ceased, and Thuradin could feel everyone's eyes on him.

"What do ye think could be the cause?" Ronorim asked.

Thuradin let the question hang for a moment, unsure if he should continue. "I cannae say for sure. But I have my suspicions."

"And they would be?"

"Burrowers," he said firmly.

There was silence. Then the dwarves from the other clans chuckled. Thuradin frowned. He had figured others would find it difficult to believe his suspicions, but he knew he wasn't the only one who thought the burrowers were the cause.

Borim, his friend since childhood, had been absolutely certain when they had last spoken that there were burrowers within the tunnel connecting Dun'Burell to Dun'Aldor. How many was a different matter, but Borim had initially guessed their numbers to be manageable. However, if it were true, the question remained how a group of burrowers had managed to pass Dun'Burell's defenses and enter the tunnel system.

"Burrowers?" one of the representatives cried. "Here? This deep inside dwarven territory? We know ye well, Thuradin, and ye're indeed an esteemed figure, but burrowers getting past Dun'Burell and inta our higher caverns without our knowing? Preposterous!"

Thuradin looked around at the gathered dwarves. The only ones not laughing at his claim were Ronorim, the royal guards, and the representatives from Dun'Burell. Ronorim seemed to notice the same thing.

"What say ye ta this claim?" he asked them.

The representatives from Dun'Burell glanced at each other nervously and spoke to one another in hushed whispers.

"We cannae report anything more than what we've already stated," one of the representatives finally said. "We've had no more word from our cavern since we arrived here a week ago."

The room was silent.

"Ye haven't heard anything from Dun'Burell in a week?" Ronorim repeated.

The representatives nodded.

"Thuradin," Ronorim barked. Thuradin immediately stood at attention and faced his King, waiting for orders.

"I want ye ta go ta all of our communication service centers and ask them if they've had the same problem. If they have, I want ye ta immediately send a messenger with an escort ta Dun'Burell ta check up on them."

Thuradin pounded his chest in salute, donned his saphyrium helm, and hurried out of the commons.

It was strange for such an active cavern as Dun'Burell to stay quiet for so long. Usually, they sent updates to Dun'Aldor at least twice a day on a quiet day. Thuradin understood the King's sudden anxiety. He knew just as well as anyone what it could mean if communications from Dun'Burell had truly ceased.

Thuradin rushed out of the royal palace and made his way through the many communication service centers in the city. He came away from each one with the same answer the representatives had given: no communications had come from any part of Dun'Burell for the past week.

Ronorim had said that if the service centers could confirm this lack of communication, Thuradin was to send out a messenger to Dun'Burell; but he wondered if he should actually do that. If the reason behind this issue was the fall of Dun'Burell—or, at least, a devastating battle had caused major disruptions—as he thought it might be, then he would be sending the messenger and his escort to their deaths.

Thuradin shook his head. He would visit Borim at the tunnel wall and see what he thought.

He made his way to the outskirts of the city and then through the rocky flatlands that separated Tinas Gran from the tunnel to Dun'Burell. He could see the gigantic gaping hole that marked the entrance of the tunnel and could just barely see the dim lights from torches mounted on the wall.

As Thuradin approached, the wall's features took shape. It was about half the height of the tunnel itself. Stairways led to several different sections, which ran a straight line from one side of the tunnel to the other. Torches burned weakly, occasionally illuminating one of the fifty wall guards on duty as they made their rounds.

Thuradin made his way through the many stairways and eventually found himself outside of Borim's quarters. If the situation hadn't been so urgent, he might have simply barged in unannounced to catch his friend off guard, but this was no time for games. He knocked.

"Borim," Thuradin called. "If ye're in there, I need ta talk ta ye—now."

The wooden door creaked opened, revealing an elderly dwarf like Thuradin with a graying beard that ran down to his knees. Unlike Thuradin, however, he was bald. His small eyes gleamed with humor, and, despite his aged and rather pudgy appearance, Thuradin could still sense the strength of a warrior in him.

"Back so soon?" Borim said, grinning.

"Urgent matters," Thuradin replied. "Come with me ta the main wall. I need yer opinion."

Borim nodded as he went back inside to put on his armor. "When don't ye need my opinion?"

The two dwarves made their way up to the main wall, which was already occupied by several of the guards. They all saluted as they saw their captain and the commander of the royal guard approach.

"What is it ye need ta talk about?" Borim asked as Thuradin looked out into the dark tunnel.

"Today at the King's yearly meeting," Thuradin said, "I brought up what ye told me about the strange noises and the creatures crawling around the tunnel."

"Ah, well that's nice that ye thought of me. Are they going ta give me more guards then?"

Thuradin shook his head. "I told them about how I thought there could be burrowers in the tunnels. They laughed at me."

"As I told ye they would," Borim said, nodding wisely. "They're fools, the lot of them. They don't know the first thing about burrowers. Not like you and I, eh?" Thuradin couldn't remember how many times they had fought those ugly things back when they were regular soldiers in Dun'Burell. He nodded in agreement.

"The representatives from Dun'Burell claim that they haven't received any communications from their cavern since they arrived here a week ago."

"Did ye check the communication service centers?" Borim asked.

"Aye. It was the first place Ronorim sent me. They've all confirmed the claim. Nothing has come from Dun'Burell in the past week. I was told by Ronorim that if the claim was confirmed, I had ta send a messenger ta Dun'Burell ta check on them. I don't know if I should."

Borim shook his head slowly. "I don't think ye should. There are very few reasons why Dun'Burell would go silent. I doubt they've fallen, or we would be overwhelmed by burrowers by now. They're probably just under heavy pressure; but I bet the burrowers are taking advantage of that to get inta our tunnels."

"What do we do then?"

"Nothing. Like I told ye before, I'm sure their numbers are manageable. There's no way Dun'Burell could have allowed too many ta sneak past their defenses. If they attack these walls, we'll stop them."

"Are ye sure?"

"Thuradin." Thuradin shifted his gaze away from the tunnel and saw Borim staring at him with an unusually serious expression. "This isn't like that time at Kul'Murdran. We had no way of knowing the attack would be that large.

Ye did all ye could ta get us out of that massacre. And I know yer father doesn't blame ye."

Thuradin looked away at the mention of his father. "Ye saw him die."

"Aye," Borim said softly. "So believe me when I tell ye he doesn't blame ye. He was as lucid as he'd ever been—I saw no trace of his madness. He was proud that ye chose ta pull yer dwarves back ta safety instead of fighting ta the death. He would be proud of what ye've become today."

Thuradin gripped the edge of the wall. "Murnir, Grath, and Doltyr. Borim, my brothers and father are dead because of me, because I didn't take the proper precautions—" he looked again at his friend, wanting to see some ray of confidence that could put his mind at ease. "So I want ta be absolutely certain. If they attack, can we hold?"

Borim was silent for a while as he now looked out into the dark tunnel.

"I don't know."

"Ye don't know."

"I cannae get a clear estimate of what their numbers truly are," Borim shrugged, his brow furrowed. "Some days there appear ta be very few of them. Other days, many."

Thuradin nodded. "So what do ye plan ta do?"

"We cannae just abandon the wall and flee back ta the city. Otherwise, if an army of burrowers were ta come through, we would have no way of knowing, and the city would be unprepared. We must stay and encounter the enemy, then run. That way we'll know enough ta prepare accordingly."

"The city will have no time ta prepare if ye run back with the enemy at yer heels," Thuradin pointed out.

"Aye. I know," Borim said softly. "Half of the wall guard

is staying to hold off whatever comes in order ta give the rest
of us time ta make our escape. All volunteers."

Thuradin glanced at his friend. Borim's somber face
struck him as odd. Normally, he was able to maintain his
good humor, even in the worst situations, to lighten the
mood. Thuradin understood how he must be blaming
himself for the fact that there even needed to be a sacrifice.

Thuradin would have tried to give some comforting
words, but just then one of the guards yelled and pointed out
into the darkness. He turned to look where the guard was
pointing and saw a nightmare.

A swarm of burrowers approached the wall. Many of the
wretched creatures walked along the ground, but many others
crawled along the sides of the tunnel and even along the
ceiling. There were hundreds of them.

No, Thuradin realized, thousands.

Borim was the first to react.

"Fall back ta Tinas Gran! Hrandir, hold them off for as
long as ye can. We're counting on ye!"

A dwarf standing at the far right side of the wall raised his
hammer in salute. He and several of the other guards spread
out along the wall, ready to intercept the enemy wherever
they could. The rest of the dwarves had already begun
running back toward the city, carrying nothing but the armor
they wore and the weapons in their hands.

Borim and Thuradin hurried to join them.

And as they ran, Thuradin glanced back just long enough
to see throngs of burrowers descend onto the brave group of
defenders manning the wall like an avalanche.

CHAPTER THREE

They ran in silence.

The only sound Thuradin could hear as the darkness of the tunnel melted away and the towering city of Tinas Gran loomed in the distance was the huffing and panting coming from those dwarves running around him.

There was no sign of the burrowers emerging from the tunnel yet. Hrandir and his fellows seemed to be holding them off for the moment. Even so, Thuradin knew it would not take them long to reach Tinas Gran. By the time they were close enough to warn everyone, the burrowers would surely be amassing themselves just outside the city.

"Borim, who's yer fastest runner?"

Borim glanced at Thuradin, then at the tunnel, then nodded.

"Molgar, go on ahead of us and warn the city of the attack. Don't stop for anything or anyone. Go!"

The dwarf called Molgar nodded and took off, steadily pulling farther away from the rest of them.

Thuradin was glad he had thought to send someone ahead. They had only just reached the outskirts of the city when a deep, echoing blast sounded from the horntower at the center of Tinas Gran, followed immediately by the loud, jarring ringing of several large bells situated throughout the city.

It was the call to arms.

Thuradin saw many guards on patrol in the streets freeze as the alarm sounded, no doubt confused. Civilians froze as well, but after the initial shock wore off, they recovered their wits and ran to the nearest armory. Dwarves of all trades, male and female, strapped on their standard, heavy plate armor. They grabbed spears, iron bucklers, swords, axes, and hammers of all shapes, sizes, and kinds.

Nodding approvingly, Thuradin led the wall guard through the city's twisting streets toward the royal palace. It was a requirement that all dwarves, no matter what sex or trade, learn to fight and take up arms whenever the city was threatened. By doing this, the number of available defenders in the city could reach up to three thousand dwarves within a moment's notice.

Once equipped with their armor and weapons, the soldiers formed themselves into separate legions. Their officers, veteran warriors, led each legion toward the tunnel where the burrowers would soon emerge.

As they neared the royal palace, Thuradin saw a large group of heavily armored royal guards pour from the main gates. Leading them was a dwarf in dark red plate and wielding a massive two-handed iron axe. The moment Ronorim saw Thuradin and the wall guard, he called for a halt and made his way to them. After a quick salute, Thuradin answered the question he knew was about to be asked.

"Burrowers," he said.

"They were all over us," one of the guards cried out. "We had no chance of holding the wall against such an army."

"How many?"

Borim stepped forward. "I cannae say for sure, my King. But it looked ta be several thousand, at least. Half of my wall guard volunteered ta stay behind and hold them back ta buy us some time ta warn the city."

Ronorim placed a hand on Borim's shoulder. "Their sacrifice will nae be in vain. We will defend this city from these savages who dare attack our home and bring honor ta the dwarves ye lost today."

Borim saluted, as did the rest of the wall guard.

"Now," the King continued. "Go on and join the main army. We have much work ta do."

Nodding, Borim turned and led his wall guard back the way they came. Ronorim turned his attention to Thuradin.

"How soon?"

"Now."

Ronorim frowned. "Nae much time then. Very well. Follow me, Commander; we have a city ta defend."

Thuradin nodded and took his place at the front of his elite royal guards. As Ronorim turned to face them, they stood at attention, slammed the edge of their large, rectangular shields on the ground, and saluted all at once. The sound of one hundred plated gauntlets slamming on one hundred breastplates was deafening. These warriors were armed to the teeth and would fight, and, if need be, die, to protect their King. Thuradin felt an overwhelming sense of pride as he saw rigid determination etched into each face.

Ronorim smiled grimly. "Lads, let's show these invaders why they have no place in our Kingdom." With that, he began to make his way through the city, and, with a roar of approval, the royal guards followed him.

Upon reaching the outskirts of Tinas Gran, however, the

mood shifted. The call to arms had not been raised in time.

Burrowers swarmed without end from the tunnel entrance. A small group of warriors had tried to confine them within the gaping hole in order to give the city more time to put its defenses in place, but their sacrifices had been in vain. Their numbers were far too few, and they were no match for the enemy. Their bodies lay strewn across the rocky flatlands where the burrowers now gathered together.

Seeing that the tunnel entrance had already been taken, the dwarven army began following phase two of the city's defense protocol. Whereas phase one would have had them amass themselves around the tunnel entrance to confine the intruders, phase two meant the dwarves would now focus on keeping the enemy from entering the city streets.

Every entrance into the city was clogged from building to building with armed dwarves. Clustered bottlenecks were created so that the fighting would be confined into small areas only. Such limited space would minimize what the burrowers could use for tactics and thus make it harder for them to breach the dwarven defenses.

As the King and his royal guards drew closer to the front lines, it became more difficult for Thuradin to see his surroundings. Soon he would only be able to see the dwarves around him. Just before losing sight of the front lines, he caught a glimpse of the burrowers gathering themselves directly across from them. And they waited. The dwarves muttered amongst themselves, wondering why the burrowers didn't just attack like they normally did.

It soon became too congested for Thuradin and his royal guards to move through the streets easily. They would have to find another way if they wanted to reach the front lines. Ronorim seemed to think the same thing. He turned to his right into an empty, narrow alleyway, Thuradin close on his heels.

As they ran through, they heard shouts coming from the army. They stopped and listened, trying to make out what was happening. The shouts continued to ring through the air but they were soon joined by angry bellows which, Thuradin guessed, came from the legion officers. This continued for a while until it was replaced by something worse, something that made Thuradin's heart drop.

The dwarven army roared a unified war cry, and the thunder of thousands of armored feet pounded against stone as the dwarves charged across the rocky flatlands.

They had done the one thing they were not supposed to do. The entire strategy for phase two depended on everyone standing their ground to cut down any attacker challenging them. Thuradin glanced at Ronorim, who looked as shocked as he felt.

Their eyes met. They both cursed.

By charging, the dwarves had just given up their most important advantage: the bottlenecks. Now, without the city's buildings at their sides, they were susceptible to flanking maneuvers. Even though every dwarf was trained for battle, none of those in Tinas Gran, except for the officers, had ever seen any action. The army would break at the slightest amount of pressure.

"Follow me!" Ronorim yelled. "We must get ta the front lines quickly. We cannae allow this mistake ta be our downfall."

They sprinted down the alley and into an empty street. From there, Thuradin caught sight of their predicament. The flow of burrowers hadn't stopped flooding from the tunnel and didn't seem to be slowing down. Thousands of them had already emerged from the darkness, ready to fight. If this continued, the dwarves would be quickly out-numbered and overwhelmed.

Thuradin frowned. He wondered if that even mattered. Their forces seemed to be dooming themselves on their own quite effectively.

The dwarves had crashed into the enemy's lines and were now cutting down any burrower they could with gusto. However, they had failed to form a single, intact line when they abandoned their bottlenecked positions. Each legion remained in its separated position, meaning only certain parts of the burrower lines were in combat, leaving the rest free to flank the individual dwarven clusters. Ronorim swore loudly at their stupidity.

"We're going ta split in half," Ronorim said through gritted teeth as he turned to face the royal guards. "Thuradin, ye take half of yer royal guards and fill in one of those damned holes in our line. Tell any officer ye see ta fall back inta the city. We're moving inta phase three. Go!"

Thuradin quickly picked out the dwarves he wanted and led them across the rocky flatlands to sections of the battle where he thought their line was weakest.

A yell escaped his lips as he drew his twin axes and crashed into the enemy. He took the first burrower by surprise, burying an axe into the creature's skull while he used the other to sever the neck. He didn't stop there. He continued cleaving his way through the burrowers with seemingly little effort. His breathing came in angry gasps, blood and sweat splashing onto his beard and face. He ignored all of this and let the adrenaline take control.

The burrowers were ugly things. Humanoid but hunchbacked, they would have been much taller than the dwarves—though even bent, they were still a head taller. They wore no armor and no clothes except thin loincloths. Their blue-gray skin was flaccid and wrinkled, giving them the appearance of old age. Their faces were similar to a dwarf's but much scruffier. Sparse hair grew on their oval-shaped heads. Their teeth, the few they had, were blackened with rot, and their eyes burned a dull yellow.

Their weapons were no better. The most formidable blade a burrower carried was a small hatchet, but that was rare. Most of them used clubs and daggers.

The state of their weapons had caused Thuradin to think that they were weak, brittle instruments when he first fought against them, but the burrowers' clubs were made of a hard material the dwarves had never seen. Their daggers were lethally sharp and were not easily broken. He learned quickly that they were as capable of killing as any dwarven axe.

As Thuradin carved his way through the horde of burrowers, his royal guards fighting right behind him, he told each officer he saw to fall back to the city for phase three.

Phase three was the last strategy in the dwarves' defense protocol before it became every-dwarf-for-themself. The outskirts of the city would be abandoned, and the dwarves would create bottlenecks farther back in the streets that led into the inner city. The dwarves' flanks would again be protected by the nearby, taller buildings, some reaching all the way to the cavern cieling. Any burrowers who tried to sneak past the bottleneck by crawling on the sides of the buildings would find themselves easy targets for the dwarven archers and spear-throwers positioned on the roofs.

Thuradin glanced across the battlefield during a lull in the fighting.

Ronorim's plan to get the army to fall back into the city seemed to be taking effect. Most of the dwarven clusters were beginning their retreat. However, a large number of dwarves had already been killed, and Thuradin feared that too many might have died to allow phase three to work effectively. Either way, he thought, they had no choice but to try.

It wasn't easy for the dwarves to reach their positions for phase three. They couldn't simply turn their backs on the burrowers and run. If they had, the burrowers would have easily slaughtered them. Instead, a rear-guard took form for each cluster. While the main body made a full retreat, the rear-guard acted as a wall between the burrowers and the retreating army. They faced their enemy the entire way back, killing any who approached but remaining in their tight formation. By the time they had shuffled back to their positions for phase three, the bottlenecks were complete.

A quick gap formed in each bottleneck to let the rear-guard through, closing as soon as the last dwarf had reached safety. The burrowers would have to fight a fresh line of dwarven warriors now if they wanted to pass. The rear-guard, in the mean time, were allowed a quick rest before rejoining the fight.

The battle raged on in these bottlenecks. The burrowers were unable to break through the dwarven shield wall and, because of the buildings, they were also unable to flank them.

With their lack of armor, the burrowers made easy kills for the first row of defenders. Some tried to climb across the sides of the buildings to attack the dwarves from above, but, as Thuradin had imagined, they were dealt with by spear-throwers and archers. There was no way past the bottlenecks except straight through. The burrower losses quickly grew disastrous, but they continued to attack.

Thuradin was now behind the dwarven lines, where he saw Ronorim talking to several officers. He made his way to the King and waited as he questioned the officers on what had started the charge. Every officer he questioned shrugged and gave the same answer, ending with the statement that it was no fault of theirs.

Several individual dwarves, "fresh greens," the officers called them, had seen the burrowers' lack of agression as a challenge which they had only been too happy to accept. This resulted in a snowball effect. The officers had tried to stop them and pull them back into line, but there was nothing they could do. Too many dwarves had already left the security of the formation, so they ordered a full charge so at least all of them could crash into the enemy at once instead of one-by-one. Thuradin saw that Ronorim was frustrated by their reports, but he had to agree with them. In the end, this was not their failure as leaders, but rather a failure of their people as a whole for an inadequate degree of training and discipline.

After he dismissed them and let them return to their legions, the King turned to Thuradin.

"We cannae hold."

"More dwarves are being armed as we speak," Thuradin argued. "We haven't yet reached our full defensive capabilities."

"It's nae enough," Ronorim shook his head, his beard flapping back and forth. "This is more than the several thousand we anticipated, and still they continue ta pour through the tunnel. We cannae hold."

Thuradin could hear the disbelief in Ronorim's voice. He understood his King's pain. It didn't seem possible that

Tinas Gran, the capital of the Dwarven Kingdom, could be taken so easily with a single attack. Yet, it was happening. Worse, with the fall of Tinas Gran, the dwarves would lose the royal family, which was and had always been a unifying force for the clans. Thuradin knew Ronorim had no intention of escaping, and, he was sure, wherever Dunkell was, the prince was of the same mind. They would die with their city.

With each passing hour, Ronorim's predictions came closer to truth. The army grew exhausted from the constant fighting, but the burrowers seemed to always be replenished with fresh fighters, no matter how many the dwarves killed.

Fatigued, the dwarves fell easily to the burrowers as many warriors simply dropped their weapons or shields, no longer able to carry them. The piles of bodies grew so high that burrowers began climbing over them and jumping into the middle of the dwarven clusters, creating havoc within the tight formation.

"Come," Ronorim grunted, swinging his large axe before him. "I'll nae let this city fall without taking as many of those ugly beasts as I can."

He let out a roar of fury and leapt headlong into the nearest bottleneck, carving a deep hole in the burrower lines with a single swipe of his axe. Thuradin had no choice but to follow, though he was more than happy to do so.

Thuradin watched Ronorim wince slightly as he applied pressure to the wound on the King's bicep. It wasn't a deep cut, but it still needed wrapping. After bandaging the wounded arm, the two dwarves made their way from the crowded makeshift hospital within the royal palace to one of the various balconies overlooking the city.

They had fought together for what seemed like hours but to no avail. The burrowers still poured out of the tunnel in a steady stream.

Thuradin looked out over the city. The outskirts were ablaze with fire, and smoke billowed high, hitting the cavern ceiling and staying there. Corpses littered the streets. Many of the slain dwarves were already going through entombment, their stone bodies mixing in with the fleshy corpses of the burrowers. Wherever he looked, he saw nothing but death and destruction and fire. The tall iron and steel buildings of Tinas Gran would soon become a ruin.

But as he continued to gaze upon the city, he noticed a flickering light from out of the corner of his eye. He looked to the north, where a second tunnel was located.

This tunnel was several hundred feet higher than the one from which the burrowers emerged. A steep set of stairs carved out of the rocks provided access to it, and it connected Dun'Aldor to Kul'Kriegar. It was normally only used for trade shipments and military expeditions en route to Dun'Burell. At a time like this, Thuradin would have expected the tunnel and stairs to remain dark and empty, but now they were glowing with light.

He soon realized the lights were coming from individual torches carried by dwarven warriors. The dwarves of Kul'Kriegar had arrived to Tinas Gran—in a most opportune time, no less—and Thuradin had no idea how this was possible. There had been no time to send for help to the other cities, yet here they were. They were the deadliest warriors the Dwarven Kingdom had to offer, and there were many of them.

The reinforcements moved into formation at the base of the stairs. The sight was overwhelming. Only a few hundred warriors from Kul'Kriegar could have saved the city from ruin, but there looked to be thousands.

Baffled, Thuradin turned to Ronorim, wondering if he could explain the unexpected but much-needed aid.

"It's the first expedition of warriors I ordered ta be sent ta Dun'Burell," the King said, smiling. "They must have been on their way there. Luck is with us today, Thuradin."

The two dwarves watched as their reinforcements charged the exposed burrower flank. The invaders didn't know what hit them. Several went flying into the air from the impact of the charge. The ruthlessness with which the dwarves of Kul'Kriegar fought was frightening, even to Thuradin. He noticed that the burrowers who hadn't been crushed by the charge began to circle around, attempting their own flanking maneuver. But at the last minute, they turned and fled back through the tunnel from which they had come.

The reinforcing dwarves didn't pursue. Instead, they curved their way around the backs of the remaining burrowers still inside the city. There were many to kill, and it would take some time to clear Tiras Gran of the remaining invaders.

"Come," Ronorim said. "I've seen enough. We should join them."

The two dwarves grabbed their weapons and sprinted out of the palace. Thuradin watched Ronorim slide his way past the faltering dwarven clusters and, upon reaching the first burrower, unleash his fury.

Burrowers fell left and right by the King's axe. He cut a path through them with a fury Thuradin had rarely seen. The dwarves behind him cheered and attacked the burrowers with renewed zeal. Thuradin saw Ronorim making his way past several more burrowers, but he soon lost sight of him as the raging battle moved them farther and farther apart.

He tried to keep up with the King, but it was hard work pushing his way through so many bodies, both living and dead. Once they reached the front lines of the Kul'Kriegaran reinforcements, he leaned on his knees to catch his breath, expecting Ronorim to do the same. But straightening up, he realized that the King had gone on without him.

A quick scan of his surroundings showed no sign of him. Thuradin looked to a nearby warrior for answers. The dwarf pointed in the direction of the retreating burrowers. Thuradin frowned. He wished Ronorim had at least waited for him instead of going off alone. He was needlessly putting himself in harm's way. He picked out a handful of Kul'Kriegaran warriors to accompany him and ran after his King.

It didn't take long for the small group of dwarves to catch up to him. Ronorim spent his time killing any burrower near him, which slowed his progress. Thuradin and his group didn't waste their energy with that.

Once reunited, they continued to pursue the fleeing enemy together rather than pulling back to the city. Thuradin noticed that Ronorim was so lost in bloodlust, his eyes wide and crazed, that he was becoming a hazard. He debated whether he should suggest going back to the city but decided against it. The bloodlust would end soon enough, but if he tried to force Ronorim out of it, he might be the one with an axe in his skull.

They chased the fleeing burrowers back into the tunnel to Dun'Burell where it quickly became too dark to see without a torch. The fires that normally burned along the tunnel walls were extinguished. They couldn't see, yet Ronorim continued to pursue the burrowers relentlessly.

"My King," Thuradin called out. "Perhaps we should

return ta the city."

No answer.

He tried again. "Ronorim, Don't ye think it's time—"

The shaking started slowly, and it was so faint at first that Thuradin could barely feel it. However, it soon grew much stronger and much more violent. The earth shook and heaved and cracking sounds could be heard coming from the ceiling.

"Cave-in!" Thuradin shouted. "Back! Out of the tunnel! Move!"

The dwarves fled as the ceiling collapsed on top of them. Rocks crashed and tumbled and shattered all over, nearly crushing them all in several instances. By the time the dust had cleared, Thuradin saw that all the dwarves who had accompanied him into the tunnel had managed to escape. All except Ronorim.

"Back ta Tinas Gran," the commander said. "Tell Captain Kalgan about the tunnel's collapse and then help clear out the city."

The Kul'Kriegarians nodded, their nerves shaken, and turned to rejoin their comrades.

Thuradin rushed back to the sealed tunnel entrance to see if there was any way through. He tried pushing and lifting some of the smaller boulders to the side, but even that took much effort and made no noticeable difference. Depending on how deep the cave-in was, it could take anywhere from days to months to clear it out, and, as far as he could see, there was only one small, unsealed gap at the top of the entrance. Small enough for a hand to fit through. He climbed the rocks blocking the tunnel entrance until he was level with the small gap and tried to peer through but saw only darkness.

"Ronorim!"

Silence. Thuradin feared for the worse. Then: "It's good ta hear yer voice, lad."

It was Ronorim. He was still alive.

"Stay put right there. We'll come get ye out as soon as we can."

"No," Ronorim said. "There are still burrowers crawling all over the place. I can hear them. In fact. . . ."

Thuradin heard a clang and then a sickening thud. Then nothing.

"Ronorim?"

"Aye, I'm still here," the King replied. "I need ye ta do me a favor, lad. I'm nae coming back through here—I cannae wait for this ta be cleared out. The tunnel has collapsed pretty far in, so I imagine it'll take at least a couple weeks ta clear everything. So, what I'm going ta do is take the tunnel down ta Dun'Burrel. It'll give me a chance ta see what's going on down there, anyway. What I need ye ta do is come pick me up from there."

"Of course, of course," Thuradin said, thinking hard. "I'll just take the outside route."

"Aye," Ronorim said softly. "Do that. But be careful. Ye know what that sun will do ta ye if it touches ye. Oh—" Thuradin heard shuffling and metal scraping against rock on the other side, "—and there's one last thing. I need ye ta take this and keep it safe."

Thuradin saw a circle of intertwining gold with a ruby in the center pushed through the small hole.

"I cannae take this. Ye're the King! Ye have ta wear this until ye die."

"Aye, but if I die here, then the crown is lost for a good, long while," Ronorim chuckled, though there was little mirth in it. "I need ye ta take it so that doesn't happen."

The crown tipped out of the hole and tumbled down the rock pile until it hit the ground where it rested, waiting for him to pick it up.

"Well, I best be off. It'll take a few days for me ta reach Dun'Burell, especially in this darkness."

"Be careful," Thuradin said. "Don't get yerself killed, ye hear?"

No answer.

Thuradin made his way down the rockpile. He looked at the crown. Gently, he picked it up and began making his way back to the city, his mind already buzzing with ideas and forming plans. He would not fail Ronorim. He would bring the King home.

CHAPTER FOUR

Thuradin couldn't help but notice the huge change the city underwent after the unexpected battle. Not only were the metal towers of the city blackened by fires but the hearts of the dwarves who lived in it were as well. Those who survived wore haunted, broken looks. For most, this had been their first battle. They hadn't expected it to be so terrible. Smoke lingered on the cavern ceiling as it slowly filtered through the dwarven ventilation system and drifted out of the mountains into the outside world.

Now the survivors put themselves to the task of clearing out the dead and putting out the fires. The burrowers would be burned together without a second thought. The dwarves who hadn't yet been entombed were carried to one of the several burial halls beneath the city. Those who were already fully entombed were left alone to stand as eternal monuments of the battle. The few dwarves who weren't partaking in this gruesome work had the simple task of extinguishing the many fires that ravaged the outskirts of the city. The Kul'Kriegarans had suffered next to no losses, and they gave their aid wherever they could.

Thuradin walked through the littered streets toward the palace. The crown in his hands was now wrapped in a sheet of cloth to keep it hidden from plain view. It was best if no one knew about what had happened at the tunnel—at least not yet.

Upon entering the palace, he headed straight for the commons. There were only a few royal guards posted—the rest were helping with the clean up—and none of them tried to stop him. But as he entered the commons, he was greeted by someone he hadn't expected to see.

"Thuradin!" Dunkell Ironaxe rose from his seat. "It's good ta see ye survived, though no one would have expected anything less."

Thuradin greeted the prince and looked around the room. It was full of wounded dwarves and the Enurg'en looking after them. A few dwarves in ceremonial armor stood at their seats by the stone table, which had been moved to the side of the room.

"What's that ye got there?" Dunkell asked, pointing at the cloth Thuradin cradled.

The commander hesitated, but only for a second. Dunkell was Ronorim's brother, after all. There was no harm in showing him the crown and if there was anyone who should know about Ronorim, it was Dunkell.

Slowly, he unwrapped the cloth. Dunkell's eyes widened and his mouth dropped.

"My brother. He isn't. . . ."

"No," Thuradin said quickly. "He's alive. We chased some fleeing burrowers inta the tunnel and it collapsed. I escaped, but he was trapped inside. He's making his way ta Dun'Burell as we speak."

Dunkell let out a sigh. "Ye scared me there, Commander." He stretched out his hand for the crown, which Thuradin handed over. A look he couldn't quite recognize covered

Dunkell's face. Regret? Envy? Sadness? Whatever it was, he didn't like it.

"Yer brother told me ta take care of that," he said, watching how Dunkell traced his fingers along the gold bands. "He'll be back soon enough ta reclaim it."

"Aye," Dunkell replied slowly. He seemed to be deep in thought. "But he's nae here now, and the dwarves cannae be leaderless . . . Ah, but we're getting ahead of ourselves. This will all be settled in the meeting I've arranged for tomorrow."

"A meeting? So soon?"

"Aye. I had originally planned it ta discuss how ta retaliate against the burrowers for this invasion, but now, with what ye've told me, we'll have more important things ta discuss. I expect ye ta be there, of course."

Thuradin was surprised. Of all the dwarves to plan retaliation against the burrowers, Dunkell was the last he would have thought of. Everyone in the Kingdom knew the younger prince had a soft spot for the barbarians. This sign that his soft spot seemed to be hardening was encouraging.

He nodded. There were now many questions in the air because of this attack and they had to be answered. This meeting would also be a good opportunity to get approval for his own plan to rescue Ronorim.

"I'll be there," he said as he reached out to retrieve the crown.

Dunkell pulled it away, just out of reach. "The crown is royal property. It belongs here."

"Aye," Thuradin said, withdrawing his hand slowly. "It's just—yer brother told me ta take care of it."

"It's quite safe here." Dunkell put the crown in a bag hanging off his belt. "Don't worry. I won't lose it. I'll be taking care of it personally."

A few seconds passed. Thuradin nodded and turned to leave. Dunkell was right; the crown would be safe enough in one of the palace's many vault rooms. Pushing thoughts of the crown out of his mind, he exited the royal palace and began helping with the city's clean-up.

After a day's work of putting out fires, Thuradin grabbed some food and went straight to his room in the palace. There was nothing left to do that day, and tomorrow was Dunkell's meeting. He bathed, washing the soot from his body, and, after giving his armor a quick inspection, went straight to bed. Sleep was the quickest way to pass the time, and he was exhausted.

He had no dreams.

He rose early in the morning with a pained sigh—perhaps he was getting too old for this warrior business. He chuckled at the thought; then the memories of yesterday's battle flooded back into his mind, and he remembered the situation. Ronorim was gone, and it was his job to bring him back.

But first, there was a meeting to attend.

After downing a small goblet of ale, he put on a clean tunic and trousers and wiped down each piece of his armor again to remove any dried remnants of blood or soot before he put them on. He left his room and began walking through the palace corridors towards the commons. On his way there, he occasionally stopped by a window or balcony and looked out over the city. The dwarves seemed to be in a more spirited mood. No one was celebrating, but he could hear chatter coming from the plaza through the open windows. A sign of normalcy. He could even make out some of the dwarves' conversations; but what he heard, he didn't like. It appeared the King's absence after the battle had been noticed. Rumors spread like a disease in Tinas Gran, and any rumors of Ronorim's death could only lead to more problems for the Kingdom.

Walking deeper into the palace, Thuradin noticed there were more royal guards on station today than there had ever been. The palace swarmed with them.

He hurried to the commons. He expected to be the first one to arrive, being the early riser he was, but he was wrong. The commons was already crowded. Thuradin saw most of the representatives who had attended Ronorim's meeting only a day ago. Some were missing though, and he wondered if they had been killed in the battle the day before.

Dunkell was also there. Thuradin saw him sitting on a throne-like seat placed in the center of a newly built stage. The dwarves made eye contact and nodded in greeting but said nothing. There would be time to talk after the meeting.

Several minutes passed as the rest of the dwarves arrived. Thuradin was surprised to see so many familiar faces.

There was Stürn Forcewielder, the Enurg'en who had crowned Ronorim only days ago. A dwarf who was known to greatly appreciate silence, he didn't speak with anyone and immediately took his seat. He was always the type to get straight to business and took everything seriously.

Thuradin remembered Ronorim's description of Stürn. He had believed his seriousness was a kind of reverence that came from his mastery in the powers of the Enurg'en. The King and Enurg'en were childhood friends, as Borim was to Thuradin. The two had seen less of each other as Ronorim had been forced to focus more on his royal duties and Stürn on his training as an Enurg'en, but their friendship was still strong.

Stürn was known as the best healer in the Dwarven Kingdom and had even been offered the position of Seer, a title offered to few Enurg'en. He had turned down the offer, though, in order to maintain his independence. Had he become a Seer, he would not have been able to travel throughout the Kingdom but instead would have been forced to reside in the Halls of Earth, where the Seers lived and communed with the god Nythirim.

Thuradin didn't know much about Stürn's family, but he did know that he came from a long line of Enurg'en. As the first son, there had always been big expectations for him. The same could not be said for his younger brother, Balig. As far as Thuradin knew, the two brothers didn't speak to each other very often.

Moving his gaze past Stürn, Thuradin noticed Borim sitting at the far end of the room. His friend had a bandaged leg but other than that had left yesterday's battle unscathed. He looked deep in conversation with another dwarf Thuradin recognized as the young Threnn Crystalshield, the apprentice of Bronn Lightninghammer, an elderly but strong dwarf who had been like a father to Thuradin ever since his real father had died.

After a quick nod of acknowledgment to Borim, Thuradin continued scanning the crowd until he saw the next dwarf he was looking for.

Ayrie Hearthkeeper.

He didn't know her personally, but he had heard promising things about the young lass. She was known as the best tracker in the Dwarven Kingdom and was fiercely loyal to the crown. Raised with nine brothers, she was forced to learn quickly how to be tough. She had achieved much, becoming a skilled fighter and the highest-ranking female dwarf in the Kingdom. Thuradin thought she was a perfect candidate for the task he would propose during the meeting.

He had spent some time last night and early that morning planning out his task and the journey it would require, and he knew he could not do it alone. He needed a small group of dwarves to go with him, and he knew who he wanted to ask. Stürn, Borim, and Ayrie stood out in his mind as his top choices for companions. He couldn't force them to go, but he was sure they would accept his invitation for the sake of finding their King.

As the last few dwarves entered the commons, a hush fell over the assembly. Dunkell stood and addressed the crowd.

"My fellow dwarves, I thank ye for coming in on such short notice. A great tragedy has struck due to this recent battle. My brother, Ronorim, King of the dwarves, has been lost—he's nae dead," Dunkell added before anyone could interrupt him with their outrage, "but he's been trapped on the other side of the collapsed tunnel ta Dun'Burell."

The assembly erupted into conversation.

"The commander of the royal guard, Thuradin Stonebeard, was the one ta give me this news," Dunkell continued over the noise. "He tells me that my brother is alive and is currently making his way ta Dun'Burell. Something must be done."

"Aye, and it will be!" one of the dwarves shouted. Chaos ensued. Arguments broke out over who would go rescue their King. Dunkell raised his hands for silence and the assembly quieted down.

"Aye," he said. "We will do something. But first, there is another issue that must be discussed."

Dunkell took out the royal crown from one of his bags.

"While my brother is absent from his throne, we dwarves must have a ruler. We cannae be leaderless. Since I am second in line for the throne, I shall be King in my brother's absence."

Without giving anyone time to object, Dunkell lifted the crown and placed it on top of his own head.

The assembly went into an uproar. Insults and threats rang out through the commons. The dwarves from the Earthwrought clan—from Dun Aldor—as well as the Guardian, and Border clans vehemently disagreed with Dunkell's spontaneous claim of the throne, saying no effort had even been made to find Ronorim, which gave him no right to take it. The dwarves from the Tiller and Oredweller clans defended Dunkell's self-appointment, emphasizing that his claim was legitimate. Ronorim was lost, dead for all anyone knew. Were they supposed to wait, leaderless, for their dead King to show up?

The noise was deafening, and Thuradin sensed a brawl was imminent. He stood. If a brawl started now, the meeting would go nowhere, and they didn't have the luxury of wasting any time.

He looked to Dunkell for help, but the self-appointed King wasn't even paying attention to the chaos. He seemed to have no interest and stared at his fingers with a grin.

Thuradin frowned and pushed his way through the assembly toward the stage. Dunkell raised his eyebrows as he approached, but Thuradin didn't acknowledge him. Instead, he faced the assembly, drew in a deep breath, and let out a loud, ringing war cry. The cry reverberated against the stone walls of the commons and stunned the bickering assembly into silence.

"Fellow dwarves," he said, his voice clear and commanding.

"While ye all stand there and bicker amongst yerselves, ye waste time that could be spent searching for our King, who is at this very moment roaming around in a dark tunnel filled with burrowers."

Thuradin could feel Dunkell's disapproving stare bore into his back.

"It's true that we need a temporary leader ta keep us in order while a search is carried out ta find Ronorim, and dwarven law does give Dunkell the right ta claim authority—but nae as King."

The silence in the commons deepened as everyone listened attentively. Thuradin saw their anxious faces and knew that they wondered what his final point would be. He had mentioned a search for Ronorim, but no one else saw how one could be carried out quickly enough with the tunnel to Dun'Burell collapsed.

"Dwarven law decrees that Dunkell will be steward of the throne until either Ronorim has returned or half a year has passed. If half a year passes without Ronorim's return, then he will be presumed dead and Dunkell will be made King."

Heads nodded as some of the older dwarves remembered what the laws said about a proper succession. There was a low buzz of murmuring in the assembly, but Thuradin pressed on.

"As for the search for our King," he said. "I will personally go and lead the search party."

He saw several heads nod again, this time more vigorously. He was the obvious and most capable of choices to go on such a mission. But he knew they wouldn't like his next statement.

"And because the tunnel ta Dun'Burell has collapsed, I've decided that the fastest way ta get there is through the outside."

For the third time that day, the assembly of dwarves burst out into a tremendous uproar. This time, however, they were united in their objection to Thuradin's plan. Thuradin raised his hands for silence and was surprised to see Dunkell doing the same thing next to him. The assembly was just as surprised, having forgotten that the prince was even there, and they soon fell silent.

Dunkell turned and faced Thuradin. "How do ye intend ta do this, considering that our skin melts if sunlight touches us? Do ye intend on taking anyone with ye?"

Thuradin searched the crowd for those he wanted. He saw several heads shake and several eyes glued to the floor, avoiding his gaze.

"I'll be taking a small group, which is all I need. And ta counter the sun, we'll simply cover every inch of our body with cloth. We cannae melt if the sun doesn't touch us."

Dunkell was already shaking his head, the disbelief clear on his face. "How do ye know that will work?"

"I don't," Thuradin said truthfully. "But it's a risk I'm willing ta take for my King."

The prince raised his hands in resignation. "Very well. Ye've decided. But who would be mad enough ta go with ye?"

Thuradin took a step forward and looked into the crowd once more. He had decided to take six other dwarves, all of whom were well qualified for the task.

"As I call yer name, step forward and stand beside me ta accept yer place in this quest."

Thuradin could feel everyone in the assembly hold their breath, hoping their names would not be called.

"Ayrie Hearthkeeper."

A path formed as Ayrie pushed her way through the assembly. Her bright orange hair, weaved into a single braid, bounced with her proud stride. She walked with a confidence her reputation as a renowned tracker merited.

She saluted as she came level with Thuradin. With sharp eyes full of purpose, she, too, faced the crowd. Thuradin noticed she had managed to avoid getting her weapon confiscated by the guards. Ever since Thelm's assassination, no one was allowed to bear arms anywhere near the royal family except for the royal guards and the royal family themselves. Her spear, a thick crescent of jagged iron set into a thick shaft of wood, was, as always, strapped to her back.

Thuradin was glad she had accepted the invitation. He was sure he would need a good tracker for the task ahead and Ayrie was the best. He nodded his thanks and then faced the crowd again.

"Borim Tomestone."

"Thought ye'd never ask!" Borim shouted from the back of the assembly. Moments later, Thuradin saw dwarves pushed over as his old friend rushed to where he was. He slammed his fist against his chest in a dwarven salute with such enthusiasm that it brought out a few chuckles from the assembly, despite the tension.

Thuradin returned Borim's eager grin. They had been friends almost six hundred long years. He had watched Borim, born into a family of poor weavers, constantly rise up the ranks during their time in Dun'Burell. Even now he knew Borim took weeks, sometimes months, away from being captain of the wall guard in order to go back to Dun'Burell and lend his support. He trusted Borim with everything that was his and couldn't imagine doing anything as dangerous as this journey without him.

"Stürn Forcewielder."

Solemn as ever, Stürn joined Thuradin without the slightest show of emotion, though he did bow his head slightly toward the commander out of respect.

"Bronn Lightninghammer."

A commotion broke out in the middle of the assembly. Thuradin saw Bronn arguing with Threnn and two other apprentices who he recognized—Murtosh Firebrand and Agrethar Kinguard. He saw how strongly Bronn was resisting and sighed inwardly. Bronn would have been a good warrior to have and, like Borim, would have been a good source for advice when he needed it. He knew, however, that he couldn't force anyone to accept this dangerous quest. He made eye contact with the old warrior and noted the pleading look in his eyes. He nodded once and addressed the silent crowd again.

"Therason Kinfriend."

A bulkier dwarf walked out of the commons and Thuradin knew at once that it was Therason. He cursed silently. He had been sure Therason would answer the call. He had hoped his sense of duty as a royal guard would outweigh his fear of the unknown. Now a worm of worry began to gnaw on his mind. If he couldn't get the next dwarf on his list to accept, then his mission would surely be suicide. But he was sure she would accept. She had never let him down even after centuries of friendship. She had always been there for him just as he always tried to be there for her. And now he needed her more than ever.

"Lyrie Swordmeist."

One of the few female dwarves present, Thuradin had no trouble finding her. His heart sank, however, when he saw her shaking head, her downcast eyes, and her trembling shoulders. For a moment, he was at a loss for words, but finally he grunted. He didn't like it, but there was nothing else he could do, no one else he wanted to call on. He turned to Dunkell, finished with his selection.

Dunkell raised an eyebrow. "Three others and yerself? That's all?"

"Aye."

The two studied each other for several seconds before Dunkell conceded. "It is done then."

Thuradin went back to his place in the assembly and tried to pay attention to the rest of the meeting, but his head was in another world—one of calculations, estimations, other names he might have considered calling upon, and his slim chances of success.

He snapped out of his thoughts once the meeting ended. The commons was empty now except for Dunkell and the three dwarves who had accepted his call. He stood to leave, but the prince—now steward—called for him.

"Ye know how dangerous this mission will be and I'll nae stop ye," he said. "But ye must know that because of the high probability that ye'll fail, ye and yer companions will be thought of as dead until proven otherwise."

Thuradin nodded, as did the other three dwarves.

"I understand."

He could see Dunkell hesitate, perhaps wondering how he would react to the next piece of news that he knew must come.

"Then ye must also understand that in yer absence, I'll be needing a new commander for the royal guard."

Thuradin tried to keep his face a blank mask as he slowly lifted the saphyrium helm from its resting position on his hip. He turned the helm in his hands, admiring its design and craftsmanship. He had been its owner for so long, he couldn't remember a time when he had not been. Now he had to part with it because, by undertaking this task to find his King, he had given up his position. Only the commander of the royal guard could wear the saphyrium helm.

He sighed deeply and, without further hesitation, handed the saphyrium helm to Dunkell. He turned to leave and was met by the companions he had chosen. They all looked at him with understanding and sympathy but also a grim determination. Borim clapped him on the shoulder. He nodded to them in thanks.

He led the way as they exited the royal palace. Without the saphyrium helm, Thuradin felt naked, but he couldn't let that distract him. Ayrie, Borim, and Stürn had put their lives in his hands by agreeing to go with him to the outside world, and he would not fail them.

As they obtained provisions and made the final preparations for the journey, Thuradin felt a firmness of purpose creep through his mind. He would find Ronorim without losing any one of his companions in the outside world. They would all return home to Tinas Gran together. And once they returned, he would reclaim his position as commander of the royal guard. He would have his saphyrium helm back, whatever it took.

CHAPTER FIVE

Thuradin held his breath as his mount—a shaggy mountain ram—lost its footing for a moment on the steep stone steps. He looked down at the many lights emitted by Tinas Gran's large braziers and grimaced. They looked miniscule now that he was so high up, and he shuddered at the thought of how long it would take for him to reach the ground should his ram lose its footing entirely. He wondered if his companions felt as nervous as he did on their mounts. If they did, they were good at hiding it.

The four dwarves were on their way to Kul'Kriegar, where they would get additional supplies needed for their journey. Since they would already have to pass through the warrior city in order to reach the tunnel that would lead them to the outside world, Thuradin thought it would be best to get battle rams, which could only be bought there.

The rams of Tinas Gran were some of the best in the Dwarven Kingdom, but they were born within the mountains and had never seen the sun, like their dwarven masters. They would be unreliable in the outside. Kul'Kriegaran rams, however, were born outside the mountains and were captured once they wandered into one of the many dwarven tunnels. They would be better suited for the sun and they could help protect their riders from any threat they might encounter in the outside world. Kul'Kriegarans trained their rams to fight alongside their riders, after all.

After what seemed like an eternity to Thuradin, they finally reached the tunnel's entrance. The climb had been a long one and he was sure he wasn't the only one who was saddle sore, so he decided to stop their progress for a quick rest. They all dismounted and sat along the edge of the stairs, facing the city far below them. They chewed on dried ram meat, which made up the bulk of their provisions.

As Thuradin chewed on the dried slab of meat, Borim sat next to him and said, in a purposefully loud voice, "Well, I see ye're still the worst at riding rams."

Thuradin could hear chuckles coming from behind him, but they were quickly stifled.

"Well, I see ye're still the worst at conserving supplies," he retorted, inclining his head toward Borim's armload of ram meat. "Leave some for later, will ye? We have a long road ahead."

Borim grinned and walked away.

After one last look at the city he was leaving behind, Thuradin mounted his ram, telling the others to do the same. Once everyone was ready to move, he led the way into the tunnel.

The path rose at a thirty degree slope the entire way, forming sharp switchbacks every now and then. They rode in silence. The light from the never-ending torches on the walls gleamed off their armor, making it look like each dwarf emitted their own light. They rode for several hours before another break was called.

"It's getting close ta dusk; we'll camp here."

As he helped set up camp, Thuradin's mind wandered to

fantasies of the outside world. Like most dwarves, he had never been outside the mountains, so he didn't know what actual night or day looked like, but he could tell what time it was. The Enurg'en said it was because dwarves had become so attuned with the mountains they had lived in for so long that the stones around them helped them sense the time outside.

"Should we light a fire?" Ayrie asked.

Thuradin nodded. "Aye, I think it's safe. We're close enough ta the surface that even the tunnels have ventilation systems which will clear away the smoke."

Ayrie took the first watch as the rest of their group lit a fire and cooked a savory ram and mushroom stew.

Normally, a watch would not have been needed in tunnels so far from Dun'Burell, but after what had happened with the burrowers in Tinas Gran, Thuradin didn't want to chance it. It was unlikely any had managed to crawl so far into this tunnel system—especially after an army of Kul'Kriegarans had marched through it—but caution never killed anyone.

They took turns with their two-hour shifts. It was silent in the tunnel, and Thuradin looked forward to a decent night's sleep. But it was not meant to be. Only hours later, during Borim's watch, Thuradin was shaken awake.

Borim, with an unusually serious face, motioned for him to follow. Thuradin obeyed, wondering what could have caused his friend to act so strangely. He knelt next to where Borim had stopped and peered out into the darkness—the torches on the walls had been automatically extinguished during the night—trying to see what had alarmed Borim.

"I heard voices," he whispered. "Nae loud enough for me ta tell ye what they said, but they're nae being too quiet about it."

No sooner had Thuradin heard this than he too heard voices coming from the darkness. They were whispers, barely audible, but they were there. He nodded to Borim, and the two sat back with their weapons drawn, wondering what to do next.

The sound could be burrowers, Thuradin thought, but there was no way to be sure. He narrowed his eyes, trying to make something out of the darkness, but he could not.

"I say we ambush them."

Thuradin jumped at the unexpected voice. He looked to his right and saw Ayrie sitting next to him, her spear in hand.

She looked back at him with her sharp eyes. "Two of us should be enough."

Thuradin nodded. "Borim, ye stay here and keep watch, just in case there's a second group out there waiting for us ta leave. Ayrie, approach along the right side of the tunnel and wait for my signal ta attack, but don't go in for the kill until we know what or who they are. They could be another group of dwarves, for all we know. I'll take the left."

Ayrie nodded once, moved away toward the tunnel wall, and began to shuffle her way toward the voices. Thuradin went to the other side and did the same.

It didn't take long to draw level with the voices. They were louder now, but Thuradin still couldn't make out any words. He waited for a minute to give Ayrie ample time to reach her position, then gave a soft whistle.

Instantly the voices died out, only to be replaced by Ayrie's and Thuradin's war cry. The two charged the center and raised their weapons, ready to strike.

"Wait!" a voice cried out. Thuradin thought it sounded familiar. "We're on yer side; what do ye think ye're doing?"

"I should be asking ye the same question," Thuradin replied as he reached out to where he thought the voice had come from. He grasped a handful of thick hair and began to pull.

"Ah! Och! That's my beard! Stop that!" the voice cried.

The lack of light made it difficult to see specific features, but what Thuradin could make out were the figures of four kneeling dwarves and another one standing over them, holding a spear above their heads.

"Ayrie, stand down. Ye four, come inta the light."

He led the four dwarves with Ayrie in the rear to make sure none of them tried to escape. Borim yelped in surprise as they appeared suddenly from the darkness, but his expression quickly changed to intrigue when he saw who they had captured.

Now that they were in the light, Thuradin recognized them and was glad to see Bronn Lightninghammer among them. The other three were Bronn's apprentices. There was Threnn, looking surprisingly calm. Murtosh and Agrethar still looked somewhat stunned and jumped at the slightest sound.

"Bronn," Thuradin said, unable to mask his relief. "What are ye doing here? I thought ye had declined my invitation."

"I did." Bronn grumbled. "I'm sorry, Thuradin, but I'm too old. I'd only cause trouble for the rest of ye. These boys, however—" he nodded his head at the three dwarves behind him who, Thuradin noticed, were all heavily armored and looked ready for battle, "—these boys wouldn't allow for no aid ta be given when the cause is ta find their King. They've volunteered ta join ye, if ye'll have them."

Thuradin studied the three dwarves. They were in excellent shape. Along with their thick armor, each carried a large, rectangular shield that covered more than half of their body. Such shields were expensive No ordinary dwarf could afford them. He knew that Bronn must have paid a hefty sum to get such a beneficial piece of equipment for all three of them.

"Bronn," Thuradin said quietly. "Can I talk ta ye alone for a moment?"

The two walked deeper into the tunnel until they were out of earshot.

"Do ye want them ta join me?"

"I have no say in this matter," Bronn said, though Thuradin could sense his anxiety. "They've chosen their own paths and I must respect their decision. The only thing I can do as their mentor is give them all the skills and equipment they need ta survive."

Thuradin nodded.

"Bronn, I know how much these three mean ta ye. We all know they're like yer own—"

Bronn glanced sharply at Thuradin. Thuradin knew he had lost both of his sons in Dur 'Burell around the same time Thuradin had lost his father. He also knew it was a touchy subject, and he had no wish to aggravate the old warrior.

"Thuradin," Bronn broke the silence. "I won't deny that I hold these three dwarves close ta my heart, but they aren't my real sons. I know that. They have their own wills and they've chosen ta follow ye." Bronn glanced at the three dwarves in question and in a softer voice said, "That being said, I want ye ta look after them. They all are young and have bright futures ahead. Murtosh is the youngest and I'm sure ye know what line of dwarves he comes from."

Thuradin did know. The line of Firebrand was famous

for their bloodlust and their tendency to go berserk in battle. He remembered that, once, the orange-haired youth had tried to join the royal guards but had given it up to be Bronn's apprentice instead.

"He is the last of his line," Bronn continued. "All of his brothers died in Dun'Burell and left no heirs. He, too, is heirless. If he dies, the name of Firebrand dies with him."

Thuradin glanced at the orange-haired dwarf. His face seemed to glow in the firelight. To dwarves, bloodline was one of the most important things in life and the thought of losing a family name was feared by many.

"I'll protect him."

"Threnn is the second oldest of the three and is the only one who has a wife and child he's leaving behind. He's a quick learner and intuitive. He has a bright future ahead of him that he has ta come back ta. He doesn't deserve that future ta be cut short."

Thuradin nodded, promising again to protect the three dwarves. Threnn, he knew, aspired to be part of the royal guard and had nearly enough experience to do so. He also knew that because he was the commander—former commander, he corrected himself grudgingly—Threnn looked up to him. He had no doubt the younger dwarf would obey everything Thuradin told him to do, no matter the consequences.

"And Agrethar," Bronn said with a soft sigh. "Agrethar is my successor, as ye know. He was an orphan when I found him, and it was so soon after my own sons died that I took him in as my own. I didn't want him ta go on this journey, but he says he must uphold my honor and go in my place since I'm unable. He looks up ta the other two—they're like brothers ta each other—and follows them everywhere. Just make sure that no harm comes ta him. I couldn't bear it if he were ta—"

"Bronn," Thuradin put a hand on the elderly dwarf's shoulder. He could feel him trembling as his old eyes looked up. "I will do everything in my power, I will even lay down my own life, if it can save yer dwarves. We will all return safe."

Bronn looked at Thuradin for a moment and let out a shaky breath, closing his eyes. "Aye, I know ye will. I thank ye, Thuradin. Yer words give me some comfort."

The two dwarves gripped each other's wrists, and after a few final words with his apprentices, Bronn departed and made his way back to Tinas Gran. The three new additions to the group sat around the campfire awkwardly, speaking in short sentences. Eventually they followed Ayrie's example and went to sleep.

Thuradin stayed awake a while longer with Borim, who was still on watch. The two sat in silence for most of the time. It wasn't until near the end of the shift that Borim finally asked the question Thuradin had been asking himself since Bronn left.

"What do ye think?"

"I think," Thuradin said, trying to keep his voice low and steady, "that they may be more of a burden ta us than a help."

The next morning they broke up their camp and resumed their journey to Kul'Kriegar. By midday, the tunnel ended and the warrior city was spread out before them.

Upon arriving, Thuradin noticed the three newest members of their party talking excitedly to each other as they took in the city. Such a reaction wasn't strange since not every dwarven city was the same, but it didn't help encourage him. The dwarves were so young, so eager to see new things. He would even call them naïve. He hoped they were prepared to face the dangers awaiting them all.

Kul'Kriegar was built for war. Several dense towers stood over the city in many different areas, and all of them were garrisoned by heavily armed dwarves. The city rang with the constant hammering of blacksmiths as they worked on weapons, armor, and other necessities for war. The sound of warriors training for battle could be heard from the various barracks throughout the city.

The city's citadel—built for the viceroy of Kul'Kriegar—was far different from the ornate and artistic architecture that made up Tinas Gran's royal palace. The citadel was surrounded by a large wall made of the mountain's hard stone, a perfect fortress. It was a sturdy, cylindrical building that acted as a support pillar for the cavern's ceiling. Windows weren't a part of the building until twenty stories up to ensure no ladders could be used to climb inside. There was only one entrance. The entire structure was a testament to the Kul'Kriegarans' determination and ability to defend themselves.

Threnn, Agrethar, and Murtosh found it impressive. Thuradin found it boring.

"Keep up, lads. We're nae waiting for ye," he called out when he saw them still gawking at the keep. His voice snapped them out of their wandering thoughts, and they hastily rejoined the group.

Thuradin led them to the stables where new battle-rams were raised and trained. After trading in their own mounts, he haggled with the stable master for new ones. It didn't take long for him to convince the Kul'Kriegaran to settle for less gold once he mentioned they were on a quest for the King.

That had been his last bargaining chip. He hadn't wanted to use it, but he was glad it had its desired effect.

The group stayed for a day in Kul'Kriegar, and by the next morning, after a small breakfast, they resumed their journey.

They entered the tunnel leading to the outside world and rode in silence. There wasn't much to say. Thuradin knew they all felt anxious for what was to come. The worst part was, he thought, they didn't know what was to come.

He wasn't much better. He had read through every old text he could find that offered information on the outside world before they had left Dun'Aldor. The last time the dwarves had regularly gone outside had been a millennium ago. Because of this, all the dusty tomes provided him with were rumors and legends and myths of terrible creatures. Beasts he couldn't even imagine were, according to these documents, alive and thriving outside—many of them had been marked as dangerous.

When Bronn's apprentices joined them, Thuradin had been both relieved and frustrated. On one hand, more fighting dwarves meant a better chance of survival in any potential battles. On the other hand, watching over three of his own members like he was their mother might prove deadly in the end. He wondered if he was up to the task. And, as his mind returned to the things he had read about, he remembered one particular bit of unnerving information.

According to the texts, there existed a small civilization in the outside world that used to trade regularly with the dwarves long ago. These beings weren't painted in a good light, and it made him wonder how those trade ties had begun in the first place. He hoped they wouldn't have to run into any of these beings, these *viatari*. He had translated most of what was written about them from the Ancient Dwarvish and was chilled by the translation of their name. Eng'Pergen. Life stealers.

Thuradin shuddered at the thought of meeting these viatari. He alone knew of their existence, and he wanted to keep it that way. If he felt so fearful at the thought of encountering them, he wondered how the others might react if he told them of their existence. Would they flee? Would they no longer be willing to follow him? He couldn't risk it. It was better to leave it to chance that they would never run into these life-stealers and hope the journey progressed smoothly.

The line of torches, which had kept them company since they left Tinas Gran, ended. The tunnel grew dark, but the dwarves continued moving forward as if nothing had changed. Soon a bright light was ahead of them. Thuradin called for a halt.

"Put on yer extra skins."

The group dismounted and took off their armor. They helped each other wrap themselves in a skin-tight cocoon of the thickest fabric the dwarves could make. After everything, except for their eyes, was wrapped in cloth, they put their armor back on.

Each dwarf had a visor connected to his helmet. The visor had slits large enough to see through, and these slits were covered by a thin fabric to block out the sunlight without completely obstructing their vision.

Now, their bodies completely covered, the dwarves remounted and continued riding toward the tunnel exit. The light of the sun enveloped every member as they traveled away from the familiar Dwarven Kingdom and into the unknown.

Thuradin noticed his companions trembling, though they were doing their best to conceal it. He imagined what was going through their heads. Within his own he could already imagine hearing their anguished cries as their protective cloths failed and the sun melted their skin. But whatever fears gripped their minds, it didn't stop them from following him. They didn't hesitate. None of them stopped.

None of them looked back.

CHAPTER SIX

Light engulfed them in its bright glory. The dwarves, unaccustomed to such brightness, couldn't help but shield their eyes. Thankfully, only a few words of complaint were all Thuradin heard as they entered the outside world. There were no cries of shock, no melting limbs. His plan to repel the sun seemed to be working. From the moment he had first thought of it, he hadn't been completely sure if it *would* work. He was glad that his gamble had paid off.

After several minutes of blinking and shading their eyes, the dwarves grew more accustomed to the light. Thuradin looked around to try and get ahold of his surroundings.

The tunnel had deposited them halfway up the mountain, which meant they had a long climb down before they could go anywhere. Once they reached the ground, they would have to find a way to circle around the mountain range in order to reach the tunnel to Dun'Burell on the other side.

It would have been shorter to cut across the mountain range, but they would have no chance of arriving to Dun'Burell if they did so. There were too many dangerous beasts they could encounter, and Thuradin didn't have enough dwarves to fight them all. They wouldn't last a day, and he would have failed his King. At least with the unknown, they didn't know their chances and could continue their journey with, if nothing else, a small hope for success.

As he looked around, Thuradin saw the tunnel entrance from which they had just exited. It was a large, gaping hole with an equally large gate in front of it. To an outsider, the open gate might look to be nothing more than a slab of stone lying on top of two upright ones. To the dwarves, however, this gate was the last sign of home that they would see for some time. Ancient Dwarvish runes ran along the top slab, which read: *Welcome friend, be warned foe, ye are now entering the Dwarven Kingdom.* On both sides of the gate stood a large stone statue of a dwarf in full armor, thrusting his warhammer triumphantly into the air.

Thuradin shifted his gaze to his fellow dwarves behind him. "Right," he said, his voice muffled behind layers of cloth and armor. "Let's get moving."

He whirled his mount around and steered it toward a narrow mountain trail. He remained wary. While they were on the safer route, there were still many dangerous and hostile creatures that liked to make their homes around the middle and lower parts of the mountain.

Their rams trotted down the rocky trail in single file. Accustomed to such uneven ground, they had no trouble keeping their footing and even seemed to enjoy themselves as they continued down. Occasionally, they bleated to each other gleefully, or so Thuradin imagined.

Like the tunnels, the trail zigzagged all the way down the mountain to maintain the same angle of descent. On one side of the trail was the mountain face and on the other, a long drop. The trail continued like this for some time, but every now and then, it led into a relatively open space where they could all gather and rest without having to worry about falling off the ledge.

Thuradin had no idea how these "resting ledges," as he called them, had formed, but he knew they couldn't be natural because they were perfectly and consistently spaced and always large enough for a moderately-sized group to rest.

They stopped at every resting ledge but never for long. Thuradin was determined to reach the base of the mountain before the day was done. He didn't want to remain in this danger zone for the night. There had already been several close calls where the most prominent danger in the area, a grattle, had come within inches of noticing them. During these times, the dwarves had to sit still and remain silent as the large reptile crawled along the mountain's face nearby. So far, they had managed to avoid detection.

Grattles were vicious beasts, lizard-like in almost every aspect but size. They averaged at about ten feet tall and fifteen feet long, much larger than the average dwarf. All it would take was for one grattle to jump into their group and knock everyone off the ledge, and their journey would come to an abrupt end.

Worse, these reptiles were hard to kill. Their scales provided a naturally tough armor for their head, back, and sides, and their scales were so thick they might as well have been made of rock.

Decapitation would have been the best method—their necks had the least amount of armor—but grattles had a defense mechanism for that. Hidden spikes of bone would shoot out all along the neck if anything or anyone came near. In most cases, this was enough to make anyone think twice about attacking one of the giant reptiles.

Through the few encounters they'd had with small groups of grattles wandering into their tunnels, the dwarves had discovered that the next best way to kill them was if they opened their mouth. The mouth and eyes were the only areas not covered in armor—easy targets for dwarves to lodge spears or axes.

It usually didn't require too many dwarves to kill a single grattle, but grattles weren't solitary creatures. Calculating and imagining scenarios as he led the group down the trail, Thuradin figured that any pack which consisted of more than three grattles would be too much for them to handle.

They approached another resting ledge, which meant another short break before pressing on. Thuradin saw that this one was situated just before a bend in the trail. He decided it would be wise to scout the next section of the mountain before they traveled down.

"Borim, with me."

Borim groaned but got up to follow Thuradin. Following the commander's example, he took out his kite-shield and strapped it snugly around his left arm, while in his right he wielded a smooth, square-faced hammer.

The two dwarves stopped at the edge of the bend and cautiously poked their heads around it. Thuradin waited a few seconds, but nothing stirred. It looked like the trail ahead was completely clear. He sighed, relieved.

"I think I'm getting too old for this."

"Ye and me both," Borim replied.

They took a couple tentative steps forward. Borim never lowered his shield or hammer, but Thuradin started to relax once it became clear there was no danger present. He was just about to mention their luck when he noticed something was wrong.

Borim stood rigidly where he was, staring, unblinking, ahead of them. Thuradin turned slowly and looked once more down the trail and noticed two yellow eyes staring back.

He tensed but didn't make any sudden movements. The grattle's gray scales had camouflaged it into the mountain face, but now that he looked closely, he could see the outline of its reptilian body. It hadn't seen them, though, or they would have been dead by now. But the beast knew something was there and stared at the spot where it sensed food, waiting for any small movement. An understanding passed between Borim and Thuradin. If either one of them moved, they would both die. The best thing to do was wait and hope that the grattle lost interest.

This grattle appeared to be young. Its size was hardly larger than one of the battle rams; yet, if anything, that only made the situation more dangerous. Because grattles traveled in packs, there was no doubt that this one's mother was nearby, and an angry mother was a dangerous thing to encounter in any species.

The grattle cocked its head to the side and blinked. Like all of its kind, its vision was so terrible it couldn't see the two dwarves in front of it. However, its sense of smell was superb. It was only by the purest luck that Borim and Thuradin happened to be downwind off the beast.

Finally, after what seemed like an eternity, the grattle shook its head and crawled away. Thuradin and Borim waited a few more minutes to make sure it wasn't some sort of trick before sprinting back to the resting ledge.

The small camp noticed their hasty return and they stood up expectantly. Some of them drew weapons.

"Grattle," Thuradin said grimly. "A wee one too, and ye all know what that means."

They nodded and moved to their battle rams to make preparations.

Young grattles never left their birthplace. A pack of grattles never left their young behind. They had to assume the next part of the trail was infested with the reptiles. Thuradin couldn't risk a fight, nor would he want to, even if the pack was small. They had to try to sneak past them during the night while the grattles slept. The rest of the day would be spent making preparations for that.

They set about using the last of their strips of cloth to cover the rams' hooves. Every single item the rams carried was tied down as tightly as possible to avoid accidental noises from shifting gear. Likewise, when the time came, everyone would tighten the straps of their own armor as much as possible to keep their plate pieces from clanking together.

When all of this was done, a watch was set up, and the rest of the dwarves went to sleep, rotating shifts every few hours.

Dusk seemed to linger an eternity.

As the dwarves made final preparations, Thuradin identified the moon. He had never seen it before, and it filled him with a sense of wonder he couldn't describe to the others. He felt encouraged by its soft glow as he mounted his ram and waited for the others to do the same.

The moon was high by the time they were ready to move out. They kept their rams at a walking pace. The normally sharp crack of hooves against rock was reduced to a soft thud. As they approached the bend in the trail, clouds floated in and covered the sky and the moon's now-unwelcome light.

Luck seemed to be with them tonight.

They rounded the bend and made their way down the next section of the mountain, making sure to keep their distance from the mountain face. Grattles had a habit of sticking to the walls while they slept. It would do no good to accidentally bump into one.

They made good progress, hardly making a sound as they passed the large beasts breathing rhythmically against the wall next to them. Their mounts seemed to understand the gravity of the situation and didn't so much as shake their shaggy manes. It was all going smoothly, just as Thuradin had envisioned it. When they reached the halfway mark of the trail, he began to think this night might be uneventful. Then Borim's stomach growled.

The dwarves stopped in their tracks. Thuradin turned to look at Borim, who rode right behind him. The darkness from the cloud cover was complete, and his friend was completely covered in armor, but he could imagine Borim's face paling significantly as he realized what had just happened.

Thuradin turned his head to the right and saw what he feared he might: round yellow orbs appeared and then disappeared in growing rapidity. Blinking. The grattles were waking up. And there were a lot of them.

"Ride!" Thuradin yelled as he spurred his ram to a full gallop.

The wind rushed past him, as did the wall of yellow orbs. He tried to keep count of how many pairs of eyes there were, but there were too many. He lost track at fifteen. He had never heard—never dreamed—of such a large pack. Now, despite the odds, his small group of dwarves had to either escape or make a stand and fight, but they couldn't do the latter on the trail. They had to find a resting ledge.

The grattles would have been far too fast for the dwarves to outrun, even on mounts, if not for their lethargy. The dwarves had to find a resting ledge before the grattles fully awoke.

They rounded the next bend in the trail and continued riding at a swift gallop. Brilliant white light lit up the world for a split second as the moon peeked curiously over the clouds, but it was enough for Thuradin to see the next resting ledge. And it was a big one.

As he rode, Thuradin loosened his armor straps, hoping the others were doing the same. There was no need for silence anymore, and their fighting ability would be hindered if their armor was too tight.

The rams slid to a halt as they entered the spacious ledge, and the dwarves immediately dismounted and drew their weapons. Thuradin turned to face the grattles, only to see that the trail behind them was empty. He looked around and saw nothing but his companions. The grattles hadn't followed them.

Borim walked up to him as they began to let their guards down. "I . . . I swear I ate. I don't understand how—" he said, bewildered, as he tried to find the right words to explain what had happened. But Thuradin just shook his head.

"Couldn't be helped. We're lucky they decided nae ta follow us."

"Commander," Ayrie called out. "I think ye'd better look up before ye say anything else."

Thuradin's stomach twisted at the words. It twisted even more when he saw what she meant. Yellow orbs appeared from the ledge above them, pair by pair, and slowly grew in size as the grattles crawled down the mountain face.

He had been mistaken. The grattles had indeed followed them, and they were hungry.

CHAPTER SEVEN

They descended slowly.

There was no urgency to their movements; after all, their prey was no match for their speed. The dwarves had no chance of outrunning them. That was why they had taken their time waking up. The dwarves were limited by the trails they had to follow; they were forced to zigzag back and forth along the switchbacks. The grattles were not hindered by such limitations.

Thuradin cursed his luck. He thought back to when he had estimated how many grattles his group of dwarves could handle at a time. What he saw now he knew for certain far exceeded any number he'd imagined. He had to think of a plan quickly if they were to survive.

An idea came to him. It was a tactical folly, he knew, but he was desperate. With no time to think of another plan or about how disastrously this could end, he put his thoughts into action.

"Split inta groups of three!" he ordered. "Stürn, stay where ye are and focus on healing. No one can die tonight. We'll keep them off ye as best we can!"

With that, he, Borim, and Ayrie jumped away to one side

of the ledge while Threnn, Murtosh, and Agrethar jumped to the other. Stürn stood his ground. As long as he remained relatively still, he wouldn't be noticed by the grattles, especially under the cover of darkness.

The grattles didn't charge down in a frenzy. Instead, they challenged each group one at a time while the others watched. Thuradin realized they were toying with them. That was fine. This would give his dwarves a chance to lower the grattles' numbers before the real attack began.

Borim let loose a savage war cry as the first grattle approached and began smacking his hammer against his shield, making a racket. The reptile, confused by the strange attack, hesitated for a moment. It was enough.

Ayrie's spear sailed through the air and ran straight through the grattle's eye, through its brain, and out the other end in a flash. The beast dropped without realizing it was dead.

The next grattle charged at the now-weaponless Ayrie, but Borim was quicker and intercepted the attack. The beast's claws deflected off his shield with a resounding *shing!* Dwarven craftsmanship was excellent, and Borim's shield was made by one of the best blacksmiths around. It could withstand most attacks without so much as denting.

Ayrie sprinted to her spear and rearmed herself. She and Thuradin circled their foe until they were on either side of it. Borim still had its attention and didn't show the slightest sign of giving it up.

Jumping onto the grattle's back, Thuradin dug his axes into its hard scales for grip as it began to buck. The grattle jerked from one direction to the next, trying to shake the new weight off, but Thuradin had dug his axes in deep. The beast turned its head and snapped at him, but he was just out of reach. An angry gurgling sound came from its throat.

Ayrie's spear sped through the air again but missed the grattle's eye as it drew its head back for another attempt at Thuradin. The reptile's gaze followed the lethal projectile and it seemed to remember there were other dwarves trying to kill it as well. It turned its attention back to them. The grattle knew its weaknesses, and the dwarf on its back wasn't too much of a threat as he was.

It whipped its tail at Borim and knocked him into a nearby boulder. The older dwarf groaned and coughed hard. By the way he clutched his stomach and struggled to lift himself off the ground, Thuradin guessed he had broken a few ribs. Ayrie, having retrieved her spear, drew the grattle's attention away from the incapacitated dwarf. She rolled left and right, barely managing to avoid the beast's sharp claws as it hissed in triumph.

Stürn watched the battle, constantly aware of where he was needed most.

As Thuradin had suggested, his sole focus here was to heal the party. Under worse circumstances, Stürn might have ignored the orders and gone down fighting with the rest of his companions. There was no point in healing a hopeless battle. This one looked bad, but it wasn't hopeless. He was one of the most powerful Enurg'en in history, and he was confident he could keep everyone alive.

Thrennn and his group had taken down their first few grattles with incredible ease. Now the beasts increased the pressure and attacked all at once, but the group of three continued to hold.

Thuradin's group was doing equally well, but once Stürn saw Borim crash into a boulder, he knew it was his turn to act.

He closed his eyes and focused on the dwarf's life-energies. He called out to them. They were scrambling all over the place, a sign that Borim had been badly injured. He pleaded with them to stay put and heal Borim quickly. They were resistant at first and tried escaping from the internal wounds. Stürn reprimanded them and cowed them into submission. He focused them onto the affected areas and watched them mend the broken bones until they were fully healed. The entire process took less than five seconds.

With Borim at full strength, Stürn turned his attention back to Threnn's group, which had been split up—each dwarf fought his own grattle. He set his focus on Murtosh and grimaced. The fool had gone berserk and now received more wounds than he gave out.

The Enurg'en sighed and wondered how the name of Firebrand had survived for so long.

A groan escaped Borim's lips as he felt his ribs break. He had been careless in thinking that his shield would protect him completely. Now he watched helplessly as Ayrie kept light on her feet and continued to move in circles to avoid the grattle's attacks. He wanted to help, to bring the beast's attention back to him, but he couldn't stand.

A sudden warmth seeped through him. His ribs hurt less and less until they didn't hurt at all. He stood up without the least bit of pain and tapped his hammer lightly against his torso to make sure his ribs were alright. He nodded, satisfied, and raised his hammer toward Stürn in thanks. He then charged the grattle, giving the reptile a mighty smack in the face with his hammer. Its attention was back on him.

* * *

Threnn grimaced as the grattle he was fighting managed to bypass his guard and slash his leg. A burning sensation erupted from the the wounded area and went all the way up to his head. He staggered for a moment, but within those few seconds the burning pain disappeared, and he knew without looking that Stürn had healed him.

The grattle hissed angrily as it realized its attack had no effect again. The two circled each other. Threnn took the lull in fighting to check on his companions.

Agrethar had been injured many times and bled profusely, but the bleeding stopped almost as soon as it began thanks to Stürn. Even after enduring a powerful blow, he didn't seem to feel or care about the pain and continued with his increasingly reckless attacks. Already he had killed two grattles by himself, and Threnn sensed that he was on the verge of going into a berserker's rage.

Murtosh, on the other hand, had already snapped.

He laughed like a maniac as he received blow after blow from the grattles he faced only to have his wounds healed immediately. His beard was a dark red instead of its natural orange because of the blood—both his own and the grattles'. Threnn watched as Murtosh managed to dodge his foe's snapping jaws and sank his axe deep into the beast's throat, killing it. He roared victoriously and ran to greet his next enemy.

Looking back at his own grattle, Threnn was thankful for the shield he carried. It was the reason he hadn't taken the same substantial damage his friends had.

Before dismounting, the three dwarves had agreed it would be best to have only one of them carry the shield and keep the grattles' attention while the other two used their heavy two-handed weapons for killing blows. While it was nice to have received fewer wounds, Threnn had only been able to kill one grattle on his own—and that by pure luck. He simply couldn't do enough damage with just his sword. The best he could do right now was keep this particular grattle busy.

With a roar, he slammed his shield into the grattle's jaw and heard bones crack.

He smiled.

His sword may not be able to do enough damage, but his shield might.

Thuradin gouged the grattle's eyes out with his axes.

As the reptile screeched in pain, Ayrie delivered the finishing blow and skewered the roof of its open mouth with her spear. It fell in a heap, and Thuradin rolled off and onto the ground.

He nursed his injured shoulder, which had been stabbed by one of the grattle's defensive neck-spikes. He had been climbing across the beast's back carelessly in an attempt to reach the head quickly and had been rewarded with a spike through the shoulder. Only after he cut it off with his axe had he been able to continue climbing onto the grattle's head.

He pulled the remainder of the spike from his shoulder and waited for Stürn to heal it. He could feel the Enurg'en's powers influence his life-energies to mend the gaping hole. The next time he looked, the wound was gone. He grinned, ready to face the next grattle, and was surprised to see there were no more.

The grattles that still lived had given up on fighting the dwarves. They realized, after losing more than half their pack, that these dwarves were far too well trained. They weren't worth the trouble. Silently, they sulked back up the mountain face to return to their slumber.

The dwarves collapsed, exhausted. But after a brief rest, Thuradin had them up again.

"Get what cloth ye can find and cover up those holes in yer armor. We have ta be completely covered before the sun rises."

It was only a temporary fix. Thuradin knew that they had to repair their armor properly before the next battle—assuming there would be one—if they wanted to stay alive. But they couldn't repair it here, where the sun could catch them off guard. For now, they needed to find a cave. Thankfully, the mountainside was riddled with them.

The sky was growing lighter as the dwarves entered one of the large holes in the mountains. As their eyes adjusted to the darkness, Thuradin saw something he hadn't expected. Anvils and forges sat in separate corners of the cave, all of which looked dwarven in style.

"This cave has been occupied in the past," he said as he trudged to the nearest forge and wiped off the layers of dust and dirt that rested there.

"They must be ancient," Ayrie noted, inspecting one of the anvils. "I remember reading how the dwarves used ta live in the outside world. I guess this is proof."

Thuradin glanced in her direction. If she had been reading about the dwarves and the outside world, he wondered if she also knew about the viatari.

"They still look like they'll work!" Threnn said excitedly after inspecting one of the forge's fuel tanks.

"Right," Thuradin said. "Well, let's light them up, then. We need ta repair our armor before we try going back outside."

For the rest of the day, they stayed in the cave, warmed by the forge's fires, repairing their damaged armor with spare metal scraps they had brought for the journey. They took off their protective cloths while they worked. They were far enough inside the cave. They didn't need to worry about the sunlight here. It almost felt like home.

After a day of rest, they resumed their journey. Having spent a day without wearing the protective cloths, wearing them now was uncomfortable. But, Thuradin reminded himself, discomfort came second to what could happen if they took them off.

The rest of their journey down the mountain was uneventful. As they reached the woods below they all looked up to see how far they had come. He couldn't make out too much detail, but Thuradin was sure he could see the smooth set of stone slabs that made up the gates to the Dwarven Kingdom. It was such a tiny thing when seen from the ground.

With Ayrie in the lead, keeping watch for any potentially dangerous tracks, the dwarves quickly found a road that led south and followed it. It was the only road that would take them completely around the mountain range, according to the old maps Thuradin had.

An itch began to gnaw at Thuradin's mind, and no matter what he tried, he couldn't distract himself from it. After an agonizing hour of suffering silently, he turned to Borim, who nodded without him even having to say anything. He had the same feeling.

Something was wrong.

As their mounts walked along the road, there were

sudden bursts of song which Thuradin assumed came from the strange flying creatures he had never seen before—they reminded him of bats, though they were much prettier—but then, just as suddenly, the singing stopped, followed by an ominous silence.

His instincts told him something was watching them, but he shrugged the thought aside. He had no idea what it was like in the outside world, and Ayrie hadn't mentioned crossing any strange tracks. For all he knew, the sporadic singing might be a natural thing. Still, he decided to remain vigilant. He glanced, every now and then, from side to side and up at the treetops to see if anyone was watching them.

After a few hours of riding, the dwarves left the wooded area they were in and stopped to set up camp for the day. They were now in an open field, with grass almost as far as the eye could see. So far, Thuradin hadn't seen any wildlife, except for the occasional flying creature, and even those he hadn't seen lately. He declared it safe to build a fire. They would have hot food today rather than the hard rations they had been forced to eat on the mountain. Soon the smell of mushroom stew and fried ram meat wafted through the air, making all of their mouths water. They washed the meal down with ale that Borim had brought on one of the extra rams.

Thuradin hadn't eaten like that in days, and the ale hit the spot. He lay back on a lonely log with a happy grin hidden under his helmet. But his smile slowly faded as the itch came back into his mind. A sound came from behind, and he whirled around to see what had made it, but nothing caught his eye. He glanced around in all directions, hoping to catch a glimpse of anything unusual but, as far as he could tell, there was nothing out of the ordinary.

Standing up uncertainly, he made his way to where Borim was lying down, humming an upbeat tune. Thuradin nudged him with his boot.

"Remain vigilant," he said.

"Oh, aye," Borim yawned.

Thuradin then made his way to where Ayrie and the rest of the dwarves were. They sat in a circle, deep in their own discussion, and stopped suddenly when they noticed him.

"Do ye feel it too?" he asked.

They all nodded. Everyone seemed to have the same feeling, and Thuradin was beginning to suspect that his initial instincts may have been correct.

Another sound came from behind. He whirled around again. The other dwarves scrambled to their feet and looked around as well, but none of them could see what had caused the sound. A creeping paranoia began forming within their minds.

Suddenly, the flying creatures burst into song again and, just as suddenly, they stopped, only to be followed by a jarring call moments later that made the skin crawl.

Thuradin frowned. There were too many coincidences, too many signs that he couldn't ignore anymore. And if those signs alone were still not enough to convince him, the fact that the flying creatures hadn't been seen since the dwarves had left the woods behind was.

They were being watched.

CHAPTER EIGHT

A watch of three dwarves was set up that night, with shifts set for every few hours. The fire was extinguished, and the three sentries watched over the rest of the group while they slept. The moon was bright and kept anything from hiding in shadow.

Thuradin was part of the first watch. He found a lone boulder several feet from the campsite and sat on it. From here, he could see almost the entirety of the plain they were in. Agrethar and Ayrie found their own watch posts, and together—along with the mountains behind them—they formed a decent perimeter around the campsite. Nothing could approach them without being seen.

Thuradin had ordered everyone to continue covering up their skin, even at night as a precaution, but he was starting to regret it. While within the mountains it was always chilly, out here, he couldn't stop sweating. It appeared that they had left the mountains during summer.

He had read about the changing seasons before they had left. Because seasons didn't exist within the mountains, he had hoped they would come out during the winter so that they wouldn't have to adapt too much to the climate. Hope, unfortunately, could only do so much when confronted with reality.

Behind him, he could hear the soft snoring of Threnn and Murtosh and the impossibly loud huffing of Borim. Stürn was as silent asleep as he was awake. It had been a tiring day of riding, and the four dwarves had fallen asleep almost as soon as their heads touched their bedrolls.

Thuradin stifled a yawn and groaned. This would be a long night. The paranoia had stayed with them ever since they had left the mountains. Even now, he could feel something watch him as he tried in vain to find the source.

Several times he thought he caught a glimpse of silver pop up from the tall grass, but almost as soon as he noticed it, it vanished. He sat there for three hours, waiting for the silver whatever-it-was to pop up long enough for him to identify it, but he could never catch a full image. He only ever saw it in his peripherals.

A hand gripped his shoulder, and he jumped. Turning, he saw Borim.

"My turn. Go get some rest."

Thuradin nodded and trudged back to the campsite, where he gratefully sank into his bedroll.

When morning came, Thuradin asked Borim if he had noticed anything suspicious. Borim said he had not, leaving him to wonder if the silver whatever-it-was truly existed or if he had just been seeing things. He had been tired, after all.

With a quick breakfast of leftovers from yesterday's dinner in their stomachs, the dwarves broke camp and continued following the road south. Every now and then, they switched from a steady trot to a walk and then back. This enabled them to cover a fair distance without expending too much of their mounts' energy.

The road followed the mountains closely for the most part, and for a long time, the terrain on their right remained a flat, dry plain. The sickly-green grass surrounding them was tall, and Thuradin could make out no sign of their stalkers in it.

After lunch, he noticed scattered trees in the distance, rising above the sea of grass. When they reached a turn in the road, they saw the beginnings of a large forest. It looked a long way away, but the trees were still incredibly tall. Thuradin thought if they looked like this from where they were at present, they had to be gigantic up close.

This was the first forest he had ever seen, and he had to admit he was impressed by its majesty. The texts he had read before their quest and the map he had stored in his saddlebag mentioned this forest, he remembered, but the descriptions did not give it justice.

After a half hour of riding, the road split into two separate trails. Thuradin checked his map. Both trails led to Dun'Burell's tunnel, but the trail on their left would be faster and would stay closer to the mountains, which gave him a sense of security.

They took the left trail. Every now and then, they stared at the forest, which had begun to feel more ominous and foreboding the closer they got to it. The sense of being watched was still there, but they could feel it fading gradually with every step they took away from the large mass of trees—though it never disappeared completely.

As they rode, Thuradin took out the map and studied it. According to it, they could go through a pass that cut straight through the mountain range. It would be a perfect place for an ambush—even the map said so—but after having survived the unprecedented grattle attack the other night, he was confident his companions were more than capable of handling extreme situations. Plus, it would be significantly quicker than going around the entire mountain range. They would reach Dun'Burell with time to spare.

However, once the pass came into view, his hopes of an early arrival vanished. In front of them, where the pass should have been, was nothing but a huge pile of rocks. He should have expected something like this. The map he was using was ancient. It dated back to a time when dwarves visited the surface regularly. It represented what the world looked like then, not now. Anything could have happened during the time in between.

In this case, it looked like rockslide after rockslide had hit the same spot over the centuries, eventually blocking off the pass entirely. The rocks had stacked on top of each other and eventually became part of the mountain.

With the pass blocked off, the dwarves would have to take their original route and ride all the way down the mountain range and then back up. And the only path that led that way was through the forest.

"Couldn't we just climb up and over?" Agrethar suggested. "There's no way the entire pass is filled."

Thuradin was considering this course of action when a chorus of loud screeches filled the air. It was a grattle's call, and it had come from the top of the blocked-off pass. He made a decision.

"Grattles have already infested this part of the mountain range. I won't risk another battle with them when they know we're coming—if we surprised them, maybe, but nae like this. We have ta go through the forest."

With that, he turned his ram back the way they came and

broke into a gallop, wanting to regain the time they had lost for coming to this dead end. The others followed.

It didn't take long for them to retrace their steps back to the fork in the road, but as they drew nearer, they noticed the feeling of being watched had strengthened. They slowed to a walk and followed the trail to the forest. They had wasted too much of the day, though. Already, the sun was descending. At this rate, Thuradin thought, they might not even enter the forest before dusk. They would have to set up camp outside its domain.

His prediction turned out to be correct. Half of the sun had already disappeared below the horizon by the time they reached the forest's boundaries.

The dwarves stared at the wall of trees before them as their growing shadows enveloped them. The eyes of beasts and critters within reflected the fading light eerily. Thuradin hoped his mind was only playing tricks on him, but he thought he could see humanoid figures high in the branches. He turned to Borim and pointed up at the branches, but when he looked back, the figures were gone.

After Ayrie performed her customary perimeter sweep of the area to check for suspicious tracks or any sign that they should leave, they split up and started setting up camp.

Thuradin was in charge of collecting firewood today. He entered the forest, with Borim as his helper, to search for fallen branches or anything that looked like it would burn. The ground was littered with them, making the collection easy, but the feeling of someone or something watching them had reached a frightening intensity. He couldn't help but look behind him every few seconds to see if anything was stalking them, and he noticed Borim doing the same.

The trees here were much thicker than the ones in the

woods they had traveled through before. Light filtered through the canopy of leaves but only fell in certain spots. The areas that weren't touched with light were covered in complete, impenetrable shadow. Thuradin imagined that these darker sections grew pitch black during the night. Anyone within them could disappear completely.

While he searched for more wood, Thuradin caught glimpses of their stalkers. They mostly hid in the shadows, and he never saw them in their entirety, only small glimpses. He would see blood-red eyes here, a flicker of silver there, but he only ever saw them for a split second.

He knew that whatever It was watching them had been doing so since they stepped off the mountain range. He now also knew for a fact that he had indeed seen silver the night he had been on watch. He double checked with Borim to make sure he wasn't alone in these sightings, and felt goosebumps rise when Borim said he was seeing the same things.

It wasn't until the second trip into the forest for more wood that Thuradin discovered what the silver stuff was. It was hair. A strand of it landed on his shoulder as he bent down to retrieve another piece of wood. He picked it off and held it between his fingers to examine it. This was no fur from an animal; it was too long and the texture was all wrong. Whatever was watching them, it was no beast.

He bumped into Borim.

"Och! Warn me if ye're going ta—"

Thuradin's words died in his throat.

A figure stood before the two dwarves, partially hidden in the shadows. It was taller than them by a few feet. Besides height, Thuradin couldn't make out any other specific details. Whatever it was, it had placed itself perfectly within the shadows so that it couldn't be clearly seen. The being stared at the dwarves for a few more seconds, then vanished with a sharp *hiss!*

The two dwarves, thoroughly spooked, agreed that they had collected enough firewood for the night and ran back to the campsite. It was one thing to face a beast like a grattle. It was another thing entirely to face something unknown and sentient.

In his gut, Thuradin feared for the worst. There were only two things he had read about that could possibly explain what they had seen, and one of them, he knew, wasn't even close to matching the description. The more he thought about it, the more he became certain that they had just survived an encounter with a viatari.

According to what he had read, these beings possessed incredible strength, were able to move at impossible speeds, and were so beautiful they could seduce secrets out of anyone with the sound of their voice. Their civilization had been described as brutal back when they were trading partners with the dwarves—though neither race had ever gone to war with each other.

The texts mentioned that the viatari didn't feed themselves normally, as dwarves did, but fed on the life-energies of living things. Their long, sharp fangs could bite into anything that was alive and suck out its energy, turning it into a dry, empty husk.

For whatever reason, the fact that what appeared to be the viatari's home was near the mountains had never been mentioned in all the reading Thuradin did. Had he known, he would have never approached this forest.

Viatari were extremely difficult to kill. They had fast regenerative abilities, which meant they could only be killed if they suffered several fatal wounds faster than they could heal. They could even survive decapitation for a time, so long as that was the only thing that happened to them.

Everything Thuradin had read about the viatari was frightening. He had hoped they wouldn't have to encounter them during their journey, but that was all it had been, hope. He didn't know why, perhaps it was because of what he had read, but he sensed that the viatari were evil beings who could very easily put an end to their mission to rescue their King.

The two dwarves returned to a completed camp utterly exhausted and still quite spooked. They wolfed down their meals more from the anxiety they felt than hunger. Despite the potential danger from what they had discovered, neither one wanted to speak of what lurked within the forest.

Another watch was set up that night. Thuradin had the second shift, so he allowed himself to indulge in some sleep. But it was a troubled sleep. He couldn't stop thinking about the horrors of the viatari, even in his dreams.

He woke with a jolt and immediately berated himself. He was the commander of the royal guard, the bearer of the saphyrium helm. He didn't have time to dwell on fear. He was a dwarf. And if anything threatened him or his companions, he would fight fiercely and with honor, as he always had.

He took his shift and relieved Stürn, who had chosen a position near the forest, no doubt to see if he could detect any strange energy forces from within. Sitting so close to the tall trees made Thuradin feel uncomfortable, especially after his encounter earlier that day. He shook his head, doing his best to clear it of all distractions so he could focus on his job.

Half an hour into his shift, the wind started to howl. The

trees whistled and moaned as it rushed through their branches. The noise set Thuradin's nerves on edge. He closed his eyes and tried to push out all the terrible things he had read in the old texts. They were what was making him nervous, not the noise. The noise was just wind, after all; it wasn't dangerous.

The wind stopped. Everything was still. He opened his eyes and stood abruptly when he noticed a shadowy figure standing in front of the tree line. As soon as he realized what he saw was real, the figure vanished, as if it had melted into the shadows. And even as he started to turn around, he knew he would be too late. Whatever it was he had seen in front of the tree line was already behind him.

A sharp, searing pain erupted along the side of his head. He had been wearing full plate armor since the day they had left the safety of the caves, as all the dwarves had, yet whatever hit him punched through it as if nothing were there.

Thuradin slumped to the ground, his head throbbing, and succumbed to the darkness.

Stürn was exhausted and had gone to sleep the moment he was relieved from his watch. Yet, as an Enurg'en, he was constantly in sync with all the energy forces around him, whether he was awake or not. He had felt a faint and strange energy signature come from the forest when he was on watch, but he hadn't been able to identify it before he was relieved.

Now, in the midst of his dreams, he felt the same strange energy, only this time it was stronger. Much stronger.

He felt this energy move behind Thuradin from the tree line in a split second. He felt Thuradin's energy flicker briefly as he lost consciousness. At that moment it became clear to the Enurg'en that the camp was in danger.

Stürn's eyes snapped open, and he bolted up from his bedroll.

"Defend yerselves! Enemies have breached the camp!"

Murtosh woke up screaming his war cry and ran off in a random direction, his arms flailing. It didn't take long for him to be subdued. Agrethar was a little slower in waking up. He might have gone unnoticed had he not proclaimed his presence with a loud yawn. He wasn't even finished rubbing his eyes clean when the intruder rushed over to him and knocked him out as well.

Stürn tried to make out details on who was attacking them, but the moon was hidden, so that all he could see was a dark figure. He would have to rely on his powers to see where the intruder was. He felt Ayrie's and Threnn's energy moving toward the camp from where they had been keeping watch.

Ayrie arrived first and attempted to thrust her spear into the being, but it was no longer there. Stürn felt the being move from in front of Ayrie to behind her faster than anyone could see with their eyes. His mind told him such a speed was impossible, but he had felt it. There was no way he could deny what he saw in the energy around him. The being struck Ayrie with a heavy blow on the back of her head, and she crumpled.

Now Threnn arrived at the camp, but before he could even register that Ayrie had been defeated, he too was struck from behind by another being that seemed to materialize out of nowhere. There were now two of them in the camp and only Borim and Stürn remained.

Borim took his time waking up so that he attracted as

little attention from the strange beings as possible. Unlike Agrethar, he remained quiet and inconspicuous. By the time Threnn was subdued, he had managed to grab his hammer and shield and now stood ready to face the attackers.

The two intruders surrounded him before he even had a chance to blink. Knowing what was coming, he lifted his shield behind his head to protect it and cried out as the impact broke his arm. His shield-arm fell limply to his side and another blow brought him to sleep.

Stürn knew resistance was futile, but he was determined to fight as best he could. He would not go down quietly.

He said a quick chant to heal Borim's arm. The manipulation of energy peaked the intruders' interest as they noticed Stürn for the first time. They moved toward him simultaneously. Stürn felt for their energy forces and knew they were on either side of him. The one on his left was preparing to strike.

He acted instantly and dove out of the way. He turned to face the attacker who now stood where he had been a second ago. He sensed that the other was nearby.

They stood there like that for several minutes before the beings began to circle him. They moved from one spot to the next at lightning speed, too fast for Stürn to follow with his eyes. Any second now, he knew, one of them would come in for the final blow. He had to be ready.

The being moved in for the strike just as he knew it would. He turned to the side as the being moved into position and swung his sword to parry the blow. But instead of parrying a weapon, the sword sliced through a hand.

The being stumbled back and hissed angrily and, before Stürn could get a good look at it delivered the final blow with its other hand. Stürn fell to the floor, unconscious.

Even so, he could still feel the energy forces around him and knew what was happening. More beings materialized out of the forest and moved quickly to tie up all the dwarves. They dragged them together and surrounded them.

And then they waited.

Stürn guessed that they were waiting for the dwarves to wake up so they could begin questioning them. He could feel conversation between two of them. One of their energy levels spiked suddenly, and the being walked up to him, hitting him hard on the head a second time. This was too much, even for Stürn, and for the first time in his entire life, he stopped seeing the energy forces around him as he slipped even deeper into unconsciousness.

CHAPTER NINE

Thuradin immediately regretted waking up. His head throbbed terribly, and he sat with his legs cramped and his hands tied behind his back. He was about to wonder aloud what was going on when he remembered.

They had been attacked. Based on their current position, he assumed everyone had been defeated just as he had. Whatever had attacked them—and he had a pretty good idea what it was—was strong.

He cracked his eyes open just wide enough to make out shapes in the night. But even with his blurry vision, he could discern silver hair and glowing red eyes perfectly. The viatari were several feet away and looked to be in a heated discussion. He tried to make out what they were saying, but they were speaking a language he couldn't understand.

He turned his head left and right to check on his fellow captives. Everyone looked well enough, except for Stürn, who had a large welt on the side of his head. However, they were still unconscious, which left him alone to deal with the viatari, who now noticed he was awake.

As he turned his head forward he saw one of them walk toward him. As the viatari moved closer, Thuradin could make out his features more clearly. He looked quite young compared to the dwarf. He had no facial hair, which struck Thuradin as odd, and he could see a few sharp fangs protrude from his upper and lower lip. His red eyes were intimidating but not hostile. There was a collective calmness in them that made the dwarf feel more curious than alarmed. He wondered what it was about them that interested him so much.

And then he realized it. The eyes were ancient. Thuradin stared at them to make sure, but there was no doubt in his mind. Though the viatari standing before him looked young, his eyes held a wisdom and pain in them that only time could bring.

The next thing he noticed was the armor. Compared to the dwarves, the viatari wore very little. It consisted of a long-sleeved, skin-tight jerkin and trousers, both made of a dark green cloth. An X-shaped leather chestpiece went over the jerkin, giving a little more protection to vital areas. Double-layered leather spaulders protected the shoulders, and a few patches of tough leather over the trousers gave further protection to the legs. The leather boots on all of the viatari looked flexible and light and were only a few inches below the knee.

Thuradin only had a few seconds to take all this in as the viatari crouched to meet him at eye level. The red eyes searched his for a short time before the viatari spoke.

"*Antha bek'sur?*"

Thuradin shook his head. He couldn't understand the soft hissing sounds the viatari made. The viatari frowned and moved to take off the dwarf's helmet. Thuradin didn't resist. There was nothing he could do at this point. He would just have to hope the night endured for as long as possible.

As the helmet was removed, the viatari's eyes widened,

and a small grin traced his lips.

"What brings you to our home. dwarf?"

Thuradin gasped. The viatari had just spoken in perfect Dwarvish. Not only that, but now the others switched to Dwarvish as well, as their muttered conversations continued.

"My name is Felix Draka. Do you know what I am?" the viatari asked.

Before Thuradin could respond, however, he felt movement come from his sides as his companions stirred.

"I've had better nights," Threnn muttered next to him.

The viatari had bound the dwarves' hands behind their backs and had connected these bindings together with more rope. Now Thuradin was jostled and pushed around as the other dwarves realized they were tied down and started to panic and struggle. The other viatari, three females and another male, surrounded the dwarves quickly and glared at them until they stopped. Even the crazed Murtosh fell silent under their intimidating eyes. Thuradin didn't blame them; even he could barely endure the viatari's gaze.

"Well, let us start again, shall we?" Felix said as his fingers tapped on Thuradin's confiscated helmet. "What are you doing in our home, dwarves? Heavily armed, if I might add."

Like Thuradin, the other dwarves gasped when they heard Felix speak in perfect Dwarvish.

Thuradin glared at Felix with as icy a stare as he could muster, but his attempt at intimidation failed as Felix raised an amused eyebrow. Finally he turned his head away. He heard Felix sigh softly as a sharp pain erupted on Thuradin's face. The other male viatari had moved in and struck him hard.

"You will answer, scum," he said.

Thuradin hated to admit it, but the ferocity with which this particular viatari looked at him now caused him to tremble, and he was sure the other dwarves could feel it, too. Looking at those eyes, he could tell this one was much younger than Felix, though outwardly they appeared to be around the same age.

However, no matter how intimidating this aggressive viatari was, Thuradin refused to offer any explanation for their presence. Doing so would mean telling them about their task, and he couldn't do that. What would happen if it became known by potential enemies that the Dwarven Kingdom was currently in a fragile state with their King missing? He would defend the secret with his life, even if it meant failing to find Ronorim.

He braced himself and closed his eyes as the young viatari raised a fist to strike again.

"Control yourself, Dragos," said a smooth yet fierce voice.

Thuradin opened his eyes and saw one of the female viatari standing next to the one named Dragos, holding his arm in place. Dragos struggled, but the female's grip was unbreakable, and she pushed Dragos aside.

Before now, Thuradin hadn't studied any of the female viatari in particular. Now that he saw one up close, however, he realized how shockingly beautiful she was. Her long, silver hair flowed with the soft wind. Her piercing red eyes, along with the glow her skin seemed to reflect from the moonlight, were mesmerizing and he couldn't help but stare.

Shaking his head forcefully, he turned his attention back to Felix. The viatari glanced between him and the female thoughtfully.

"Victria, if you do not mind, would you kindly ask our

friend what he and his fellows are doing in our home?"

Victria nodded her understanding and crouched down next to Felix, moving her face close to Thuradin's. Now that she was closer, he could smell the forest on her. It was a hearty scent, and it filled his nostrils, intoxicating him even more to her charm. Even though her red eyes were fierce-some, there was also a softness in them that made the dwarf feel as if he could trust her.

"Why are you here?" she asked.

It was only four words, but they were the sweetest Thuradin had ever heard. It was over. There was no way he could resist. Whether by some spell or his own weakness, Victria had managed to break down all of his mental defenses. He eagerly explained their presence.

He told the viatari everything: the death of Thelm, the attack on Tinas Gran, Ronorim's absence from the throne, and their journey to the outside world up to the present. He spared no detail. When the explanations were finished, a moment of pure silence ensued as both dwarves and viatari realized what had just happened.

"Well," Borim said in an amused voice, "Thuradin never could resist women very well."

"Shut up, Borim," Thuradin muttered.

No sooner had the silence been broken than the viatari moved away from the dwarves and again had a heated discussion among themselves.

"What have ye done, Thuradin?" Ayrie hissed.

"Don't blame him!" Threnn hissed back. "That whatever-it-was must have used some sort of magic ta force it out of him."

"Enough about that," Thuradin said before the two dwarves could continue. "These ropes are weak, and I have just the right angle ta cut into them with my gauntlets. Everyone should try ta do the same."

"How?" Ayrie grumbled.

"Just find a sharp edge on the metal and start rubbing it against the rope! Do it quickly, before they return. We aren't going ta wait for them ta decide on what ta do with us."

Now that the secrets had been spilled, Thuradin had to make sure the viatari didn't interfere and keep them from completing their quest. They would sneak away without a fight. It was their best chance. All they needed was a little more time to cut through these ropes.

But Felix, followed by his companions, strode back to where the dwarves sat and stood over them with a small grin on his face.

"It has been quite some time since contact between our two races was made. A little over a millennium, in fact."

Thuradin and the other dwarves moved more cautiously, trying not to make it obvious that they were cutting through their bonds.

"We were once great allies," Felix continued. "And above all, friends. It is through this friendship that I can speak your language. A dwarf who went by the name of Hroth Ironwall taught me, and I, in turn, taught my people so we could all speak it. I am sure you have many questions, but they can be asked and answered as we make our way, so let us stop wasting time."

"Make our way ta where?" Thuradin asked.

"To our city." Felix's grin broadened

Without another word, the viatari pulled each dwarf to their feet and went to untie their bonds only to discover that most of them were either already cut through or close. The viatari chuckled at the dwarves' efforts. Only Dragos looked peeved by their attempted escape.

Together, the viatari led the dwarves into the dark forest. Thuradin, after scanning the group, found Victria and hustled forward to walk next to her. Victria noticed his presence and stifled a grin. The dwarf glanced around to make sure no one was close enough to hear.

"What sort of magic did ye use ta get me ta talk?"

Victria laughed, causing Thuradin's insides to melt against his will as the melody reached his ears.

"There was no magic," she said. "Though I am flattered that I was able to seduce such a strong-looking dwarf so easily."

She winked. Thuradin looked at her in disbelief, trying to read her face, to see if she was lying. But the truth was in her smile. Silence followed for a time as the group of dwarves and viatari made their way deeper into the forest.

"His name is Dragos?" Thuradin finally asked, nodding his head in the direction of the viatari who had struck him.

"Yes, Dragos Duskhunter. He may seem a little harsh at times—and violent—but try not to think too badly of him. He's just young. I apologize for his treatment toward you, but I think he was a little upset that one of your companions sliced through his hand during our little scuffle."

Victria's voice softened as she spoke. Thuradin noticed the change but only briefly wondered what the cause behind it might be.

"What about the other two?"

A smile jumped back onto Victria's face. "The one with the shoulder-length hair is Tessa Shadoweaver. Don't let looks fool you; she can be nice when she wants to be. She only *looks* like she wants to kill you. The one with the braid is Natiari Lunglow. She's spirited and energetic but shy around strangers. I've known both of them since we were young, and they're like sisters to me. My full name is Victria Bloodletter, by the way, in case you were about to ask."

Thuradin absorbed all of this information as he continued to walk with Victria. He wondered why she and the other viatari had opened up so quickly and easily to the dwarves, but it was just a brief thought. For all he knew, the dwarves were being led to their doom, and it was his responsibility to figure out a means for their escape. But he had no idea how such a feat could be accomplished. The viatari had wisely surrounded the dwarves as they led them through the forest. Eventually he left her side and returned to his companions to share what he had learned. They agreed that the viatari were all equally dangerous after he had finished telling them everything.

The deeper they went, the darker the forest became, the thicker the trees became and the more menacing the situation seemed to be. There were several instances where a slight rustle of the forest's undergrowth or a movement of shadows caused the dwarves to jump in fright.

"Do not fear the forest. You will not lose your way so long as you follow us," Felix called out.

Thuradin couldn't tell how long they had been walking before the trees began to thin and light began to shine through the treetops. The forest transformed almost instantly from a place of darkness and fear to one of peace and comfort. Even the undergrowth, which had been full of dead twigs and leaves, thornbushes, and vines of all kinds a moment ago, changed. Fresh grass grew in place of weeds. Flowers grew in place of vines. Thornbushes disappeared.

Eventually they reached the end of the forest but then found themselves standing over the edge of a cliff. Thuradin's eyes widened in awe. Before him was a deep ravine which encircled a large mesa. On this mesa stood a city of white walls and towers. And beyond the city, more forest.

What shocked him more than the location of the city was how it was built. It was unlike anything he had ever seen. The dwarves were masters of creating impossibly tall structures but typically shaped them into pillars that helped support the cavern ceiling. In that respect, the viatari's city was no competition. But the dwarves were rarely ever creative with their architecture. This place had buildings of all shapes and sizes and each one with a different style, giving the eye something new to behold every time it moved from one cluster of buildings to the next. And yet, though it was so unfamiliar, Thuradin thought he saw a hint of dwarvish craftsmanship in the masonry.

Connecting the isolated mesa to the cliff edge was a single wooden-plank bridge. Straining his eyes, Thuradin could see two other bridges far off to the right and left, and he guessed that there was another on the opposite side.

"Welcome to Aleganthia," Felix said without breaking stride. The viatari began to cross the bridge, and the dwarves followed, stumbling over themselves as they stared at the viatari's city.

Thuradin didn't know how he hadn't realized it sooner, but it suddenly dawned on him that the light of the sun was touching his face. Felix still possessed his helmet. He stopped in his tracks with a gasp and fell to his knees, expecting his skin to melt off at any moment. He waited—but nothing happened. He opened his eyes and saw the viatari look at him quizzically. Behind him, the dwarves took off their helmets one by one as they realized what had just happened—or rather, what hadn't happened. They squinted at the sun. A soft breeze caressed their faces with its cool touch. Sounds were now crisp and loud, instead of muffled as they had been within their helmets. It was as if they had again stepped into a new world.

"I don't . . . I—" Thuradin stammered. Felix moved his way to where Thuradin still knelt and asked what was wrong. Thuradin was in no condition to speak, however, so his companions explained the dwarven belief of the sun to the viatari. After hearing the explanation, he gave a hearty laugh.

"Do not worry, friends, the sun will not harm you as your race has come to believe. How such a ridiculous belief began—Ah, but we are getting ahead of ourselves. We have much to discuss and I am sure many of the things I tell you will help ease your confusion." The viatari smiled, turned, and continued making his way to the city.

As they passed through the gates, Felix told them they would head directly to the keep, which was the largest building in the city. Once there they would eat and drink and then decide on what to do about the current situation. Thuradin was only able to catch glimpses of the city within the walls as he was rushed toward the keep. Bustling streets. Markets full of live, braying animals. Crowds upon crowds of viatari.

The keep was indeed the largest building in the city. Outside, it didn't appear extraordinary in any sense except size. Inside, however, the building transformed much like the forest had. Huge stairways, enormous pillars, and expensive-looking vases and paintings covered every inch of the interior.

The dwarves were led to the second floor and into the dining hall, which was no less impressive. They all sat on one side, facing the viatari on the opposite end of a long, rectangular, wooden table with a red tablecloth with intricate golden designs draped over it. The food was served almost as soon as they sat down.

For the dwarves, plates heaping with roasted meats, fresh bread, and steamed vegetables were presented. Thuradin and his companions wolfed down their food without a second thought, only stopping when the viatari were presented with theirs.

The dwarves watched curiously as live rabbits and deer were brought in. The deer were left tied to the viatari's seats and the rabbits on their plates. Without missing a beat, each viatari grabbed a hold of their rabbits, exposing the neck. Then, gently, almost reverently, they bit into them. The dwarves watched in horror as each rabbit aged in seconds. Fur fell off like dead pine needles, and they soon were unable to support their own weight. Eventually they sunk onto the plates, empty vessels.

The viatari moved on to the deer. They bit into the neck as they had with the rabbit and immediately the deer aged. Each one stumbled about as it felt its life being taken from it, but the viatari had a firm hold on their prey. Soon, they sank to their knees as much a lifeless husk as the rabbits.

The viatari returned to their seats as if nothing had happened and looked at the dwarves expectantly, waiting for them to finish their meals. Instead, the dwarves dropped whatever food they had been holding, their appetites long gone.

"What . . . was that?" Thuradin asked, unable to mask the horror he was feeling.

Felix nodded solemnly.

"I am sorry, friends," he said. "I assumed you already knew. We viatari do not eat as you do. We feed off the life-energies of other living things. It is our only sustenance."

"That—that was monstrous!" Threnn cried out. "These animals had no chance to save themselves."

"That is true," Felix admitted. "Regardless, we need to eat in order to live just as you do. Is our method of eating truly any worse than yours? These roasted meats were once a living, breathing animal. That animal was killed and butchered. Personally, I think being butchered into food is much more terrible than simply having the life-energies sucked out, yet I do not criticize your eating habits. Instead, I accommodate them for your benefit."

The dwarves glanced at each other.

"While our eating methods may seem cruel, do not believe that we do this and relish it. We honor the animals that are brought to us as food, and we give them proper thanks for their sacrifice. In your language, the word 'Eng'Pergen' can be broken up into the words 'energy thief.' However, in our language, 'viatari' means 'life' because we carry the life-energies of everything we eat. But if it is truly too disturbing for you, we will refrain from eating in your presence while you stay here. I hope this is satisfactory."

"I hope ye know we don't plan ta stay here long," Thuradin said.

Dragos scoffed. Felix sat expressionless as if he hadn't heard Thuradin's words.

"We need you dwarves to help us with something, and you will stay in our care until that task is complete," he said, his voice neutral.

"I don't think ye understand," Thuradin replied with a little more force. "We have our own task ta complete, and we have ta do it within a certain time period or it is all for naught. We don't have time ta help ye with yer problems."

"It is you who does not understand," Dragos said with a dark edge in his voice. "You dwarves are under our care until we say you may go." He took a moment to glare straight into the eyes of each dwarf as he rose from his seat. "You cannot escape."

CHAPTER TEN

Everyone looked at Dragos as the echoes of his dramatic proclamation died down. Noticing that all the attention was now on him, he sheepishly sat back down, his face red, and refused to make eye contact with anyone. Victria and Natiari tried to suppress a fit of giggles.

Thuradin was not amused. He jumped up from his seat and slammed his fists on the table. Though not tall, the force with which he acted caused everyone in the room to flinch.

"Who are ye ta hold us captive after showing us hospitality?" he growled. "I've already told ye that we don't have time ta help with yer problems. Ours are more important. They take priority. We won't help ye and ye won't keep us here as hostages."

"Will you fight all of us, then?" Dragos asked smugly. Thuradin thought he had recovered from his embarrassment rather quickly.

Viatari guards burst through the door, armed with long, thin blades and diamond-shaped shields and blocked the exit, their weapons lowered but ready to be used at any moment. The dwarves, realizing they were trapped, began shouting in protest. Dragos was the only viatari to respond in kind. The others remained composed, sitting with straight backs and hands folded across their laps. They watched the shouting match with what Thuradin thought was slight amusement. Several minutes passed with no end to the arguing—which had, by this time, turned into a contest of insults.

Felix stood up slowly and waited for the room to quiet down. It took some time, but patience eventually won, and silence settled around the table.

"My friends," the viatari said, spreading his arms toward the dwarves. "We have no hostile intentions toward you or your quest—but I will not deny that your help is so badly needed that we cannot allow you to leave our presence until the task is done. We will even go so far as to drag you with us to secure your aid. But you need not fear for your lives; we mean you no harm."

"Ye say that, yet ye've called in yer guards ta keep us from leaving. Ye should know that we'll fight ta the death if we're provoked," Thuradin snarled.

"Your stubbornness would be your own undoing. I am not to blame for any rash actions you and your companions may take. However," Felix nodded to the guards by the door and, one by one, they filed out, "consider this an act of goodwill and trust that we mean you no harm."

Thuradin hesitated. He tried to think of a reason why he shouldn't trust Felix, why the viatari might be lying, but no reason came to mind. Slowly he took back his seat. The other dwarves followed his lead.

"Now," Felix continued as he and Dragos took back their own seats. "There is an area south of us that we call *Inadarim*—'The Cursed Hole' in your language—and in this area lies an artifact, inside of which dwells the Creature, a being of powerful darkness. The Creature has the power to spread chaos and destruction in his wake, which we became all too familiar with a thousand years ago. For a long time, chaos reigned in this world as we fought the Creature and his darimun. We eventually managed to put him to sleep with the help of the dwarves but at a great cost. Have you never wondered why your kind retreated into the mountains and broke ties with us?"

"That would be yer doing, wouldn't it?" Borim said uncertainly. "It says so in our historical texts that we had ta leave the outside world ta escape yer kind."

Felix nodded with a sad smile. "I understand why your ancestors would think that, but your history is not accurate. In fact, I would go so far as to say it is a complete lie. The dwarves and the viatari initially encountered each other by pure chance, yet no hostilities ever broke out between us. In fact, our two races were so close that we even lived in the same cities for a time."

"Purely by chance?" Ayrie repeated. "Ye speak as if ye were there yerself."

"That's because he was," Natiari said. "We may not look it, but almost all of us have lived for more than a thousand years. We age much more slowly than other creatures. But even we are young compared to Felix."

Felix nodded. "It is true; I was there when our two races first met. At the time I was the leader of a scouting party. We had already been fighting the Creature for a millennium, and we were losing. Several of our older viatari were dying in battle on a daily basis, and, because we do not reproduce easily, our population declined. My scouting party was in charge of finding a strong, easily defensible area where we could build a city, a safe haven for what remained of our race. This was that location—Aleganthia.

"We saw the mesa first but we had to scout the surrounding forest as well to see if there was any reason why we could not make our home there. That is when we met the dwarves. In those days, your race had several settlements in the outside world as well as within the mountain range. You were a sturdy people who had only recently begun fighting the Creature. I remember our first encounter involved much shouting and threatening with weapons at the ready. We might have started our relationship by fighting each other had we not been attacked by the darimun first.

"In that moment, we banded together and fought off the enemy. After that, my group was brought to the deepest parts of the Dwarven Kingdom where we formed an alliance with your people in hopes of defeating the Creature together. It was then that I was taught the dwarven language by Hroth."

The dwarves sat in silence as they absorbed Felix's story. Thuradin was especially troubled by this tale. The historical texts he had read before the quest had said the alliance with the viatari had been out of necessity, and it had never mentioned anything about their two races getting along with each other. Indeed, he had always come away in a foul mood after reading what their alliance involved.

"So then, what happened?" Stürn asked.

"We fought together for many centuries, and with the help of the dwarves, we finally managed to make some progress in defeating the Creature. We reached the wastelands of Inadarim and fought off the remnants of his forces together. Unfortunately, some of the dwarves, including Geothur Ironaxe, your King at the time, split off from the army during the battle and made their way to face the Creature directly. I cannot say what happened to them individually, but their actions triggered some sort of explosive reaction from the Creature, the consequences of which spread to every dwarf in the area and affected their minds so that they cursed us and feared us and fled from us as if we were the monsters. I led a group to where your King had led his dwarves, and upon arriving, I saw what had happened. Your King had foolishly opened the artifact. Not only that, but he had also gone inside. The only thing that remained of him was his royal crown, which I personally returned to his son, Ranth."

Felix sighed as if remembering some past regret.

"In any case, after that the dwarves who returned from Inadarim told everyone what I assume were terrible stories about us, and the dwarves all retreated into their mountains, isolating themselves for a millennium. No doubt, Ranth ordered his scribes to write what had happened based on the corrupting lies the Creature had put in your people's minds to convince any future reader that the outside world was no place to live."

His eyes shifted between the individual dwarves. "And now that you have heard what really happened, what do you make of it?"

The dwarves were silent, but they couldn't hide their confusion. Thuradin glanced around and could see their minds at work as they tried to comprehend everything they had just been told.

"Whether what ye say is true or nae," Thuradin said slowly, "it still doesn't explain why we must help ye."

Felix nodded. "For the past nine hundred years, the Creature has slumbered in his artifact, dormant; however, recently, reports have come from the south of darimun roaming the lands surrounding Inadarim. It appears that the Creature is coming out of his dormant state. The viatari are not as powerful as we used to be. If the Creature is waking up, that means another war is coming. And if there is another war, we will perish. We had to find some way to lull the Creature back to sleep, to avoid war. Scouts I had sent to Inadarim returned with news that the artifact remained as it had been left at the final battle—with its lid half open. With no other ideas available, we reasoned that the open lid must be the reason behind the Creature's return. We lost many viatari trying to close that lid. The artifact responded violently to our touch and struck out like a cornered animal."

Here, he grimaced.

"And it was all in vain. The lid was finally closed, but the corruption continued to spread. More darimun were formed from animals in the area as the corruption consumed them. The Creature was still active. We had to look for another solution. We began to go through every historical record we had, looking for some clue that might guide us to a solution. Eventually, in a fragment from an ancient tome that had, by the time we found it, mostly turned to dust, we found what we were looking for:

Lords of the Mountains opened the cage.
Children of Nythirim must end the rage.

"Dwarves," Threnn said. "Ye need dwarves ta put the Creature back ta sleep."

Felix nodded. "I do not know what exactly it is that you must do. All I know is that dwarves are the only living beings in this world who can end the Creature's destructive influence. Of course, your race has been isolated and hostile toward us for the past thousand years, so we were unsure how we would ever gain a dwarf's help until you left your mountains. And when we saw you and your companions wandering so close to our forest, we knew it would most likely be our only chance, so we decided to bring you with us to Aleganthia."

Thuradin stared across the room through a window overlooking the city. The sun was much lower in the sky, and he estimated there were only a couple of hours before night fell. Much had been said, most of which he had trouble taking in, but the desperation in Felix's voice was unmistakably genuine. There was truth in the viatari's explanation.

He understood why the viatari were unwilling to let them leave. Their mere presence gave them hope for a better future. But still, why should the dwarves care about what happened in the outside world? Thuradin directed this question to Felix, but it was Victria who answered.

"You may believe the Creature's actions in the outside world won't affect you in your mountains," she said. "But why do you think your mountains have been left in peace by the horrors we've described? The Creature only knew of your race for a short time before he was put to sleep. Don't you think he will want revenge against you for ending his rein all those centuries ago? He's not at full strength yet, but once he is, we are the only thing keeping him from attacking your mountains, and we will be wiped out. Then he can invade your home and do the same to your people. Surely you have some beasts in your mountains that you would not want to be imbued with the Creature's corruption."

The burrowers.

Like Ronorim, Thuradin was of the opinion that the burrowers should be crushed. There simply wasn't enough room in the mountains for the barbarians. But if burrowers came under the Creature's influence, as Victria suggested they could, it would spell disaster for the Dwarven Kingdom. Finding Ronorim before the deadline was important, but what good would finding him be if the Kingdom was destroyed?

He glanced at his companions. They all looked at him with expectant gazes. He thought he saw Ayrie shake her head slightly, but it didn't matter; his mind was already made up.

He turned to Felix. "There is nothing more important ta me than the safety of my home and fellow dwarves. If they are truly in as much danger as ye claim, then it is our duty ta help ye with your quest in order ta ensure their safety from this Creature."

Felix nodded, visibly pleased. "It is settled, then. I am sure you have all been worn out by the past few nights. We will escort you to your rooms, where you may rest for the upcoming journey. We will meet tomorrow to discuss plans."

The dwarves were led out of the dining hall and, after being split up into two groups of three and four, were escorted to their rooms. Thuradin was roomed with Ayrie and Borim. He didn't know what to expect, but he was surprised to find the room they were given was to his liking.

There were several windows, all covered with scarlet drapes. They glowed like embers under the fading sunlight. There were three large, soft beds, a welcoming sight after having spent the last few nights on hard earth. Several pieces of ornate furniture lay about the room, each one having a different set of designs on the fabric. It was a room Thuradin thought should have been reserved for a king instead of three weary dwarves.

They were left to do as they pleased. They took the opportunity to finally get out of their oppressive armor. They removed the metal plates gently and laid them out on the nearby tables, then ripped apart the black cloth they had thought was protecting them from the sun. They were left only with their tunics and trousers on and felt freer than ever before.

Thuradin sunk into the nearest chair and made himself comfortable. He was about to doze off when he noticed Ayrie standing in front of him, looking sternly down at him.

"Yes?"

"Why did ye agree ta their demands?" she asked.

"What choice did we have?" Thuradin lifted his heavy shoulders in a shrug. "If it's ta protect our Kingdom, I'll gladly do anything they ask of me. Besides, they would never have allowed us ta leave if we continued ta deny them."

"How do ye know if what they told us is even true? They could have been playing us for their own needs for all we know."

"Aye," Thuradin conceded. "That may be. But as I said before, what choice do we have? If it eases your mind, though, know that I believe Felix's tale. He seemed genuine."

"We know nothing about them and ye're going ta risk everything because ye *believe* they were genuine?" Ayrie asked incredulously. "It should worry ye that they know so much about us."

"Why? They're ancient—ye can see it in their eyes. They've seen more in their lifetimes than we can ever hope ta see."

"I still think this is a mistake," Ayrie muttered. "We should be focusing our efforts on finding and rescuing our King." She walked off to the farthest bed.

Borim, who had been watching the argument intently, now plopped himself onto the chair next to Thuradin. "She's just worried. The lass is young and already knows she has a lot ta live up to."

Thuradin nodded but said nothing. He closed his eyes, quickly falling asleep, and dreamed of monster-size burrowers toppling the towers of Tinas Gran.

The next day the dwarves were taken to a different room in the keep, where a map of the surrounding area was laid out on a table. All the viatari from yesterday were gathered around it, along with five new ones. As the dwarves entered, introductions were passed around, and it was announced that these new viatari would join them on their journey.

Thuradin tried his best to remember what Felix told him about them. There was Biranar Longblade, one of the town's blacksmiths, whose strong, broad arms made all of his admirers jealous of his wife. Anadyr Skysong was one of these admirers, and Thuradin could see her luscious eyes constantly wander over to where Biranar stood, nodding her head absently to whatever it was Victria was saying to her.

There was Galyres Steadheart, one of the keep's guards and a personal friend of Felix's. Thuradin was shocked by his booming voice, which contradicted his thin stature and boyish face.

Daleres Cloudshade was another surprise. With a bearing as impressive as Biranar's, Thuradin had expected him to be a carbon copy of the blacksmith. He hadn't expected the viatari to be a mute.

The last viatari introduced to Thuradin was Pulaneus Stargaze, who had been one of the scouts sent to Inadarim to get more information on the Creature's activities. Unlike the others, Pulaneus had shaved his head, which Thuradin thought made his red eyes look all the more disconcerting.

As Felix continued to introduce these new viatari and their personal lives, their families, their pasts, Thuradin's eyes passed over each one again. They all knew how dangerous this was, how likely the odds were they would never see Aleganthia again. And yet here they were. They reminded him of his dwarves, who had volunteered to help him save Ronorim despite facing the dangers of an unknown world. He nodded his approval.

"Well," Felix said, clapping his hands together. "Now that introductions are finished, it is time to plan for the task at hand: how we will get to Inadarim and put the Creature back to sleep or destroy him altogether."

As the sun made its journey across the sky, it was agreed that the time it would take for them to travel to Inadarim was about four days. The journey back was another four, so it was estimated their task could be completed in a little more than a week—provided everything went according to plan. Thuradin saw most of his companions nod approvingly at the estimation, thinking the less time they spent on this task, the more they could spend on their own. The only dwarf who remained disgruntled was Ayrie.

The dwarves were told of another race called humans. They were considered barbaric by the viatari, who emphasized their dangerous and clever nature. They posed a potential threat because they always tried to kill any viatari they could find. They were a xenophobic people, wary of strangers, and the dwarves were told to keep low profiles when they had to pass through a town—of which there were many in the plainlands.

Thuradin noticed the meeting didn't cover what they would do once they actually arrived to Inadarim, which worried him, but he didn't dwell on it. It could be explained later. They had to reach the place first, anyway.

When the meeting was finished, the dwarves were led back to their rooms to rest, though Threnn and Murtosh declared they were going to explore the city. As the rest of them approached their rooms, Ayrie split from Borim and Thuradin and went over to Agrethar.

"I need ta speak with ye," was all she said as she led him farther down the hall and into his room.

Thuradin glanced at Borim, who looked just as curious as he was.

"It's probably nothing," Borim shrugged.

Thuradin nodded absently and entered his room, ready to fling himself onto his bed.

A large bonfire raged in the center of Aleganthia's crowded plaza that night as the city's inhabitants celebrated and wished luck upon the dwarves and viatari who would be going to Inadarim.

As Felix had promised, none of the viatari ate in their usual method around the dwarves but instead nibbled on simple foods like bread and fruit. Thuradin felt somewhat guilty for being the cause of this fasting, so he encouraged his companions to also abstain from eating as a sign of solidarity. They all agreed grudgingly and walked off, grumbling about how they had been starving themselves for the feast.

Only minutes after walking off, Agrethar had already

passed out from drinking too much. Several viatari surrounded him with interest, expecting the dwarf to jump back up at any moment, ready for more.

The other dwarves took to Agrethar's example and drank themselves into sleep in an attempt to alleviate their hunger. By the time the celebration was half-way over, almost all of them had passed out. The only ones left standing by the end were Thuradin and Ayrie.

As the celebrations ended and the viatari returned to their homes and the cleanup crews put out the bonfire, the unconscious dwarves were carried into their rooms to rest, their drunken snores the only thing breaking the silence of the night.

The next morning the dwarves rose from their slumber without so much as a groan. None of them seemed to have any sort of headache from the night of drinking. The viatari chuckled in envy as they rubbed their own heads.

The dwarves strapped on their armor—now without the protective cloth—and headed outside where their mounts waited, along with the viatari who would accompany them on the journey. Victria and Felix greeted the dwarves as they made their way to the group and explained how they had taken the liberty of retrieving the mounts they had left behind. The rams bleated happily as they reunited with their riders, and their horned heads bobbed up and down as the dwarves mounted them.

Thuradin noticed that the viatari rode animals that, though resembling a ram, didn't have the same shaggy fur or horns on their head. Felix explained that they were called horses, and they were the standard mount for both viatari and humans in the outside world.

It took most of the first day to ride through the forest.

They rode in silence. The forest seemed to demand that all who entered its domain remain silent. Nothing could be done by the dwarves or viatari, or even their mounts, to disobey it.

The forest began to thin as the sun sank toward the horizon. Felix called for a halt and decided they would make camp within the protection of the trees for the night. The real traveling would start tomorrow.

As they set up camp, the dwarves looked around with a new awareness. What they had learned about the humans had troubled them more than they cared to admit. The viatari had said they were dangerous, but they couldn't see how humans could stand up to the speed and strength the viatari possessed. Surely no amount of them could stand up to a group of ten viatari and five dwarves.

"We're strong enough, aren't we?" Threnn said aloud as the others prepared the camp. "With our combined forces, we should have nothing ta fear from these humans, right?"

The viatari stopped what they were doing for a moment. They chuckled and shook their heads. Tessa moved to where Threnn stood and knelt so that she was eye-level with him. Her eyes were unnerving enough, but she gave the dwarf such a cold stare that he took a step back.

She smiled, but it was not one of warmth or humor. "There are many more things to fear in the outside world, dwarf, than just humans. We would not have enough might even if we took with us every single viatari that lived in Aleganthia."

CHAPTER ELEVEN

Thuradin woke to the smell of frying meat.

Several minutes passed before he remembered the events of the past couple of days. He sat up and took hold of his surroundings. The dwarves were huddled around a fire, where he could hear a faint sizzling. The viatari were nowhere in sight.

"Mornin' ye sloth!" Borim called as Thuradin approached the fire. "Had a nice beauty's sleep?"

"Sloth?" Thuradin repeated.

Borim held up a finger and lifted his eyes to the treetops. Minutes passed, and Thuradin was about to ask what they were waiting for when he saw a quick flurry of movement out of his peripherals and heard a hard thud to his side. He turned and saw a . . . thing.

It was an ugly beast with a face that made Thuradin shudder. Light brown fur covered its body, and its nails were incredibly long and thick. He nudged it cautiously with his boot. The beast didn't move, which was enough to convince him that it was dead.

Borim burst into laughter. "That beauty there is what they call a *sloth*. I was woken up by one of them falling on me. Gave the viatari a fright when I started yelling my head off—

which I'm surprised ye were able ta sleep through, by the way."

Thuradin raised his eyebrows as Borim continued chuckling at the sloth's misfortune.

"Borim, when ye're done enjoying the deaths of these little creatures, would ye mind telling me where the viatari are?"

Borim took several deep breaths and wiped the tears from his eyes. He had never been one for composure.

"They went inta the woods ta hunt. Told us ta prepare our own food and that they'd be back soon enough."

Thuradin nodded and took a seat next to his companions by the fire. They ate their breakfast in silence, waiting for the viatari to return. It wasn't until after they finished their meals, and the viatari still hadn't returned, that Agrethar suggested they escape.

"Why should we?" Thuradin said. "This task will only prolong our own by a week at most. We'll have plenty of time ta find Ronorim after this is over."

"That's nae what I have a problem with," Agrethar replied. "I'm wondering why we even have ta partake in this quest in the first place. Ayrie mentioned it ta me a while ago, and I say she's right. Everything they told us could have been made up ta get our help. They've given us no evidence ta prove what they say, and by aiding them, we're playing right inta their hands while we could be traveling ta Dun'Burell."

Thuradin glared at Ayrie, who met his gaze with an equally fierce one.

He turned back to Agrethar. "Even if that were the case, what do ye propose? They're quicker and stronger than we are—than anything we've ever encountered. One of them alone is enough ta kill us all. If we escape, they'll chase us and catch up ta us, and they would kill us if they didn't need us for their own purposes. I don't believe we should risk making such dangerous enemies while we're in their world."

Agrethar opened his mouth to argue, but Thuradin wasn't going to have it. He jumped up from his place at the fire, stomped over to Agrethar, and slammed him into the ground with his boot.

"I've decided for us ta join in this task because I believe it is the best way ta keep us alive." Spittle flew into Agrethar's shocked face. "Bronn told me ta do whatever I could ta protect ye, and helping powerful beings like the viatari instead of going against them seems ta me like an obvious choice, but if ye have a problem with my decisions, then go. Leave us and find Ronorim on yer own." He spat the last words out in Ayrie's direction. Her gaze dropped to the ground.

Thuradin looked around at the other dwarves. All of them avoided his gaze, though Threnn and Murtosh looked ready to come to Agrethar's aid.

"I want ta find Ronorim more than any of ye," he said, taking his foot off Agrethar. "But I also want ta make sure we live through this. It's my fault that he was lost. It's my fault we have ta be out here risking our lives ta find him. Know that I take responsibility for each and every one of ye, so believe me when I say I do nae make my decisions lightly."

With that he walked away from them and began preparing his ram for the day's ride. The dwarves around the fire were still at first, like statues. Then, one by one, they too walked over to their rams and readied their belongings.

It was a silent camp the viatari returned to. If they noticed the tension in the air upon arriving, they didn't mention it.

Felix made his way to Thuradin, who was already mounted, and gave him a knowing look and an encouraging pat on the shoulder. The viatari packed their belongings quickly, and soon, they too were ready for the day's ride.

The trees continued thinning out as they rode on. The sun was high in the sky by the time they exited the forest. Before them lay hill country. It was a stark contrast to the flat plains Thuradin and his group of dwarves had been traveling in before entering the forest.

They rode in single file, with the first and last members of the line riding several hundred feet away from the rest to keep a lookout for possible threats.

Hills rose and fell in every direction, a perfect area for an ambush. Thuradin thought if he were in charge, he would have taken more precautions and placed lookouts on the flanks as well instead of just the front and rear. He wondered what made Felix feel confident enough to ride through this area with so little security.

It wasn't long before the hills left Thuradin completely disoriented. There were no unique reference points, just hills. There were no trees, just hills. There was nothing interesting at all in this land, just hills. He was sure the constant rising and falling of the earth would drive him insane, so he was relieved when he noticed thin trails of smoke rising from behind one of the many hills in front of them.

Felix called for a halt. Their lookout, who Thuradin remembered to be Anadyr Skysong, had already dismounted and crawled up the hill to determine the source of the smoke. She now made her way back.

"Settlement ahead," she said. "Humans."

Felix nodded and told everyone to dismount. The mounts

were herded together by Biranar and taken away a short distance. Thuradin watched the blacksmith cup his hands and put his mouth over the ears of one of the horses, staying in that position for several seconds before moving on to the next. Victria explained to the dwarves that the horses knew certain words of their language—enough for the viatari to tell them to ride around the town without being seen.

"What about our rams? Will they understand yer language?" Borim asked.

"We shall soon see," Victria said.

When Biranar finished giving instructions to the last ram, the group of horses whirled around and started running, the rams following close behind.

"It appears they do understand after all," Victria noted before leaving to join the rest of her kind.

Borim turned to Thuradin. "I like that one a lot, I do."

Thuradin nodded. He didn't have the slightest doubt that Borim was charmed by Victria much in the same way he had been during their first encounter.

Soon after Victria left, Felix walked over to the dwarves and dropped a bag he had taken from his own horse in front of them. From it, he took out long, black, hooded cloaks and passed them out.

"Put these on."

"Are there enough for everyone?" Thuradin asked, slightly concerned that there was only one bag, now empty, and that only the dwarves were the ones with cloaks.

"We do not need them," Felix replied. "This is only a precaution for your kind. As we have said before, humans are not known for their hospitality to strangers, especially those who are not like them. We cannot hide your size, unfortunately, but we can hide your appearance. Hopefully that will be enough."

"What about ye, then?" Murtosh said, struggling to walk in the long cloak. "Ye look different from humans as well, don't ye? Even if we have these cloaks, they'll recognize ye before we can even—"

Murtosh and the other dwarves' mouths popped open in surprise as the viatari transformed before their eyes. Their bodies shimmered and then seemed to fade. When it was over, the viatari looked nothing like themselves. Their silver hair and red eyes were gone, and their fangs had flattened out.

"What?" Thuradin said incredulously.

Victria, who now had chestnut-brown hair and startling blue eyes, simply smiled. It was Felix, now with dull, dark hair and green eyes, who explained.

"Humans are formidable opponents in battle. What they lack in agility and strength, they make up for with cunning and poisons. That is the only way they manage to kill us. Luckily, we viatari have the ability to create illusions of any kind, so we use that skill to temporarily change our appearance to look like them. It makes it harder for them to identify us for what we are."

"Don't get the wrong idea though," Dragos scowled, his hair now jet-black, "We don't do this all the time. It would be disgusting to look like a human on a daily basis."

"Not all of us think so," Anadyr said quietly.

Thuradin looked around to see what all the others looked like in their human form. Tessa had black hair like Dragos but green eyes like Felix. Natiari had brown eyes like Dragos but fiery red hair, the likes of which Thuradin had never seen before—it was even redder than Murtosh's beard.

Pulaneus still had no hair, but his eyes were a deep blue.

CHRONICLES OF THE FIRST GODS BOOK ONE   137

Biranar's hair was now blond and his eyes were such a light blue they looked like the sky. Even in human form, his appeal was unmatched. Thuradin noticed Anadyr, whose hair and eyes were now brown, stare numbly at Biranar as if in a trance. Galyres' eyes were green, but his hair was a darker black, making him appear much younger. Daleres stood as silently as ever, stroking his long, braided, orange hair while watching Anadyr's attempts to capture Biranar's attention with his soft, brown eyes.

While Thuradin observed the changes in each viatari, Felix dug through several different bags and pulled out an assortment of odd-looking clothes. The viatari put these clothes on over their leather armor. If they hadn't looked like humans before, they certainly did now.

Once everyone was ready, they hiked their way over the hill and continued on into the human town.

As he beheld the town, Thuradin thought it was nothing like the dwarven cities and only slightly resembled what he had seen in Aleganthia. People milled about in congested, muddy streets, haggling in a strange language to merchants who held up their goods with smiles on their faces. Men with large swords patrolled the streets and the rooftops of the wooden and stone buildings, looking for signs of trouble and occasionally harassing random townsfolk.

The dwarves and viatari stayed close together and pushed their way through the crowds. They received ugly glances from those they pushed, mixed with suspicion when the dwarves were noticed. But hidden under the hooded cloaks as they were, no one paid them too much attention.

It seemed an eternity before they reached what looked to be the main plaza of the town. There was much more open space here and fewer people due to the lack of shops. Felix told them most of the buildings here housed the town's leadership. They decided to rest for a short while before attempting to move through the next few streets.

Some of the viatari had managed to procure money during their trek through town by pickpocketing random townsfolk they passed. They entered what Thuradin thought looked like a bakery and bought several pastries as well as what appeared to be a type of meat on a stick. Thuradin was suspicious of everything in the town, but that didn't stop him from admitting that humans were excellent at making food. He thought the tender, juicy meat on a stick surpassed the tough ram meat from the Dwarven Kingdom effortlessly, and the pastries were fluffy and sweet. Both delicacies melted in his mouth as he ate them.

Felix wanted to leave the town before it turned dark, so he urged everyone back to their feet and led them through the next street, which was now much less crowded than the ones they had traveled through before. Judging from the sun's journey downward, Thuradin figured most of the townsfolk would have finished their shopping and gone home by now.

They walked through several sections of town, most little more than rows upon rows of worn-down wooden huts. They moved with ease and little to no harassment. The townsfolk barely noticed the dwarves in their cloaks, and they didn't seem to suspect the viatari for what they were at all. Thuradin began to think they might pass through the entire town without incident.

It wasn't until they were walking through a final row of houses toward the open gate that led out of town when voices called to them from behind. Thuradin couldn't understand what was being said, but the viatari stopped in their tracks.

Felix turned to face the voices and stepped forward to address them. Thuradin took a look at the men who had ordered them to stop. There were three, all armed with large swords and small shields. The bald man in the middle appeared to be the leader of the three and was the one who spoke to Felix now.

As Felix and the man spoke, the man's voice grew more aggressive. Though Thuradin couldn't understand what was being said, he could read body language, and he could hear Felix's confidence falter. The men seemed to be demanding something of them before they left town. Whatever it was, Felix didn't think it was a good idea, and he tried to persuade them not to pursue the matter. The men didn't like this, and their voices grew low and threatening. Their hands moved to rest on their weapons.

Finally Felix turned to the dwarves and explained the situation.

"They have challenged us to a competition of strength between the strongest of theirs and the strongest of ours."

"Very well, I'll—"

"Be quiet, Dragos," Felix said sharply. "He wants to challenge the dwarves." He turned to Thuradin. "He sees your size as an oddity. My guess is this trial is a way for them to figure out your strengths and weaknesses, to see what you are made of and try to figure out what you might be."

He hesitated. "Since this is a competition of strength, I believe this may be a battle to the death. Would any of your dwarves be willing to fight, Thuradin?"

"Couldn't ye just tell him we won't do it?"

"I have," Felix shook his head. "But they will not accept that. They will not let us leave unless we leave as victors or we fight our way out."

"Why can't we do that, then?"

"Because the minute we use our skills to fight and escape this place, they will know we are viatari, and they will know our disguised identities. These towns are always under observance by those who run them. I have no doubt our presence and what we look like has been documented at some point during the day. We cannot risk losing our disguises unless we have to."

As Felix said this, Thuradin heard the gates behind them close with a heavy thud. He turned and saw two bulky men lock them, grinning smugly as they leaned against the large, wooden doors.

"I'll go," Stürn offered.

"Are ye sure?" Thuradin asked the Enurg'en. "Ye don't have ta do this, any one of us can—"

Stürn held up a hand to silence him. "I am an Enurg'en. I can heal myself if necessary, which will be ta my advantage during a fight. With my healing abilities, victory is certain, and we can leave this place sooner rather than later."

Thuradin nodded slowly. He knew Stürn was right, and if he thought he could win the battle easily, Thuradin would trust him.

"Very well," Felix said. "I suppose I shall go tell them."

Stürn walked with Felix away from the group so that Felix could introduce him as the competitor. The humans laughed as Stürn approached.

After an agreement was made, they turned and began walking back into town, still laughing. Felix and Stürn followed. Thuradin intended to keep everyone else near the gates and wait for their return, but the men behind them had different ideas. Several more jumped out of the shadows and grabbed the viatari and dwarves and dragged them forcefully back to the town's plaza. Whatever was going to happen, it looked like they had no choice but to watch.

CHAPTER TWELVE

A crowd formed around the plaza as long, thick tables and huge kegs of ale were hauled through. Thuradin and the others were dragged in front of the forming crowds where they could get a clear view of what was happening. Thuradin expected to see Stürn and the man he would face preparing weapons for a dual. Felix had said this would be a test of strength, and he assumed that had meant a duel to the death. Instead, he saw the long tables placed in front of them, the kegs of ale following close behind.

Stürn looked uneasy. He too had thought this challenge would involve fighting. Thuradin doubted the Enurg'en had imagined any other possibility. He certainly hadn't.

Felix walked over to the man who had issued the challenge and demanded an explanation. The man replied smugly in words only Felix understood. The viatari returned to Stürn's side and relayed whatever new information he had learned. Stürn frowned, obviously troubled by what had been said, and began to protest, but Felix raised a hand to stop him. A few more words were exchanged, and then the viatari was making his way back to join the others.

"What's happening?" Thuradin asked.

"It appears I misinterpreted what the humans said before.

They indeed want a test of strength, but not through combat, like I originally thought. They are having a drinking contest. I imagine the first person to collapse is the loser. It is probably better this way—after all, Stürn *is* a dwarf." Felix grinned at these last words. Thuradin guessed he imagined the humans would be flabbergasted by the dwarf's drinking ability.

"This is bad," he said, snapping Felix out of his daze.

"What is?"

"Stürn isn't a drinker. He's notorious in our Kingdom for nae being able ta keep it down. He had a lot of confidence winning the competition before because he thought it would be combat. Now look at him—"

Felix turned to look at Stürn and seemed to notice for the first time the lines of worry on the dwarf's face, lines which became more pronounced as he glanced at his opponent—a huge man, thick with muscle.

The man wore simple trousers for the competition, leaving his chest bare and exposing his many scars. He seemed to be proud of them as he pointed each one out and showed the crowd, nodding as they cheered him on. Veins popped out of his shaven head as he looked down and grinned at Stürn, who looked no taller than a child compared to him.

The two contestants were presented with large, empty tankards. A loud, high-pitched horn blew from somewhere behind the crowd, and the contest began. Both the man and Stürn quickly filled their tankard to the brim with their first drink and downed it just as quickly. Stürn still looked discouraged about the odds of him winning, but now that the competition had begun, it didn't look like his doubts would keep him from trying.

He held his opponent's hostile glare as he filled his

tankard a second time and chugged down the contents. Not once was eye contact broken.

Oblivious to the mental battle being waged between the two contestants, the crowd cheered and placed bets on who would win. The cheers turned into chants for the man, and the chants grew in volume as Stürn began to slow down and sway in place. The man took the opportunity to spur the crowd further and raised both hands up into the air. He gave a mighty roar before downing his fifth drink.

Thuradin stamped his foot in frustration. He was helpless. There was nothing he could do that could help Stürn get out of this situation. All he could do was watch.

"You should have picked me," Dragos muttered. "I wouldn't have succumbed so easily."

"If we had picked you, defeat would be certain," Felix replied curtly, more than annoyed at the current situation.

The crowd chanted incessantly, but their confidence and excitement faltered as Stürn regained his balance and began to consume the ale faster and with more vigor.

His opponent saw this change in composure and increased his own pace as well, but he couldn't last. Thuradin could see the effects of the alcohol already taking hold of the man's mind and body. Before long, Stürn had regained lost ground and was now even with the man in the number of pints of ale consumed. But unlike him, he showed no signs of wavering.

Silently, the crowd watched as the short figure downed tankard after tankard of the town's ale. Someone his size shouldn't have been able to do such a thing. The amount of alcohol Stürn was consuming was much more than his body weight. The spectators murmured amongst themselves. The stranger should have blacked out by now, but he didn't even look tipsy. Suspicion spread through the crowd as they wondered at the dwarf's endurance.

Thuradin and Felix glanced at each other.

"How is he doing that?"

"I cannae be sure . . . But I think he's using his power as an Enurg'en ta heal himself from the effects of the drink."

"I thought so. That is not the smartest thing to do. Look at the crowd. They grow suspicious. I would advise your companion to be careful; we do *not* want to start a conflict here."

"And how would ye like me ta relay that message?" Thuradin said through clenched teeth. "Ye should've warned him earlier when ye had the chance. There's nae a thing we can do now but watch. We just have ta trust Stürn's judgment and be prepared for whatever consequences may follow."

Stürn's opponent swayed heavily. The man brought a newly filled tankard of ale to his lips, gave Stürn one last look of pure hatred, and crashed onto one of the tables, smashing his head on the corner before reaching the ground. If the alcohol hadn't rendered him unconscious, the impact with the table certainly had.

The crowd was ominously silent. They watched Stürn carefully as he finished the contents within his tankard and walked back to Thuradin and the others. Thuradin ground his teeth as the Enurg'en walked normally, with no indication of intoxication at all. No heavy breathing from having to fight the effects of the alcohol, no stumbling around as he made his way back. It looked to everyone present as if he hadn't consumed a single drop of ale.

Stürn frowned as he sensed the tension in the air. He glanced around and noticed for the first time the crowd watching him with suspicion in their eyes. Thuradin hurriedly pulled him back in with the rest of the group before the Enurg'en could do anything else and put a finger to his lips. Felix took a step forward and said a few words in a loud, clear voice, which, Thuradin guessed, announced that they would be taking their leave. Taking Felix's lead, they turned to go.

Then one of the spectators said something. Thuradin had no idea what it meant, but soon more people were saying it until the entire crowd had joined in and chanted it angrily. The group stopped in their tracks and turned to face the humans. The viatari glanced nervously at one another as they listened to the angry crowd.

"They are calling us cheats," Felix translated.

"Is that bad?"

"No matter what I say now, I cannot convince them otherwise," the elder viatari muttered to himself. He glanced at the dwarf. "Yes, it is very bad. In their eyes, we just cheated our way to victory. Humans do not appreciate being fooled, especially by strangers, *especially* on their own land. We have just made a dangerous enemy. We need to run. Now—"

They all turned to run but found their way blocked by a group of heavily armed guards.

"Form pairs," Felix ordered. "To the roofs!"

The viatari paired up immediately, as if they had planned to do so all along. Two of them acted as diversions, attacking the guards so that the others had enough time to grab the dwarves and jump onto the roofs of the nearby buildings. Once that was done, the two diversion groups disengaged, knocking their opponents to the ground, and joined the others.

Thuradin didn't enjoy being manhandled, nor did any of the dwarves, but they didn't complain. They knew the humiliating act was necessary since they couldn't jump as high as the viatari had. Necessity demanded they swallow their pride. For now.

They ran along the rooftops, hopping from building to building toward the gates. They had a head start on the guards, but they weren't the only ones in the town. Already, Thuradin saw several more guards climb onto the buildings ahead to try and intercept them.

Natiari ran ahead and confronted them, dodging their lethal attacks and quickly knocking them off the roof with some well-placed kicks. Short barks of surprise escaped their lips as they fell to the ground. The dwarves and viatari continued their escape like this, with Natiari running just far enough ahead so she could deal with anyone who tried to slow their progress.

Thuradin was impressed by her fighting ability. She would weave around attacks and use her opponent's momentum to her advantage. Occasionally, she retaliated with her fists or even her whole body, knocking her opponents back several yards in any direction when she tackled them. There was no need for her to use any weapons. She was one.

Now he realized why the viatari didn't carry heavy weapons as the dwarves and some humans did, but instead chose to arm themselves only with a long, slender dirk which they kept sheathed in a scabbard hanging from their hip. Their supernatural strength made any other weapon virtually unnecessary.

They ran as far as the roofs would allow, but eventually they reached the edge of the human town. Before them lay a small stretch of space and then the town wall. Below them were several clusters of armed men forming together and looking up, yelling taunts. Those who had bows used them.

Were it not for the shield wall Threnn, Murtosh, and Agrethar had set up along the edge of the roof, the dwarves and viatari would have been picked off to the last member.

Thuradin was wondering how they could get out of the town when he felt himself being lifted up by one of the viatari again. The wind rushed through his beard as the viatari jumped into open space. It felt like they were flying. It was an impossible jump he would never have been able to make himself. They passed the mob of men below them, passed the wall, and continued on for a little bit until the two finally landed onto the hard earth beyond.

As soon as everyone landed safely past the wall, they turned and rushed away just as the town's gate swung open and the swelling mob of humans chased after them. Felix whistled sharply. Minutes later, their horses and rams were running alongside them. They mounted quickly and shot off into the hills before they could be targeted by the town's archers.

They rode hard for an hour to put as much distance as they could between them and the town before stopping for a short rest. Looking at his fellow dwarves, Thuradin could tell they were all thoroughly shaken by their first encounter with the humans.

"They . . . remind me of the burrowers back home," Agrethar said numbly.

"Aye," Threnn agreed. "If the burrowers were more organized, they would be the spitting image."

"Will we have ta go through that in every town?" Borim asked.

"It probably would not be wise to enter another town for some time," replied Galyres, whose arm had been cut open by a sword during the escape. Thuradin watched in wonder as it quickly healed itself, new skin forming over the open wound and thickening until he couldn't tell where the viatari had been cut.

"I'm ta blame," Stürn said somberly. "If I hadn't dispelled the toxins from my body, we wouldn't be in this situation."

"If ye hadn't done that," Thuradin reminded the Enurg'en, "ye would have lost the competition, and we'd probably have been in an even worse situation. They had no intention of letting us leave without a fight. Ye did what ye had ta do."

There was a small pause as Stürn let the words sink in. Then he nodded, accepting them.

"Unfortunately, that does not change the fact that we are in a dangerous situation now," Tessa said. "We've made enemies of those humans, and making enemies of one town makes you enemies with all of them. They'll send out hunting parties for us, and they'll send couriers to nearby towns for aid. If there's one thing humans are good at, it's hunting down their prey. Things will be more dangerous from here on out. We must be cautious, or we will perish."

The people of Halshire bustled about, bringing water to the wounded, wrapping up injuries, and covering up the dead. So much had happened in so little time in what had seemed like a perfectly normal day. It was the strangers' fault. They had come into town, cheated their way through a friendly competition, and then attacked without provocation.

Simon walked through the streets, helping out where he could and giving words of comfort when they were needed. He was the town's chief. These people were his responsibility. Had he been less welcoming to the strangers that day, perhaps this destruction would not have happened. But curiosity had gotten the better of him.

Among the group of strangers, there had been seven short figures covered in black cloaks. Simon had sent his men to spy on these strange "dwarves," as the scouts said they had been called, to try and see what they might be like. But even during the drinking game, the dwarves had refrained from taking off their cloaks, including the one who had been drinking.

That's when they had attacked. And now he was angry. They hadn't caused many casualties, but they had caused much property damage and many injuries. Not only that, but in the fighting, he had realized that the strangers who hadn't been cloaked were viatari. The cursed things! They may be able to change their appearance to that of a human, but he knew what they looked like in their true form: silver hair; red eyes; long, sharp fangs. Monsters.

Simon hated the viatari with a passion, and he had been fooled into letting ten of them enter his town today. He would not allow the trickery to go unforgiven.

"Gather the couriers," he told his servant as he entered his home. "I want them to ride out to the neighboring towns to ask for assistance in hunting down a group of viatari. Tell them to inform the other town chiefs of the dwarves we saw today as well."

"Yes, sir," the servant replied, after scribbling down the instructions on a piece of paper.

"Ah, Gabriel," Simon called as the servant was leaving the room.

"Yes, sir?"

"Tell the couriers to inform the town chiefs about this as well." He handed Gabriel a separate piece of paper he had just written several lines on himself.

"Yes, sir," Gabriel said.

"That will be all."

"Yes, sir."

Simon smiled grimly as the boy left to deliver the message. They would hunt down the viatari responsible for today's destruction and kill them, along with the dwarves in their company.

He was confident the other town chiefs would answer his call for aid, especially now that they knew what to look for. With the descriptions of their human features he had just passed on to Gabriel, they would ensure the viatari could no longer enter any more towns in disguise. With their aid, he had no doubt they would have enough men to kill the viatari. After all, they were strong and could endure quite a bit of damage, but they were not invincible.

CHAPTER THIRTEEN

A day passed with no signs of a hunting party. They had left the hill country and now rode in the middle of a giant plain. For Thuradin, it was worse than what he had gone through before the dwarves encountered the viatari. These grasslands seemed to stretch out for miles and miles without end. Since morning, he had seen nothing but tall, yellow grass and clear, blue skies. It felt like he would never see the mountains again.

Despite not having had any more encounters with humans, they remained cautious. They would take no chances. At night, a watch large enough to encircle the camp was set to make sure nothing could enter without being seen. During the day, there were now lookouts on the flanks as well as the front and rear. The lookouts rode at lengthy distances from the main group so they would have more than enough warning if someone were to show up. If a human hunting party was following them, they would be seen no matter which direction they came from.

It was around midday when Thuradin saw the smoke in the distance. It drifted slowly skyward and faded into the clouds. The lookouts rejoined the main group and made their reports. They were approaching another human town, smaller than the one before. Felix asked if there was any place they could observe it from afar. Daleres, who had already scouted the area, nodded.

They all dismounted and followed Daleres through the tall grass. They were forced to leave their mounts behind while they crept forward in these flat lands. Thuradin's stomach was in knots. He didn't want to enter another human town. It was asking for too much trouble. They walked for some time before coming to a stop behind a small incline—the first rise in the landscape Thuradin had seen in hours.

They lay low so they were well hidden from any watchful eyes as they peeked over the small hill to see what was ahead. It was indeed a small town, less than half the size of the last one they were in.

"Is there any way around it?" Felix asked.

Daleres shook his head and made several motions with his hands. Thuradin had no idea what was being said, but the elder viatari watched him intently. After a couple of minutes of signing, Daleres shrugged and turned his gaze back to the town.

Felix sighed and turned to Thuradin. "It appears if we went around this town, we would have to go far around in order to not be seen. However, Daleres says the land turns into a dense wood at the distance we would need to go on both sides of the town."

"A perfect place for an ambush," Threnn muttered.

"That is correct, young dwarf," Felix said. "If we go around, not only would it add time to our journey, we would also run the risk of running into any ambushes set up by the humans who may be hunting us. However, if we go through the town, we risk walking into an area that has already been warned of our presence. I have no doubt the leader of the last town we went through included a description of you dwarves in his report."

"Why don't we send in a scout first, then?" Anadyr suggested. "One of us could go in disguise and eavesdrop, see if there is any talk of dwarves amongst the townsfolk. That way we can see how safe it is to enter."

Felix nodded. "That is a fine idea. I will go, then, and—"

"No, Felix," Biranar said, laying his hand on the viatari's shoulder and shaking his head. "It should be one of us who goes into town, not you. You are our leader, and if, by some misfortune, we lost you, we would be lost ourselves. I will go in your place."

Felix opened his mouth to argue but Victria beat him to it. "Biranar is right, Felix. It is us who should take this risk, not you."

The other viatari nodded in agreement, giving Felix no choice but to concede.

"Very well," he said. "But do not take any unnecessary risks, Biranar. The moment you sense danger, get out of there. If there is even the slightest bit of suspicion from the townsfolk, you need to escape."

Biranar nodded and, without another word, began to shimmer and fade and transformed into his human disguise. As soon as his blue eyes and blond hair were fully developed, he stood up and made his way toward town. There was nothing anyone else could do but wait. Everyone took the opportunity to rest their eyes except Anadyr, who said she would keep watch over the town to see if anything happened. No one objected. Thuradin couldn't help but note the worry in her voice.

He wasn't sure how long he had been asleep, but when

he woke up, it was to the sound of Anadyr crying out. A quick glance at the sky told him the day was almost done— the sun was sinking below the horizon; quite a bit of time had passed since Biranar went off into the town.

Everyone had woken up to Anadyr's cry, and they rushed over to see what was wrong. The scene before them was enough to even make Ayrie feel sick.

Before them, in front of the town's gates, Biranar was held by several large men, who threw him onto the ground where he was then restrained with thick ropes. Thuradin could see the viatari struggling to break free, but the men had a firm hold on him.

"Why doesn't he break free and fight back?" Murtosh growled. "He's a viatari, for Nythirim's sake; he has the strength ta kill all of them if he wanted."

There was no answer for several minutes. Many of the viatari knelt speechless, their mouths hanging open in disbelief and shock. Anadyr trembled violently as she watched. Felix's hands covered his face, and he muttered something about how he should have gone to the town.

"They must have poisoned him," Victria finally answered. "It is the only way they could have weakened him enough to capture him. How they did it, I don't know, but I have no doubt that he has been stripped of his strength."

Thuradin's gaze returned to the town, where he now saw one of the men holding a large double-bladed axe, which he swung masterfully. He raised the axe high over his head and swung it down at the struggling viatari.

The town was a fair distance away, but they could still hear Biranar's cry as his arm was severed. Felix, Pulaneus, and Galyres turned their heads, unable to watch anymore. Daleres and Dragos shook in silent rage, their faces dark with hatred. Tessa, Natiari, and Victria were all holding back Anadyr, who was trying to break free to rush to Biranar's aid. Thuradin heard them trying to comfort her with soothing words, but they had no effect.

Looking at his own dwarves, he noted that despite the disgust etched into their faces, they couldn't turn away, no matter how much they might want to. They sat there, still and transfixed.

The man with the axe moved to the other side of Biranar and quickly severed the other arm. Another cry. More struggling between Anadyr and those holding her, determined to keep her in place.

"Let me go—Let me go! I need to—Before he—"

The man moved on to Biranar's legs and brought his axe down two more times. Two more cries, now weaker. Anadyr stopped struggling and now sobbed into the earth. Victria, Tessa, and Natiari continued to stay with her, each one with their arms around her as if trying to shield her from the reality of it.

Finally, the man positioned himself next to Biranar's head. Thuradin could see the mutilated viatari shake his head slowly as the man lifted his axe for the killing blow. There was no cry of pain this time.

Without wasting a moment, the men gathered the body parts and drove stakes through each one of them. They then set the stakes into the ground outside of the town's gates. Before returning to their homes, they nailed a sign onto each one. Thuradin was too far away to see any words, but he guessed they had left a warning to show the viatari what would happen to them if they were caught.

Only the dwarves, Daleres, and Dragos had watched the execution to the end. Anadyr lay still on the earth as if she, too, were dead. Victria, Tessa, and Natiari lay with her, tears silently rolling down their cheeks, their fangs bared. Felix gazed into the landscape, his face blank. Dragos smashed his fist into the earth and cursed in his own language.

"How did they know he was a viatari?" Ayrie asked softly.

"I doubt it was something he did," Felix said, his face void of expression. "They must know what our disguised forms look like . . . The humans in the last town must have taken note of our appearances and spread the information to the others." He looked back at the gruesome scene for a few moments and shook his head. "We are in the middle of enemy territory with nowhere to hide."

For the rest of that day, they stayed in place, too shocked to do anything. But as soon as night fell, Felix was up, encouraging everyone else to follow him. Everyone did, except Anadyr, who had to be carried by Tessa and Natiari.

They walked back to where they had left their mounts in silence. To an outside observer, they might have looked like walking corpses. By the time they made it back, the moon was high in the sky, its warm glow giving them a small sense of comfort.

Felix walked over to the horse that had belonged to Biranar. He took off all the baggage, the saddle, everything, and whispered into its ear. After he had finished, the horse rose up onto its hind legs, gave a mournful cry, and galloped off into the wilderness.

The next morning they continued their journey. It was obvious the towns weren't safe, and everyone agreed that they would have to go around and take their chances with the woods. They rode away from the human settlement at a fast pace and within a few hours saw trees looming in the

distance. Once they were closer, they noticed a small trail
leading deep into the thicket. They brought their mounts to
a stop just before entering. The trees weren't as tall or as
thick as those in the viatari's forest, yet they seemed darker
and more ominous. They twisted in all sorts of directions
and angles, creating several possible hiding places. It was
indeed the perfect place for an ambush.

Without a word, Felix spurred his mount forward and
entered. Everyone followed his lead. They soon found that
the trail narrowed significantly the farther in they rode, and
soon they were riding two abreast. Felix and Thuradin
shared a glance. They were much too exposed and spread
out. Felix gave the order for weapons to be drawn, just in
case. The sound of blades sliding out of sheaths filled the
still woods. Thuradin noticed an eagerness in Anadyr's face,
like she wanted a battle to occur, a chance to extract revenge.
He couldn't blame her.

Eyes watched his every move, he could feel it. He
swiveled his head left and right, trying to spot something that
would give away an enemy's position, something that just
wasn't right. It was impossible. He was out of his comfort
zone, and the foliage was too thick. He couldn't recognize
any oddities. In a cave or tunnel, where the rocks and stone
were all more or less the same, he would have been able to
spot an ambush with just a glance. Here, he felt blind.

Thuradin knew Felix was certain they were walking into
an ambush by coming here. He waited to see if the viatari
might point something out that would take away the enemy's
element of surprise. Unfortunately, it looked like even he
was having trouble making anything out in this place. Leaves
fell from the trees incessantly, creating a natural screen for
anything hiding in the shadows.

The attack began with a single arrow. Whether it was an intentional shot or an accidental slip of the hand, the lone arrow whistled past Felix and slammed into Galyres' shoulder. Galyres fell from his horse, grasping at the arrow and pulling it free. He tried to stand again but stumbled as humans appeared from all sides, yelling war cries and brandishing swords and axes and spears.

"Their weapons are poisoned!" he managed to cry out before a man jumped out behind him and ran his sword through the viatari's midsection.

Felix yelled furiously, his horse rearing back.

There was no time to sit and watch. The remaining viatari jumped from their mounts and began to fight for their lives. The dwarves dismounted and met the men with an even more ferocious war cry. The battle rams joined the fray with wicked screams. The humans hadn't expected animals to join in the fighting and scrambled back in confusion as they tried to avoid their sharp hooves and horns.

Unlike the last battle they were in, Stürn couldn't focus solely on healing. There were too many enemies, and the humans were much smarter than grattles. At one point in the battle, Murtosh had received a brutal blow to the head, and the helm he wore crumpled. Stürn quickly called on the life-energies around him to heal the injured dwarf. The humans took notice of the healing and soon identified him as the source. After that, they kept pressure on him to keep him from healing anyone else.

But the dwarves fought with strategy this time. Thuradin led them like they were his own royal guards. He put them in a wedge formation with himself at the point and had them slowly advance. They cut down men left and right as their discipline persevered. Even so, more men poured from the trees endlessly, and the formation was quickly overwhelmed.

As they broke ranks Murtosh immediately went berserk and started slaying every man he could find in his savage bloodlust. Agrethar lay on the ground, struggling to pull an arrow out of his shoulder while Threnn stood over him, protecting him from anyone who tried to approach. Ayrie masterfully hurled her spear at the archers hiding in the trees, retrieving her weapon quickly as it returned to the earth with her kill. Borim and Thuradin stuck together and defended each other from anyone who dared approach.

As for the viatari, from the few moments Thuradin could spare to look around, he could tell they were intent on extracting revenge for the deaths of Galyres and Biranar. They moved so quickly, they seemed to teleport from place to place. They would kill a man in one part of the forest and the next second be fighting another on the other side.

Natiari and Tessa fought as a ruthless pair, cutting down the enemy with their dirks. Dragos and Daleres fought with a calm fury that was unnerving to all they faced. Felix sometimes fought with the dwarves, saving many of them at the last second from a fatal blow, but more often he was alone against large groups of the humans and with an even deadlier calm than his companions. The men around him panicked as they sensed their doom.

Victria and Anadyr took to the trees to help Ayrie flush out the archers. Anadyr lashed out with a mad fury that matched Murtosh's berserker's rage. Her short, silver hair flew in all directions as she maimed and finished off every human she could find.

The dwarves and viatari weren't invincible, however. The human archers wreaked havoc with their poison arrows. Any viatari who was hit or even grazed by one of their missiles wouldn't be seriously injured, but the contact was enough for the poison to enter their system—and the poison acted quickly. It weakened them significantly and made them much more vulnerable to attacks.

Thuradin saw an arrow strike Daleres in his calf. The viatari fell to the ground and broke the wooden shaft in half, leaving the poisoned tip in. Pulaneus came to his defense and tried to protect him from the huge onslaught of men; but, weakened and slowed, Daleres couldn't defend himself as well as he used to. He was too slow to dodge the giant axe that bit deep into his chest, nearly cleaving him in half. Pulaneus wasted no time in avenging him, stabbing the human responsible several times in the chest with his own blade. But there was nothing he could do for Daleres, who lay in the forest's undergrowth, as silent in death as he was in life.

The humans kept coming. Thuradin didn't know where they were getting their numbers. There were far too many for this to be a simple hunting party. At this rate, if they didn't escape soon, they would be overwhelmed. He looked for Felix to tell him this, but the elder viatari was already of the same mind.

"Mount up!" Felix yelled over the noise of battle. "Ride! Ride out of this forest!"

Everyone followed Felix as he mounted his horse and rode straight through the line of men blocking their path, swinging his slender blade in lethal arcs as he went. The dwarves called the remaining rams from battle and mounted them, following the path the viatari had created. They sped through the forest, avoiding their attackers where they could and crashing into them where they could not. They burst out of the twisting trees at a full gallop and continued until the mounts were on the verge of collapsing from sheer exhaustion.

They dismounted and set up camp. Victria took the watch while others who weren't wounded pulled down supplies and started a small fire. The wounded were immediately looked after by Stürn.

Felix walked around the camp, conducting a head count.

". . . twelve . . . thirteen—we're missing one. Where is Anadyr?"

"She stayed behind," Dragos mumbled. "I couldn't get her to leave. She said she would stay in that forest until every human was dead. She's with Galyres and Daleres."

"I see," Felix sighed.

For a moment, everything was silent and still as they imagined the gruesome demise Anadyr must have faced fighting the horde of humans all on her own. Was she weakened by an arrow and killed with a quick, clean sword stroke? Or was she captured and butchered like Biranar?

Felix began pacing, glancing up at the sky and then into the distance. "That hunting party was larger than any I have ever seen," he muttered. "This does not bode well. Pulaneus?"

Pulaneus looked up from where he was helping Stürn with the injured. "Ride back to Aleganthia. Tell them of the current situation. A hunting party this large, spread across the area like this, is dangerous—they could easily stumble upon Aleganthia if they go too far north. Tell them to take every precaution necessary to avoid discovery."

Pulaneus nodded and, after a few quick farewells, galloped away from them with a small supply of food and water. Felix went back to his agitated pacing.

"Thuradin," Stürn called. "It's Agrethar."

Thuradin rushed over to where the young dwarf lay by

his battle ram. He was clutching his shoulder, and a steady stream of sweat dripped from his brow. He looked feverish. He groaned in pain as Thuradin removed his hand from the wound. A gasp escaped his lips.

The young dwarf's skin had turned black. He could see the wound was severely infected already. The stench was almost unbearable.

"Why haven't ye healed him?" he finally asked.

"The humans use a poison I'm unfamiliar with, and its been in him for too long," Stürn said. "I'm calling on his life-energies ta heal him, but so much has already been corrupted by it that they aren't responding ta my pleas. I've never seen anything like it."

Agrethar reached out weakly with his hand, which Thuradin took. "I know how bad it is," he said in a weak voice. "If even Stürn cannae heal me—find a cave for me," his voice became strained, "ye know what happens ta us if we're entombed outside the mountains."

Thuradin nodded. If a dwarf were entombed outside the mountains, he would eventually erode away. To be eroded away into dust instead of preserved forever in the mountains was one of the worst fears a dwarf held. It was the most severe punishment sentenced only to the worst criminals in the Dwarven Kingdom.

"Stürn, keep working on him," Thuradin said. "We cannae let ye die, Agrethar. I won't let it happen."

"Commander," Agrethar whispered. "Whether ye let me or nae, death comes for me. I can feel his gaze upon me—and he does nae obey yer commands."

A day passed, and Agrethar's condition only worsened. He turned a sickly green, and the stench from his arm grew more potent by the hour. If it hadn't been for Stürn's continuous healing, he would have undoubtedly passed hours ago.

On Thuradin's insistence, they stopped for the tenth time that day so that Agrethar could rest and Stürn could perform stronger healing chants.

Felix, followed by Dragos, approached Thuradin as everyone else worked on building a small camp.

"We cannot continue to travel this way," Felix stated. "I am truly sorry about Agrethar, but he is slowing us down significantly—we should already be at the border to Inadarim by now."

"What can we do?" Thuradin shrugged, frustrated. "The poison is impossible for Stürn ta heal, and we're certainly nae going ta leave him here ta die by himself."

Felix sighed with some exasperation. "Well, something must be done. We cannot continue moving at a snail's pace or the humans will catch up to us, and next time, they will destroy us."

"Agrethar already knows he's going ta die," Thuradin said, thinking fast. As much as he wanted to believe the young dwarf would eventually pull through, the realistic part of him knew it was unlikely. "If we could find him a cave ta die in, then we could leave him there and continue on with our journey; that way—"

"Absolutely not," Dragos seethed. "The nearest caves are back in the Silent Mountains. You would have to ride back the way we came for half a day and then east toward the mountains. It would add an entire week to the journey."

"Well, what will ye do? Leave him here?" Thuradin retorted angrily. "I tell ye, we won't leave him out in the wilderness where he can erode away inta dust. He deserves better than that!"

"I consider myself quite patient, but even I am nearing my limit," Felix said. "I will not have your injured friend endanger this quest and our well-being."

"Oh, ye won't, will ye?"

Thuradin drew his twin-axes and would have tried to plant them into Felix's skull then and there had Victria not stepped in and grabbed his arms to stop him.

"Now, now," she said, picking him up from the ground with ease and turning him to face her. By now, Thuradin had grown accustomed to the viatari's eyes, enough to hold Victria's gaze with his own.

"Put—Me—Down," he commanded. "I don't enjoy being lifted."

Victria laughed softly and winked but obeyed his wishes and lowered him to the ground.

"Forgive me for eavesdropping, but I couldn't help but hear your complaints," she said as she turned her attention to Felix and Dragos. "And I believe I may have a compromise."

CHAPTER FOURTEEN

Victria proposed they split up into two groups. One would make their way to the mountains so a cave could be found for Agrethar to die in. The other would continue with the journey to Inadarim and wait for the rest to reunite with them before pressing on into the Creature's domain.

"How is that any different from all of us going to the mountains, then?" Felix asked.

"The group taking Agrethar will only consist of a few members. Obviously, Stürn will need to go so he can heal Agrethar for the journey to keep him from dying. I will go with them to lead them around the human towns in the area. And I'm assuming Thuradin will want to go?"

Victria turned to Thuradin, who still glowered at Felix with both of his axes gripped tightly. He nodded.

"Then it's settled," Victria clapped her hands, closing the matter. "The four of us will find a cave for Agrethar. That way, too many aren't taken from the main group to the point where you are unable to protect yourselves."

Dragos looked like he was about to argue, but a look from Felix stopped him. "This does not change the problem of time, Victria. This little excursion will still add at least a few more days to the quest. That is time we do not have."

Victria turned her gaze back to Felix, the brightness in her face rapidly evaporating. There was no longer any tone of compromise in her voice as she spoke.

"If you wish to not waste time, you may go into Inadarim without us. As I said before, losing only four members—one of whom will soon be dead—will not seriously weaken the party, and you have plenty of dwarves to take care of the Creature when the time comes."

Felix seemed to notice the change in Victria, the sudden chill that had come into her words. "Very well, but Dragos is going with you."

"We don't need him," Thuradin said as he made his way to his ram to prepare his things for the journey.

"I insist," Felix replied. "Consider this my . . . condition for letting you do this."

Thuradin's eyes narrowed. He didn't appreciate the idea of Felix forcing Dragos onto them, no doubt to keep an eye on him, but he appreciated even less the way the viatari implied that he needed his permission to do this in the first place. Once again, before he could retaliate with something a little sharper than words, Victria intervened, accepted the condition, and told Dragos to hurry and ready his mount.

It took some time for the five of them to leave. Stürn had trouble keeping Agrethar balanced on the ram they shared, and Dragos kept arguing with Victria over . . . something. Several minutes passed before he finally threw his hands in the air and headed for his horse. A quick glance at Victria told Thuradin she wasn't going to share the nature of their argument. At least, not yet.

They rode off, Thuradin quickly taking the lead as he urged his mount forward. He was furious with Felix and wondered now if perhaps Ayrie had been right to mistrust the viatari's intentions. Would Felix dispose of the rest of them once they had served their purpose? He could not help but think of the possibility.

It was some time before he calmed down enough to let Victria ride ahead and lead the way. The landscape was a blur as they rode at full speed. Several hours passed before they began to slow down and Victria called for a stop. They rested and nibbled on some of the food they had brought.

"We'll be arriving to *that* area soon," Dragos warned, looking at Victria.

"What area?" Thuradin asked, confused.

"This place has long been in the hands of the humans. They've spread like wildfire, and villages and towns have popped up everywhere," Dragos explained. "It's a dangerous and difficult area to travel through. which is *why* I suggested we take the other route."

"Dragos," Victria said. "I know you did not wish to come, but now that you are here, you will listen to what I say. We are going through the plains because it is faster. As you and Felix said, time is of the essence. If we went your way, we would add *another* week to the journey. This way we only spend a few days traveling."

Dragos's scowl deepened. "But the risks—"

"—are great, yes," Victria interrupted. "Which is why we will travel during the night from now on. I suggest you all sleep for the rest of the day so you have plenty of energy for tonight's ride."

She dismounted and led her horse away so that it could graze, followed closely by Dragos and his own mount. Thuradin let his ram wander aimlessly as he turned to Stürn, who had resumed healing Agrethar.

"Will ye be alright?"

Stürn nodded. "Don't worry about me. I can handle being awake for a few days. Worry about Agrethar. He's in a much worse state than we will be."

Thuradin nodded and turned his attention to the sick dwarf lying stiffly on the ground. Agrethar was paler than before, but his color came back a little thanks to Stürn's healing. He was already asleep, and Thuradin could hear him mumble like he was trying to tell him something, but he couldn't make out what was being said. Finally, after being chased away by Stürn for being a nuisance to his charge, he found a soft patch of earth and closed his eyes.

The moon was rising slowly when he was gently nudged awake by Victria.

"We must resume our journey."

Thuradin nodded, yawned, and rubbed his eyes slowly before he got up and started preparing his ram, who bleated a soft greeting. He took out some more of the dried ram meat they had packed and ate it before mounting. Once he was atop his mount, he steered it around to join the others, who were waiting on him.

"I've already told the others this," Victria whispered as he came alongside her. "We must stay as quiet as possible while we travel. Sound travels for miles in this area, and the towns and villages will all be asleep, so they won't be making much noise themselves. If we're too loud, our hoofbeats will be noticed. We won't ride faster than a trot, and when we near a town or village, we slow down to a walk. Do you understand?"

Thuradin nodded and spurred his mount forward as Victria led the way through the darkness. They stayed at a trot for some time and slowed to a walk as they neared a town, just as Victria had said. They traveled like this the entire night, veering far around several human settlements to avoid them.

Most of the time, Thuradin could only see a soft glow on the horizon rather than the town itself, but even at that distance, he could hear some noise coming from it. The clattering of plates as the watchmen on the walls ate. A sudden burst of laughter.

It wasn't until dawn that Victria began to search for a place where they could rest out of sight. Darkness faded as the sun peeked over the plains and continued to rise. An hour passed, and Thuradin worried that they might be seen if they continued traveling in the daylight like this when Victria saw something to her liking. She pointed it out.

About a mile to the right of them was a cluster of stones jutting out of the ground, a perfect cover from wandering eyes. They urged their tired mounts toward the stones, and within minutes, they were dismounted and looking for soft places to sleep.

The animals moved under the shadow of one of the larger boulders to sleep. Victria threw herself to the ground as soon as her feet touched it. Had Thuradin not noticed her deep, rhythmic breathing, he would have thought she had died.

It didn't take long for him to realize that she had been on watch the entire day as the rest of them slept, and had stayed awake all night to lead them through the dark plains. This would be her first chance to sleep in at least two days.

Dragos sat near the outskirts of the stone formation, looking outward. This time he would be the one staying awake for the day and following night. Thuradin silently thanked both of them for the sacrifices they were making to help bury Agrethar. He dared not think what might have happened had Victria not intervened.

Walking near the center of the stone formation, he came across the place Stürn had brought Agrethar for healing. The stones surrounded them completely, giving the Enurg'en the necessary cover to heal the young dwarf without any interruptions from the outside.

Thuradin knelt next to Agrethar, who was breathing heavily. His eyes drooped slightly.

"How are ye feeling?"

"Nae terrible for someone who is near death."

Thuradin didn't meet Agrethar's steady gaze. The crystal-blue eyes that were so young and normally so full of life were now dull. A shadow had passed over them.

"Bronn . . . I promised him that I'd keep ye safe. He made me promise that before he handed ye and Murtosh and Threnn over ta me."

Stürn kept his gaze on Agrethar's wound as he communicated with the young dwarf's life-energies, but Thuradin knew he was listening. Agrethar remained motionless, staring at Thuradin intently as he waited to hear more about Bronn.

"I never meant for this ta happen," he continued. "Perhaps if I hadn't been so stubborn, if I had listened ta ye and Ayrie when ye told me ta be cautious with the viatari, this wouldn't have happened."

"There's no need ta apologize," Agrethar said softly. "Threnn, Murtosh, and I joined knowing we may never return. It was nae for adventure or fun. We aren't fools. We joined ta help find our King because it was our duty ta do so."

Thuradin placed his hand on the young dwarf's forehead,

which felt dangerously hot, "Ye had no such duty, dwarves as young as ye are."

Agrethar shrugged weakly as he turned his gaze to the cloudless sky.

"What else did Bronn say about me?"

Stürn glanced at Thuradin.

"He wished ye hadn't gone," Thuradin said, ignoring Stürn's cue to leave. "But I know that didn't stop him from being proud of ye. I could see it in his eyes as he left ta return ta Tinas Gran. I don't think any father has ever loved a son so much. I remember the day he took ye from that orphanage. He wouldn't stop talking about ye; I don't think I've ever seen him so happy since before his own sons died that day—"

"Thuradin—"

Thuradin glanced up at Stürn and then down at Agrethar, whose eyes had filled with unshed tears.

He cleared his throat and patted Agrethar lightly on the shoulder. "Ye should get some rest. It's been a long night and there are sure ta be more."

He got up to leave, shooting Stürn an apologetic glance for upsetting his patient, and walked over to a secluded spot that looked to be out of sight from everyone else. He quickly found a place where he could lie down and sleep, but his head was filled with thoughts of the future.

What would he tell Bronn? The thought of losing any of the three dwarves Bronn had entrusted to him had crossed his mind, but never had he thought it would truly happen. Now, sometime in the future, he would have to face the elderly dwarf and tell him that he had lost not only one of the three dwarves, but his heir. Thuradin could only imagine two scenarios: one of utter rage, one of complete despair.

Accompanied only with these thoughts and the sound of a blacksmith's hammer coming from a town miles away, Thuradin fell asleep.

He woke to see Dragos glaring at him. There was nothing sinister in his eyes as far as he could tell, but he thought he detected a hint of contempt, and he wondered, not for the first time, where such resentment against him and his kind had come from. None of the other viatari seemed to have it.

It was night now, and Thuradin had slept through the entire day, as had Victria. He saw her now as she mounted her horse. She gave a small nod in his direction and a flash of a smile before bringing her focus to Dragos, who gave a report of the day's occurrences. No sign of any humans nearby.

Thuradin also mounted and watched as Agrethar heaved himself onto Stürn's ram and then turn to help the Enurg'en get on. It looked as if their roles had reversed. After a day of healing, Agrethar was the one full of energy, while Stürn looked to be on the verge of death.

They continued their slow journey with Victria in the lead once again. Before leaving, she had told Thuradin they would be out of the plains by the end of the night, which made him feel slightly better about their situation. The sooner they were out of this region, surrounded by hostile towns, the better.

The night wore on, though the moon and stars were nowhere to be seen—thick clouds floated overhead, obscuring the natural light of the sky. They were still there hours later when the sun rose.

Ahead of them, Thuradin saw the Silent Mountains growing larger and clearer the closer they rode. The snowy caps were covered by clouds, but that didn't stop him from admiring their beauty as he saw his home for the first time in what seemed like years.

The landscape changed as they continued their journey in the daylight, no longer worried about the human towns they had left behind. The long grass of the plains grew sparse. Hills took shape, rising above the rest of the earth only to fall back down again like waves. Every now and then, there was a patch of wooded area within the small valleys the hills created.

Victria led them into one of these copses and declared they would make camp there. Dragos slid off his mount and walked off deeper into the brush, disappearing from sight. Thuradin watched him go, figuring he wanted a more secluded place to sleep.

As soon as he dismounted, Stürn went back to healing Agrethar, whose skin had returned to its ashen-gray color. The Enurg'en spread his arms out, palms facing the earth, and resumed muttering his chants.

Victria walked away and sat on a fallen log some distance from the camp to keep watch. Thuradin swore to himself that he would stay up and keep watch with her this time, determined not to be the only one enjoying the comforts of sleep. He would join her, but first he went to Agrethar's side.

"We're nearing the mountains," he said.

"Aye, I saw them as we approached. Beautiful, weren't they?" Agrethar gave a sputtering cough.

Stürn glanced at Thuradin warningly, which told him not to push the young dwarf too far, as he had done yesterday. Thuradin nodded.

"I wish ye could have seen the snowy peaks one last time. It seems unfair that this world would block such a sight from ye when yer time is so near its end."

Agrethar smiled weakly. "I thank ye, Thuradin. I didn't think I would be able ta smile at all, so close ta the end as I am. But don't blame the world. It's such a beautiful place, much more than we could have ever imagined."

Thuradin wondered when the young dwarf had started feeling that way. It was true the outside had its own sense of beauty. But it was dangerous, much too dangerous. Compared to the dwarven caverns, Thuradin thought there was no comparison. He mentioned this to the dying dwarf, not sure what sort of response he expected.

"Aye," Agrethar agreed, his eyes closed as if he were asleep. "'Tis a dangerous world, but that's what makes it all the more beautiful. The fact that everything around us, the different colors and smells, can disappear in an instant—such a dangerous beauty."

Thuradin nodded. He thought perhaps Agrethar's mind was beginning to drift because of the poison. Guilt washed over him again. Surely, he would carry this guilt to his own grave, whenever that time came.

He shared a few more words with the young dwarf before leaving him to rest. He then went over to where Victria was keeping watch and sat on the opposite end of the log. The viatari greeted him with a warm smile. She was the only one who ever did so, Thuradin realized. He grinned back halfheartedly.

"Is it Agrethar?" she asked, noticing his lack of spirit.

Thuradin nodded.

"You blame yourself for his coming death."

Again, Thuradin nodded. "My companions are the bravest dwarves in all the Dwarven Kingdom. They joined me on this foolish quest, despite the dangers, only because I asked them to. I'm nae worthy ta be their leader."

Victria sat in silence for a while before replying. "Humility is good, but you should not fall into despair. Insecurity can be dangerous when in a position of leadership. You must believe in your own abilities. After all, they are what earned you the title of commander of the royal guard, are they not?"

Thuradin looked at Victria, surprised. "How do ye—"

"Your friend, Borim. He's told me quite a lot about you, enough for me to guess some things. I don't think you're weak, or unworthy. In fact, I don't believe anyone else could have led them as far as you have."

"I'm nae so sure," Thuradin sighed.

Victria turned her gaze to the treetops. "When I was young—very young—I was filled with pride—that is how the youth are, after all. When viatari are born, they are abandoned by their parents in their first years of life and forced to learn how to survive in the wilderness on their own. I was no different."

Thuradin glanced at her. She sat still as she continued to look up into the trees and the falling leaves. Her voice had turned soft as she was pulled into the memories of her past.

"It wasn't until I was forty-eight years of age that I was finally discovered by a group of older viatari. They took me in, gave me a home, taught me how to fight, and turned me into a fully fledged viatari. Still, I kept my pride even after being taken in. It wasn't until the Creature began his war against us that I learned to put my trust in those around me. Even then, pride, my insecurities, weren't completely gone. I kept it all hidden, in check for over a millennium. But they eventually resurfaced and led me to one of the greatest failures of my life."

"Wait," Thuradin said hesitantly, not wanting to seem

like a fool for asking. "Ye said ye were found?"

Victria nodded. "Like I said, viatari are abandoned early on in life and left to survive on their own. Many of us have to do this for centuries before we're found by those who are already established viatari. It's not until we're found that we can be established ourselves and join a community. At least, that's how it used to be."

There was silence for a moment. Thuradin felt he knew the answer to the question he was about to ask, but that didn't stop him from asking it.

"Who was it that found you?"

Victria turned to him, a nostalgic smile on her face as she was pulled back to a different time.

"It was Felix."

CHAPTER FIFTEEN

It felt like boulders had been tied to Victria's legs as she burst through the undergrowth in a mad dash, the wolves following close behind. She heard them howling at the moon as they pursued her and occasionally heard a sharper yowl or bark as they communicated with each other. Based on how close their voices sounded, she figured it wouldn't be long now before they caught up to her and began tearing her apart.

This had been Victria's life for the past forty-eight years. Over the course of that time, the young viatari had grown accustomed to this life full of constant struggle, danger, and death. In fact, it wasn't even the first time she had been in this sort of danger, the kind where a pack of wolves chased her, wanting to kill her for invading their territory and stealing their food.

As far as she knew, this was how life was supposed to be. She met few other viatari in the wilderness, but the ones she did meet had all been in the same predicament. Abandoned orphans. Surviving by luck. Alone.

Despite that, for whatever reason, everyone she met had wanted to form some sort of pact with her, much to her distaste. For as far as she could remember, she had always survived the dangers of this world by herself, with her own strength and ability. She saw no reason to change that. She was her own most reliable ally.

She often abandoned her newly found companions once they offered the idea of a partnership. It usually took only a few days more before she discovered their bloody remains. She never felt guilt when this happened, only confirmation that her initial impression of their weakness had been correct.

Now it was her turn, once again, to prove to whoever was watching—and she knew someone was watching, for she always felt eyes upon her—that she had what it took to be a viatari, that she was not weak.

She had noticed, while wandering the woods earlier that day, that she was near a well-known and particularly dangerous piece of wolf territory. Entering alone was enough to ensure she would be hunted down and devoured by the wolves living there. Even now she didn't quite understand what drove her to do what she did—there were surely other ways to prove one's strength than by outrunning a pack of wolves—but she had entered their territory and provoked them by making her presence known and stealing their food.

The wolves had waited for night to fall before they began their hunt. With a unified howl, they bounded after the intruder, death in their minds. Victria had heard the howling and began running as fast as she could out of their territory and through the forest she had lived in for her entire life. She started with a huge lead on the hunters, but they quickly closed the gap as the moon crossed the sky. Now they were nearly on top of her. She sensed several of them right on her heels and occasionally caught a glimpse of a couple of them running a few yards to her side.

Victria knew she was close to collapsing from exhaustion and letting the wolves have at her. She looked for a tree she could climb and hide in for a few days. Surely that was her only hope of survival. If she couldn't lose the wolves by running away, she would wait them out. She found the perfect one a few dozen yards ahead and put every ounce of energy she had left into a final sprint to reach it.

The wolves must have sensed what she was planning. One of them running to the side of her drew near and tried to pounce on her, its sharp fangs glistened in the moonlight. Victria easily dodged the attack, positioning herself behind a tree the second the wolf lunged. The wolf's fangs bit into nothing but bark.

Not even looking back to see if the wolf would lunge a second time, Victria jumped as high as she could to reach the lowest branch of the tree she saw as her sanctuary. Once she grabbed hold of it, she began to climb. Her tattered clothes clung to her skin and made the climb easier than it otherwise might have been. She didn't have to worry about any of it snagging on a branch, making her lose her balance. She ignored the wolves' frustrated growls as they reached the tree, worried that any lapse in focus might cause some misstep that would lead to her death.

The wolves tried to reach her, but they could only reach as high as their hind legs would lift them. Victria stopped climbing once she was sure she was at a safe height and watched them as they continued jumping, trying to snatch her out of the tree. Finally, the wolves settled down, and the long game of attrition began.

Several days passed, and Victria's small food supply, live animals she had managed to steal from the wolves' territory, ran out. Their dried carcasses littered the floor, where she tossed them after all their life-energies were consumed.

Now she was hungry and thirsty and her body felt sore from sitting on a tree branch for so long. Her eyelids were heavy as the lack of sleep continued to take its toll. She had stayed up every night since the hunt began, worried that if she fell asleep she might accidentally roll off the branch and into the maws of the wolves below.

Meanwhile, the wolves continued guarding her tree, determined to rip apart the body of the one who dared enter their territory. A few split from the main pack every once and a while to go hunting while the others continued to watch their prey. They would take turns doing this so that none of them ever became too hungry or thirsty or bored.

Victria began to think that perhaps she had been a little too reckless with this stunt when she heard voices nearby. They were cheerful, unaware of the danger the wolves presented. The wolves heard these voices as well and growled, pricking up their ears at the newcomers' arrival. Victria looked down over her branch to see a small group of viatari facing off against the pack of beasts.

Victria noted the silver hair and sharp red eyes. There was no way she could be wrong. The newcomers were definitely viatari, just like her. But they looked different somehow.

The viatari showed no signs of hostility. They were quiet as they discussed what to do and looked completely relaxed in their movements. There were only four of them, and Victria saw that they were greatly outnumbered, since several of the wolves that had gone off hunting had just returned, surrounding the viatari. She called out for them to run, but only one of them seemed to hear her.

This particular viatari looked up to where she was. He nodded his head at her and smiled reassuringly before bringing his attention back to the wolves.

The wolves attacked first. Victria covered her eyes as she saw them rush toward the viatari. She expected to hear snarling and smell blood as they tore into their unsuspecting victims. She hadn't expected to hear yelps of pain from the wolves. She uncovered her eyes and saw blood cover the forest floor.

The viatari were only blurs as they moved around and attacked at lightning speed. The wolves hadn't expected their opponents to be so fast or strong, and fear quickly made its way through the few that remained. They fled the scene, leaving their decimated pack behind. Those that remained whimpered at the pain of their broken bodies.

The viatari made their way around the fallen wolves on the ground and ended their misery as painlessly as they could. The wolves may have attacked first, but the viatari were not sadistic.

The one who had heard Victria's call walked over to the tree and called for her to come down. Suspicious, she didn't move or respond at first. For all she knew, these viatari might be like the others she had run into: scared and weak, trying to form some sort of partnership for their own survival. She quickly dropped that idea, though, as she remembered how they had handled the wolves. They had been quick, violent, and precise in their attacks—far more powerful than any viatari she had seen in her short life.

She made her way down the tree.

She hadn't realized it until she began to move, but she had lost more strength than she previously thought. If these viatari hadn't saved her, today might have been her last day in this world. Her hand slipped on one of the lower branches as she was making her way down, and she fell. She would have fallen headfirst into the ground had the viatari below not caught her. She squirmed and cried out, trying to free herself from his clutches. He set her down gently and stepped back a few paces to give her space.

"Who are you?" Victria asked after she had finished sizing up these four strangers.

"My name is Felix," said the one who had first noticed her. "And these are my friends. We were scouting these woods to see if there were any good hunting grounds around when we came upon your little . . . stalemate."

Victria didn't believe him. Why would a group of *four* viatari need to find hunting grounds? It didn't make sense. They looked friendly, but something inside her refused to trust them.

Felix seemed to sense this, but that didn't stop him from making an offer. "We have a village a few miles from here. Would you like us to take you there?"

This piece of news surprised Victria. In all her life, she had never seen as many viatari in one place at one time as she did now, but a village of them . . . that was impossible. She didn't believe this 'Felix,' but she also didn't understand why he would offer something like that if it wasn't genuine. Curiosity eventually won her over, and Victria accepted the offer, albeit hesitantly.

Felix smiled again, which Victria thought he seemed to do a lot. The other viatari came up to her and introduced themselves. She didn't bother to remember their names because she didn't care. Despite their offer to take her to their village, she didn't plan on staying. She just wanted to see if what they said was true.

Looking up close, she could see how much older these viatari were. All of their eyes were old, showcasing the wisdom and hardships they'd had to endure throughout their lives, but Felix's were far older than the other three. She saw more wisdom and hardship in his eyes than in any other, but she also saw something that the others didn't seem to have. Exhaustion.

"How old are you?" she asked as Felix picked her up and began to carry her on his shoulders through the woods. The other viatari went the other way, delving deeper into the trees.

Felix didn't answer; he didn't even appear to have heard the question—or rather, he chose not to hear it. "We should get you washed up first," he said, maintaining a cheery tone.

He carried her to a nearby stream which ran through a small clearing and dropped her into the water. It felt like a swarm of bees had enveloped Victria, stinging her at the same time everywhere, as the icy water touched her skin. She came up sputtering and glared at Felix, who only grinned.

"Wash yourself," he said as he sat down on a nearby boulder. "Or do you need my help?"

"I can wash myself!" Victria replied angrily. "I just—a little privacy would be nice."

Felix laughed and turned to face the other way. Victria sighed, annoyed, but took off her tattered clothes and sunk into the frigid stream.

She couldn't remember the last time she had done this. It felt strange to part with the dirt and grime that had been a part of her life through her many years of surviving in the wilderness. It had concealed her scent when she needed to hide and had helped her in many other ways. Now it crumbled off her body, like dead skin, and washed away in the stream's current.

New clothes were laid out for her while she bathed. She got out of the water and quickly put them on. They were soft and simple and reminded her of the large ferns she would use as a hiding place when in danger. She didn't know what the material was, but it fit her perfectly, and it was warm.

"Now you look like a proper viatari," Felix said as he turned to see her. "My friends will return shortly. They had to complete our scouting mission. We can't go back empty-handed, after all."

Victria nodded absently and sat down on a separate boulder next to Felix. She watched the stream pass by. An awkward silence ensued as the two waited for the others to return.

"How did you kill those wolves so easily?" Victria asked, unwilling to endure the silence any longer.

Felix raised an eyebrow. "What do you mean?"

"You were outnumbered, yet you killed so many of them in a flash," Victria remembered the startled cries of the beasts. "How?"

"Do you not know how to fight?" Felix asked. "Such a thing is natural for a viatari. How have you been surviving all this time?"

"Luck," Victria shrugged. "I never needed to fight."

"And how would you have dealt with the wolves, then, if you had not had our aid?"

Victria was silent.

"We viatari are very strong, very agile individuals," Felix said. "With the proper training, we can smash boulders like the one I am sitting on now. We can jump far distances; we can run almost faster than the eye can see; we can create illusions to trick the mind. We are born with these abilities, but it takes years of training for them to be unlocked. It takes many more to grow and perfect them."

"Where can I get this training?" Victria asked eagerly. The thought of being able to protect herself even better than how she had been in the past interested her. She would never again need to rely on another for help like she had been forced to today.

"You can get it at our village. It is not a large village, mind you, but it is enough to help any young viatari unlock his or her potential. You can train there, if you like."

Victria didn't answer immediately. She still doubted Felix, but if what he said was true, going to this village might help her become stronger. Learning the skills and abilities he said she had would be beneficial when the time came to return to her lifestyle of survival. Just as Felix had pointed out, the situation with the wolves proved that.

"My parents abandoned me," Victria said, not quite sure why she felt the need to explain her life to the older viatari. "I can't remember their faces, or what they were like. All I know is that I've had to rely on only myself to survive. I can't let myself trust anyone, because it'll only lead to me getting hurt if that person betrays me. I could never dream of living in a village . . . But if it's to get stronger, to give me the tools I need to survive, then I'll go to your village and train. Just don't expect me to ever trust you, or even to stay once I finish my training."

She turned to see how Felix would react. She was surprised to see him nodding, an expression of sad understanding on his face.

"It is the way of the viatari," he said, his voice softer than Victria thought possible. "We abandon our children in the woods very early in their lives to see if they have the ability to survive. Only after surviving for at least twenty years can they then be considered a true viatari. It is a sad and brutal trial that has existed since the birth of our race that I regret . . . you may not trust us for a long time, that is to be expected. But you will, eventually. And you may even end up considering the village we take you to as a home, given time. However, if in the end you decide you truly wish to continue living alone, I will not try to stop you."

With that, Felix's carefree grin returned and he turned his gaze back to the tree line, where three figures emerged.

"Ah, they've returned!"

Felix called out to his friends cheerfully, but Victria wasn't fooled. She had noticed the sudden change in topic. She wondered what it was exactly that Felix regretted about this so-called viatari tradition.

She didn't have time to think too much on the matter. Felix picked her up and put her on his shoulders again, carrying her through the forest as he explained everything about the viatari to her. There were so many things she was hearing for the first time about who she was that she could hardly keep up with all the explanations, and she quickly forgot her suspicions. By the end of the trek, her head swam with so much new information that she felt dizzy.

They traveled like this for a couple more hours before the trees thinned out and revealed a village. Victria stared in awe at the cluster of buildings before her. For so long in her life, she had been alone and had seen so few of her kind. Here she counted nearly fifty viatari, all with the same silver hair and red eyes that she had.

The village lay in a small meadow within the forest. There were several wooden houses and larger buildings scattered throughout. They were simple structures, made only to serve as shelter from the elements for the villagers. Even so, Victria was impressed. Felix had spoken the truth. There really *was* a village of viatari.

Some of the villagers noticed Felix's arrival. As they approached, Victria suddenly felt out of place, as if she were some unwanted intruder. Felix set her down as he greeted some of the people and she began to back away toward the treeline. She was a stranger here; she would be stared at like some kind of pet, and she wouldn't have it. But before she could make up her mind to run away, Felix grabbed her and, once again, put her on top of his shoulders.

"This is Victria," he called out in a loud voice so everyone could hear. "We found her in the woods, but from now on, she will be one of us."

The villagers welcomed her with smiles and friendly pats and a couple of hellos. Victria didn't know how to respond. She had expected them to look at her with distaste or disinterest, anything but open arms. She sat on Felix's shoulders, dazed. The villagers already saw her as one of their own, not as an outsider. Distrust and misgivings still thrived within her, but she felt much of the weight she'd had living alone in the forest leave her. And for the first time in a long time, she smiled.

Just as Felix had predicted, Victria quickly came to consider the village her home. She met some of the viatari who were her age and quickly befriended them. There were two she especially grew to like: Natiari Lunglow and Tessa Shadoweaver.

The three met for the first time during training. They would often spar each other and help each other grow.

Eventually Victria started to consider Natiari and Tessa her sisters, and they in turn considered her theirs.

It was often remarked with wonder by the other villagers how different the three girls were from each other yet how well they got along. Natiari was energetic and took on all challenges with great enthusiasm. Victria was more reserved and cared only for victory in all that she did. Tessa was quiet and seemed like a nice girl, but her true ferocity and viciousness showed during training, often leading to several injuries for the viatari she fought. The only ones who seemed to always leave a fight against her unscathed were Victria and Natiari.

A century passed, and Victria didn't leave the village as she had said she would. She trained every day and grew stronger, faster, and more intelligent. The trainers often remarked on her ability to learn a concept or technique faster than most. Soon, she caught up in skill level to Tessa and Natiari, who had been training longer than she had, and eventually, she surpassed them.

"Today we will be testing you on your agility," their instructor, Thymos, announced as Victria and the other trainees near her age lined up on the training grounds, a small clearing separated from the rest of the village.

"Being able to move from one place to another quickly is a great advantage in any fight. You must be quick so you can deal damage without receiving any. Today, you will face me in combat, and you will use your agility to land a blow on me before I land one on you."

Victria grew anxious as the trials began and ended one after the other. Many trainees couldn't match Thymos' speed and failed the trial. Natiari was the first to pass and that was purely by luck. She had jumped back to put some distance between Thymos and herself but tripped on a rock.

Thymos hadn't expected this and ran straight into Natiari's boot as she flailed around in midair.

After Natiari, some of the other trainees began to pass the trial, including Tessa, who left Thymos with a bruise forming on his shoulder. Before long, it was Victria's turn. She walked calmly from the line of waiting trainees and turned to face the older viatari. A horn was blown to signal the start of the trial, but no one moved. Thymos stayed in place, ready to see what Victria would do. However, Victria also stood her ground, waiting for Thymos to make the first move.

She saw him coming at top speed, just as she predicted. She stepped to the side and ducked, knowing he would expect the first move. Hopefully it was all he anticipated. She felt his fist fly over her head as he swung into empty space. Just as she thought.

With a triumphant grin on her face, Victria jumped up from her crouching position and rammed her knee into Thymos' unguarded stomach. She could feel the air escape his lungs as he gasped in surprise. Before giving him time to retaliate, she jumped back quickly and put distance between them.

Thymos knelt on the ground, trying to catch his breath.

"Well done," he said with some difficulty. "Incredible—I never expected something so simple."

Victria passed her trial with a faster time than anyone else, which was what she had wanted. At Thymos' bidding, the entire class went over to her and congratulated her, though some seemed to clap her on the back harder than was necessary. She thanked them and took her place back in line. The rest of the trials went smoothly, with only a few of the viatari failing.

Afterwards, Thymos told the class they would learn more

about how to create illusions. They were separated into pairs and told to practice the concept they had learned the day before. Victria was paired with Natiari and was trying to focus on creating a second, false sun in the sky when she heard screaming. Everyone stopped what they were doing and looked in the direction of the village. More screaming met their ears, along with the snarls of beasts.

"Back to the village," Thymos said calmly.

Training was over. The class ran back only to enter a scene of chaos. Beasts rampaged out of the woods in droves, but they weren't like any Victria had ever seen before. These were giants and had a purple aura about them. Their eyes glowed a dull yellow, and they all had the same snarling, blood-thirsty face. They tore the village apart with their giant bodies, ramming into buildings and rearing back their heads with ferocious roars.

The villagers tried to defend themselves, but these beasts were far more powerful than any regular wolf or bear, and it took several viatari just to kill one. Victria rushed in to join the battle, followed closely by the other trainees. She jumped onto the back of one of the beasts and tried to snap its neck, but it shook her off easily. She was surprised by its strength, but that only made her put more effort into her attacks. She ran around the beast in fast circles in an effort to confuse it. Once it was thoroughly confused, she went for its neck again and this time succeeded in snapping it in half.

Natiari and Tessa were soon fighting by her side. The three of them killed many of the strange beasts, but more came to take their place.

"It's as if the entire forest has turned against us," Tessa muttered as she gouged a wolf-like creature's eyes out. It howled in pain but continued to attack until she finally managed to kill it.

"We cannot fend them off."

Victria turned to see Felix standing behind her, a grim expression on his face.

"The village is lost. We must abandon it and meet at the Lone Tree. Tell everyone you see to regroup there. Go, now!"

Victria hesitated, but she trusted Felix a lot more than she had when they first met. She took Tessa and Natiari by the hand and led them away from the battle. The three ran through the burning village, telling everyone they could to meet at the Lone Tree. Once they passed the last building, they made a dash for the treeline. Victria looked back one last time at the small village she had called home. The only place she had ever called home. Smoke bellowed from some of the buildings that had caught fire. Many of them were demolished by the beasts as they broke inside. Several viatari she had known for the past century lay on the ground, dead, their blood turning the grassy meadow a dark, sticky red. Fury rushed through her and she vowed to avenge the village, even if it cost her her life.

A tug on her frayed shirt pulled Victria out of her daze. She turned to see Tessa, whose face was also marked with lines of dark anger. *Together,* her gaze seemed to say, *we will avenge our home—together.*

CHAPTER SIXTEEN

Darimun. That is what they had named the unnatural beasts that had attacked them. After their village was destroyed, Victria and the other surviving viatari rendezvoused at the Lone Tree just as Felix had ordered.

The Lone Tree was the most ancient tree in the known world. Many thought it was the first to come into existence. A pine of giant proportions, it stood tall over the surrounding forest, almost touching the sky. Its trunk was a giant pillar, as wide as a mountain. Victria had only seen it a few times since Felix had found her, but each time she had been filled with the same sense of wonder. The giant pine stood in an isolated part of the forest often used as a refuge for the viatari when they needed it, though, those times had been rare.

Now it stood over hundreds of refugees from neighboring viatari settlements as they milled about. Victria, Tessa, Natiari, and the neighbors they had managed to save were the first from their village to join the chaos. There was a cacophony of noise, and no one seemed to be able to understand what was going on or what they would do next. It wasn't until Felix arrived that order began to take hold in the mass of misplaced viatari.

Felix quickly found himself the de facto leader of the refugees. He suggested they leave the Lone Tree and make their way to one of the larger villages where they could hopefully gain the advantage of numbers against the darimun. Several of the other refugees opposed the idea, feeling they would be safer if they stayed and defended the Lone Tree. He ignored their objections and declared he would leave the next day. Anyone who wanted to join him could. Most did, leaving only a fraction of those gathered behind to make their last stand at the Lone Tree.

Felix led them for many days and through several of the larger villages only to see the same sight: burning houses, mutilated bodies strewn across the ground, and, not too far from the fires, they would always find the survivors. There were occasional encounters with the darimun, but the refugees were enough in number now to defend themselves successfully against small attacks.

Over the course of a few weeks, the viatari transformed into a race of nomads. They could do nothing but wander the land and fight off the enemy whenever they met. They tried several times to settle and build a town where they could bunker down and fight off the enemy, but they were always eventually overrun.

It was noticed by some that the darimun attacked with a larger force every time the viatari tried to settle somewhere, and Felix eventually realized it was because towns made them stationary targets. Wandering the lands and never staying in one place for too long made it difficult for the darimun to pinpoint their position. And so they continued to wander with no end in sight.

A thousand years passed after the first attacks by the

darimun. During these turbulent times, Victria continued to grow stronger. She excelled in fighting and, with Tessa and Natiari by her side, could fight several darimun at once and defeat them without receiving so much as a scratch. Together, the trio made a vicious group, and their peers respected and admired them for their efforts in guarding them against the darimun.

Now Victria was on a perimeter patrol for the huge column of refugees. She had aged over the centuries, appearing more mature, no longer stuck with the mischievous, impish appearance of adolescence. But though she no longer had the looks of youth, she still had the spirit of one. Often she charged eagerly into battle and was known for making risky, if not rash, decisions. The refugees saw it as zeal. In reality, it was hatred. Victria hated the darimun with everything she was, and she would do anything she could to kill every last one of the monsters.

But not at the expense of her own kind. She saw their protection as her first priority. These days, though, it was becoming increasingly difficult to maintain a secure perimeter. The number of refugees swelled well past the thousands, but many of them couldn't fight. As a result, the darimun's raids were starting to take a toll on them. They suffered more losses, often spending the evenings burying any who had died during the raids.

The last attack had been almost a week ago. Victria had a gut feeling that another raid was imminent. After all, the Creature, the being who controlled the darimun, never allowed his enemies to rest for more than a week.

For the first few centuries of fighting, no one knew what the darimun were, what created them, or why they seemed so bent on hunting the viatari. It was only by a chance scouting mission that Victria had uncovered their secret.

Wandering around for centuries had brought the viatari to a new, unknown land. Despite this, days after entering this land, they had suffered from a large, coordinated attack by the darimun. This went against the pattern the darimun usually followed and gave Victria the feeling that something had changed. Perhaps this new land was their home. And if it was, maybe they would finally have a chance at retaliating, taking revenge for all the times the darimun had attacked them. With this in mind, she had quickly formed a small scouting party and went off to explore. It didn't take long for her to find what she was looking for.

She and her scouts had exited a wooded area nearby and found themselves standing at the edge of a massive crater. The crater went on for as far as the eye could see, but it wasn't deep. Victria saw that there had once been tree life within the crater in the past, but now it was a wasteland. Dead trees were everywhere. The ground was nothing but hard, cracked earth. A small, lonely mountain stood in the center.

It was on this mountain that Victria discovered the Creature and his desire to destroy the viatari race. She saw firsthand the Creature unleashing his tendrils of dark energy to transform regular animals into darimun. A passing bird had been caught by one, and the corruption had transformed the animal into one of the large, yellow-eyed monsters she had been fighting for so long.

Several times its original size, the bird-like darim swooped down and carried off two of her party members to their deaths. Luckily those had been the only two casualties. Victria and the remainder of her party quickly escaped the Creature's crater—*Inadarim*, they called it—and headed back to the main host to tell Felix everything they had discovered.

Now, at least, they knew who their enemy was.

Coming back to the present, Victria heard screaming. She turned in the saddle and saw a pack of darimun charging down a hill on the left side of the refugee column. Victria leapt off her horse and charged the enemy without a second thought. Some of the guards were already fighting them, doing what they could to keep the refugees safe, but they were being overwhelmed. Many fell under the sharp claws and fangs of the darimun. The line wavered, and the viatari were pushed back closer and closer toward the mass of cowering civilians behind them.

Fortunately the raid was a small one, with only five darimun. Once the initial surprise of the ambush faded and more viatari arrived to fight, they were easily dealt with. All but one were killed, the last managing to escape back into the hills.

"We should camp here for a while, scout the area before we move on," Felix said as he picked his way over the dead toward Victria. She nodded and turned to the nearest guard to relay the orders. A large watch was established to protect the camp while everyone else went about their duties.

Temporary tents were set up and livestock were gathered as word spread that the refugees would be camping in the area for a few days. Victria helped around where she could with the small chores and tried her best to keep a positive attitude so as not to spread any more worry than was necessary.

She was walking through camp looking for something else to do, when she noticed some of the Elders entering the large command tent in the center of the camp with Felix. Curiosity aroused, she made her way to them.

The command tent was only used when there were meetings between the Elders—the oldest of the viatari. It wasn't set up very often, and no one other than the Elders could enter to discuss the future of the column. What roused Victria's interest, however, was that Felix had gone in with them.

Felix was not an Elder, despite being older than all of them, and so was usually not present during their meetings. However, despite this, the Elders often came to him for advice. To see Felix enter the command tent of his own accord had to mean this meeting was of the highest level of importance, and Victria refused to miss a single word.

She walked around the tent casually to see how many guards, if any, were stationed around it. But if any were to come, they hadn't arrived yet.

After making sure she wasn't being watched, she jumped lightly onto the tent's roof. She was lucky the Elders' tent, as she called it, was made of taut leather instead of cloth or she would have fallen through and crashed into the middle of the meeting. She crawled slowly and carefully toward the center, where there was an opening to let light in. It was a perfect perch for eavesdropping.

The meeting had already begun, but nothing important had been discussed as far as she could tell; there was no arguing yet.

"My friends," Felix began. "We cannot continue living like this—like nomads."

There was silence. Victria dared not poke her head over the hole to see the Elders' reactions.

"We have lived like this for a millennium, for one *thousand* years! We should not be living like the humans do. We must create a permanent settlement where we can live for generations to come, a place we can call home."

"But Felix," one of the Elders spoke up. "We've tried this in the past, and no matter what we do, we're always eventually overrun by the darimun. Is it really wise to waste all the time and work and lives necessary to build such a settlement, only to have it taken away from us and destroyed again?"

There were murmurs of agreement from the other Elders.

"This time will be different," Felix said, the confidence clear in his voice. "I will personally lead a scouting mission and find an area where we can build a permanent settlement, one that can be easily defended. And believe me, I will not be negligent with my choice."

There were some low mutterings.

"You go on a fool's errand," one of the Elders said. "But you have led us this far, Felix, and we will trust your judgment. The Council of Elders hereby gives you approval for this task and we hope—"

Victria made her way back down to the lower edge of the tent and jumped to the ground. She had heard all that she needed to hear. Felix was going to explore the surrounding area, and she would go with him. She agreed with him about the necessity of building a permanent settlement for their people. They wouldn't be able to last forever as nomads. Eventually they would die out, and the Creature would win.

She kept her distance from the Elder's tent and pretended to be busy stacking buckets as she waited for the meeting to end and for Felix to come out. It didn't take long. As soon as she saw him, she ran to his side and began walking next to him. They walked side by side like this in silence for several minutes.

"Yes?" Felix finally asked, eyebrows raised.

"I know you're going to look for a new home for us, and I want to be a part of it."

Felix stopped in his tracks. "How do you know about that? This task is a secret—not to mention the decision to do it has just been made."

Victria turned away, an impish smile on her face. "I . . . overheard it."

Felix sighed. "I suppose the Elders should start stationing guards outside their tent during meetings to thwart the curious."

He began to walk away, but she followed closely, peering over his shoulder and trying to read his face.

"Well, can I come?"

"No."

"Why not?"

"I need you to stay here and protect the refugees from raids like the one we had today," Felix said, coming to a stop once again. "As I am sure you heard, they consider this task foolish. You will be much more useful here than out there with me. And you must keep this a secret. We are going to keep these plans from everyone for as long as we can."

"Why?" Victria asked, disappointed. Her breath came more rapidly. Her fists clenched. She could feel tears spring to her eyes, but she held them back. She didn't want to look like a child who didn't get her way, not in front of Felix.

"Because this plan has never worked before. I will do all that I can to make this dream of having a home a reality, but even I cannot promise anything. It is best not to get everyone's hopes up. Come now, cheer up," Felix's voice softened, "it is not the end of the world if you do not get to come with me this one time."

Victria nodded and tried to swallow her bitterness as she walked away.

* * *

Felix did not come back for weeks.

Victria had wanted to maintain the camp for a while longer to see if he would return, but it became more and more dangerous. Darim raids grew stronger and more frequent as they realized the viatari were still in the same location, but she didn't want to risk leaving Felix behind. She feared that if they moved on, he would come back to an empty campsite, left to wonder where they had gone. Eventually, however, they had to move. Felix's task should have only taken a few days at most. Victria worried that something terrible had happened to him while he was out scouting and now she wished more than ever that she had insisted on going with him, even if she would have had to sneak off to do it.

Everyone shared her gloom. Mourning saturated the air as many assumed the worst. One did not have to travel far within the camp to hear someone lamenting the loss of Felix. Many tears were shed, and the camp as a whole lacked energy in all its daily chores. Felix had led them through the hardest of times over the past thousand years, and they had never thought that he, too, would eventually become a victim of these terrible times.

Now Victria sat on a ledge on watch duty, but she wasn't paying attention to what happened around her. Instead, she stared at the huge, snow-capped mountain range ahead and wondered how things had gotten so bad. They were in a strange land. They were constantly on the run from the Creature and his darimun. They never had peace.

She would have sat on the ledge for the entire day, thinking of all the negative aspects of life, had it not been for the commotion going on behind her. She turned and saw that everyone was crowded around a single spot near the edge of camp. There was a buzz of excitement. A burst of energy seemed to run through the entire camp. The change in mood was enough to bring Victria away from her wallowing thoughts. Now she was curious.

She made her way to the crowd and gently pushed through to see what the commotion was about. She broke through the final few viatari and saw Felix and all those he had taken with him on his scouting mission alive and well.

She ran to him and gave him a giant hug. With it, she tried to relay the amount of distress she had felt over his disappearance and the enormous relief she felt for his return. All through one single squeeze. But no matter how long or hard she held him, it would never be enough.

"I thought you died!"

Felix laughed. "No, I am in perfect health and so are the others. And what is better is that we found what we were looking for!" He moved his lips closer to Victria's ear and whispered, "We found the perfect spot."

Victria was about to ask for more details when she noticed the five strange beings Felix had brought with him into camp. They were short, stout figures with incredible amounts of facial hair. Their small, pudgy eyes showed signs of long life, though she doubted they were as old as the viatari. They all wore strange, thick armor, which appeared to be made out of some form of metal. It was smooth and looked heavy, but the beings carried themselves around as if they wore nothing at all. Each one also carried large, incredibly lethal-looking weapons she had never seen before.

"What are these . . . things?" she asked.

Felix turned to the short beings and spoke in a strange, guttural language. Victria couldn't understand a word of it, but the dwarves responded in kind and marched off to the Elders' tent.

"They call themselves *dwarves*," Felix said, turning his attention back to her. "They are quite impressive, are they not?"

Victria glanced at Felix to see if he was really alright. Something must have happened for him to have brought these strangers into their camp.

"I need to speak with you alone," she said after a while and moved to a more secluded spot. Once they had walked what she thought was a safe distance away from everyone else, she faced him.

"What happened? Why would you bring those things here? They could be an enemy."

"Calm down," Felix said, grabbing her shoulders to steady her. "These 'things,' as you call them, are now our allies. We ran into each other in a forest we were scouting, and they helped fend off a large group of darimun that attacked us. They then took us to one of their cities, right next to that mountain range."

He nodded his head toward the snow-capped mountains in the distance.

"It was there that I was taught their language, and after I learned enough of it, they took me to their capital *inside* the mountains—Tinas Gran, I think they called it. It was a sight to behold. You could never imagine what I saw down there. Even for someone as old as I am, it was unbelievable—"

"And?" Victria prompted, trying to get Felix back to his story. "What happened?"

"They took me to their capital and, after a few explanations, their King and I wound up forming an alliance to fight the Creature. They even offered to build a city for us at the location we found as a sign of friendship."

"We shouldn't trust them."

Felix frowned, confused. "Why do you say that? They were nothing but hospitable and generous during my stay in their Kingdom. Is it because they are not viatari? Because they are strangers?"

Victria's answer must have been plain on her face because Felix didn't wait for her to respond.

"I have only known them for a few weeks but I know they are a trustworthy people. They are the reason I was able to come back despite the camp moving to a different location. I see no reason *not* to trust them."

He took a deep breath to calm himself. "Victria, I know from personal experience that it is hard for you to trust. But you will learn to trust them, just as you learned to trust us after we found you in the wilderness."

"That was different," Victria shook her head. "At least *we* were the same. These dwarves aren't viatari. They're more likely to betray us than to help us for all we know."

Felix's face grew stern. "They are our allies, Victria, and whether you like it or not, you will respect them as such. Is that understood?"

Victria nodded numbly, shocked that Felix's attitude had become so firm toward her. She couldn't remember the last time it had happened, if ever.

"Good. Now, about the settlement, continue to keep it a secret. The less who know about it, the better. The dwarves are in the process of building it for us as we speak, but I still do not want anyone to know about it until some progress has been made in its construction. Do you understand?"

Victria nodded.

"Good," Felix turned to walk away but hesitated. "I know

it is hard, but you must learn to trust those around you, even those who may seem strange to you. They are not always bad.'

That night, Felix introduced the dwarves to the entire refugee camp and announced that the viatari were now allied with the Dwarven Kingdom. There was no mention of a future home for the viatari nor any mention that the dwarves would build it. But the Elders who stood next to Felix grinned knowingly. Victria guessed that they, at least, had been told.

She looked around at the gathered refugees. They all seemed to take the news of new allies well, much to her disappointment. If even one viatari had shown some sign of disapproval, she would have felt justified.

Felix went on to announce that he would personally teach them all the dwarven language, so communication could flow easily between the two races. This got Victria's attention and further darkened her mood. She didn't care to learn the language, and she was angry that Felix had decided this for everyone without offering a choice.

"We will also begin carrying out offensive attacks against the Creature," Felix went on to say. "The dwarves have promised to lend us as many soldiers as they can, but they cannot be the only ones fighting and dying. We need more viatari who are willing to fight. Please lend us your strength so we may rid this world of the Creature and his evil."

Cheers broke out among the assembled camp. Even Victria temporarily forgot her anger and beamed at the news. She liked the idea of taking the fight to the enemy and looked forward to finally being able to extract some revenge against the monsters that took her home.

* * *

The next few months were a flurry of activity. Victria and all of the fighting viatari were taught the dwarven language first so they could communicate with their dwarven comrades. The language was strange and guttural and completely different from her own, but she quickly learned all of its patterns and could soon speak it decently. Tessa and Natiari had a harder time with it, but they eventually caught up to her as well.

The viatari who wouldn't or couldn't fight were sent to live with the dwarves in their cities temporarily. It would be impossible to attack the darimun while defending the refugees from them at the same time. Now with the refugees safely behind dwarven walls, they could focus all their resources on attacking the enemy.

Victria noticed that Felix only ever sent out parties large enough to carry out small raids against the darimun instead of a large force for a full attack. However, as long as they did some damage, she didn't really mind. But she did mind the fact that no matter what the situation was, the raid parties always consisted of both viatari and dwarves. It was done, she felt, so she had no choice but to interact with these strangers, and she hated it.

The dwarves were lazy, weak creatures, in her mind. The only thing she enjoyed about having them around was the ease with which she could intimidate them. For whatever reason, the viatari's red eyes stirred a natural fear inside them, but they were especially intimidated when it came to Victria. She would purposefully leer at the dwarves anytime one was near. Unfortunately, even that small joy soon disappeared as the dwarves grew accustomed to her kind.

"Why do you harbor such hatred for them?" Natiari

asked her one day as they kept watch over the construction of the city that would soon become the viatari's home.

Victria shot her an incredulous look. "Just look at them."

Natiari did for a long time. "I don't see what it is you see. They seem just like us in every way but appearance. Whatever it is you hate about them, take care that you don't let it control you. A mind that runs on hate can only lead to loss."

Despite Natiari's words, Victria couldn't bring herself to restrain how she felt. Every chance she had, she would do what she could to provoke some inner, evil nature she was sure was hiding deep within them. She just needed this nature to show itself once so that she could justify her feelings. But no matter what she did, the dwarves always took it on the chin, nodding to her as if they thought it was her way of showing affection.

Years passed, and the raids continued with no change. Enough time had gone by for Victria to see a pattern in what they were doing. All the raids were far from the mountain range and the forest within which they were building their city. In fact, there wasn't a single skirmish that took place *anywhere* near the forest. It hadn't taken long for her to realize all these strikes they carried out were just distractions to keep the darimun's attention away from the forest. Felix was buying time, but Victria wondered if that was a wise move.

The raids hardly lowered the darimun's numbers. In fact, every day there seemed to be more. Felix may have been buying time for the dwarves to build their city, but in doing so, he was also giving more time for the Creature to build his own strength.

CHAPTER SEVENTEEN

"We will strike here and here," Geothur Ironaxe, King of the dwarves, pointed at two separate locations on the map before him. The assembled mixture of dwarves and viatari listened with the utmost attention. This was the meeting to determine how they would face the Creature and his darimun in one final battle. Everyone had to know what to do and when to do it if they wanted a chance at victory.

After two long centuries of constant work, the dwarves had finally finished constructing the viatari's city, which the viatari named *Aleganthia*, or 'haven' in their language. With the city complete, they no longer needed to keep most of their forces guarding the refugees, and the workers who had been building the city could now join the war effort. Now, with both dwarven and viatari armies at full strength, the time to attack the Creature's home had come.

As all the commanders and officers sat within the city's newly built keep and listened to what they would have to do, Felix left his seat and joined Geothur by the map, pointing to the center of Inadarim, where a small mountain was drawn in.

"It was discovered centuries ago that the Creature dwells on top of this mountain at the center of the crater. We will surround it and any darim that dares to try and block our path, and we will destroy them."

Many of the viatari in the room nodded thoughtfully. The dwarves grinned at each other, eager for the coming battle.

"Unfortunately, our enemy is still quite strong, despite the raids they have endured over the past two centuries. It is essential that our march to Inadarim be thought of as another raid by the Creature so as not to attract too much attention before we arrive."

He unfurled a large scroll of paper and began reading names. They were a mixture, as always, of dwarves and viatari. Then, he announced that those who had been called would be the leaders of their own "raid parties."

"The parties will be the usual size, between twenty to fifty individuals. Each one will leave at a different time of day tomorrow and will take a different route to Inadarim. This way, the Creature's spies will not see us all gathered together as one force, and we may keep the element of surprise. Remember, our main priority right now is to attract as little attention as possible while on the move."

Everyone murmured agreement and began to leave the room to make preparations and pick out who they wanted to include in their parties. Victria was about to leave when Felix stopped her. "You will lead a raid party to Inadarim as well," he said. "Can I trust you with that?"

Victria nodded.

Over the past two centuries of fighting together, she hadn't changed her feelings about the dwarves. She continued to despise them. The only difference now was she was better at hiding it from Felix and the others. Nothing had changed. She left the meeting room and made her way through the keep to her room to think about who she would bring along.

The keep was by far the largest structure the dwarves had
built for the viatari, so Felix had decided it would be where
all the important matters were discussed and events held and
where the leadership of the viatari would stay, as well as
officials from the Dwarven Kingdom. The walls were lined
with large, crystal-clear glass windows, which allowed Victria
to gaze out on the new city as she walked. She was glad they
no longer had to be constantly on the run, grateful to have a
home again, but she loathed the fact that it had been built
completely by the dwarves.

Tearing her gaze from the shining white buildings and the
forest that surrounded and protected them, she opened the
door to her room and walked in, determined to find a way
to keep any dwarves from being part of her party to
Inadarim.

The next day the city was a bustling mass of armored
dwarves and viatari as they rushed around making final
preparations for the march to Inadarim. The raid parties
had been leaving the city two at a time every fifteen minutes
since dawn. Already more than a thousand viatari and
dwarves were en route and the morning had only begun.

Victria picked her way through the crowded streets
holding a list of the names of those she wished to take with
her. Felix sat on his horse in the middle of Aleganthia's
plaza, shouting orders and letting party leaders know when it
was their turn to head out. When he noticed Victria
approaching, he let Geothur take over for a while and met
her halfway.

"Here is the list of those I wish to take with me."

Felix scanned the names she had written down, then
looked quizzically at her. "These are mostly viatari. There

are only three dwarves on this list."

"Yes," she said. "But there's still a mixture of dwarves and viatari. Does it really matter how many there are of each?"

Felix frowned disapprovingly, and rolled up the list with an exasperated sigh. "It has been two centuries, Victria. You must put away these feelings, and whatever else is getting in the way of you accepting the dwarves as our friends and allies must be overcome. This is no time for your pride."

Victria was silent. She wanted to disagree, to argue with Felix until he finally conceded to her point of view. But this was a military matter, and he was in charge.

"I already had your party picked out for you last night, anyway. You will find them near the south gate, which is where you will depart from within the hour."

She turned without another word and stomped her way to the south gate. She heard Felix call out to her one last time, but she didn't acknowledge him.

It didn't take long for her to find the party she would lead. It was unique among the others. Whereas everyone else had an equal amount of either race in them, hers mostly consisted of dwarves. In fact, she counted only five viatari. Her face flushed with embarrassment at having to lead such a party.

Without making eye contact with anyone, Victria stiffly walked to her charges, muttered about how they should begin their march, and quickly darted through the open gates. She didn't even glance back to make sure they were following her.

Once they were out of the city, her embarrassment faded and turned to anger. She made a point of only speaking to the few viatari under her command, ignoring the dwarves.

She set the pace of their march in such a way so it could be followed easily by her kind but made it difficult for the dwarves to keep up. Every time a dwarf approached her, she would glare, making things uncomfortable to the point that he would forget whatever it was he wanted.

But the dwarves never complained. They continued their cheerful act as always and responded respectfully the few times they were addressed by Victria.

It took a week for them to arrive to Inadarim, longer than Victria had wanted, but she blamed the dwarves in her party for that. Much of the army had already arrived and had set up camp on the outskirts of the crater. Victria searched for the command tent while her party joined the rest of the host. As soon as she found it she made her way over and entered.

Felix, Geothur, and all the dwarven and viatari officers and commanders within looked up from the map they had been studying.

"Ah, you have arrived. Any problems?"

At first, Victria thought Felix was referring to the dwarves in her party. Then, she realized he was asking about her journey to Inadarim. Probably wondering if they had encountered any darimun.

"No. We didn't see the enemy on our way here. It was a smooth march."

Felix nodded and beckoned for her to join them.

"Others have not been so fortunate," he grimaced as she walked over to his side and studied the map of the surrounding area. "It seems we will not have the numbers to carry out our original plan of surrounding Inadarim. We will have to face the Creature and his armies head on."

Victria looked up in alarm. "Why? What's happened?"

They had been planning this battle for decades, and

everyone agreed surrounding the Creature's home was the strategy with the highest chance of success. She couldn't imagine what might have happened that would force them to alter the plans at the last minute.

"Many of our raid parties were wiped out," Geothur said. "There was an unusually large force of darimun roaming around the countryside ta the west, and they decimated the dwarves and viatari they encountered. Our lines would be stretched too thin if we continued as we had planned."

Victria tried not to acknowledge the dwarven King, but she hadn't expected to hear such disheartening news. This was turning into a disaster.

"What do we do now?"

"As Geothur has already said, we do not have the numbers to surround the Creature and his forces initially, so we must meet them head on—in a manner of speaking. I have come up with a new strategy. It is risky, but if it works, we could still win this battle. Victria," Felix's tone was firm, uncompromising, "I need your full cooperation. You have a very critical role in this fight, and I need to know I can trust you to not be reckless or rash."

Every eye in the room focused on Victria. She looked around, taking in their stern faces. The viatari had the same serious expression that was chiseled onto Felix's features. The dwarves were no better. For once, they looked like they might end their policy of tolerance toward her if she wouldn't agree to comply with their plan. Finally, she agreed to restrain herself, no matter the circumstances.

Felix's features relaxed for a second, but then he frowned as his focus returned to the map. "We have decided to split our forces into two sections: one large, led by me, and one small. The larger force will meet the enemy head on and will allow itself to become partially surrounded. The smaller force will move its way around into a flanking position on the darimun's right. You will be in command of half of this smaller force, Victria."

Victria listened intently. She could already see how risky the plan was. Felix was going to let the darimun surround them, and if they ended up completely surrounded, it wouldn't be long before they were annihilated. The timing for her flanking maneuver had to be perfect.

"Once they have surrounded us," Felix continued, "you will charge into their backs and crush their flank as quickly as you can. After you have dealt with them, you and our freed left flank will swing around and wash over them like a crushing wave. In the end, we should be able to destroy the darimun and any form of resistance the Creature has between us and the mountain."

Felix looked up to see everyone nodding. It was a good strategy, but it all rested upon the timing and discipline of Victria and her command.

"We will march down into the crater tomorrow where the enemy will undoubtedly meet us. I recommend everyone rest and prepare. Tomorrow will decide whether we survive or fall to the Creature's onslaught."

Everyone began to file out of the tent except for Victria and Felix.

"I assume you already have my command picked out for me, as usual?" Victria said, a little more sarcastically than she intended.

"Yes," Felix replied. "And as before, there are significantly more dwarves than viatari."

She glared at him, waiting for some sort of explanation. None came. Felix didn't look at her as he packed away his things and prepared to leave. But after rolling up the map and putting it away, he finally faced her. "Do not forget your promise. This battle determines the fate of all of us. Do not let something so petty as your racial hatred for the dwarves get in the way of *our* survival."

With that, he left the tent, leaving Victria lost for words. She wanted to follow him out and have the last word, to respond with some biting remark, but her words failed her once again.

The next day Victria found herself standing among nearly one thousand dwarves and only a few hundred viatari. This was the smaller part of the force that would carry out the planned flank attack, and she was in charge of two-thirds of it—mostly the dwarves and a few dozen viatari. The other third was under the command of a dwarf by the name of Brenna Firebrand.

Victria had spoken briefly with Brenna before they began their march. The dwarven female seemed strong, her flaming orange hair and fiery demeanor establishing an intimidating aura which even Victria could appreciate. By the end of their short conversation, however, the only thing she'd learned was that Brenna had a son by the name of Murgran waiting for her back home. The dwarf had promised to perform her duty to the utmost ability in the name of her son. Such sentimental feelings Victria could not understand, but it did clarify one thing for her: she didn't trust Brenna to do her part.

The two began their march around the crater before the sun rose. They wanted to be in position for their attack as soon as possible. Moving far enough east to a position where the darimun's right flank would be exposed, they entered the crater and made their way forward until they were hidden within a thick cluster of the dead trees that littered Inadarim.

From their position, Brenna and Victria watched Felix lead the coalition of dwarves and viatari into the crater. Not long after that, the darimun appeared. They came in droves from the mountain and the surrounding areas. Felix called for a halt as the darimun formed their own battle line.

The two armies faced each other for what felt like hours. Neither side seemed willing to make the first move. Strange yips and yowls came from the darimun as they grew impatient. Their bloodlust, ferocious in nature now that they were imbued with the Creature's essence, began to overcome whatever control the Creature exerted over them.

The darimun charged.

Felix had his battle line shift into a semi-circle, with the outward curve facing the enemy, inviting them to surround his waiting forces. The mindless beasts crashed into the front line with such force that they sent some dwarves and viatari flying through the air.

There was an intense struggle as the coalition fought with everything they had to maintain their ranks against the weight of the charge. As the middle section of the line held its ground, the darimun crept their way around to attack the curved flanks. The coalition was slowly surrounded, as intended.

Victria tensed. It was almost time to carry out their own attack.

"We should move farther behind their lines," Brenna suggested.

Victria glanced at her, not in the mood for last-minute suggestions. "And why would we do that?"

"If we attack from here, they'll see us comin'. It looks as

though the darimun have some reserve forces waitin' farther back. But if we move behind *them*, they'll have their backs completely turned ta us. They won't see us comin', and we'll keep the element of surprise."

Victria scoffed. She had seen the darimun's reserve forces, but unlike Brenna, she didn't see them as a major threat.

"This is no time to change position; it's already time to attack! If we move now, we'll arrive too late. Everyone will be completely surrounded before we can reach them."

"Maybe," Brenna replied. "But if we attack now, we'll be flanked by *their* reserves, and our charge will have less of an impact on the battle as a whole."

This was too much for Victria. Even now the darimun were getting closer and closer to completely surrounding Felix's forces. Brenna may be right about the darimun reserves intercepting their charge, but Victria was confident they would be easy enough for her to handle on her own.

"I have no time to argue with the likes of you, dwarf," Victria said with a note of finality.

Brenna's brow furrowed as she opened her mouth to reply, but Victria called for a charge and started running across the open field before she had a chance to speak. The dwarves under her command followed without hesitation as did the few viatari, though they exchanged worried glances. Brenna cursed under her breath but didn't follow. She would have to carry out the flanking maneuver by herself, with her own section of warriors, if it were to be done properly.

The wind whistled past her ears as Victria ran across the open field. The viatari under her command caught up with her, but there was a considerable gap between them and the dwarves.

"Victria, their reserves are coming," a viatari next to her warned.

She looked to her left and saw what he meant. Several hundred darimun were running across the field toward them. She calculated the darimun's speed and compared it with their own. There was no helping it; they would have to fight through these reserves, and with the several dozen viatari she had beside her, she was confident they could finish the job without wasting too much time.

"Kill them as quickly as you can. We must attack their exposed flank before Felix is overrun."

The darimun crashed into them with a crazed fury. Victria weaved her way through the chaos, evading their lethal claws. When she was forced to fight, she made quick work of her enemies, launching herself at them and using her speed and strength to snap their necks. Eventually it became impossible for her to do this as the mass of bodies closed in on her. She had underestimated the size and strength of the reserve, and, looking around, she realized she was now surrounded. Several of her viatari had been killed in the first few minutes of the battle. The beasts snatched them out of the air like fish in a river as they tried to avoid their attacks. Their superior strength and agility did nothing to combat the sheer bloodlust and ferocity the darimun possessed. They growled menacingly at Victria and the few surviving viatari as they closed in for the kill, and she wondered for the first time if she had made a mistake.

A loud, earth-shattering cry erupted from nearby, and Victria caught a glimpse of something crashing into the darimun's backs. The dwarves had finally caught up to their commander, and now they fought furiously to free her from the enemy's grasp. Axes sliced through distorted flesh, shields protected their carriers from sharp claws, hammers crushed skulls and bones. The dwarves were turning the reserve of darimun into dust but not without losses of their own.

Several dwarves snapped in half as darimun wrapped their fangs around their bodies. Several more were impaled by abnormally sharp claws, which passed through their armor as if it were made of cloth. Others were sent high into the air only to come crashing back down to the earth.

Despite their losses, the dwarves killed the darimun at an incredible rate, but there was still a large chunk of them they had to get through before they could save the viatari.

Victria heard the last of her viatari cry out as he intercepted a darim that had tried to pounce on her from behind. She leaped onto its back and quickly snapped its neck before it could try again. She looked around. All she could see was a ring of darimun around her, dark clouds overhead, the rim of Inadarim reaching for the sky in the distance like mountains. She was wounded in several places and bled profusely. Her regenerative abilities were healing her but not fast enough. She couldn't move her left arm, and she was having trouble standing. She heard the dwarves fighting on the other side of the wall of darimun facing her, but she didn't expect them to actually save her. Why would they after how she had treated them? What she had done was beyond reconciliation; she knew that now. They had all the reasons in the world to let her die.

The darimun prepared to pounce. Victria bared her fangs as she readied herself for one final fight. She would not go down quietly. Suddenly several darimun howled into the sky as the dwarves cut their way through them. There were only a few dozen left from the hundreds she had originally commanded, but they fought with the strength of forty dwarves each. They quickly rushed through the path they had made and formed a protective circle around her.

"Rest and heal yerself, lassy," one of the dwarves said to her. "We'll protect ye until yer well enough ta come back inta the fight."

Victria didn't know what to say. After everything she had put the dwarves through, she hadn't expected them to come to her aid so willingly when she had needed it most. They had lost hundreds of their brothers and sisters because of her recklessness, and still, here they were. After several minutes, she finally found her voice.

"Why are you doing this?" she asked, surprised at how weak it was. "I don't deserve your help. Because of me, hundreds of your kind lie dead. Save yourselves while you can, and leave me. I accept my fate."

"What are ye talking about, lady?" the dwarf exclaimed as he bashed his heavy hammer against the face of a nearby foe. He stepped back to face her as another dwarven warrior took his place in the circle. "It has been our highest honor ta serve under a commander such as yerself. Ye don't bat an eye when things get rough, and ye just dive in. We've admired the strength ye've shown since the beginning. Aye, many have died, but it wouldn't be a battle if none did, now would it?"

He turned to his dwarves, "*Ergath hüld!*" The dwarves locked shields to ward off another assault as the darimun regrouped.

His words surprised Victria. Blood rushed to her face, and it felt as if the Creature himself was ripping into her heart as she recalled every moment she had mistreated her saviors.

Then, for the first time in her life, she felt shame. She was ashamed at her behavior toward these brave warriors when they had genuinely looked up to her. She'd had no legitimate reason for her hatred against them, and she knew there was no way she could ever forgive herself. But she could still change and do her best to make amends. And that started with making sure these dwarves didn't die because of her mistake.

She gripped the dwarf by the shoulder before he could rejoin his comrades. "What's your name?"

The dwarf grinned at her. "Khalran Stonebeard, commander. Now go on and heal yerself. My boys will keep these beasties off ye!"

The darimun attacked, and the dwarves held their ground. Victria willed herself to heal faster, but she had received too many wounds for that. The dwarves were holding off the darimun as they had said they would, but she could tell they were exhausted. If she didn't heal soon, fatigue would claim her protectors if the darimun did not.

She focused her regenerative abilities into her legs. If she could just move around, she could fight with her legs as her upper body healed. She closed her eyes and concentrated. She imagined the gashes and bruises on her body disappearing. A warm trickling feeling rushed through her legs, and when she opened her eyes, they looked as if they had never seen battle.

Victria jumped over the dwarves and ran into the nearest darim. She used her legs to attack, kicking and slamming her knees into the darimun while the dwarves broke their protective circle and helped cut them down.

The enemy was no match.

Finally, the way for them to execute their flank attack was

cleared. Victria looked at the few dozen dwarves still standing, Khalran at the head of them, and, for the first time, regarded them with a cheerful smile.

"Shall we continue?"

The dwarves grinned, a few chuckled, as they followed her into the fray once more. Looking to her left, she saw Brenna Firebrand crash into the darimun's backs with her own command at full force. It was a much stronger attack than her own, but Victria didn't care. The flanking maneuver was complete, and even though it wasn't as strong as originally intended, it had its desired effect.

The darimun panicked as they wondered which side they should attack. Thanks to the confusion, it took only minutes to annihilate their flank. The plan proceeded smoothly from there. The freed left flank swung around the battlefield with a victorious war cry as they surrounded the remaining darimun. With the enemy surrounded, the only job left was to cut them all down.

The crater was littered with the corpses of darimun, viatari, and dwarves.

Victria made her way carefully toward Khalran and the surviving dwarves in her command. They greeted her as she approached, and she returned the greeting happily.

"Quite the battle, aye?" Khalran said.

Her lips curved slightly but she made no reply. She was still thinking about what Felix had just told her.

After the battle, Victria had gone looking for the elder viatari to apologize for the way she had been acting for the past two centuries and for her reckless charge. As she had gone deeper and deeper into the ranks, though, everyone grew more and more panicked. She overheard dwarves talking about their King going off on his own, but she didn't pay too much attention to the mutterings. She was too intent on finding Felix.

She was glad to see Tessa and Natiari had survived the battle, though she never doubted their ability to do so. She only spoke briefly with them before continuing her search.

She finally found him, after what seemed like ages, but he looked distracted. She soon learned why.

Geothur had split from the main army with a small group of dwarves and had made his way toward the crater's mountain. Felix feared the King would do something foolish, like trying to defeat the Creature on his own. After a few more words, Victria was sent back to her own command to wait for orders as Felix took several viatari with him to go to the King's aid. The time for apologies would have to wait.

Khalran and the other dwarves in her command seemed to have not heard about their King yet or they would have been talking about it. Instead, she listened as they recounted stories of their heroic actions in past battles.

A tremor went through the earth, catching everyone by surprise. Victria looked at the crater's mountain and saw a stream of purple light shoot into the sky. The stream burst, and a wave of purple mist washed over the entire area. It enveloped both the dwarves and viatari. She expected pain or some sort of anguish to sweep through her as the mist touched her since its source could only have come from the Creature, but she felt nothing except the cold touch of something evil.

The light and mist faded, and when Victria opened her eyes, she saw that the surrounding landscape was the same as before.

But not everything was the same.

Wails and cries of anger erupted from the dwarves as they backed away from the viatari with looks of fear. The viatari remained where they were, confused, as their allies began to run away like their lives depended on it.

Victria had no idea what was happening, but it was happening everywhere. She turned to her own dwarves, dreading what she might see, and flinched when she saw the looks of fury on their faces. Fury directed at her. Many of them stomped their booted feet into the ground in frustration as tears ran down their faces.

"Ye killed them!" Khalran roared at the top of his lungs. "*Ye* killed our brothers and sisters! *Ye're ta blame!*"

Victria was at a loss for words. Khalran's words had a profound effect on her, though. The shame and guilt she had felt during the battle washed over her once again. She was no longer the tough, pitiless killer she had grown up as. Unfamiliar emotions flooded through her as she tried to find the appropriate response to his accusations.

Though she wasn't sure what drove her to do it, she reached her hands out to Khalran, hoping he might take them. Instead, his face turned fearful, as did those of his fellow dwarves. They began to back away.

"Run for yer life, lads!" Khalran cried out. "She'll take us next!"

Victria felt her eyes sting. Guilt hung heavily, overwhelming. She stood there, her hands still reaching out as she watched the dwarves run away in a panic. Finally it all became too much for her, and she sank to her knees.

It wasn't long before Felix returned, looking disappointed. He didn't seem surprised that the dwarves had disappeared and that those still in the area were running away as fast as their little legs would carry them. He found Victria, who was still on her knees with a dazed expression on her face.

Gently, he placed his hand on her shoulder, trying to snap her out of her shock. She turned to him with a stricken face, full of the emotions she had been hiding all her life.

"What have I done?"

CHAPTER EIGHTEEN

Thuradin glanced at Victria as she concluded her tale. Her face was mostly concealed in shadow, but he was almost sure he saw a single tear glisten in the filtered sunlight as it slowly made its way down her cheek.

"No one knows for sure what that wave of light actually was," she said in a calm voice. "But there's no doubt it was related in some way to the Creature. I don't know why it didn't affect us, but when it touched you dwarves, it instilled within you all an unnatural and extreme fear and hatred for our race. That is why your historical texts are so inaccurate. Your ancestors were, in a way, infected by the Creature, and because of that, our two peoples lost contact and were separated. However—"

Victria paused and took a deep breath to steady herself. Thuradin pretended not to notice. He imagined sharing this was difficult for her, and he didn't want to make it any harder by interrupting.

"The dwarves under my command . . . your father, Khalran . . . the Creature influenced them too, obviously, but I think it affected them differently. It's always been my impression that the Creature simply fueled their anger so they could unleash their true feelings toward me. I do not hold it against them. They had every right. It was my fault so many of their companions died. My pride had me believe I was better than them because I was a viatari. I didn't trust anyone but myself. I didn't have to let so many of them die. I should have listened to Brenna, but my pride . . . so I made that reckless charge."

Thuradin could feel Victria trembling next to him. If he was honest with himself, he was surprised to hear about her past nature, which sounded more like it belonged to someone like Dragos. However, he didn't feel any differently toward her for it. These things were in the past, and it was clear she had changed for the better since then.

"It wasn't until much later that I realized all the mistakes I made in those times—my pride, my contempt, all of my weaknesses—were because of my own insecurities. Khalran and the other dwarves I led were the first ones to unlock the feelings I had stored away deep within me, and they were the first to take away some of the bad ones. They are the reason I am who I am today. Thuradin—"

Thuradin turned to meet her gaze. Victria's eyes were as deep as the rarest gems, and a sadness lived within them that reflected his own.

"Do not doubt yourself," she said with some force. "Do not give in to your insecurities as I did. Believe in your abilities, and you will make the right decisions in the end."

Thuradin looked away. He hadn't expected for Victria to open up to him like that, but he was glad she had. He also hadn't expected to hear about his father, especially not during a time four hundred years before Thuradin was even born. He felt some comfort in hearing how his father was once a good, strong dwarf instead of the broken one he had known for a majority of his life. And now he knew the reason behind his father's madness.

The advice Victria had given him and the concern she had shown also helped chase away many of the doubts he had been feeling. He still felt responsible for Agrethar's coming death, but he realized now it would be an insult to wish he had turned the young dwarf away when he had the chance.

Victria and Thuradin tensed as footsteps came from deeper within the woods, but they relaxed when they saw it was only Dragos returning from wherever he had gone. He made his way toward the camp, his face marked by an ever-present scowl.

"He reminds me of myself when I was his age."

Thuradin looked at her with some alarm, then at Dragos, then back.

A knowing grin played gently on her lips as she watched the younger viatari. Thuradin wondered what could be going through her head to make her grin like that, like she was basking in the nostalgic feel of old memories. He didn't think there was anything to grin about. It was dangerous. After hearing what someone like Victria had done with this kind of attitude, he decided it might be best to keep a close eye on Dragos. He didn't trust him, and he no longer knew if he could trust Victria to keep him under control.

It was an uneventful day. Thuradin and Victria decided early on to take separate watches every couple of hours so that at least one of them could sleep for a while. Even so, the day dragged on much too long for Thuradin's liking. Once he noticed it was getting darker, though, he woke everyone up, and they began packing for the night's ride.

As they tied down the packed camp materials onto their

mounts, the viatari suddenly stopped what they were doing, their bodies rigid. Thuradin followed their example but motioned for Stürn to carry on with his healing. Victria turned her head back and forth, trying to detect what it was that made her feel uneasy.

"Take him," she whispered, pointing to Dragos, then Agrethar, and then to the treetops. Dragos made a sign that clearly meant he wouldn't do it. Victria sighed as she continued to sign to him that he needed to take Agrethar and hide in the trees. The younger viatari refused again. The signing grew more intense.

Finally, Victria lost her patience. She rushed over to Dragos and shoved her face into his with a fierce expression. "Get—up—there—now," she seethed.

Even Dragos was cowed by her sudden transformation. He walked to where Agrethar lay, avoiding Victria's eyes. After scooping the incapacitated dwarf into his arms, he jumped up high and landed on one of the lower branches of a nearby tree. Thuradin saw him jump one more time before losing sight of him in the intersecting branches.

"Right," Victria said in a low voice. "Our turn."

She scooped up the remaining two dwarves, one in each arm, and jumped into the tree next to Dragos. Thuradin felt his beard fly up and down as Victria jumped from branch to branch, gaining more altitude each time. She stopped when she was high enough to be hidden but low enough to keep an eye on the camp. They were on one of the thicker branches, so Victria let the two dwarves go so they could stand for themselves.

Thuradin looked down at the camp, waiting to see whatever it was that had panicked the viatari. At first, nothing appeared, and he wondered if maybe they weren't getting enough sleep.

Then the first human walked out of the shadows.

The human carried a short spear and was lightly armored—a scout. Three more scouts came cut of the shadows to join him and searched through the remains of the camp. Thuradin heard them murmur to each other, but he couldn't understand what they said.

They continued searching, emptying bags, scanning the ground for tracks. The horses and rams didn't put up any resistance and even allowed the strangers to go through the supplies on their backs. Luckily, nothing of importance was currently tied to them, so the scouts came up empty-handed.

"Humans!" Dragos hissed, coming out of the shadows on Thuradin's right. "What are they doing here?"

"Looks like a scouting party," Victria suggested, then cocked her head to the side. "Whoever they are, they don't seem to have expected to run into our camp, if what I am hearing is correct—" she looked to Dragos for verification. Dragos nodded quickly.

The scouts met at the center of the camp and spoke in hushed tones. Thuradin saw Victria lean in, straining her ears so she might catch what they were saying. Suddenly the humans split up and trudged off in different directions, vanishing from sight as they reentered the undergrowth.

"We'll stay here," Victria said, an uncertain frown crossing her face. "I believe their plan is to wait and see if we will come out of hiding."

"How would they know we were here—unless they have some means of detecting our life-energies?" Stürn asked, thinking of his own powers as an Enurg'en.

"No," Victria replied, narrowing her eyes as she stared at a bush nestled between a trio of trees. "They don't have any talent like that, which means they don't *know* if we are here, which is why they are waiting to see if anyone will come out."

Sure enough, after almost half an hour, the scouts left their hiding spots to meet back at the center of the camp. Thuradin noticed the bush Victria had been staring at so suspiciously had in fact been hiding one of the scouts.

The humans huddled together, no doubt discussing what they should do next. But it appeared they couldn't come to a consensus, as they eventually walked off into the undergrowth and disappeared from sight once again.

"They're gone this time," Dragos said.

Victria nodded. "We should still wait here. They may come back again to make sure the camp is truly empty."

Time passed slowly as they waited in the trees. The scouts returned once more, several hours after they had left, and stayed in the camp for only a few minutes before leaving for a final time.

Even after they had left for what Thuradin was sure was the last time, Victria didn't suggest climbing down until it was well into the night. Eventually, the viatari scooped up the dwarves again and jumped down from their high perches, setting the dwarves down gently as they touched the ground.

"Those scouts seemed familiar," Dragos murmured.

"It's natural they would seem familiar after what we've been through," Victria said.

The viatari shared an uncertain look before Victria returned to packing up the rest of their camp. Dragos helped her with a troubled frown on his face.

After the remainder of their belongings had been packed and tied to their mounts, they rode out of the woods as quietly as they could. Silence reigned as each member of the party thought of the consequences the scouts' discovery could mean. For their sake, Thuradin hoped Victria was right and that the four scouts were nothing to worry about.

It was midday by the time they arrived to the base of The Silent Mountains. They had ridden at a slow pace with no breaks the entire night and morning in order to arrive.

Now they dismounted, leaving their mounts hidden behind a cluster of craggy boulders, and hiked around the face of the nearest mountain for a while before Thuradin spotted a good cave not too far above them.

The viatari took turns carrying Agrethar as they climbed, while Stürn muttered quick healing chants every now and then to keep the unconscious dwarf alive.

Thuradin was first to reach the cave's mouth, and he immediately liked what he saw. The cave was deep, wide, and spacious. Stalactites and stalagmites jutted out all over the ceiling and floor. The rich minerals inside glinted as the little sunlight that managed to sneak its way inside touched them. It was no Hall of Kings, but it was as good a cave as he was likely to find in the middle of the mountain range. As he continued looking around, Thuradin noticed the viatari struggle to drag Agrethar into the cave.

"He's getting heavier," Victria grunted. "I think he's reached his limit."

"Aye," Stürn's sad voice echoed through the stone walls. "My chanting is having no effect. His life-energies have grown deaf ta my pleas."

"Then we must hurry," Thuradin said. "Bring him here, by this stalagmite—" he pointed to one of the smaller formations near the cave's entrance. It was deep enough so Agrethar would be comfortable but also close enough to the cave's mouth so he could have a good view of the outside world.

"Thuradin," Agrethar called out, eyes fluttering madly as the young dwarf struggled to remain conscious. His breathing was heavy and ragged as he forced out what he wanted to say. "Find Ronorim. . . . Find him and bring him home."

Thuradin clasped Agrethar's outstretched hand and knelt beside the dying dwarf.

"Rest easy, my friend. I'll find him. Yer death will nae be in vain."

Agrethar nodded in thanks.

"Thuradin . . . Tell Bronn—tell him I'm sorry."

The older dwarf, no longer able to speak, nodded several times.

Agrethar's eyes shifted to the outside world. A soft groan escaped his lips. His chest rose and fell more irregularly than before, and his breaths came in stifled gasps as the poison spread through the rest of his body

"I don't blame ye, Thuradin."

The young dwarf's breathing became softer and less frequent.

"Without my healing," Stürn said quietly, coming up beside Thuradin, "he will deteriorate quickly. The poison is rushing through his veins as we speak, and very soon it will kill him."

No sooner was this said than Agrethar let out one last shuddering gasp and breathed no more. The dwarves bowed their heads in respect. Thuradin was sure he saw Victria bow her own head out of the corner of his eye. As for Dragos, no trace of him could be seen.

It didn't take long for Agrethar's body to entomb. His legs and feet were the first to harden and turn gray. The gray slowly crept up the rest of his limbs as the process continued until what had once been Agrethar was now stone. He was part of the mountain, part of the stalagmite he leaned on. Thuradin stared at the soulless eyes as they looked out at the outside world.

"The sun is setting," Victria said from behind. "We will stay here for the night and set out in the morning. Is that alright?"

Thuradin nodded.

When he asked where Dragos was, she answered with a shrug. Apparently, while Thuradin had been speaking with Agrethar, Dragos had suddenly run out without any explanation. This wasn't particularly worrying to the dwarf, who thought a few moments without the viatari's attitude was nothing to complain about.

After having nothing but cold rations on their difficult journey to the mountains, they all agreed it was time for a nice, hot meal. Victria left the dwarves to their own devices as she exited the cave to hunt for live prey.

As Felix had promised back in Aleganthia, none of the viatari ate their food in front of the dwarves, even during their journey to Inadarim. Victria made it a point to make sure she and Dragos continued to follow these rules, even though they weren't under Felix's supervision.

Stürn started a fire close to the mouth of the cave so the smoke could escape into the air rather than remain inside. He then began frying all kinds of meat which they had brought from Aleganthia. The aroma from the pan intensified as the Enurg'en added potatoes, greens, and a savory sauce to the mix. Thuradin couldn't help but peek over Stürn's shoulders to see how soon the food would be finished.

After he was yelled at by a hungry, and therefore grumpy, Stürn that the food wouldn't cook faster just because he kept looking at it, Thuradin decided he would pay his ram a visit to retrieve one of the small kegs of ale he had brought with him for the journey. It would go excellently with the hot meal.

He was trying to remember the last time he'd had a chance to drink in peace when he ran into a breathless, angry Dragos.

"Put that fire out, you fools!"

Stürn looked up from his cooking, not in the mood to be taking orders. "We're cooking. Leave us alone."

The viatari kicked the pan, scattering its hot, greasy contents all over the cave's floor. He then took one of the large, thick blankets from his bag and smothered the fire.

"How could ye—"

"Quiet, dwarf!" Dragos hissed. "The smoke from your fire has attracted unwanted guests. How are we supposed to leave this cave alive if we corner ourselves by showing everyone where we are?"

Victria walked in at that moment, licking her lips in satisfaction. It looked like she, at least, had had a good meal, though Thuradin wondered exactly how the life-energies of different animals differed in taste—or if they had a taste at all. As soon as she saw Dragos towering over Stürn, the slight smile she'd had vanished.

"What's happened?"

"Didn't you see them when you came in?" Dragos asked incredulously.

Victria shrugged, oblivious to what the younger viatari was talking about. With an exasperated grunt, Dragos led her to the mouth of the cave, followed closely by the dwarves. Thuradin's eyes widened when he saw what lay before them.

Below them, near the base of the mountain, was an army of humans. Many fires burned as they set up their camp for the night. Though he couldn't count every single one, there looked to be at least several hundred, all of whom were armed and armored even as they sat around their fires to eat.

"Look what these dwarves have done."

Normally, Thuradin would have defended himself against such an outrageous claim. To think that it was his and Stürn's fault alone that they were now in this predicament? That was a ridiculous notion. But he was too much in shock to say anything.

"No," Victria said, clearly shaken by what she saw. "I don't believe the smoke is what attracted them to us."

"But there's no other reason for them to have come. Everything was fine when I first left the cave, and the minute I return, I see smoke coming out of it and this huge—"

Victria raised her hand to silence Dragos. "No," she said again. "The dwarves may have given away our position, but they did not attract the humans here."

"Why are they here then?" Dragos demanded.

Victria sighed. "They are here because of my serious lack of insight back in the woods. That scouting party didn't just happen to stumble upon our camp. They were *looking* for us."

"But they looked so surprised when they found our mounts."

"Yes. . . ." Victria agreed thoughtfully. "I don't think they expected for us to be so close. They may have been looking for signs of our presence, not our actual whereabouts. Most likely they have been following us since the very beginning— since we split up from the others."

"What are we going to do then?" Dragos asked. "We can't have this army follow us back to Inadarim. They'll kill us before we get there."

"Well, at this point there's nothing we *can* do. They are too many, and we are too few."

Victria walked back into the cave with the others following close behind. As she went deeper into the darkness, she explained her plan for their escape.

They would sleep inside as originally planned and, despite their current situation, wouldn't have a watch—since the cave would be so dark during the night, any scouts the humans sent up wouldn't dare go inside for fear of an ambush. It was a gamble, but Victria was sure it was a good one. Besides, they all needed to rest.

When the sun rose the next day, they would climb down the mountain as quickly but as stealthily as possible to reach their mounts without attracting attention from the camp below. Once mounted, they would ride for Inadarim at a fast pace to put as much distance as they could between themselves and their pursuers.

"I recommend we sleep now. Tomorrow is going to be a a difficult day, and we will need all our strength for it."

Thuradin and Stürn ventured off deeper into the cave than Victria had already taken them and looked for good stalagmites to lean on. From the outside, they could hear a distant rumble, as if a storm were coming.

Trying not to think of storms or assassins during the night or of the amount of luck they would need to escape tomorrow, Thuradin closed his eyes and drifted off to the sound of Stürn grumbling about their wasted dinner.

CHAPTER NINETEEN

Felix turned in his saddle and watched the cloud of dust made by Victria's group settle back down. He could no longer see the riders who had made it, but before they had completely disappeared, he had noticed one particular rider had broken off from the others as he charged across the countryside in a furious rage.

"It appears I have upset your commander," Felix said to Borim.

"Aye."

Felix raised an eyebrow. "Just 'aye'? You are usually much more talkative, Borim."

Borim glanced sharply at Felix. "Don't pretend. Ye showed yer true colors in that petty argument with Thuradin. Ready ta kill us on a whim when we start ta slow ye down, are ye? I warn ye, viatari, there's only so much we dwarves will put up with."

Felix frowned. He hadn't expected a reaction like this from the dwarves. Yes, he had spoken rather harshly with Thuradin, but it had been with the greater good of the group as a whole in mind. "I admit I lost my temper, but I assure you I had no intention of killing Agrethar myself. That would be ridiculous!"

"Oh, well then that makes it all better! Please, ye said ye would nae allow anything ta endanger this quest, and ye've made it clear that 'anything' can include us. We're only tools for yer use."

Felix shook his head. He had spoken out of place, that much was true. The stress from recent events and the loss of so many viatari and then their constant breaks for Agrethar, which only helped the humans catch up to them, certainly hadn't helped. But he hadn't meant to sound like he didn't care for the dwarves. He had always considered them friends, even after they retreated into the mountains all those centuries ago.

He tried to tell Borim this. "I have always been a friend to the dwarves, ever since the beginning. I fought with them—"

"Aye, so ye've told us. And I'm sure ye thought of us as tools then as well. Easily disposable, nae worth the time or effort it takes ta bury us. I'm one of the more patient of my kind, but even I have a limit ta the insults I can take."

Borim turned away and spurred his ram to join the other dwarves, all of whom were making an effort to keep their distance from the viatari.

Natiari and Tessa rode up next to Felix. They said nothing at first, but one look at their faces and he knew they sympathized with him.

"Don't take their words personally," Natiari said. "Isolation has made it hard for them to trust anything new, and the trust they do have is fragile. In many ways, they remind me of Victria when we first met."

"They don't fully understand what their race and ours went through together all those centuries ago," Tessa added. "Even though the memories of those trials still live within us like it happened yesterday, to them it never happened. We can't blame them for not understanding."

Felix nodded.

Such wise words from viatari much younger than he was. He marveled, not for the first time, at the transformation that had taken place within the girls since he first met them.

He remembered when he and Pulaneus had stumbled upon a young, disheveled Tessa for the first time. She had just managed to snap the spine of the bear that killed the last of her three sisters. He recalled how sullen and introverted she used to be, how she always ran away from those who tried to approach her, even during training.

He also remembered Natiari's dark history. Instead of losing sisters attempting to protect her, she lost the sister *she* was trying to protect, her only sibling. He recalled Thymos, the trainer who honed every viatari's skills, telling him about how he had found this thin girl draped over the even thinner corpse of her sister, screaming loud enough to attract every dangerous beast within a ten-mile radius.

By Thymos' account, the two sisters had been ambushed by a formidable pack of spiders the size of boulders. Natiari was skilled enough to deal with most of them, but three escaped her attention, and, before she knew it, her sister had been stabbed through several times by their enormous stingers. In the end, their poison, rather than the wounds themselves, proved to be the killing blow. And like Tessa, Natiari had sunk into her own shell of solitude because of the loss.

He remembered thinking that nothing would ever bring these two out of their mourning. And then he found Victria.

The minute she, Tessa, and Natiari met, they became inseparable. In fact, Felix was fairly certain that Tessa and

Natiari had, in their minds, adopted Victria as a sort of replacement for their slain sisters. As for Victria, he suspected the two girls were the family she never had.

It had always been a pleasant feeling watching the three previously lost souls laugh away the pain of the past as they played in the green meadows that used to be their home. And now, he was the one comforted by those who knew and shared his own pain.

After hours of riding, they stopped for the day and pitched camp near a small gully.

A watch of two was set up for the night with a rotation every few hours. Tessa and Borim were the first on watch and situated themselves on high ground so they could spot anything sneaking up on their camp from a distance. As the sun slowly drifted downward, nothing of import registered on either one's mind. But as soon as the sun disappeared, the two sat up straight as a sea of lights lit up north of their position.

"What is that?" Borim said.

The lights looked a fair distance from the camp, so there was no sense of immediate danger, but it was still a curious sight.

"Humans, possibly," Tessa replied. "It looks like they've set up camp near where we split into two groups. I bet that confused their trackers. If we can see them from here, though, there must be a fairly large host. Maybe hundreds."

"Should we be worried?" Borim asked, not liking their odds for survival should they have to confront that many humans out in the open.

But Tessa shook her head. "They're still a fair distance away, and they will move slower than us since they have a larger force. As long as we keep moving at the same pace we have been, we should be fine. . . . Still, it probably wouldn't hurt to tell Felix in the morning."

They continued to stare at the shimmering lights in the distance, so focused on it they were unaware of the long, dark figures rustling about in the tall grass behind them. As the next watch—Ayrie and Threnn—took over, the dark figures moved away from the camp, out of sight.

Felix drove them hard and fast to cover as much ground as they could before they had to set up camp again. After hearing about the shimmering lights in the distance, he had come to the same conclusion as Tessa. With the possibility of an army of humans chasing after them, he declared that Inadarim was only two days away—provided everything went smoothly—which meant they couldn't allow the humans to catch them.

So they rode hard through the plains until they were no longer surrounded by the tall grass. Flat land turned into hills and tall pines jutted out of the earth, at first individually, then in large clusters. Far off in the distance, Felix could see the sky fill with clouds and the land lose the vibrant colors of life that it normally had—the first signs they were nearing Inadarim.

Everyone was ready to collapse by the time Felix said they could stop for the day. He pointed out a small depression to their right that would keep them hidden and they set up camp. Ayrie made a perimeter sweep to make sure they were truly alone, just in case human scouts were nearby, but she found nothing threatening.

The watch was the same as the previous night. Borim and Tessa decided to keep an eye on their surroundings from one of the nearby hills that overlooked the area. Night fell, and Borim could once again see evidence of the humans following them. This time, however, instead of a sea of lights, only a faint glow indicated their presence.

"They're farther away from us now than they were last night," Borim noted, distracted enough to forget his grudge against the viatari.

"Yes," Tessa agreed, narrowing her eyes. "In fact, they're farther than they should be, even with the pace we rode at today. They must be moving away from us, which means they're following Victria's party, not us."

Borim glanced at Tessa and saw the small but noticeable worry lines forming on her face.

"Don't worry," he reassured her. "Thuradin would never let any harm fall upon her. I'm sure they'll be safe."

Tessa grinned, the worry lines disappearing. "I wasn't worried, but thank you."

They continued their vigil in silence.

The night wore on, and the glow in the distance grew fainter as the fires making them died down. Borim was growing tired and wondered when his watch would end when he heard a loud, sharp hissing coming from somewhere on his left. Tessa, too, had registered the sound. The hissing stopped only to be followed by a menacing growl. Borim had never heard such noises come from regular animals, and he could see their mounts in the depression below them shift about nervously.

No matter which way he turned, though, he couldn't spot any sign of a threat lurking near them. Thinking hard, he reasoned that whatever was making the noise must be quite large to be heard from such a distance.

"Don't panic," Tessa said as he continued to turn in circles. "What you're hearing is a darim. The fact that we can hear them now means we're close to the Creature's domain. They won't attack yet. We're still not within their borders."

Borim nodded and sat back down, though he kept his guard high for the remainder of the watch. He looked around every now and then, but never caught a glimpse of the darimun he had heard so much about. For now, they would still have to exist only in his imagination.

The next morning they told Felix about the noises they had heard. Felix nodded knowingly, not a hint of surprise crossing his face. He had been wondering himself, before the camp was even set up the night before, when they would start encountering darimun.

They rode cautiously that day.

Felix had everyone spread out so they could cover a larger area, lowering the chances of anything sneaking up on them easily, or, at least, he hoped that's what it would do. However, he made sure to emphasize that everyone stay close enough together to come to the aid of the others should a need arise. They were to stay alert for any signs of movement because the only thing that would be moving toward them in this place would be a darim.

The dwarves continued to ride sullenly but significantly less so than the previous couple of days. They still listened to Felix when he gave instructions or orders, but other than that, they hardly acknowledged him or the other viatari— except for Borim who was often seen now chatting with Tessa. Felix wasn't exactly happy that the dwarves continued to distrust him, but he was grateful their grudge against him appeared to be fading, at least gradually. Perhaps after this task was over, after more time had passed, they would be willing to forgive him for his outburst.

"The birds," Ayrie said, snapping Felix out of his thoughts. "They've stopped singing."

They all listened, but what Ayrie had said was true, not a single chirp or trill could be heard. But not only had the birds stopped singing; crickets stopped their chirping, squirrels quit jabbering, all the wildlife noises they had grown so accustomed to suddenly stopped. It was an unnatural silence, and Felix felt the thin hairs on his skin rise.

"My friends, we have arrived. Welcome to Inadarim, the Creature's home."

It wasn't long before the landscape began to change dramatically. Trees continued to dominate the land, but they were now dead and barren or, at best, sickly. The vibrant, green grass that covered the hills they had been riding through transformed to a nauseating yellow as the land itself flattened. The dirt they trod on looked to be nothing more than ash.

Horses and rams fought against their riders. Their sudden resistance caught the dwarves and viatari off guard, and they struggled to reestablish control. One of the pack horses darted ahead of the group, eyes wild with fear. Felix saw it go and watched as a giant snake lunged out of the tall grass and tackled it.

Only it was no ordinary snake. It was larger than any he had ever seen. Its body was immensely thick, and as it reared back to its full height to deliver a final blow to the gasping pack horse, he noted it was nearly as tall as the nearby trees. A purple haze surrounded it, seeming to emanate from its own body. That, along with its dull, yellow eyes, was enough to tell him what this was. A darim.

The dwarves gaped at the giant snake, too stunned to

realize it was rearing back to attack again, its attention now on them.

"Move!" Felix yelled. His voice snapped them out of their trance, and they moved into action, riding around the darim in circles in different directions to try and confuse it. And it seemed to be working, initially.

The darim hesitated as it tried to decide which target it should strike. Wanting to take advantage of this distraction, Felix tried to urge his horse toward it for an attack, but his mount refused to move. Instead, it stumbled and slid backward. Looking behind him, he saw another darim, also a giant snake, glare back hungrily into his eyes as it continued dragging his unfortunate horse through the grass.

He jumped off his mount hastily as the darim let go and tried to lunge at him, narrowly avoiding its powerful jaws. His horse wasn't so lucky.

Natiari and Tessa had already dismounted and ran toward the darim attacking Felix. They moved around in rapid, random patterns, a battle tactic developed millennia ago, which involved one viatari acting as a distraction while the other waited for a chance to deliver the killing blow. After glancing at the dwarves and seeing that they were holding their own against their opponent, Felix joined Tessa and Natiari in their fight.

Tessa taunted the darim by standing in one place, only to move at the last second as the snake attacked so it smashed its face into the ground every time. Felix helped by slashing at the tough snakeskin with his blade and then jumping away when the darim tried to strike back. With the enemy distracted, Natiari crept behind it and leapt onto its scaly back.

The situation appeared under control and Felix was

about to leave and give the dwarves assistance when he saw the darim's thick tail wrap itself around Natiari's climbing figure. She screamed as it plucked her from its back and began crushing her body.

Her eyes wide, disbelieving, Tessa stopped her distraction tactics and charged the darim head on, but she was knocked back by its swinging head.

Felix took action. He jumped around the darim, disappearing and appearing in several different places so fast he looked to be standing in them all at once. The snake looked this way and that, trying to pinpoint where Felix was but to no avail. Satisfied that his plan was working and deciding the darim was confused enough, he jumped straight onto its head.

The darim shook its head wildly and hissed. Felix held on, searching for a good enough handhold that would allow him to execute the next part of his plan. He found one in the darim's right nostril and tried to yank its head to one side to break its neck, but the snake realized too quickly what he was trying to do. It stiffened its neck muscles and fought Felix's pull as it continued to crush Natiari. Even with all his strength, Felix wasn't able to force the snake's head to turn enough to break it.

"Tessa!" He shouted, hoping she could hear him. "Make its head turn left. Quickly!"

He waited, struggling to maintain his hold. There was a sharp whistling sound to his left and then a sudden *smack!* as a projectile hit the darim's face. Tessa had thrown a rock at its left eye.

The darim hissed furiously and, momentarily forgetting about Felix, turned its head to the left to face Tessa. As it did this, Felix switched his grip to the left nostril and used all his strength and the darim's own momentum to twist its head all the way around. The darim went limp, and its head crashed to the ground.

The two viatari, breathing hard, rushed to the coils where Natiari was buried and pulled them apart. She was still there, unconscious but breathing. Felix and Tessa felt lightheaded as relief flushed through them.

Remembering the dwarves, Felix turned and started running to their aid but stopped when he realized they didn't need him. Their darim was already dead. Its severed head rested several feet from the rest of its writhing body.

He walked over to the huddled dwarves, who were panting heavily and cursing. They stood crowded around Murtosh, who lay on the ground with a large gash on his forehead, his eyes closed.

"Is he dead?" Felix asked, concerned.

The dwarves shook their heads in unison.

"Just knocked out," Ayrie panted. "That beastie whipped him on the head with its tail before hammering him into the ground. But he's a Firebrand. He'll live."

Felix nodded. He didn't say it, but from what Ayrie had just told him, he was surprised the dwarf's head hadn't come flying off after being dealt such a blow.

"How did you manage to kill it?" Felix asked, shifting his attention to the now-still carcass next to him.

"We cut off its head," Threnn said casually. "Took a few tries ta sever it completely, though."

Felix nodded again like this was a perfectly normal explanation, but inside he marveled at the dwarves' fighting ability. It had taken three fully trained viatari to take down one darim with some difficulty, yet the dwarves had managed to decapitate theirs in just as much time and with only a few cuts, bruises, and, of course, the gash on Murtosh's head to show for it.

Tessa carried Natiari and laid her down next to Murtosh.

"They're both unconscious," Borim noted.

"Aye," said Threnn. "They'll slow us down."

Felix glanced at Tessa, who was clearly trying hard to suppress a smile. He would get no help from her. He turned to the dwarves, who looked at him expectantly, daring him to suggest that they abandon their companions again.

"Of course we are not going to leave them," he said. "We will take them with us."

The dwarves looked at each other with raised eyebrows as if this was the strangest news they had ever heard. Felix rolled his eyes in exasperation and turned to Tessa. "Ride with Natiari on her horse. I will take yours."

They all mounted. Natiari and Murtosh woke up during the process but they were weak and groggy. It took some effort to put them into the saddle and even more to keep them in it as they all continued their journey deeper into Inadarim.

There were no other encounters with darimun as they rode. Luck, Felix thought. If they had been attacked again by a larger force of darimun, he wasn't sure they could have walked away with only some scratches again.

His heart began to beat faster and his stomach twisted as the land rose, leading to a ledge. Once they reached the top of this slope, he knew, they would be standing over the crater. Glancing around, he tried to spot some sign that Victria was close by but found none. He hoped she and the others were alright.

Purple lights flashed in the distance. He didn't remember seeing them the last time he had come here, and he wondered what they might mean. Whatever they were, he was sure they were not a good sign.

They crested the slope and looked down into a scene of decay. The crater looked worse than Felix remembered. He saw the dwarves stare uncomfortably at the dead earth. The ground was littered with large cracks, sharp rocks, and dead trees, most of which were now just cracked stumps. At the center of the crater, they saw a small, lonely mountain. The flashes of purple light were coming from it. Felix saw several more flashes crackling around it, shooting into the dark, cloudy sky in a thin beam of light. The Creature was making his presence known.

"Come," Felix said. "We will not go farther until we are reunited with the others. Besides," he nodded his head at Murtosh and Natiari, who still wore dazed expressions on their faces, "those two need rest until Stürn can come back and heal them. For now, we will search for a place where we can make a suitable camp."

He led them to a clump of trees not too far from the crater's rim. He had told Dragos and Victria they would rendezvous there. All he had to do now was wait and hope that they all returned alive.

It was a stressful week for Felix.

Tessa and Natiari took turns keeping a lookout for Victria, but for the last six days they had come back with no news.

Meanwhile, with each passing day, the darimun grew more aware of a foreign presence in their land. Several times, they'd had to hide in the trees because large packs of darimun had been spotted roaming nearby.

There had been the occasional battle with a stray darim

or two, but no one, so far, had been seriously injured. However, over the past six days, they had lost three of their pack horses. Felix wondered if they would have enough provisions for the return journey and figured if they kept losing horses, they certainly would not.

He hoped Victria would pull through like she always did and arrive soon. It was only a matter of time before one of the herds of darimun discovered their camp and killed everyone, and if that happened, the one good chance they had at stopping the Creature would be gone. He would have failed his people.

Felix climbed one of the trees overlooking the crater and watched the purple lights dance around the central mountain. He still didn't know what was causing the display or what the lights were made of, but they gave him an ominous feeling. There was something sinister about them, something foreboding, but he couldn't figure out what it was.

"No sign of them today either," Tessa reported from a lower branch. Felix was surprised he hadn't heard her approach.

"They will come."

"That won't matter if they come too late."

Felix nodded, conceding the point. "We will wait for them for a few more days before we try to go in by ourselves. How are Natiari and Murtosh?"

Tessa grunted, which meant they were fine. The two had woken up again only a few hours after the camp was established. Natiari had suffered a few broken ribs, but they were easily mended by her regenerative abilities. Murtosh's gash, on the other hand, continued to bleed and looked infected. It would have to stay that way until Stürn returned, Felix thought. They had tried treating the wound with some pastes made from healing herbs they had packed with them, but nothing seemed to work against the infection.

The flashes of purple light grew brighter and more intense, drawing his attention to them once again. He didn't know what had caused the sudden change, but like everything in Inadarim, he didn't like it. As he continued watching the lights dance around the crater's central mountain, he wondered what was taking Victria so long.

CHAPTER TWENTY

Simon was resting in his tent when the report came in.

Things had been busy since their encounter with the viatari in the forest. Simon had been disappointed when they managed to escape his ambush, but that disappointment quickly turned to satisfaction when he learned three of the viatari had been slain. Now he was determined more than ever to hunt down the rest of them.

Of course, their deaths weren't cheap. He had lost many men in the battle, and many more were wounded. He remembered walking through the forest as his men finally managed to decapitate and skewer the last viatari, a female whose face, covered in blood but fixed with a perfect look of fury, had even managed to make Simon not want to approach her. Laying in a ring around her were several dozen of his warriors, most of whom were dead.

After the battle, Simon had decided the best course of action would be to bury the dead and treat the wounded, rather than give immediate chase to the viatari. They would have a head start, but he was sure he would eventually be able to catch up to them. The viatari couldn't run forever.

Now, however, he regretted not sending at least one or

two scouts to keep an eye on them.

The hunting party had grown exponentially since their hunt for the viatari began. The surrounding towns Simon had sent messages to had responded with incredible speed and generosity, and their hunting party had quickly grown into a small army.

At first their trackers followed the viatari's path with ease. Now, however, a day and a half later, their progress came to a halt. The trail they followed had split in two.

A poor tracker himself, Simon let those trained in the skill go about their work while he walked through camp, encouraging everyone to keep their spirits up and comforting those who had lost friends or family in the recent battle. Eventually, seeing that the trackers were not going to come to a decision on which way to go any time soon, he went to his tent for a nap.

He woke up to find William, the head tracker, inside his tent waiting for acknowledgment. A quick glance outside told him it was already dark.

"Have you made a decision?"

"We sent some scouts to follow both trails for a distance to get an idea of where they might go," William answered. "The one that splits off seems to lead to the mountains. The one that continues leads to the *Forbidden Lands.*"

Simon sat up in his cot. No one went to the Forbidden Lands unless they wanted to die. It was a dangerous place filled with mystery and evil. No one knew what really resided in the area. Only rumors existed from those few survivors who had come back from there insane.

"I believe the path that leads to the Forbidden Lands is a distraction, a false trail," the head tracker continued. "I don't know why they would make for the mountains, but I believe that is the trail we should follow."

Simon nodded slowly. "I trust your judgment. Gabriel—"

The servant Gabriel entered his tent. "Yes, sir?"

"We've already set up camp, so we might as well stay here for the night. Tell everyone that we move out at first light tomorrow."

Gabriel nodded and left the tent to carry out his duty.

As the days progressed, it seemed that their choice to follow the mountain tracks was the correct one. The trackers constantly kept their eyes on the trail, which was easy now since the viatari didn't seem to realize they were being followed. There were no twists and turns, no more attempts at evasion since the initial split.

They marched all day and some of the night, stopping only to eat, and they would have continued had the trackers not suddenly realized a change in what had previously been an easy trail. Simon saw William speaking with one of the other trackers near the outskirts of the camp and rode up to him.

"Is there a problem?"

William shook his head. "Not a serious one, but if we're not careful, we could lose their trail in the dark, which would mean wasted time when we have to try and relocate it. It looks to me like the viatari are avoiding the towns—wise of them—but this makes their path unpredictable. I recommend we rest here and start again in the morning."

"Very well," Simon pursed his lips. They had crossed quite a distance in one day and deserved their rest, but he would have preferred to continue the march, even at the risk of losing the trail. He would trust William's judgment, however, and hope it didn't keep them from catching up to the viatari in a timely manner.

"If there's a town nearby, go and tell them what we're doing. Ask them if they're willing to give us any aid and if they have any information or if they've seen the viatari. If they haven't, tell them to remain vigilant and to spread word to the other towns in the region."

William nodded and rode off into the night toward the faint glow of torches that outlined a town. The thud of his mount's hooves against the ground could be heard long after they disappeared from view.

They continued marching the next day.

The trackers spoke excitedly to one another as the day progressed. They pointed at certain parts of the earth and ran their bare fingers along individual prints, feeling the soil. Simon was pleased when they told him the tracks were getting fresher.

Occasionally, the army would run into a traveling merchant or farmer, and Simon would stop to ask them if they had seen any sign of the viatari or dwarves. Most answered with a shake of their head and moved on, except for one farmer.

"I di'n see 'em with my own eyes," the farmer said, bringing his hands up to his face and pointing at his eyes to emphasize the point. "But durin' the nigh' I hears people ridin' hard an' fast across these lands, and I 'hough' it was strange tha' someone would be ridin' so hard so late. Sound to me like was a few of 'em too."

This news bolstered everyone's spirits, especially Simon's. This meant the viatari were only moving during the night. It would be easy to catch up to them as long as the host continued to march all day and into the night for the next day or two. The viatari had the disadvantage of having to remain undetected by the surrounding towns. Simon didn't have that disadvantage.

They marched with renewed vigor, Simon leading them with an eager grin, as the thought of catching the viatari soon gave them a new sense of urgency.

Two days passed and the tracks remained fresh. They led to a patch of woods in a small valley. Simon was eager to catch his prey, but he didn't want to go blundering into a wooded area without sending in some scouts first. Otherwise, he would just be making the same mistake the viatari had made days earlier.

As scouts were sent into the woods, the army rested where they were without setting up camp. Simon was sure the woods would be cleared by the scouts quickly, and he didn't want to waste precious time setting up a camp only to have it taken down soon after.

However, as the sun continued to sink closer toward the horizon, Simon was forced to give the order to set up camp, since the scouts had yet to return. They must have found something if they were taking so long, and Simon had a suspicion that something was the viatari. He worried for them, hoping they hadn't accidentally run into their quarry and perished.

Finally, as the sun flashed its last rays of light, he saw them emerge from the woods. They trudged toward the camp, exhausted from the day's march and their recent expedition. They were covered in sweat and dirt and leaves stuck to their skin because of it. Their weapons hung loosely from their belts, and their steps were taken with great pain, as if each one was a result of a sheer force of will. He let them rest and eat before he asked them for their report.

"They're here," one of the scouts said through a mouthful

of his second bowl of potato stew. "We ran right into their camp. It was deserted, though, couldn't find any clues as to where they had gone. We decided to separate and keep a watch on the place until they returned—try to ambush them if we saw the chance—but we hid for maybe an hour before deciding it would be wiser to scout the entirety of the woods, just to see if we could find anything else."

"We didn't," another scout continued with a scowl. "So we returned to where we found the campsite. It was gone. They must have packed up and left while we were scouting the rest of the woods."

Simon nodded and patted each scout on the shoulder encouragingly.

"You did well," he said. "We're very close now. That's all we needed to know."

The next morning, Simon had his men comb through every inch of the wooded valley as they passed through. They checked every tree, every log, stone, and bush as they searched for any sign of the enemy. Nothing.

The scouts led Simon and the trackers to where they had found the campsite, and from there, the trackers picked up the trail and moved on ahead to see where it led.

It was midday by the time the host reached the other side of the valley. The trackers still hadn't returned despite the hours Simon had wasted going through every inch of the wooded area. He worried he had wasted too much time and had given the viatari a chance to slip away. But those worries were soon quelled by the sound of hoof beats and a hazy picture of a small group of riders in the distance.

"Well?" Simon demanded as soon as William was within earshot. The head tracker pointed behind him toward the mountains that now loomed over them.

"The tracks lead straight to the mountains. I rode ahead to see how far they were, but they were already in one of the caves by the time I arrived."

"Come then," Simon said as he mounted his horse and signaled for the march to continue. "If we hurry, we can surround and trap them and finally put an end to this wild chase."

They set out once again and, after a few hours of marching, set up camp a few hundred feet from the first set of mountains.

The sun was lower now. There was still enough daylight to send in a strike force, but Simon wouldn't dare risk such a move without first sending in scouts to find out exactly which cave the viatari hid in, and that would take time.

"If we wait too long, we could lose them just like we did in the valley," William warned as they walked through camp. "You're being too cautious."

"We know they're here, but we need to know where *exactly*," Simon pointed out. "What if the sun sets while our men are still searching for the cave these viatari have burrowed away in? Then they're on their own, and we both know the mountains are a dangerous place at night. No, I think—"

Shouts rang out through the camp and men pointed upward as smoke began drifting out of the mountain closest to them. Simon couldn't tell where exactly the smoke originated from, but it narrowed down the area in which the viatari could be hiding. His enemies had just saved him several precious hours.

"Well, I suppose *now* we don't need a scouting party," he muttered.

He walked through the camp, hand picking those he thought were his best fighters, and told them they were to search the mountain for the viatari and kill them. They were only too happy to do it. The small force sprinted off toward the mountain with nothing but the armor and weapons they managed to get their hands on before leaving.

After they left, a large watch was set up, encircling the entire camp. Simon didn't believe they were going to be attacked. But he wanted to make sure nothing escaped from the mountains. He needed eyes to stay on them even through the night.

Looking at the peak nearest the camp, Simon could see the men he had selected climbing its face. To him, they looked like tiny specks, like ants on a hill, but he could tell by their progress that they would be able to search the entire summit and find the viatari's cave before it grew dark. They were already almost level with the first set of caves.

Fortune was not on Simon's side, however. The weather had been charmingly clear for the past few days, but now clouds moved across the sky in increasingly large clusters until it was completely covered with them. Their color changed from white to gray as they blotted out the sun.

A storm was coming.

Frowning, Simon hoped the men he had sent into the mountain had enough sense to find shelter instead of continuing with their task, but they didn't seem to be slowing down.

Thunder rumbled as the storm prepared to release its pent-up rage. The rain came in single drops at first. Then in pairs. And then it turned into a torrential downpour. Lightning flashed. Luckily it didn't strike the camp, but it did strike the mountains several times. Simon heard rumbling in the distance like a giant stampede of horses as large boulders tumbled down the mountain, instigating larger rock slides. It was as if the earth itself roared.

The wind grew strong and blew the rain in all directions. Soon it wasn't even possible to make out the outline of the mountain they were camped under, so heavy was the downpour. The watch was called in and everybody went about staking everything into the ground.

In response, the winds grew even stronger. It lifted some of the unstaked tents into the air and tossed them out of the camp for several hundred yards. Horses cried and rose onto their hind legs in a wild panic as they tried to escape their restraints. The ground turned muddy and men stumbled about and fell as they rushed around, trying to prevent as much damage as they could. Specks of mud flew everywhere, leaving nothing unstained. The rain did nothing to wash it all away, only adding to the misery.

This lasted for several hours.

Once it was over the watch was reinstated, but they were all so tired no one really cared when they saw that each and every sentry had fallen asleep at their post. Exhausted beyond measure, everyone went into any tent still standing and instantly fell asleep. Even Simon found it difficult to stay awake long enough to change into dry clothes before crashing onto his cot.

The clouds dispersed completely by morning. One by one, those within the camp woke up and milled about as they performed their morning duties. Some lit fires to cook breakfast. Others gathered up and organized the supplies that had survived the storm and threw away those that had not. Others just kept sleeping. Those on watch woke up and carried on their duties as if they had been standing there vigilantly all night.

Most of the camp was breakfasting when the sentries

started shouting. Simon, who had just woken up, stumbled out of his tent in a daze. He made his way to the nearest point in the perimeter to ask what was happening when he saw the scene unfold before him.

Four riders were storming away from the camp as hard as their mounts—two rams and two horses—would go. There was no doubt in his mind. These were the viatari and dwarves they had been chasing for the past several days.

He watched in dismay as some of his men chased after the fleeing riders in vain. Some tried to shoot arrows, but they were too far away, and the arrows fell short.

"After them!" he yelled, but it was unnecessary. Already, a group of twenty men mounted on horseback were riding hard after the fleeing figures, who were already only dots in the distance. Their horses were lightly packed, and the men themselves lightly armored, so they could ride as fast as possible. It wasn't long before they too disappeared in the distance.

The rest of the camp packed hastily and struck tents, but there was no way they would catch up to the viatari like this. Simon sighed, knowing there was nothing he could do. An army this size just couldn't give chase to those fleeing on mounts. He would have to put his faith on the advance guard—the twenty men who had gone on ahead—to catch up to them and hold them long enough for the rest to join them.

They followed their quarry at the quickest pace they could, but even that was nothing to the speed with which the viatari rode. Days passed and Simon had nothing to show for his chase except sore feet. They had marched back and forth through the area, often returning to places they had already been as they followed the fleeing viatari, but to no avail. Simon hoped the advance party was having better luck.

"Sir," William said quietly to Simon on the third day of pursuit. The path they were following that day had been relatively straight. "If the trail continues like this much longer, we will enter the Forbidden Lands."

Simon scowled. He was sure it wouldn't be too difficult to convince everyone to follow him into the Forbidden Lands, but even he didn't know what they might face should they enter them and he didn't like facing the unknown. Still, if it had to be done. . . .

He called for a halt and turned to face his men.

"My friends," he said loudly, his voice carrying. "William has informed me that we will soon enter the Forbidden Lands if we continue to pursue our enemy."

Murmurs broke out among the men. He had no doubt they were recounting horror stories, planting even more fear and uncertainty into their own minds.

"I know the stories as well," he continued. "I would be lying to you if I told you I had no fear. But we must remember what these wretches constantly do to our towns, our people. They are a blight to this land. They terrorize us for their own amusement, and they must be eradicated. We cannot give up the chase just because evil beings have taken refuge in evil lands. We must fight our fear! Together, we are strong! Together, we will survive!"

The men forgot their previous doubts and fears and roared their approval. The sound was deafening. Simon hoped the viatari could hear it, wherever the blasted leeches were.

The march continued.

As the days passed, the land they marched on turned into

rolling hills. And as the trackers, always leading the host in their march, crested one of these hills, they stopped in surprise.

"Sir!"

Simon could hear muttering come from those behind him as they speculated what the trackers had found. He rode up to William on the hill and immediately his face fell.

Before him lay the advance guard. Dead. But not just dead, he noted, mutilated, ripped to pieces. This wasn't something the viatari had ever done. Even they weren't *that* savage. Whatever had struck down the advance guard, it was something else. Something truly evil.

"How recent?"

"Recent."

"Let's take a closer look before everyone else sees," Simon said, glancing back the way he'd come as his men began cresting the hill. Soon they too would witness the awful scene, and he knew they would want to turn back if they saw an example of what might happen to them should they continue their journey into the Forbidden Lands. He had to find a way to turn this situation to his favor.

He dismounted and knelt by one of the bodies. The corpse was a mess of ragged gashes. There were also several bite marks. Chunks of flesh were missing. Was the advance guard slain by a pack of wild beasts? And if so, what kind of beasts could have killed twenty men?

"Simon, . . ." William murmured warningly, inclining his head toward the army waiting on the hill.

They stood frozen in their tracks. A wave of fear rushed through the ranks as they saw the bloody mess. Simon realized he had to say something now if he wanted to keep order. What it was, he wasn't sure, but it had to be *something*.

His instincts took over.

"Everyone here who has fought the viatari before knows this is not their work."

There were nods from the host. Most had fought the viatari at least once before and all agreed that even they had more honor than this.

"So what could have caused this tragedy?" Simon asked, though he expected no answer back. "It was the dwarves who we saw in the company of the viatari. Those of you from my town, you saw their weapons, their armor. They are a savage race, no doubt. They must be the ones responsible for this outrage done to our brave brethren."

He could feel the anger rippling through the host.

"Will you let these brave men die in vain? Or will you continue onward with me to exact our revenge on these outsiders?"

Everyone lifted their weapons and, once again, roared their approval. Simon sighed in relief. His instincts had pulled through. He had managed to keep control over the host, but now he had to figure out what to do from here.

He sent William ahead over the next few hills to see if there was any sign of their quarry. He needed to know what might be waiting for them before deciding what they should do. But the head tracker still hadn't returned from what should have been a quick job. Wondering what could be keeping William so long, he rode out to join him, spotting him and his mount standing like a statue again on the crest of a steep rise. He sighed, exasperated, wondering what the problem could be this time.

"What is—Oh. . . ."

Before them was a huge crater that continued for as far as the eye could see. It was a wasteland as far as he saw, but the landscape didn't interest him. What interested him was the small group of figures moving within the crater toward the lone mountain at its center.

They had finally caught up to the odd group of viatari and dwarves. There were no more doubts. The path forward was clear. He would lead the host down into the crater. He would make one last attack. And he would finally kill the strangers who had dared set foot in his town.

CHAPTER TWENTY-ONE

Thuradin had never felt so saddle-sore in his entire life.

They had been riding for the past several days trying to lose the human riders closing in from behind. As they crested one of the many hills that rose out of the land like small, rounded stalagmites, he glanced back. Only a few miles behind them, he could see their pursuers' dust cloud. They were close enough now that he could hear their mounts as they galloped across the land.

He was surprised and impressed by their determination. Victria had led them for many days, back and forth in a zigzag pattern, and their pursuers had followed every step, their mounts showing no signs of slowing down. He felt his ram shudder under him as it fought the urge to collapse. Because of this chase, there had been little opportunity to rest. Thuradin could only hope their pursuers were just as tired.

As he urged his ram to keep up with his companions, he thought back to when they had escaped the mountains, wondering if there was anything they could have done to avoid this costly chase.

Victria had woken everyone up before the sun had even

risen. After eating what Stürn sarcastically called "a wonderfully delicious and hearty" breakfast of cold rations, they had left the safety of the cave. Since there hadn't been a watch that night, no one had been awake to witness the storm, but they immediately knew it had been devastating.

Many of the paths they had taken the other day to reach the cave were buried under piles of rock. This meant the only way off the mountain was to climb down.

They made their way slowly and carefully. They had to reach the ground without announcing their presence to the humans below, and none of them wanted to be the cause of another rock slide.

As they descended, they passed several dead humans. Many had been crushed by falling boulders. A couple were face down in large puddles of water, their bodies bloated. Thuradin counted five total by the time they reached their mounts, but he was sure there were others he had missed.

The climb down took longer than expected. By the time they were mounted, the sun was already casting a gentle morning glow over the stirring camp.

"Looks like they will notice our departure," Victria said. She turned to Dragos and the dwarves. "We will ride hard and fast straight to Inadarim. There will be very few breaks if we are pursued, so I suggest you lighten up the loads on your mounts as much as you can."

They discarded their bedrolls, miscellaneous items, and, much to the dwarves' dismay, the kegs of ale, along with several scraps of metal and leather they had used to repair their armor and anything else that could weigh them down before they charged out into the open. The camp's sentries spotted them immediately and wasted no time in sounding the alarm.

Thuradin followed Victria's lead as she rode around the camp's perimeter. A few arrows flew past them, but most fell short. The sentries were still a fair distance away, so chances of being hit by one of their missiles were slim. To his right, however, he saw a group of mounted humans setting out to give chase. All with bows slung over their shoulders.

He grimaced. If they caught up to them things would not end well. He could already imagine the whistling of arrows flying past him, just missing him. His back suddenly felt bare, as if he were shirtless, and his skin tingled in anticipation of being pierced by sharp arrowheads.

Victria broke off from her orbit around the camp and began riding south. Her three companions followed her lead, and soon the camp disappeared from sight, but they could still see a dust cloud as their human pursuers followed.

Now, days later, they were still on the run.

"We're nearly there," Victria shouted encouragingly. "Just beyond this next slope is the crater."

As they prepared to spur their mounts for one last push over the hill, they stopped suddenly and pricked their ears. The viatari and dwarves tried to get them to move, but no matter how hard they tried, they refused to obey. Thuradin was about to ask what was going on when he heard a clashing noise coming from far behind him. The others heard it as well and froze.

It was the sound of battle.

Somewhere behind them came the sound of weapons being drawn, hissing, howling, growling, yelling, and many other visceral sounds Thuradin couldn't describe. The worst were those horrific screams that were cut far too short. He didn't know what exactly was happening, but it sounded like their pursuers were under attack. He looked at Victria.

"Darimun," she said nervously. "And it sounds like a lot of them. We should go—"

But before she could finish her sentence a sharp, piercing bird call came from a nearby clump of trees to their right. Victria and Dragos sat up straight upon hearing it. Whatever the call was, they recognized it. Victria cupped her hands to her mouth and responded with a high-pitched, animalistic cry that sounded to Thuradin like the noise rams made when they were strangled to death.

The dwarf waited to see what would happen next and was surprised when Felix and the others emerged from the nearby trees. There were embraces and smiles as everyone saw that they had survived their time apart. Upon seeing Murtosh, Stürn immediately began wording healing chants. Soon his infected gash was nothing more than a small scar.

"It's good to see that everyone is safe," Victria said. "But we're being followed by an entire army of humans, and they're probably not too far behind. We need to move on as soon as possible."

Felix shook his head. "Before we continue, you should have some time to rest and eat. I imagine it has not been an easy time for you four."

"Nae that we've had it any better," Ayrie muttered.

"But the humans—"

"Aye," Borim interrupted. "We saw them the night after our two groups split—"

"Then you should know we cannot fight against them and survive," Victria said, unable to comprehend why everyone was so calm. "Which is why we should leave now, before the gap between us gets any smaller!"

"Victria," Tessa's voice was firm as she stared deep into her eyes. "Calm down. I watched everything from the trees. The humans are still several hours away. Their main force was much farther behind that of the smaller group chasing you."

"*Those* humans almost caught you," Natiari added as she led their exhausted mounts to the wooded area they had been hiding in. "If it hadn't been for that huge pack of darimun running into them, we'd probably be fighting them right now instead of having this lovely reunion."

"The point is," Felix said before anyone else could chime in. "We have plenty of time for you to rest."

Thuradin watched Victria's eyes shift from one person to the next as she thought about whether she should continue arguing. After a few seconds, the tension left her shoulders and she slumped to the ground, exhausted. Felix nodded knowingly.

"Threnn, if you are not too busy, could you get a fire going?"

"Already on it."

Within minutes everyone was back among the trees, around a large fire enjoying large helpings of a hot stew Borim had cooked with his own personal ingredients. Thuradin wondered if they shouldn't be worried about the darimun that had killed their pursuers, but based on Felix's easy demeanor, he figured there was no point in worrying. They told stories of what happened to them while they were separated.

As Victria recounted their own adventure, Stürn chimed in every now and then, reminding everyone about the hot meal they never had because of Dragos. But as the story went on, Thuradin noticed Victria left out the part where she'd had to comfort him from his own insecurities. He was grateful for that. He didn't want his dwarves to know about what he saw as his moment of weakness.

Finally, after a few hours had been spent resting and recovering, it was time for them to move on.

"The final leg of our task is here," Felix said. "Once we enter the crater, we will be in constant danger of being attacked by darimun, so be on guard. We will travel on foot. I think that will make it easier for us to keep a minimal presence."

Everyone nodded.

The mounts were moved deeper into the clump of trees they had been hiding in for the past several days. They decided to leave their provisions. If everything went according to plan, they wouldn't have to stay in the cursed crater for too long.

The climb down was easier than Thuradin had expected. There were plenty of footholds and handholds to grab onto, and even though the sky was filled with ominously dark clouds, there was no rain. Not even a gust of wind dared enter the Creature's domain.

Thuradin had seen what the crater looked like from the rim, and he immediately disliked it. But now that he was inside it, his dislike grew. The ground was littered with white, petrified branches from long-forgotten, long-dead trees that cracked under his plated boots like bones. Cracks ran along the stumps, which were all that remained of them, forming faces of agony and despair. Termites crawled out of those gaps.

As they walked on, random stones began to jut out of the ground. Thuradin found it strange that they were all similarly shaped and sized. They were smoothed out ovals and seemed to spread across the landscape in no particular order. They were like tombstones. As he came to inspect one, he made out faint lines and broken features as if someone had taken a chisel and sculpted every stone here to look like. . . .

"By Nythirim. . . ."

He walked over to the next stone and examined it as well to see if his realization was correct. He looked at every line and every crevice. He checked every inch of the gray stone, hoping he was wrong, but he still came to the same conclusion: these were entombed dwarves.

Their features were so weathered from erosion they were hardly recognizable anymore, but a thick nose here and a beard there were enough to confirm their identities. *This* was the reason why he had insisted Agrethar be entombed in a cave, so that he would never weather away like this, unrecognizable.

"That's nae—" Borim started to say.

"It is," Thuradin replied.

"Then that means they're all—"

Thuradin nodded grimly.

He looked around. Hundreds. Thousands of smooth boulders jutted out of the earth. All with the same weathered features. All dwarves. He looked at the viatari. They, minus Dragos, looked around sadly, as if this part of the crater were bringing back terrible memories.

"I feel that I must apologize," Felix said. "This is the place where we battled the Creature's forces a millennium ago. Many dwarves died here as well as viatari. I cannot say I understand how it must feel to see your kind in this eroded state since our dead have long since turned to dust. However, if anything, know what these dwarves died for. An end to the Creature's reign. Let that give you the resolve you need to defeat this monster once and for all."

Thuradin looked at his companions. They all nodded. They would help defeat the Creature, not just so they could continue with their quest to find Ronorim but to avenge all those dwarves entombed here.

They continued their trek to the central mountain. Flashes of purple light danced around it and now shot into the sky more frequently than ever. At one point, Victria stopped suddenly and stared at a single, irregular cluster of eroded dwarves.

"Victria—" Felix began to say, but she ignored him. She walked in a trance toward the cluster and knelt, reaching for the first of the oval stones. She placed her hand on its side and bowed her head. Words in her own language floated out from her lips. They were foreign to Thuradin, but he felt like he knew what was being said.

It suddenly dawned on him that this particular set of entombed dwarves must be the ones she had led in that final battle against the Creature so long ago. Their remains were completely rounded off by the elements of the past thousand years—no clear features existed. Though the memories of her failure in the past would stay with her for the rest of her long life, it was clear the consequences from it would disappear with a few more centuries of wind and rain. He could only imagine the enormous guilt she felt.

Thuradin didn't know how long she knelt there, but by the time she got up, the clouds were much darker. The sun was already setting. They walked on in silence. Even in the darkness, he noticed her normally sharp, red eyes were puffy; she had been crying.

The dwarves, except for Thuradin, had no idea what had just happened, but they knew enough to keep quiet about it.

Thuradin sympathized with the viatari. He understood her pain and admired her for pushing through it. To have confronted her dark past, her failures—he wondered if he would have the courage to do that.

The central mountain cast its shadow over them as they moved along its base. It hadn't looked large when Thuradin saw it from the crater's rim, but now it towered over them—though it was still much smaller than any of the Silent Mountains.

"I thought ye said we would be in greater danger of being attacked by darimun once we entered the crater," Murtosh said, sounding somewhat disappointed as they made their way up the mountain's path, "but I haven't seen a single one since we were attacked by those two snake beasties days ago."

"This is probably why," Natiari said, beckoning for everyone to join her near the edge of the path. From their vantage point, they could see the entirety of the area they had come from. It didn't take long for Thuradin to see what Natiari had noticed.

The humans had followed them into the crater and now stood in a battle line as they faced off against a small force of darimun.

"The perfect distraction," Tessa mused.

"Indeed," Felix agreed. "It looks like the humans' hunt for us worked in our favor in the end. Not only do they give us a needed distraction, but our enemies can destroy each other while we continue with our task."

"Think again," Victria pointed to the two armies. They had already begun fighting, and the darimun were tearing through the humans' lines. Some darimun would be killed here and there, but for every one killed, twenty men went with it.

"They won't last long. We need to use the time they gave us wisely so we can reach the Creature's artifact before the darimun realize where the real threat is."

They picked up their pace as they climbed the mountain path, which became steeper and narrower the higher they went. Soon they were forced into a single file. The dwarves were used to hiking up mountains, but even they began to pant and sweat and grow tired.

"I've been meaning ta ask ye this for a while, Felix," Thuradin said as they huffed up the path. "But what exactly do we do once we reach the artifact? How do we defeat the Creature?"

Felix was silent for several minutes. Thuradin was about to ask again, thinking he hadn't heard the question, when the viatari finally spoke.

"I do not know, exactly. I am sure we will discover the answer when the time is right."

Thuradin was sure he had heard wrong, but one glance at his companions and he knew that was not the case.

"Ye don't know?" he repeated incredulously. "Ye forced us inta this damned quest ta defeat this Creature and ye don't even—"

Something large tackled Thuradin and threw him over the edge of the mountain. He felt himself fall for a little bit before landing hard on his back. His armor absorbed most of the damage, but the impact was still enough to knock the breath out of his lungs. He lifted himself shakily and saw he had been knocked down to a small ledge jutting out of the mountain. If it hadn't been there, he was sure he would have fallen to his death.

He checked to see if anything was broken, and when

everything seemed to be working properly, he climbed back up. He heard fighting above him, as well as bestial growls. As soon as he lifted himself back onto the path, he took stock of his surroundings.

He found himself in the middle of a battle. He saw his companions fending off several feline-like darimun. The darimun had the trademark purple haze about them as well as the glowing yellow eyes the viatari had told him about, and their look was so vicious, it made Thuradin's blood freeze. He shook off his fear, remembering what Victria had told him in the woods. With his twin axes gripped tightly in his hands, he charged.

The darimun lashed out with their savage claws and fangs. They were agile and strong, dodging the dwarves' heavy attacks with ease.

Thuradin quickly grew frustrated. He hadn't been able to land a single direct hit on the darim he was fighting. The darim, however, had managed to rip through his legs with ease, despite his thick plate armor. If it hadn't been for Stürr's quick healing, he would have been easy prey for the darim to finish off.

His foe circled for another attack when Felix came out of nowhere and mounted its back like a horse. The darim snarled and tried to shake him off.

"Go," he grunted. "These darimun must be some sort of guard, otherwise they'd be fighting the humans right now. We'll handle them. You take your dwarves and get to the artifact. Your kind are the only ones who can stop it—do whatever you can!"

Felix looked like he wanted to say more, but at that moment the darim ran off with him still on its back.

Thuradin called for his dwarves to disengage and to

follow him up the path. They weaved their way through the melee. Several darimun tried to pounce on them, but the viatari managed to intercept their attacks every time. Legs pumping, they broke through the last lines of combat and ran up the path, not caring that they were tired and short of breath. Adrenaline was their fuel now, and they had plenty of it.

The path wound back and forth across the mountain, and soon the dwarves were disoriented. The air grew thinner the higher they climbed. The sky grew darker. Thuradin knew they had to be near the mountain's peak by now.

"Draw yer weapons," he said. "I don't know what we'll be facing, but I know that it won't be friendly."

They continued rounding corners, expecting to meet a pack of darimun or the artifact, but they were disappointed each time. Finally, completely out of breath, Thuradin decided they had to have a quick rest. The others agreed readily and sank to the ground, exhausted.

"Stürn," Thuradin said, the thought coming to him suddenly as he saw how tired everyone was. "Will ye be able ta heal us all?"

Stürn turned his blood-smeared face to Thuradin. "Aye, commander. I'm tired, but I can still heal just fine. Just try nae ta die in one hit."

Everyone grinned.

"Well then," Thuradin said as he stood up. "Let's get this over with. The sooner we finish, the sooner we can find our King and go home."

They all nodded and continued their way up the path. After rounding a few more corners, they found themselves standing in a rocky clearing. The path ended. They were on the mountain's peak.

Ahead of them, alone in the center of the clearing, sat a large, rectangular chest made of bronze. There were undecipherable inscriptions, engravings, and designs all over the sides. He thought they looked like pictographs, similar to the murals within the Dwarven Kingdom that depicted their own histories; but what the pictographs were meant to represent, he had no idea. They were alien, as far as he was concerned. The lid slanted upward like a pyramid with its point cut off. He estimated the chest itself could fit three dwarves comfortably.

The purple lights they had seen dancing around the mountain leaked out of the bronze chest and surrounded it, despite the lid being closed. Many beautiful jewels, cut into ovals and diamonds and squares and all manner of shapes and sizes which the dwarves had never seen before lined the box in a repeating pattern of purple, black, and yellow. But despite its beautiful appearance, an oppressive aura emanated from the chest and reached out to the dwarves. It was an evil presence. It encouraged them to turn on each other and offered the world to whoever was left standing. It encouraged them to jump off the edge of the mountain and promised they would survive. It promised lies.

Thuradin could see some of his fellows shake their heads hard, as if they couldn't believe they could think such terrible thoughts. There was no doubt in Thuradin's mind. This was the artifact—there was nothing else it could be. And inside dwelled the Creature they had to defeat.

CHAPTER TWENTY-TWO

The purple light leaking out of the artifact took the form of thick, transparent tendrils. They twirled around in the air as if grasping for something, anything that it could then squeeze the life out of. The dwarves stood back uneasily, unsure of what to do. Every time a tendril passed by them, the ominous feeling that had tried to tempt them before intensified.

"What should we do?" Borim asked.

In answer, Murtosh hefted his giant, two-handed warhammer and charged the artifact. He lifted his weapon up high, leaped into the air, and brought it crashing down. There was a loud *smack!* and a small flash of purple as the hammer made contact, but no sign of damage to the artifact. Instead, cracks formed and spread along the face of Murtosh's hammer.

"That's nae possible, . . ." he said in disbelief. "This hammer is made of reinforced steel and crystal. It's supposed ta be unbreakable."

Threnn walked up to Murtosh with his own two-handed weapon—a large, double-bladed axe—in hand.

"Perhaps if we do it together?"

Murtosh looked at him blankly at first. Then, slowly, the

light came back into his eyes and a smile crept onto his face as he nodded in agreement.

The two dwarves moved to opposite ends of the artifact. They lifted their weapons high and brought them down in unison. There was the same, loud *smack!*, the same flashes of light, yet still no visible damage. They didn't stop, though. They continued striking the artifact, the cracks on their weapons spreading with each strike.

After the tenth attempt, their weapons shattered. Shards of steel and crystal scattered across the rocky clearing. The two dwarves gawked at what little remained in their hands and slowly backed away from the pristine chest before them.

"Impossible," Murtosh said.

"Impossible," Threnn agreed.

"Well, that obviously won't work!" Ayrie said angrily. "So what are we going ta do?"

Thuradin didn't have a clue. He wished Felix or Victria were here right now; surely they could figure something out. But no sooner had he wished this than he heard hurried footsteps and heavy breathing from behind. He turned and saw Dragos round the last corner into the clearing.

"You need to lift the lid," the viatari said as he tried to catch his breath.

"What are ye doing here?" Thuradin asked, hoping he wasn't the only one who would be rounding the corner. "Shouldn't ye be back with the others?"

"I escaped," Dragos said. "Felix said he wasn't able to tell you all the information he had and that he needed one of us to join you to give you guidance. I saw a chance to slip out of the fighting and took it. Now I'm here to tell you that attacking the artifact will do nothing. You must lure the Creature out by lifting the lid if we are to destroy him."

Thuradin glared suspiciously at Dragos. What the young viatari was saying might have some merit, but was there something he was holding back? He remembered what Victria told him of herself when she used to use dwarves for her own purposes, not caring if they were injured or killed in the process. Felix had mentioned in Aleganthia how the Creature had lashed out at the viatari when they had returned to close the lid; could something similar happen to his dwarves for opening it?

"Well, Thuradin?" Ayrie said. "Are we going ta do what he says or nae?"

Thuradin didn't like it, but he had no other ideas. He couldn't think of any other way they might try to destroy the Creature, and he couldn't just sit there for hours waiting for the others to join them. He had to trust that Dragos knew what he was talking about.

"Do it."

Murtosh and Threnn moved cautiously toward the artifact. Purple tendrils passed through them harmlessly—they seemed unable to make physical contact with objects—and continued to twirl in the air. The two dwarves reached out to grip the lid hesitantly, as if they feared something might pop out and attack them.

"Stop!"

Thuradin turned again and saw Victria round the corner into the clearing. She was panting hard, and her legs shook as she struggled to remain standing. Thuradin saw a few gashes on her body, but other than that, she appeared to have left the battle relatively unscathed.

"Do *not* open that lid."

Threnn and Murtosh tried to step away from the artifact, but they couldn't let go. It was as if their hands had been glued to the metal. They struggled desperately, trying to free themselves from the trap, their eyes wide and angry with betrayal.

"Don't listen to her!" Dragos said, a touch of madness entering his voice. "We must open the artifact if we are to destroy the Creature!"

"What are you doing?" Victria demanded, pushing Dragos so that he faced her. "You know what that will do to them."

"Yes, but I also know it's necessary. And these dwarves are expendable," the young viatari spat. "Their sole purpose in this task is to open the artifact just as their foolish King did a thousand years ago so that we, the viatari, can enter the Creature's lair and defeat him."

Thuradin balled his hands into fists. He shook with rage as he listened to Dragos. Threnn and Murtosh were now in danger, and it didn't look like there was anything he could do to help them. He glanced in their direction and saw them still struggling to free their hands. Their faces were grim but determined. He looked to his right and saw Stürn muttering chants in an attempt to use the life-energies around them to help the two trapped dwarves. However, despite their best efforts, he had a feeling it would all be for naught.

Dragos pushed Victria to the side as he made his way closer to the two struggling dwarves. She looked as shocked and furious as Thuradin felt. As he came within feet of Threnn and Murtosh, Dragos addressed them one last time.

"Open it."

Threnn and Murtosh groaned and howled as they tried to fight it, but their will was not their own anymore. Their arms shuddered as they lifted the heavy lid. With one great heave, it slid off the artifact and fell with a loud *clang!*

For a few seconds nothing happened. Thuradin watched

anxiously, wondering if Threnn and Murtosh would drop dead or, worse, transform into some abomination that served the Creature, but they seemed to be fine. Their hands were no longer stuck to the artifact's lid, and their will seemed to be their own again. They glanced at each other in surprise and grinned.

And then everything went wrong.

A small orb of purple light floated out of the artifact. Threnn pointed at it curiously, his lips forming the words needed to ask what it was, when it exploded.

Thuradin, Victria, Dragos, and the other dwarves were all still a fair distance away. The blast's shock wave only sent them flying back a few feet. Threnn and Murtosh, however, were not so fortunate. The two dwarves were thrown back in opposite directions at fatal speeds.

Threnn crashed into several large boulders, shattering them all into a million pieces, before he skidded to a stop. Murtosh was thrown completely off the mountain. His arms flailed frantically as gravity took him.

Stürn was the first to recover from the shock. He lifted himself up quickly, planted his hands into the earth, and immediately began chanting in Ancient Dwarvish. The Enurg'en was directing all his efforts into healing Threnn, but Thuradin knew it would be no good. The young dwarf wasn't moving at all. He could see the body already turning to stone.

"I can't heal him fast enough," Stürn said. Frustrated tears crawled down his dirty face as he realized his powers were useless. "His life-energies are disappearing faster than I can command them."

Thuradin put his hand on the Enurg'en's shoulder. "And Murtosh?"

"I cannae sense him," he replied miserably. "He must have fallen all the way ta the bottom."

Thuradin felt numb. Two more of his companions, both Bronn's apprentices, were now dead.

Bronn.

What would the old dwarf think when he told him not only had he failed to protect his heir, but that all three of his apprentices had fallen?

To make matters worse, Threnn and Murtosh had died outside, and there was no way he could move their bodies to a cave before they were entombed. Their bodies would erode away into nothingness, just like all the dwarves in the crater below them. They hadn't deserved that fate.

He gripped his twin axes and turned to face their killer.

Dragos laughed. "It was all for the greater good, dwarf," he said. "Look, the way into the Creature's lair is open."

It was true. The artifact no longer had tendrils swinging around in the air. Instead, the inside emitted a soft purple glow, as if inviting them to enter. Flashes of light continued to flicker inside and around the artifact's mouth, but they no longer shot dramatically into the sky.

Thuradin didn't care. All he wanted to do now was avenge the dwarves he had let down. He lifted his two weapons and prepared to attack, knowing he had no chance in defeating a viatari on his own.

Dragos laughed again. "You know you are no match against me. My strength far exceeds yours. But if you insist, dwarf, I will grant your wish to join your dead compan—"

As quick as lightning, Dragos was sent flying into the nearest boulder. Thuradin stood frozen, still trying to process what had happened. Victria had come from nowhere and tackled the younger viatari so hard, the dwarf was surprised his body hadn't snapped in half. Now she stood in front of him, her fangs bared furiously at Dragos, ready to rip him to shreds. He had never seen such a frightening visage.

"You," she growled as Dragos stood up and dusted himself off. "How can you be so arrogant? How could you repeat my mistakes after *everything* I did to keep you from doing so? Everything I told you. You are a disgrace to the viatari."

Dragos smirked. "Your obsession with these dwarves is what's a disgrace. They're beneath us. I remember learning about your past from Felix when I asked him about our war with the Creature, and I admired the you of then. You were the only one who realized our superiority over these *things*."

He waved his hand dismissively in the direction of the dwarves, all of whom drew their weapons and looked ready to help tear Dragos apart. "Now, it seems I must bear the weight of this realization alone. I will prove that we don't need their help or help from anyone else. I, alone, will defeat the Creature and save our people."

"You've done nothing but bring shame to our people," Victria seethed, her jaw clenching, "and we will not tolerate your reckless behavior any longer." She drew her blade and settled into a fighting position.

Dragos raised an eyebrow and chuckled. "Do you intend to fight me in that condition? You can barely stand."

He was right, Thuradin realized. Victria had been able to tackle Dragos before because she'd had surprise on her side and anger to fuel her. Now, as more time had passed, her body remembered how exhausted it truly was. She wouldn't last long in another fight after dealing with the darimun. Dragos, on the other hand, looked much better, with hardly a scratch on him. Thuradin wondered if he had even fought when the darimun attacked them on the mountain path.

The dirk was knocked out of Victria's hand and clattered on the ground as Dragos suddenly dashed through her defenses and disarmed her. Victria dodged the following attack but couldn't avoid the one after. His knee slammed into her head and sent her reeling. He tried to finish with a high kick to the back of the head, but she managed to roll away at the last minute, giving herself a small moment of respite.

Victria had no chance of defeating Dragos alone, Thuradin knew. She needed help. And he would gladly give it.

"No," she held out a hand as he started to move in for his own attack. "I will deal with him. He is my responsibility."

Thuradin hesitated. He wanted to join the fight, but the way she sounded right now made him think she might attack him too if he tried to interfere. Slowly, he stepped back next to Stürn, who knelt on the ground with his eyes closed and his fingers just barely brushing the earth, no doubt trying to send some energy to Victria as inconspicuously as he could.

The two viatari charged each other so fast Thuradin could barely follow it. They moved faster than the wind, jumping from one place to another and then to another in a matter of seconds, all the while grappling with each other or throwing punches and kicks with incredible strength.

They were blurs to the dwarves' eyes, but even they could see that one of those blurs was slowing down in its movements. Victria's body had reached its limit. She tried to kick Dragos' legs out from under him but he jumped to avoid it and dropped down hard onto her outstretched leg. The loud snapping of bones was only drowned out by Victria's scream. Thuradin heard Stürn's muttering increase in pace as he intensified his healing.

Dragos stood over Victria for a few seconds, disappointment clouding his eyes, and Thuradin feared he might deal a killing blow. But he did not. Instead, he turned away, shaking his head, and walked toward the open artifact, only stopping once he was close enough to touch it.

"What—are you doing?" Victria croaked out the words, grimacing in pain.

"Ending this," Dragos said without turning around. The younger viatari slid his hand along the side of the artifact, as if admiring it. And after one last wicked grin to the dwarves, he jumped inside.

The moment Dragos was gone, Thuradin and Stürn rushed to Victria and knelt by her side. Stürn dug his hands deep into the earth and chanted without restraint. The viatari groaned as Stürn's healing and her own regenerative abilities fixed her shattered leg and the several bruises darkening her skin.

"I'm so sorry," she said miserably, avoiding the dwarves' eyes.

Thuradin could tell she was in shock. "It wasn't yer fault; ye had no control over what path he chose ta take."

"But it *is* my fault," she said softly. "He was exactly as I used to be. I should have done more to turn him from that dark path. If I had tried harder—but I thought it was just his youth that kept him this way—six hundred years is still quite young for a viatari, you know. I chose to ignore the warning signs. I should have *seen* it. Now two more dwarves lie dead because of me."

Thuradin put his hand on her shoulder comfortingly. Her tear-ridden eyes looked into his, fearful of any anger or resentment they might find. He smiled reassuringly, something he had never felt the need to do with her before. "I'll see ta it that they didn't die in vain."

Victria took several deep breaths as she tried to block out the pain and hold back her emotions while nodding her understanding.

"Be careful. Even I don't know what will happen or what you may encounter."

"Aye," Thuradin said. "I'll just have ta believe in my own abilities, won't I?"

The briefest smile flickered across Victria's face. With a gentle touch, Stürn nudged Thuradin to the side so he could begin performing direct healing on the viatari.

Without mentioning anything to his fellow dwarves, Thuradin made his way to the artifact. Ayrie and Borim knelt mournfully over Threnn's entombed body and didn't notice their commander's disappearance. Stürn, too, was too occupied with healing to notice anything else. Only Victria watched as he climbed over the artifact's side and dove headfirst into the soft purple glow.

Thuradin opened his eyes and saw nothing but darkness. He raised his hand to his face to see if he could at least see an outline of it. He could not.

It felt like he was floating. His feet weren't firmly placed on any sort of ground; they just hung there. He couldn't tell if he was moving or still. He wondered if perhaps this was how he was to live the rest of his life when he spotted a small, dull purple light in the distance. Not knowing what else to do, he tried to move toward it.

He didn't know how he moved—it certainly wasn't by walking—but he found that all he had to do was will himself toward the light and he would move. He noticed the closer he was to it, the more his senses were restored. He started to hear small, indistinct voices whispering through the darkness around him, but he couldn't see where they came from. The stench of death surrounded him, as if he were floating above a sea of corpses.

As he drew even closer, the light grew in size until it was larger than anything he had ever seen. It towered over him. It dwarfed whole mountain ranges. Eventually, the light was the only thing Thuradin could see, so large had it become.

He stopped moving forward.

Before him, he saw the silhouette of someone, though he couldn't tell how far in front of him it was. He couldn't make out any details of the silhouette, but he could hear voices. It sounded to him like whoever this silhouette was, was communicating with the large orb of light like it was a sentient being.

Straining his ears to hear what was being said, he thought the voice of the silhouette sounded familiar. However, no sooner had he focused on certain features of it than it burst into flame. His mouth opened in horror. Screams of pain and terror battered his ears as the silhouette burned to ashes.

Something tugged at Thuradin and pulled him closer to the orb. No matter how hard he tried to resist, he couldn't escape the grip of whatever had him, and soon he was what felt like only inches away from it.

Hmm, a voice said inside his head. *So, the accursed dwarves have reemerged from their holes.*

The voice was deep and ancient. Thuradin shivered as he felt the hairs on the back of his neck shoot up, but he kept himself from succumbing to fear. He had to keep his wits if he wanted to have any chance of surviving.

"Who are ye?"

Can you not guess?

Thuradin gulped. He had hoped he was wrong, but the way the voice had asked the question confirmed his suspicions. There was nothing else this orb *could* be.

"Yer the Creature?"

And you are Thuradin Stonebeard, commander of the royal guard, bearer of the saphyrium helm. Now that formalities are out of the way, I want you to give me a reason why I should not kill you now as I killed your viatari friend just a moment ago.

"That was Dragos?" Thuradin asked, shocked for a moment. Then, he remembered what had just happened outside of the artifact, and he no longer cared about the fate of the silhouette.

"Dragos was no friend ta the dwarves," he said through gritted teeth. "And yer the one who will be killed today. Ye'll no longer threaten our world."

Oh? I am the threat? That is rich.

Thuradin heard the Creature chuckle in his mind. It wasn't a pleasant sound.

"Why do ye laugh?"

Foolish dwarf, the Creature's voice turned hard. *Your race, the viatari, even the humans, they are the threats to this world. I only try to rid it of your taint, to eradicate it of your evil.*

"That's a lie," Thuradin said. "All ye've done is send yer darimun ta attack the viatari ta exterminate them, as ye've done before, and after them, ye would attack my home and my people, all without any provocation."

You know not of that which you speak.

"Of course I know. The viatari told me everything!"

The Creature chuckled again. *Listen well, then, little*

dwarf. *The viatari, as well as the humans, are guilty of evil. The viatari wish to wipe humans from the face of this world while humans wish to do the same to the viatari. If either got their way, the result would be genocide. I cannot allow such evil to exist. Your race is guilty of this as well, so you, too, must be eradicated.*

"The dwarves have never willed the extinction of another race," Thuradin said proudly. "Ye are wrong ta accuse us."

Am I?

Inside his mind, Thuradin saw images of burrowers being slaughtered, but these were different from any he had ever fought before. These had families and were unarmed. They lived in a community—a city. They had their own government, their own language and writing system. They were civilized.

"These are nae the burrowers we fight," he said, shaking his head. "The ones we fight are savages. They constantly attack us ta quench their uncontrollable thirst for blood. They're animals."

What makes you think of them as animals, as savages? Because you've only met them on the battlefield? Because they're different from you? You have not seen how they truly live. However, I have. . . .

The Creature's voice grew dangerously loud inside the dwarf's head. *I have seen how they live. I have seen how they suffer under the persecution of your people. Your race would commit genocide upon them, and they know it. That is why they fight you so fiercely. They fight for their own survival.*

Thuradin was speechless. He, like most dwarves, had never thought of burrowers as anything but animals. Now the Creature was telling him they were actually a civilized race like his own. He didn't know what to think. If what the Creature said was true, then his race was indeed guilty of genocide, but how could he trust the Creature's word? He was the enemy. The dwarf had already experienced his evil and deceitful aura when he was outside the artifact. He was lying; he had to be. Surely. . . .

Now, puny dwarf, the Creature continued. *You may believe me or not, it does not matter. At present, we have come to a crossroads. I could kill you now as I killed that arrogant viatari and the other dwarves foolish enough to enter my realm one thousand years ago. But I have an idea that can both spare your pathetic life and entertain me at the same time.*

Thuradin didn't respond. He didn't like the options the Creature was presenting but knew he had no say in the matter. His fate hung on the whim of the giant orb in front of him.

I will return to my dormant state. Your viatari friends— the Creature said it like the idea of the viatari being friendly amused him, *—will believe you have ended me. You will be allowed to continue your foolish quest to find your genocidal King.*

But I will curse you. You will find your beloved King, yes, but you will be seen as a traitor by your own kind. You will realize what I say about the burrowers is true, and you will try to wash away your guilt by bringing peace between your two races, but your guilt will only increase the more you try to right what is wrong. You will never find peace within those mountains you call home. By the end of this, you will wish I had decided to kill you instead.

Thuradin stared blankly at the orb in front of him. Both options were grim and he would have preferred to not pick either one. But he had no power here; there was no way he could kill this being by himself like this. Dying now would accomplish absolutely nothing. It would be better to risk the curse. This way, he could try to find a way to break it before the Creature's prophecy came to pass.

"I choose ta be cursed," he said, trying to sound braver than he felt.

An amusing choice. Very well. But know this: though I shall be dormant, I will still watch your every move during every moment of your journey. Be sure to entertain me, or I shall be sure to reawaken and finish what I started. Do not think you can escape my curse so easily.

And with that, Thuradin was sent away from the Creature's presence. The orb shrank in size as the dwarf sped away through the darkness until it was only a small, purple pinpoint of light. There was a rushing movement below him, and he felt himself move upward.

A new light became visible. Unlike the Creature's, this one felt warm and safe. It was an exit, a means of escaping this terrible place where the Creature dwelled. Thuradin tried to will whatever was propelling him to move him faster, but nothing happened. Instead, he slowed down until he was floating in place again. The exit was tantalizingly close, but no matter how hard he tried, he couldn't reach it.

Do not forget, the Creature's voice rang in his head one last time. *I am always watching.*

Thuradin shot straight up into the light and was free at last from the Creature's clutches.

CHAPTER TWENTY-THREE

Thuradin didn't know how long he was inside the artifact, but he distinctly remembered it being afternoon when he had entered. Now it was night, and though the moon was partially covered by the clouds above, its light still managed to bring a soft, white glow over the landscape.

As he stepped out of the artifact, he noticed the rest of the viatari now stood in the rocky clearing. They spoke in hushed tones and glanced sadly at Threnn's unmoving body, which was still surrounded by the other mourning dwarves.

Victria was the first to notice Thuradin's return. Her eyes widened as if she saw a ghost.

"Almost twelve hours," she said as she made her way to him. "What happened in there?"

Dragos? her eyes seemed to ask.

Thuradin shook his head quickly and Victria nodded, though her lower lip trembled slightly. He looked back at the artifact. It no longer glowed with a purplish light. Everything about it seemed less magnificent: the gems, the metal, everything. It was now just a dull, empty shell. And as he thought that the Creature had truly come to an end, he remembered the curse and the promise the giant orb had made to him.

I am always watching.

After settling down and satisfying his hunger with a stale chunk of bread and some dried meat, he told everyone what had happened. The viatari listened apprehensively, and even the dwarves left Threnn's side momentarily to listen as he explained everything from what the Creature looked like to the helplessness he felt as he floated within the artifact just inches away from the exit.

He even spoke of Dragos' terrible, though well-deserved, demise. The only part he left out was the curse. He gave no hint that he had been utterly helpless in the Creature's lair. Instead, he told a story of a mental battle between himself and the Creature which resulted in the Creature's ultimate defeat. He didn't know why he left out the curse. He could have asked for help, but he felt that he should figure out a way to thwart it on his own. The less people involved, the better. He didn't want them to share in his misfortunes should he fail.

By the end of the story, relief washed over everyone's face. The Creature was finally defeated, and as far as they knew, never to return. The quest was over.

Thuradin felt guilty letting them believe the Creature was gone forever; after all, if he failed to "entertain" him, he had promised to return and finish what he had started. He didn't know what else to tell them, though. His only option was to find a way to escape the curse while entertaining the Creature at the same time.

"What happened while I was gone?" he asked, desperate to find something to distract his mind. He didn't want to think about the Creature or the curse anymore. It would drive him to insanity.

Felix told the story.

After Dragos and Victria had escaped the battle, he, Natiari, and Tessa had continued to fight until all the darimun were slain. They had run along the mountain path as fast as they could but were too late. They entered the scene to find Victria healed but still in a mental state of shock and all the remaining dwarves, minus Thuradin, kneeling around Threnn's stone body.

They had decided to wait and see if Thuradin would return from the artifact. During this time, Tessa had gone to check on the humans to see how they were faring down in the crater below. Natiari had gone, on the insistence of Victria, to search for Murtosh's body near the base of the mountain.

Tessa came back with good news. The humans had been devastated by the darimun. Very few had survived. The darimun were also gone. As far as she could tell, there wasn't a single shred of evidence that they had even existed. It was as if the Creature's servants and the taint of the Creature himself had blown away with the wind.

Day turned to night, and Natiari returned with her own report. She couldn't find any "complete" signs of Murtosh. However, she had found several . . . pieces. A nose here. An arm there. It wasn't long after delivering this report that Thuradin had stepped out of the artifact.

Thuradin grimaced when he heard about Murtosh. He hated to think about the young dwarf killed by the blast and then entombed while midair, only to shatter into pieces as gravity thrust him into the ground. No, it was better to think Murtosh simply couldn't be found. He would remain lost forever.

However, he did appreciate hearing that the darimun were gone. That meant there would be no further threat from them, which meant one less danger to worry about for their return journey. There most likely would no longer be any threat from the humans, either, since so many had been killed in the battle against the darimun.

Thuradin stood and went over to Threnn's body as everyone else prepared for the trek back to their mounts. He couldn't tell for certain, but he imagined a peaceful expression was etched into the face of stone.

"I am so sorry, Threnn," he said quietly, "and Murtosh. Ye both deserved better than this."

He felt a hand on his shoulder and turned to see Borim looking down at him sadly.

"What will I tell Bronn?"

"The truth," Borim replied. "He knew the dangers his boys would face out here. Ye did yer best ta protect all of them, but the fates wouldn't have it. He will grieve, perhaps even hate ye, but he will understand."

Thuradin nodded, though he wondered if he would even have the courage to approach the old dwarf when the time came.

Making their way down the mountain was much easier now that they didn't have to worry about darimun attacking them. It wasn't long before they reached the crater floor.

They walked at a leisurely pace back the way they had come. There was no need to hurry anymore, much to Thuradin's annoyance. He was eager to return to Aleganthia. Once they arrived, his companions would finally be able to rest for a few days in comfort before they resumed the search for their King, but until then, no progress could be made.

"What is that?" Ayrie asked, pointing to an area along the

far end of the crater's wall.

Everyone turned to see what she was pointing at. Thuradin couldn't see very well, but it looked to him like little dark specs were moving slowly up the crater's wall.

"Humans," Tessa said after one quick glance. "They must be stragglers. The majority of them have already left the crater." Within minutes the last of the figures in the distance disappeared from sight over the crater's rim, and the party walked on in tired silence.

At one point, Thuradin walked alongside Victria to ask how she was feeling. After the betrayal by Dragos and the battle right after, it was no wonder she had gone into a state of shock.

"I'm . . . better," she said, forcing a small but sad smile. "It will take some time, but I will eventually come to terms with what happened. I have to."

They left it at that. Victria looked fragile, like she might break down at any second, and Thuradin preferred not to be the cause of that.

It took most of the night for them to leave the crater behind and retrieve their mounts. The horses and rams nickered and bleated cheerfully when they saw their masters. A quick count showed that all of them were accounted for. Thuradin was glad nothing had happened to them while they were gone.

Felix said they would all rest before they began their return journey to Aleganthia. Each member of the group found a soft patch of earth to collapse in and quickly fell asleep. No fire was lit. No food was eaten. No words were said.

Thuradin wasn't sure how long they slept but he knew it couldn't have been for very long. The sun, which had just been peeking over the horizon when he lay down to sleep, was now only a little ways above it.

As they all tiredly mounted up for the ride back to Aleganthia, he felt a sudden, deep, unnatural chill course through his body. It felt like a current of lightning raced from his head to his feet and back again. The shock sent him reeling, but no one noticed what could have easily passed as a fatigued shudder.

He turned in his saddle to look back at the Creature's home and frowned. For reasons he couldn't identify, he was sure this cold shock had come from there. And again the voice of the Creature rang through his head.

I am watching.

Simon was furious. He had led his men into a slaughter. How many women had just lost their husbands, sons, fathers, brothers? But what could he have done? The evil creatures had come upon them swiftly and brutally, like a plague. No mercy.

He thought he'd had more than enough men to push back the large gathering of the evil beasts. He quickly realized how wrong he was. The *demons*, as the men around him called them, had charged with vicious cries, causing many of his men to panic.

Simon remembered his astonishment when he saw their speed and strength. The only other beings he could think of that were as fast or as strong were the viatari, but he hadn't seen them on the battlefield.

Men died left and right. The demons were unstoppable and killed with a never-before-seen bloodlust. In only an hour, most of his forces had been massacred. Only a handful continued to fight with Simon, but they were becoming fewer and fewer.

Then, almost as if by some miracle, the demons had faded away into nothingness. They left nothing except a thin purple haze behind to show they had ever existed, and even that soon disappeared. Simon and the remaining survivors looked on in shock, unable to comprehend why the demons had suddenly vanished.

Fearing this was some sort of ploy to catch them off guard, Simon had ordered a retreat. The survivors scrambled back the way they had come, constantly looking over their shoulders to see if the demons would suddenly materialize behind them and resume slicing them to shreds.

Now Simon stood over the edge of the crater, encouraging the stragglers to climb faster. The sooner they were gone from this cursed place, the better. Once he was sure they had all joined him on the crater's rim, he led them back to camp.

He had left a troop of fifty men behind to watch over the camp while the rest pursued the viatari. Now the guards gawked in disbelief as they saw the few survivors return. None of them would ever admit it out loud, but they were glad they had been chosen to keep watch over the empty camp.

The dejected survivors plopped down by the nearest fires and did their best to forget the day's events. Simon looked around grimly. This colossal failure would cost him dearly. At best, he would only be relieved of the leadership position he held in his town. At worst . . . Well, he didn't want to think about that.

As he sat alone by his own fire, he felt icy stares penetrating his back as everyone settled down enough to realize who was to blame for this. All of them had lost friends or relatives in that battle, and if they couldn't be consoled by some sort of tangible reward for their efforts, such as the heads of the viatari, they would console themselves by seeing the one who had failed them punished.

Simon couldn't hold it against them for feeling that way. They had trusted him, after all. He had insisted they would be fine because they had strength in numbers. He had done anything and everything to make sure they stayed with him. And how had he repaid them for their loyalty? By leading them into a slaughter.

After a while, several men started to move, packing up their belongings and camping gear. Simon saw by the ferocity with which they packed that they were done. They had set their minds on returning home. They could no longer see a reason to continue the hunt. The viatari were surely lost to them by now.

"It's them!" one of the sentries suddenly yelled, looking back at the camp. "It's the viatari!"

The camp stopped what they were doing, wondering if they had heard correctly. Simon stood and walked over to the sentry. From his vantage point, he had a good view of the surrounding hills.

Not too far from their camp was a line of mounts, a mixture of rams and horses, walking casually northward. The viatari and dwarves were still within grasp.

Simon made his way back to camp, his mind racing. He noticed the men were frozen in place, looking at him expectantly, waiting for his orders. He allowed himself a small smile. After all they had been through, they were still willing to follow him on his hunt. Perhaps they could continue. After all, they still had enough numbers to do so.

But he didn't give the order. Instead, he went over to his

fire and began packing his own things. The men continued to stand still and wait for a command, but one by one, they, too, resumed their packing.

The message was clear. They weren't going to continue their hunt for the viatari. They were going home.

It took two days longer than it should have for them to return to Aleganthia. The delay was not due to any attack or sickness. It was not because the weather had become so severe it had forced them to dig in for a few nights, either. No, it was because Felix had insisted on going no faster than a snail's pace.

Thuradin regretted his decision to come back to Aleganthia, wishing instead he had departed from Inadarim to immediately resume his own quest. If they had come back two days earlier as they *should* have, the dwarves could have already left the city well rested by now. But Felix thought it would be a good idea to enjoy their return trip by taking their time.

He understood why the elder viatari thought this. Moving slowly would give Victria more time to get over the state of shock she had fallen into. She was well known and liked in Aleganthia, and having her return in a state of despair would do no good for the mood of the city. In the end, it looked like the prolonged return journey had paid off. Victria smiled more often than she had in the past few days and the look that warned of an imminent break down showed itself less and less.

Thuradin was happy for her. She was healing.

Still, he couldn't help but drop disgruntled hints that he wanted to move faster by yelling things like, "Move faster!" every now and then.

Now, as they reached the end of the forest surrounding Aleganthia, they could see the first signs of the city. A section of white wall reflecting the light from the sun. A spiral tower that made up part of the large keep. Residential buildings made of white stone and, sometimes, clay.

They exited the forest and crossed the southern bridge that spanned across the deep ravine surrounding the city like a moat. Bells rang as they approached. The thick, wooden gates opened, and they were greeted not with a jubilant crowd but with an air of solemnity.

Apparently, Pulaneus had told everyone in Aleganthia about the misfortunes and the losses they had suffered. The entire city was eerily quiet, despite the bells, as the citizens respectfully watched them make their way through the crowd and into the stables.

Even after they had put away their mounts, the crowd continued to watch them. Thuradin felt uncomfortable with every eye trained on him as he made his way to the city's keep. Felix had told him during their return journey that there would be a huge feast to celebrate the defeat of the Creature and the success of their quest, as well as to honor those who had died. Now that he felt the sadness in the air, he wondered if a feast would be a good idea.

As Felix left them to comfort the families of the companions they had lost during the journey to Inadarim, Victria, Tessa, and Natiari led each dwarf to his own room before going off to find their own.

Thuradin was left alone. His thoughts were scattered, thankfully. He didn't want to have to deal with them since most had to do with the Creature and his curse and the deaths of the three young dwarves under his charge.

Light filtered in through the windows, making everything

shine brightly, as if it were trying to cheer him up. It didn't work.

Thuradin stripped off his heavy armor, letting it clatter to the floor, until he was in nothing but trousers. He had been wearing it the entire time, and it felt good to finally let his body breathe a little.

He hopped into the nearby bed and closed his eyes as he sunk into the soft mattress. He would bathe later. He would let the water wash over him and clean his body of all the dirt and grime he had acquired over the past couple weeks. He would be comfortable later. Right now, he just wanted the blissful feeling of unconsciousness. He just wanted to disappear from this world, if only for a little while.

Aleganthia was alive that night. The viatari were no longer solemn. They cheered and laughed and danced as they celebrated the defeat of the Creature and the return of the survivors. Unlike the last feast, however, this time the viatari fed on the life-energies of any wild animal they could get their hands on.

Before the night had begun, Thuradin approached Felix to tell him he no longer cared about the viatari's eating habits, much to Felix's delight. Now wild animals roamed aimlessly through the city streets with the sole purpose of providing a meal. There were already several dried-up carcasses lying all over the city—the cleaning crews couldn't keep up.

The dwarves joined in on the fun too, happy to get away from their worries, even if for a little while. Many viatari foolishly asked Borim for a match in a drinking game. Naturally, he humored them. By the next morning, ten viatari would wake up wondering why their heads hurt so much and how they had ended up sleeping piled up on top of each other.

Looking around, Thuradin saw Ayrie dancing with Stürn in the crowd. He had never seen the Enurg'en have any sort of fun before, and he clapped along to the music, grinning as the pair swept across the plaza, dancing without reservation. His grin grew wider as he watched Stürn repeatedly trip himself and many of the viatari around him.

Despite the festive atmosphere, Thuradin didn't partake in any of the dancing or drinking. His thoughts had finally caught up with him. He was excited that tomorrow they would finally be able to resume their journey, but he was also sad to be leaving the viatari for what would probably be forever. They were a good people, and he couldn't understand how the Creature could label them as evil so easily—nor, for that matter, could he understand it when it came to his own race.

He sighed as his thoughts drove out the last vestiges of humor from him.

"You should enjoy it while you can."

Thuradin jumped as he noticed for the first time that Felix was sitting next to him.

"What do ye mean?"

"I mean," Felix said. "Your journey is not over yet. You still have a long way to go before you accomplish what you set out for. For the viatari, however, it is over. The Creature is gone. We will be able to have many more celebrations after this. But when will you be able to relax enough to celebrate something again? My guess is not soon. That is why you should enjoy the present, the now."

"I have responsibilities," Thuradin said.

Felix nodded. "As do I, but those responsibilities do not

need to be attended to right now." He brought his face closer to Thuradin's, his red eyes searching. "But responsibility is not what is holding you back." He paused, thinking. "So what is?"

Thuradin wanted to tell him about the curse. If there was anyone who would know what to do about it, it would be Felix. But before he could say anything, the same cold shock he had experienced when they left Inadarim coursed through his body. An ominous presence seemed to materialize and perch itself on his lips, preventing him from replying truthfully.

"It doesn't matter," he said hastily. "I—I think I'm done for the night. I'll be in my room."

He stood up quickly and walked back toward the keep.

Viatari danced excitedly around him. Borim won his third consecutive drinking game with a victorious roar. His opponent collapsed onto his two predecessors with a heavy *thud.* Stürn tripped over Ayrie, and the two of them crashed onto the floor in a tangle of arms and legs, much to the amusement of those around them. Thuradin didn't focus on any of it. The only thing he could focus on was Felix's gaze stabbing into his back.

The dwarves were ready to leave before the sun had even risen. They were all back in their armor and were about to exit the keep to get their mounts when Felix stopped them. He walked up to them and regarded each dwarf as if he were deciding whether he should actually let them go.

"Before you leave, I must thank you for going through with our demands," he said. "And I must apologize that it resulted in the loss of three of your fellows. I am truly sorry."

The dwarves shifted uncomfortably at the mention of

their dead companions. After a night of jubilation, they didn't want to bring such dark thoughts into their minds quite yet.

Felix looked like he wanted to say more, but, instead, he simply stuck out his hand. Each dwarf grasped it firmly. No words were needed.

When it was Thuradin's turn, he noticed the viatari was looking at him curiously, like he was some sort of puzzle that needed to be solved. Quickly, without giving him any more chances to delay their departure, he turned and left the keep without another word. He felt Felix's eyes on his back the entire time.

The dwarves entered the stables and got ahold of their rams. Taking only a few moments to tie their new supplies down, they mounted and headed for the city's eastern gate. Riding east would take them directly to the Silent Mountains, which they could then use as a reference point when they needed to start riding south.

As they rode for the last time through Aleganthia, Thuradin searched for Victria. Of all the viatari he now knew, she was the one he wanted to say goodbye to. She was the one he had bonded with the most during their quest. From the beginning, when she had seduced him into explaining everything about the dwarves' quest, to her reliving her past in order to comfort him, to him comforting her upon the rocky clearing after she had lost her battle against Dragos, they had gone through it all together.

Unfortunately, he didn't see her anywhere. The dwarves arrived at the eastern gate, and Thuradin sat glumly on his saddle as it opened. He glanced back one last time, hoping to see some hint of her presence before leading his companions away, but there was none.

But when they were halfway across the bridge, he noticed three figures on horseback waiting at the end of it. From where he was, he couldn't tell who they were, but he had a pretty good idea.

Victria smiled as the dwarves approached. Natiari and Tessa were at her side, looking annoyed.

"Where are ye off ta?" Thuradin asked.

"We're going to lead you to the tunnel entrance you're looking for," Victria replied as if the answer was obvious.

Now that he looked closer, Thuradin noticed she and her companions were dressed in their own armor; they had their long, slender dirks strapped to their thighs; and their mounts carried enough supplies to last them for a long journey.

"We don't need help finding our own tunnels," Borim said with a small chuckle.

"Aye," Thuradin agreed. "We appreciate the thought, but—"

"Please," Victria insisted, her lightheartedness gone. "Consider this my way of making up for . . . for Threnn and Murtosh."

"That wasn't—"

"I know you don't blame me," she continued, interrupting the dwarf's protest. "But I do. That's why I'm offering to help you in any way I can."

Thuradin hesitated. He looked at Borim, who shrugged unhelpfully.

"What about those two?" he asked, referring to Natiari and Tessa.

"We couldn't let Victria do this on her own," Tessa said, her tone surprisingly tender. "So we offered to go with her."

Natiari nodded.

Thuradin thought for a moment longer but realized he had no real say in the matter. He was sure Victria would just follow him anyway, even if he said no.

"Come along, then."

Victria's smile returned, and she dipped her head gratefully. The viatari's horses nickered appreciatively, as if they understood they were being given permission to follow their new ram friends once again.

As they rode through the forest, Thuradin told Victria which tunnel they needed to reach and which route they planned to take. Victria shook her head and took out a map of the surrounding area, pointing to several parts of the mountain range. According to her, many pathways existed which cut straight through the mountains and would shorten their travel time significantly. Thuradin wasn't convinced, remembering the one time he had tried to take a shortcut, but Victria wouldn't be swayed.

She took the lead as they changed direction for one of these paths. Soon, the forest gave way to clear skies and mountains in the distance. Thuradin was glad to be so close to home again. The mountains gave him a sense of security that he couldn't feel anywhere else, and he was sure his companions felt the same way.

Unfortunately, they also presented a problem. The first pathway Victria led them to was blocked off by a rock slide. In fact, it was the same rock slide Thuradin had discovered before he and the dwarves had encountered the viatari.

"Hmm," Victria said. "I suppose we'll have to go to the next one."

They moved on to the next closest pathway, but it was also blocked. As was the one after that, and the one after that, and the one after that. Each time they came across a blocked off path, Victria would say the same thing about moving on to the next one and then would continue leading them as if she wasn't at all surprised to find them all impassable. Natiari and Tessa glanced at each other, grins forming on their faces. Thuradin began to get the vaguest impression she was doing this on purpose.

In the end, all the shortcuts that supposedly existed were blocked off one way or another. The group of dwarves and viatari ended up having to go around the southernmost tip of the Silent Mountains, as was originally planned, in order to reach the tunnel.

It took two weeks longer for them to reach the tunnel entrance to Dun'Burell than it should have. Thuradin might have raged at the unnecessary delay, if he hadn't understood why Victria had done it. Their days traveling together had been filled with stories and laughter, and he would be lying if he had said he was eager to part ways with the viatari. There was no telling when they might see each other again, if ever.

As they approached the tunnel, they set up camp one last time to share a meal and rest a bit before moving on. Once he had finished eating and they had shared stories from the festivities in Aleganthia, Thuradin thought now was as good a time as any to say their farewells.

He stood up and grabbed the things he needed to tie down to his mount before turning to face the viatari. "I want ta thank ye for leading us here."

Victria looked at him quizzically. "You sound as if you're saying goodbye."

The dwarf nodded. "I am."

"But we're coming with you."

There was silence for a moment, though Borim stood up and walked away as a fit of laughter took him.

"Ye're coming with us . . . ta Dun'Burell?" Thuradin repeated.

Victria nodded. "Yes. Felix gave me the task of reestablishing ties with the dwarves. We may not have anything to worry about from the Creature anymore, but it would still be a good thing to become friends with the dwarves once more."

"She has a point," Borim said, wiping the tears from his eyes. "Plus, many of the things we lack, such as food, could be gained through trade with the viatari."

Thuradin shook his head as he tried to think. "But I thought ye were just leading us ta the tunnel because ye felt guilty about Threnn and Murtosh."

Victria's face grew solemn. "That wasn't a lie. That was true, but it was not the only reason. Felix knew I was already doing this so he asked me to do him this favor. Naturally, I said yes."

Thuradin nodded, accepting the explanation, but he still felt hesitant. He worried how the other dwarves might react when they saw the viatari walking around in their cities. Surely because of their false perceptions, the dwarves would see the viatari as a threat and attack them. Then again, not many dwarves read those old texts fully. It was possible most wouldn't even know about them. But their intimidating nature might be enough to trigger one dwarf to attack, and then another—

Victria seemed to sense what he was thinking. "Don't worry, I'm sure the dwarves will not attack us on sight. What's more likely is that our initial presence will make them too afraid to even approach us. That should give you the breathing room you need to explain the situation to your leaders."

"I agree with her," Ayrie said. "It's a good idea. We could use their help should the burrowers attack us within the tunnel."

"I agree as well," Stürn mumbled.

It looked as if Thuradin, again, didn't really have a say in the matter.

"Very well," Victria said cheerfully. "Then tomorrow we enter the Dwarven Kingdom, and we will help you find your missing King."

CHAPTER TWENTY-FOUR

Thuradin had waited for this day for the past several weeks, the day he would finally return to his homeland. He had come to enjoy what the outside world had to offer, but he was a dwarf. He was made to live in the mountains. In the earth.

Everyone looked about their surroundings one last time as they approached the dark tunnel ahead. For the dwarves, they likely wouldn't see the outside world again for a very long time. They wanted to have images of the trees, the sky, and the sun burned into their memory. The viatari looked around and wondered how much time would pass before they could return home.

Without a word, Thuradin spurred his ram forward, and the rest followed. The sun's light retreated as the tunnel's darkness began to envelope them. He sighed with pleasure when he was met with the musty smell of the earth.

A sharp whine came from behind, and, turning, he saw the viatari struggling with their horses. The mounts fought against their riders' coaxing as if their very lives depended on it. They stamped their feet, kicking up dust. Their eyes rolled and tails twitched. They looked to be on the verge of rearing up and running away. They utterly refused to enter the tunnel.

After several minutes of watching this chaotic struggle, Ayrie dismounted and searched through her bags. She pulled out a few apples and held them out to the animals. They stopped struggling and perked their ears as they smelled the treat. The first horse approached hesitantly. It grunted softly as it leaned its head in to try and snatch the snack from Ayrie's hand without entering the tunnel, but the dwarf expected this. Every time the horse's mouth came close, she would pull the apple back toward her, drawing the horse in little by little.

Eventually all three horses were inside, munching happily on their well-deserved apples as they walked calmly next to their ram companions.

The tunnel grew exponentially darker the farther inside they went. The light from the tunnel's entrance, a shrinking speck of light as they continued on, eventually disappeared completely as the tunnel fell into complete darkness. Thuradin raised his hand to his face to see if he could see it. Unlike in the Creature's lair, he could still see a slight outline of it waving in front of him.

"How do any of you see where you're going?" Victria asked. "It's so dark in here."

"Our rams know where ta go," Stürn answered. "Just as yer horses do. They have keener senses than us. Besides, we should be reaching the torch-point soon."

"The what?"

"It's when the torches along the wall start ta show up," Thuradin explained. "They're what give us light in these dark tunnels."

No sooner had he said this than the first torch came into view.

"See?"

"Not really," Natiari muttered.

The torches were more frequent with every step they took until most of the tunnel blazed with the individual flames. Only the ceiling remained hidden in darkness.

"Be wary," Thuradin said. "There are probably burrowers crawling all over the place looking for unsuspecting travelers ta kill."

"Burrowers?" Victria repeated.

"Aye," Borim said sadly. "They are ta us what humans are ta ye."

They rode through the tunnel for what seemed like hours. Thuradin found he had difficulty telling time in the mountains now, and he guessed that was because he had spent so much time in the outside world. He would have to stay underground for several more days before he could re-attune himself with the mountain and properly sense time again.

"Can ye sense the time?" he asked Stürn, whose powers as an Enurg'en made him more attuned to the mountains than anyone else.

But Stürn shook his head. "Even with my powers, it's still hard ta tell."

Thuradin frowned. Not being able to sense time was a problem. This was the longest tunnel in the Dwarven Kingdom, and if they couldn't tell when night fell, they wouldn't know when to stop and rest. The possibility of suffering from severe fatigue was high. If they started experiencing it too early in the journey, they could wander through the tunnel aimlessly until they died.

"How long will it take us to reach Dun'Burell?" Victria asked.

"About five days," Thuradin answered, already thinking of what they could do to try to conserve their energy.

"Five. . . ."

He turned to see Victria looking like she was going to be sick. Even Natiari and Tessa looked startled at his answer.

"Well, it *is* the longest tunnel in all the Kingdom," Borim said as if that explained everything.

"And you can't tell time." It wasn't a question. Victria spoke more to herself, and her forehead creased as she understood the problem.

The first two days passed without incident. The third day brought the burrowers.

As Thuradin had feared, because they couldn't tell when night fell and day came, they started to suffer from fatigue. They would ride through the tunnels for hours without knowing whether or not it was time for them to sleep. And when they occasionally did sleep, they never knew for how long, but it never felt like it was enough.

That's how the burrowers managed to sneak up on them.

The group rode along tiredly, not paying attention to their surroundings and certainly not looking up at the tunnel's ceiling. Stürn and Borim were asleep on their saddles. Thuradin had been wondering if Stürn could still sense the life-energies of anyone approaching them when the burrowers attacked.

They dropped down onto the unsuspecting group, their ugly cries startling everyone and managing to wake the sleeping dwarves. If the dwarves had been by themselves, they most likely would have been slain while they sat on their rams, confused, trying to understand what was happening. Luckily, the viatari reacted instantly to the threat, despite their own exhaustion.

Victria, Natiari, and Tessa moved about swiftly, killing every burrower they met with ease. The burrowers didn't know what hit them. They had ambushed this weary group thinking they would be easy kills. Now they scampered away, whimpering as the viatari killed their brethren as easily as they would kick a rock down the tunnel.

The viatari remounted as if nothing had happened, but Thuradin noticed their shoulders drooping and their labored breaths. They were getting more fatigued by the minute, and having to fight off burrower ambushes wasn't helping. They wouldn't be able to defend everyone like this forever.

They pressed on with renewed urgency. They had to reach Dun'Burell within the next few days or they would surely be helpless, even against the smallest of ambushes.

They continued riding through the tunnel without knowing the exact time of day, but as they neared the end, Thuradin felt he was more attuned with the mountains again.

Around what he thought was midday on the fifth day of travel, the torches disappeared, and they exited the tunnel. Thuradin heard the viatari behind him gasp as Dun'Burell came into view. He grinned and remembered his own similar reaction the first time he had seen the gigantic cavern.

Huge braziers hung on thick chains and swung gently from the cavern ceiling, illuminating an area ten times larger than the cavern of Dun'Aldor. Enormous stalactites jutted out from the ceiling, glittering as their minerals reflected the nearby light. Yet, despite their enormous size, they didn't even come close to touching the cavern floor.

The floor was a mess of jagged stalagmites and winding roads. The roads curved around huge sections of these rock formations and connected the several visible steel fortresses as well as all the other defensive towers and bunkers hidden within the landscape. Blasts of fire burst randomly from a few towers built along one side of the cavern all at once. A few seconds later, an area farther in front of the blasts exploded, and chunks of rock and dust flew into the air.

"What was that?" Victria asked, her eyes wide as she took everything in.

"Cannons," Thuradin replied with a small hint of pride. "They're quite a sight aren't they? They use a flammable rock we call *dynath* ta send projectiles flying inta our enemies. They're very deadly if they hit."

Another volley of cannon fire—this time from some of the defensive structures farther back from the original cannon blasts. The floor shook as the explosions caused a large stalagmite to topple over and crash onto the ground. A wall of dust was thrown into the air and hovered like a cloud, keeping everything within hidden from view.

"What are they firing at?"

"Probably burrowers," Ayrie yawned.

Thuradin nodded. "This cavern is almost always under attack by those—savages," he hesitated in calling them savages as he remembered the images of civilization the Creature had shown him. Another one of the cold shocks—which he now assumed came from the Creature reminding him of his presence—coursed through his body. He shuddered.

"Thuradin, are ye alright?"

He turned to see Borim looking at him, his sagging, tired eyes full of concern.

"Fine," he replied, breaking eye contact before he could give any indication that he was *not* fine. "Come, we should start heading for Kul'Burell—the capital of this region," he explained to the viatari.

They found a road leading to Kul'Burell and followed it. As they traveled, they occasionally passed lines of dwarven warriors marching along the same road. These dwarves were armed to the teeth with plate armor so thick, they made Thuradin and his companions look like they wore everyday clothes. Despite this, every time they encountered a troop of dwarven soldiers, the Dun'Burell dwarves would step off the road and cower. Thuradin couldn't blame them. He remembered his own initial fear the first time he saw the viatari.

Victria often raised her hand in greeting and smiled in a friendly way to try and calm the dwarves down, but it never worked. The Dun'Burell warriors only shrank back in even more terror with every movement the viatari made, no doubt thinking they were about to be attacked.

Because of this fear, the dwarves they encountered never showed any signs of hostility toward them, and they made their way to Kul'Burell undisturbed. Thuradin wondered how the soldiers might have reacted had they known the viatari were the *Eng'Pergen* that dwarven historical texts spoke about. He wondered if they would have attacked and killed the viatari in brutal ways like humans did. He wondered if they might have become savages.

He thanked Nythirim he would never have to know that particular what-if.

They arrived at Kul'Burell after only a few hours of riding. As they neared the city gates, Thuradin rode ahead to give the guards outside some warning so they didn't try and shut them in a panic. The guards looked at him skeptically at first as he explained what the viatari were, but their faces soon turned fearful as the viatari themselves approached and passed through the gates. Thankfully, word about them spread through the city like wildfire so Thuradin didn't have to explain their existence to every single dwarf he met.

As he looked around, he noticed how much the city had changed since last he had seen it a few centuries ago. In the past, it had been easier to distinguish between civilians and soldiers. Now everyone wore armor, even if they weren't on duty. It spoke volumes to him about the dire situation these dwarves were in. They had to be ready for battle constantly, no matter what. No one knew when the next burrower assault would occur.

He saw several dwarves in heavy armor running small shops in the street or standing on balconies sipping pints of ale as they enjoyed a little free time. Many of them stopped what they were doing to stare at the strange outsiders entering their city. Several mouths popped open in surprise, and some in horror, as they noticed the viatari.

Victria's face was a mask of calm. Thuradin understood why. She was trying her best to show the dwarves that she wasn't dangerous, despite her intimidating appearance. She intended to prove the viatari were calm, peaceful beings. Unfortunately, Tessa and Natiari had no intention of helping her and glared at the gathering crowd in front of them, no doubt thinking they might have to fight this growing mob. Several dwarves gasped as they noticed the red eyes.

"Outta my way! Move it! Make way!"

A high, piercing voice cut through the crowd, and Thuradin saw a stocky dwarf making his way to them. He would have thought this one was no different from a regular soldier had it not been for the slightly different style of helmet—smoother near the top, where it ended in a point—

and the dark green cape.

"Behave," Thuradin muttered pointedly to Tessa and Natiari. "Ye are now in the presence of a viceroy."

The viceroy, Kul'Burell's highest head of authority chosen directly by the King, stopped as he noticed the viatari. Shaking his head quickly, he brought himself back to the present and looked at Thuradin.

"Baleth Shieldlord," he said, extending his hand. "Chief Commander of all the armed forces in Dun'Burell, and viceroy of Kul'Burell."

Thuradin gripped Baleth's hand firmly and shook. "Thuradin Stonebeard, former commander of the King's royal guard."

Baleth's eyes widened. "It is an honor ta have the bearer of the saphyrium helm in our city," he said, pounding his fist to his chest in salute. "But, did ye say *former commander?*"

"Long story," Thuradin waved his hand dismissively. He didn't want to discuss the business of Ronorim's disappearance and the temporary stripping of his rank in public. "I have some business I must see ta here. If ye could take us ta the citadel, I can explain everything."

The viceroy nodded and yelled at the crowd to make a path as he led the outsiders through the streets toward the towering metal structure at the center of the city.

Kul'Burell's citadel was a massive collection of structures. It consisted of a mixture of thick, cylindrical towers, a sprawling web of tiered ramparts, and a relatively small, square-shaped building at the center of it, the commons, for meetings and living quarters. Like most dwarven buildings, the towers of the citadel stretched from the cavern floor to the ceiling, making them the tallest structures in all the Dwarven Kingdom. The viatari looked on in awe as they passed the massive towers.

After they handed their mounts over to the stable hands, Baleth led them to the commons. Despite its small size in relation to the massive towers, the commons was still a significant building, nearly the size of the royal palace itself. Baleth led them through its winding passages for several minutes until they found themselves in a large stone room where they were told they could rest and tell their story. Chairs and a stone table were brought in, and once everyone had situated themselves around it, Thuradin told the story of the past few weeks.

He talked about the burrower attack on Tinas Gran and how Ronorim had gotten himself separated from the city after the tunnels caved in. He explained the King's plan to continue on through the tunnel to Dun'Burell where he hoped to find some help. He talked about starting a quest with seven dwarves, including himself, which involved taking the outside route to get to Dun'Burell and how Dunkell had taken the throne as steward in Ronorim's absence. He also mentioned as a quick side note that the prince had taken away his rank as commander of the royal guard on the assumption that he would die outside the mountains.

After some minor details about the outside world and how it wasn't the inhospitable place the dwarves had thought it was, he talked about being captured by the viatari and forced to aid them in their task to end the Creature. He explained what the Creature was and how it was because of his influence in the past that the dwarves now had a misconstrued idea of what the viatari and the outside world were really like. Thuradin spared no detail when it came to their encounters with the humans, the events in the crater, and the deaths of Agrethar, Threnn, and Murtosh. He did, however, hold back on talking about his curse again. At the thought of mentioning it, he had begun to feel the early signs of another cold shock, so he decided to hold his tongue.

After he finished talking about how Victria had volunteered to lead him and his companions to Dun'Burell and how they had entered the Dwarven Kingdom in the hopes of reestablishing a connection with the dwarves—perhaps even forming another alliance—Baleth gave a low whistle.

"That is some tale . . . Hearing yer story, I know ye must be extremely tired and want nothing more than ta find a nice bed ta sleep in for the next few days. But I think I have some news that'll wake ye right up," Baleth smiled. "The King is here. He's been here for quite some time now, waiting for ye ta show up."

Thuradin sat up straight. The viceroy was right. Whatever drowsiness he had felt vanished instantly. "He made it here?"

Baleth laughed heartily. "Of course he made it here! He isn't an Ironaxe for nothing. He's been staying with us for the past few weeks—helping us with our battles, too."

A guard was called in and given instructions to bring the King from his living quarters. Moments later, Ronorim came striding in, wearing his blood-red armor, exactly what he had been wearing the day he was lost in the battle of Tinas Gran. He grinned as he laid eyes on Thuradin, but his grin changed to a puzzled frown when he noticed the three viatari.

"Thuradin," he said. "Would ye care ta explain ta me who and what our—guests—are and what they're doing here?"

Thuradin did. He recounted once again all the events of his quest for the past few weeks. Everyone listened attentively, even Baleth who had just heard the story. When he finished,

Ronorim sighed heavily and took a seat at the head of the table, near where the viatari sat.

"As King of the dwarves, I feel obligated ta apologize for what happened between our two peoples," he said. His steadfast gaze met Victria's without flinching. "If it is any consolation, I vow ta do whatever I can ta reestablish ties with the viatari so things might return ta the way they were before our retreat from the outside world."

All three viatari bowed their head in gratitude.

"Your majesty," Victria said. "We thank you for your kind words and we hope, now that you know us for who we truly are, that you are in agreement that we might form an alliance."

Ronorim waved a hand in the air dismissively. "Believe me. If I could, I would make an alliance with ye right now. Nythirim knows we need help with our war against the burrowers. But first, I must reclaim my throne before I can make any promises."

"Speaking of which," Thuradin said before Victria could continue with her diplomatic pursuits. "Why *are* ye still here? Baleth tells me ye've been here for almost as long as I've been in the outside world. Aren't the tunnels cleared out yet?"

Ronorim shook his head. "No. If what ye've told me is true, my brother will plan ta take as long as he can with the tunnels in an attempt ta reach the required six months before he can crown himself King." He frowned disapprovingly. "If he starts now, it'll take a couple more weeks before the tunnel is completely cleared."

"A couple more weeks just for that small cave-in?"

"It was much more than a small cave-in, Thuradin."

Ronorim explained what had happened to him while he

was in the tunnel.

After he had left Thuradin at the cave-in site, he began to make his way to Dun'Burell. As he had expected, the tunnel was swarming with retreating burrowers, but because they were retreating in a panic and could see just as well as Ronorim in the dark tunnel—which was not at all—they were easy to deal with.

He kept his hands on the walls, which guided him safely down slopes and sudden twists and turns. He walked without stopping, not even to rest or eat, trying to reach Dun'Burell as quickly as his tired feet would take him.

Occasionally, a burrower grew bold enough to try and attack him, but he always managed to defend himself. He could smell them coming from far away, which wasn't necessarily a good thing. It did, however, give him sufficient time to prepare for any attack.

After two days of this, he saw a dim light in the distance. The light grew larger and brighter the closer he got to it. It was the exit to Dun'Burell—there was nothing else it could be.

As he realized this, the ground started to shake. Rocks crashed and broke apart as they fell from the ceiling and hit the floor behind him. He ran. The entire tunnel was collapsing. He put every ounce of strength and speed he had left into his legs, and even then, it was barely enough to stay ahead of the collapsing tunnel. He leaped in desperation as the rocks fell dangerously close around him, and managed to roll out just as the exit disappeared.

Now it was Thuradin's turn to whistle. Ronorim's story, though not as long as his, was still impressive. But it posed another problem in his mind. He remembered how Dunkell had acted after hearing the news about his brother. He hadn't been particularly worried. Granted, he may have thought that Ronorim could handle himself, but then he remembered how the prince had so abruptly claimed the throne.

"I think we should get back ta Tinas Gran through the outside," he said. "It'll be faster than waiting for the tunnel ta be cleared."

Ronorim frowned. "But I told ye it'll only take a couple weeks for that tunnel ta be cleared. That's only a little more than what it will take for us ta go through the outside. Why are ye in such a rush?"

"Don't forget, Ronorim," Thuradin said, too worried at this point to remember to call the King by his title, "we're on a deadline. Already, a little more than three weeks have passed out of the six months that we have. I know there's still plenty of time, but we don't want ta gamble it away. What if the tunnel isn't cleared out in time? What if the couple of weeks turns inta months? Ye said yerself that Dunkell will try ta prolong clearing it out for as long as he can."

Everyone assembled looked nervously between the two dwarves, wondering if the King would reprimand his subject for being so bold as to argue with him.

But Ronorim just laughed.

"I know ye've done nothing but worry about me for the past few weeks, Thuradin, but everything will turn out fine. Believe me, I know my brother, and I know the dwarves of Tinas Gran. He may try ta reach the six months by delaying the inevitable, but the people will grow impatient and will clear the tunnel out themselves. And don't worry," the King wagged his finger knowingly, "I plan on giving Dunkell a nice, long chat about his taking so long with that tunnel when we get back, ye can mark my words on that."

Thuradin wanted to try to convince Ronorim to listen to him, but he could see that nothing he said would change the King's mind. Besides, his fatigue had returned and made it hard for him to think. He would just have to hope that everything turned out alright, just like Ronorim said.

The conversation was over. A meal was brought in, and the three viatari were treated to some of the finest brews of ale that the dwarves were willing to part with. Victria had one drink out of politeness, but Thuradin could tell the stuff made her nauseous. Natiari and Tessa barely touched theirs. In fact, they spent most of their meal glaring at their steins with curled lips as if they thought they had just been fed poison.

At the end of the meal, Ronorim stood and—having already consumed several pints himself—gave a few final words, thanking Thuradin for his efforts and the viatari for their presence.

"Now then," he said after he finished with the formalities. "I imagine everyone is tired from the long journey ye've had. The guards will take ye ta yer rooms. Rest easy during these next couple of weeks. As soon as that blasted tunnel is cleared, we're heading straight through it for Tinas Gran."

He smiled drunkenly and stumbled out of the room with his ninth pint still in his hands.

Thuradin sighed. He hoped a couple of weeks was all they had to rest for. But in the back of his mind, he had a feeling things were not going to go as smoothly as Ronorim planned.

CHAPTER TWENTY-FIVE

The few weeks Ronorim predicted for the tunnel to be cleared out came and went, but it still remained blocked off. Weeks turned into months, and it wasn't until the beginning of the fifth month that word came of the tunnel finally being cleared.

The dwarves and viatari rode out from Kul'Burell immediately. They all knew the deadline to get Ronorim back on his throne was too close for comfort. A little less than one month remained. Thankfully, it would only take a few days to reach Tinas Gran, but Thuradin didn't like what the months-long delay in clearing out the tunnel meant. He'd had plenty of time to think during their time in Dun'Burell, and he had a suspicion that something nefarious was taking place in Tinas Gran that was being orchestrated by none other than Ronorim's own brother, Dunkell.

He hoped he was wrong and that his suspicions turned out to be nothing more than a conspiracy theory, but he remembered the odd look Dunkell wore when he learned of Ronorim's fate. He remembered how the prince had so easily forgotten dwarven laws of succession and how he blatantly claimed himself as King instead of steward in his brother's absence. Lastly, he remembered how he had seemed so bent on postponing the clearing of the tunnel to Dun'Burell, as if he wanted Ronorim to stay lost.

Their time in Kul'Burell hadn't just been for thinking and meditation, though. There had been many battles in the cavern. Thuradin and his companions had joined in on defending Kul'Burell as often as they could while they waited for the tunnel to clear out. Ronorim was impressed when he saw the viatari's speed and power, and Thuradin couldn't help but agree. The viatari took down dozens of burrowers with little effort, their dirks lashing out quicker than a serpent's strike.

Even with the viatari's prowess in battle, though, many dwarves died as the months wore on. The number of defenders grew fewer and fewer each day, and with the tunnel still caved-in, there were no reinforcements from Kul'Kriegar to relieve them.

Thuradin reasoned that this, more than anything, was why Ronorim looked so furious as they rode to the tunnel of Dun'Aldor. He knew his King had always had a soft spot for the dwarves of this cavern. After watching many of them die in battle and seeing the hope run from their eyes as they realized no help was coming from the other cities, Thuradin was just as determined to punish whoever was responsible for the months of isolation.

They arrived at the tunnel's entrance. A small, narrow passageway was dug out in the middle of the rubble that looked just large enough to let them pass through, but the rest of the entrance remained blocked off.

Thuradin saw only a few dwarves working on clearing out the blocked areas. When the tunnelers noticed Ronorim approaching, they immediately stopped their work and stood at attention, saluting their King. All of them looked on the verge of collapse.

Ronorim dismounted and walked up to one of the tunnelers. "Why are there so few of ye?"

"Orders by the steward of Tinas Gran," the tunneler replied. It sounded like the dwarf hadn't had water in days.

"The steward?"

"Yer brother, Dunkell, sir."

Thuradin saw Ronorim furrow his brows and stroke his beard as he began to think.

"And what exactly do these orders say?"

"No more than five dwarves may work on clearing the tunnel and only during the day. This ensures that there are plenty of dwarves available ta help repair the structures in the city that were damaged during the burrower invasion." The tunneler sounded as if he were reciting a mandate to them.

"Help repair?" Ronorim repeated. "The city is still being repaired so long after the battle?"

The tunneler's face darkened. "No, my King. The city has been fully repaired for months now, but the order still stands."

Thuradin shook his head as he heard the news. It seemed to him that his suspicions of Dunkell were turning out to be true. Ronorim, however, still seemed not to fully grasp the situation as he continued to barrage the tired worker with more questions.

"Ronorim," Thuradin said gently. "I don't believe yer brother ever wanted ye ta return ta the throne. He's been delaying yer arrival so yer deadline passes so he can become King."

"Aye," the tunneler said, the disgust evident in his voice.

"We could have cleared this tunnel out in a few weeks at most if we'd had more workers. But with only a few of us at a time, it took months. If the other tunnelers had followed the steward's orders and not helped us when they weren't supposed ta, the project would probably only be half finished by now. Ye wouldn't be able ta return ta yer throne in time."

Ronorim looked at the tunneler, then at Thuradin, then back. Betrayal was written in the stones around them, but the King did not wish to see it.

"I cannae believe this," he said quietly. "But if what ye tell me is true, then my brother is a traitor, and I will make sure he is properly dealt with."

He briskly mounted his ram and guided it toward the tunnel's narrow entrance.

Thuradin moved his own mount up to one of the other tunnelers, who were all still standing rigidly at attention. "How is it?"

"Clear," the dwarf responded confidently. "There's a very low chance of another cave-in, and no chance of meeting any burrowers. Yer journey should be smooth."

Thuradin nodded. "Thank ye, friends. Ye've done yer King and Kingdom a great service by clearing this tunnel in time. I'll make sure ye are all well rewarded."

They grinned up at him.

"No reward is necessary!" one of them said.

"Aye, just getting that blasted Dunkell off the throne will be reward enough."

Thuradin grinned and saluted before turning to follow his companions into the tunnel.

The journey to Dun'Aldor took less time than Thuradin had

expected. Ronorim set a fast pace for the majority of the ride, but instead of tiring out the mounts, the pace enlivened them. The viatari's horses had grown accustomed to living underground, but they hadn't been able to run as freely nor as often as they would have been able to outside. Now they snorted happily, flaring their nostrils as they ran alongside their ram companions.

Tinas Gran stood before them only a day later, its tall, steel structures gleaming in the light of the city's many braziers, looking like a cluster of glimmering jewels. Thuradin thought it was beautiful. He had been gone for so long he had almost forgotten what his home looked like. As soon as he thought that, however, he realized something was wrong. He looked around, trying to determine what it was, but couldn't come to any conclusions.

"No guards," Ronorim stated.

That was it, Thuradin realized; there were no guards in sight. No patrols or sentries—not even here by the tunnel entrance. This was strange, considering the city had been attacked only months ago.

Ronorim shook his head sadly. "What has my brother been doing?"

They rode slowly through the city, their eyes taking in every detail. The buildings damaged during the battle months ago were rebuilt; not even the smallest of scorch marks remained. The streets were clean and clear of all signs of the fighting. The city looked like it had before it was attacked. Civilians walked through the city streets going about their daily lives. The air hummed with the sound of business as the various markets conducted their trades for the day. Money exchanged hands for spongy mushrooms or pounds of ram meat. Many dwarves watched the happenings on the street from balconies in the taller buildings, drawing on pipes or sipping ale from tall steins. Everything hinted of normalcy.

Soon the royal palace loomed over them, and it was just as Thuradin remembered it.

Small balconies protruded out of every window with one large balcony in the center where Ronorim had been crowned King. Statues of famous dwarves lined the pathway into the building. Each one held up hammers or axes into the air in triumph. Tall arches and ornate columns made up most of the entrances and doorways with detailed faces or weapons carved into them. Beautiful carvings and murals on the walls displayed some of the heroic tales from dwarven history. Seeing them now, Thuradin wondered how many of them were based off of the false history the Creature had put into their minds.

He was quick to notice, with some relief, the royal guards stationed at every entrance of the palace. The guards let them pass without hesitation when they saw Ronorim, though they eyed the viatari suspiciously. Victria, as always, tried to ease their fears with a friendly wave.

Their mounts were taken by some of the guards and brought to the nearest stables. Now on foot, Ronorim led the way through the palace's many hallways and corridors. They encountered a royal guard every now and then, but were never troubled by them once they recognized the King and former commander.

Several twists and turns later, they entered a long, spacious hall. In front of them stood a large set of metal doors guarded by several royal guards. Inside those doors was the throne room, and inside there, they would find Dunkell.

Ronorim burst through the doors, scattering several of the startled royal guards as they tried to get out of his way. Thuradin and the others followed close behind but stopped to block the entrance in case Dunkell tried to escape.

The throne room made the spacious hall they had just exited look like a closet. It was gigantic. A circular room filled with large, thick columns dispersed evenly along the walls. Two larger and thicker columns stood several yards apart in the center of the room. Ahead of them, the crystal throne glowed from the surrounding torchlight.

Dunkell sat in front of them, shock written on his face. Next to him stood a dwarf wearing the saphyrium helm with a similar expression. Thuradin recognized him to be Therason Kinfriend, one of the dwarves he had called upon to help him find Ronorim. He was one who had rejected the call.

"How did—" Dunkell started to say. His mouth refused to stay shut for more than a few seconds at a time. "The tunnel—"

"—has been cleared out," Ronorim finished. "Aye, and I came back as soon as I heard."

Dunkell shifted uneasily on the throne.

"I'll get straight ta the point and ask," Ronorim continued as he marched to the center of the throne room. "Why did it take so long for it ta be cleared out, brother?"

Dunkell glanced uncomfortably around the room as Therason and the royal guards inside all looked suspiciously at him. The prince stood up, breathing deeply as he tried to calm himself, and walked over to where Ronorim stood, an innocent smile plastered onto his face.

"I'm sorry it took so long for ye ta return, truly, I am," he said. "I put as many dwarves as I could spare inta clearing out that blasted tunnel, but it kept collapsing. No matter what those workers did, they could never make too much progress. That's why it took longer than it should have ta clear it. But in the end it was done! And now, here ye are."

Thuradin thought this was a poor lie. He wouldn't have believed it even had he not talked to the tunnelers in Dun'Burell beforehand. Apparently, Ronorim was of the same mind.

"Don't ye dare lie ta me," he growled. "I spoke with the tunnelers who were working on that tunnel. They told me everything. I know the city has been fully repaired for several months now. Ye could have opened the way for my return so much sooner, but ye didn't. Now tell me why."

Dunkell stared blankly at Ronorim for several minutes in silence. He opened his mouth a few times, as if he was going to start explaining his actions, but no words ever came out. There could be no excuse that would satisfy his brother, except the truth. And the truth was perhaps better left unsaid.

Ronorim sighed heavily, his angry eyes losing much of their fire. "Whatever yer reasons were, we'll discuss them later—in private. For now, I've come ta reclaim my throne. So," he held out his hand, "give me my crown."

There was a moment of silence.

Thuradin could sense Dunkell's mind racing as he tried to think of some way to delay the inevitable. The air was suffocating as the silence continued. The slightest cough sounded like cannon fire and made everyone in the room jump. Ronorim stared down his brother.

"Well?"

Realizing no brilliant ideas would save him from this moment, Dunkell hung his head in resignation.

"No."

Ronorim cocked his head to the side. "I'm sorry," he chuckled. "Could ye repeat that? It sounded ta me like ye refused ta give me back *my* crown."

"I did."

The King's smile faltered as his eyes stared deep into Dunkell's. "Brother, do nae be a fool. Ye know the laws of succession as well as I. I was gone from my throne for less than six months. I am *still* King. Ye must return the crown or face the consequences."

Thuradin noticed Dunkell glance in his direction, as if he were asking for aid. Of course, there was no way he would give any when it looked to him like the prince had just tried to hijack the throne from Ronorim. And now he would pay the price. However, Thuradin wondered why he so adamantly refused to give back the throne, as if his life depended on it. Or perhaps something more than his life.

Seeing that no help was coming, Dunkell turned his gaze back to Ronorim.

"I know the laws. But I cannae give ye back this throne. Ye'll ruin all the progress I've made over the past few months."

"Progress?" Ronorim repeated, narrowing his eyes suspiciously. "Tell me, brother, what progress would I be disrupting? What have ye been doing these past few months with my crown?"

Dunkell took a shaky breath. "If I give it back, ye'll ruin all the progress I've made with the burrowers."

There was a pause as everyone let this sink in. Thuradin looked around the room. Therason and the royal guards looked just as shocked about the news as he was. They, evidently, hadn't been aware of the actions Dunkell was taking as steward.

Borim and Stürn frowned like they had just eaten something rotten. Ayrie glared at the prince, her hands balled into fists. No doubt she would have executed him as a traitor right then and there if she could. The viatari stood behind the dwarves, silently watching the scene unfold before them. All three looked interested, though Thuradin thought he saw a hint of concern in Victria's face.

During the silence, Dunkell appeared to have rallied some of his courage. His voice was stronger and more confident, and he held his head higher as he said his next words.

"While ye were gone, I was busy," he said. "I've always known the burrowers were an intelligent race and nae just a bunch of savages. I had secret tunnels that lead from here ta the burrower caverns built, and do ye know what I found, brother? I found their city!"

Dunkell looked around as if he expected to see some form of approval. But there was none.

"After finding it, I decided ta start diplomatic negotiations with them ta try and end our war peacefully. The negotiations haven't taken place yet, but in the meantime we've created a trade agreement as a sign of good faith. I have a feeling that soon we'll be able ta create a lasting peace that will end this useless war. But if I give yer throne back now, all of that work will be undone. Ye'll attack them, and everything I've been working on will have been in vain."

Thuradin ran his fingers through his beard in apprehension as Dunkell's explanation came to an end. What the prince had just said sounded too much along the lines of what the Creature had told him. He, too, had said the burrowers were a civilized race. He had even shown the dwarf images to prove those statements. Now that Dunkell claimed he had found a burrower city, Thuradin wondered if the Creature's words were true. If they were, that meant he was also correct about the dwarves being guilty of intending to commit genocide. He felt another one of the Creature's cold shocks about to overtake him, but he shifted his focus back to what had been said and the shock receded.

He didn't think Dunkell was lying. The Prince looked like he truly believed in what he said. But even if Thuradin wanted to believe him, he knew Ronorim, and he knew what was coming.

The King, who had been standing like a statue for the entire story, breathed deeply for the first time in minutes, trying to control his rage. Everyone, even the viatari, took a step back as they sensed what was about to happen. Dunkell remained where he was, oblivious.

"What—" Ronorim took another deep breath to try and keep from shouting, "—*what* have ye been giving ta the burrowers?"

It was a simple question. Unfortunately, it also acted as the trigger for an imminent explosion. Thuradin had a feeling Ronorim already knew what Dunkell was going to say. He silently prayed that the prince would come up with some simple but clever lie to avoid the coming rage. He didn't particularly like Dunkell, but even he pitied the prince's situation.

"Armor scraps, weapon scraps, things we don't need or have plenty of. Basically—"

That was as far as he got.

Ronorim let out an animalistic roar.

The Prince stepped back, his eyes as wide as they could go as he recognized his brother's fury for the first time.

Thuradin sighed. Out of all the ways to phrase the answer, the prince had chosen to use the words *armor* and *weapon*, the only two that seemed to register in Ronorim's mind. He could only watch now as the King threw curse after curse at his poor sibling.

Everyone in the room glanced around uncomfortably as Ronorim continued to shout creative profanities. Thuradin had been friends with him for a long time, but even he was surprised by some of the things said. Many of the words he had in his vocabulary he hadn't thought of as curses before now.

Minutes passed and Ronorim finally calmed down, but only after he realized he had depleted his entire vocabulary and was repeating curses. He breathed heavily, his eyes searching the room. His gaze fell upon the royal guards, who were trying their best not to be noticed.

"Restrain him," he said in as calm a voice as he could muster—which was still a shout.

The guards shuffled over to Dunkell, who was sitting on the floor with an empty expression. He looked as if he didn't know who he was, where he was, or what was happening anymore. He didn't even resist when the guards took hold of him.

"Ye've betrayed us," Ronorim said, this time managing not to shout. "Ye've betrayed yer kind, and ye are hereby banished from the upper regions of the Dwarven Kingdom. Ye will be sent ta Dun'Burell where ye'll stay until I see fit. Perhaps spending some time with the dwarves who actually have ta suffer from the burrowers every day will make ye open yer idiotic eyes."

With that, he walked over to his stunned brother, plucked the golden crown from his head, and put it on his own. He then walked over to the throne and, for the first time in a long time, sat down. Only then did Dunkell snap out of his shock.

"No!" he cried. "*I'm* yer King, ye cannae do this ta me! Ye'll ruin everything!"

"Take him away," was all Ronorim said in reply.

The royal guards dragged a flailing Dunkell out of the throne room. His cries soon disappeared. Having known Dunkell for as long as he had known Ronorim, Thuradin felt a mixture of pity and satisfaction. He felt sorry for the prince's predicament, but was also glad that he had been dealt with after the power grab he had made for the King's throne. A quick look around revealed that only Victria seemed to have any sort of pity in her eyes. Everyone else still looked like they were trying to get over Ronorim's outburst.

"Therason."

Therason jumped as Ronorim called his name. "M-my King?"

"I don't suppose ye'd mind giving Thuradin back his saphyrium helm?"

It was more of an order than a question. Therason gulped several times before he finally got the words out. "O-of course nae, my King."

Therason walked over to where Thuradin stood and quietly returned the saphyrium helm. Thuradin accepted it as graciously as he could to try and keep the dwarf from further embarrassment. He looked at the winged helm in his hands. He had promised himself he would get it back, and now he had fulfilled that promise. It felt like ages since he had made it. But here he was, the commander of the royal guard once again.

He took off the regular helmet he had been wearing for most of his time in the outside world and let it fall to the ground. Its clanking reverberated across the spacious throne room like a slow clap. Then, reverently, he raised the saphyrium helm above him and slid his head into it. The fit was as perfect as he remembered.

Victria leaned in next to him and grinned. "So this is what the commander of the royal guard truly looks like. It certainly makes you taller." She pointed at the two wings on the sides of the helmet.

Thuradin was so pleased to be wearing the saphyrium helm again, he couldn't even think of anything witty to reply with.

During this exchange, Ronorim called for a courier.

"I want ye ta go ta Kul'Kriegar,' he told the dwarf. "Ask them for all the soldiers they can give me. We're going ta march ta Dun'Burell and drive the burrowers from this world permanently."

The courier nodded and hastily ran out to perform his duty.

Ronorim now turned his attention to the viatari. Victria ceased her teasing and made her way, flanked by Natiari and Tessa, to the center of the throne room, where they all kneeled.

"Hail to you, Ronorim, King of the Dwarven Kingdom," Victria said. Her voice rang clear as a bell.

Ronorim laughed, which, Thuradin was pleased to see, took Victria off guard, since he had been in such a fury only moments ago.

"There's no need for such formalities," he said, shaking his head. "I think we've become good friends over the past five months, don't ye agree?"

"Well, yes, but—"

"So we should just be frank with each other."

The King hopped down from his throne and walked over to Victria, who was still kneeling. He urged her to stand and, after some persuasion, she complied.

"I've come ta trust yer kind," the King said. "And I assure ye, eventually the rest of the dwarves will come ta be of the same mind."

A table and several chairs, as well as a gigantic keg of ale, were brought in by some of the royal guards at Ronorim's request.

"Now, I believe I promised ye that we would work on forming an alliance once I returned ta my throne. So," he sat down on one side of the table and poured himself a pint of ale. "Shall we begin?"

Victria shot Thuradin a look with eyes that clearly asked, *Are all dwarven politics like this?*

Thuradin nodded with a knowing grin.

The viatari glanced at her two companions, who looked back at her expectantly. They all nodded in unison.

Victria took a seat on the opposite side of the table, poured herself a pint, and downed it all in one fluid motion. Ronorim raised his eyebrows, impressed. Thuradin was also impressed. He knew Victria didn't particularly enjoy the taste of ale, but even so, she looked determined to do whatever it took to reestablish old ties.

She hiccupped as the alcohol settled in her stomach but quickly regained her composure and refilled her mug.

CHAPTER TWENTY-SIX

Whether making treaties, forming alliances, or negotiating a simple contract, dwarven politics always came down to the same basic principle: both parties were to get as intoxicated as possible to ensure the fairest deal was made.

There were many times in Thuradin's life where he had witnessed this form of diplomacy, though more often than not, those negotiations ended with high-ranking officials yelling obscenities at each other, getting into brawls, or passing out before a deal was struck. If he could use a single word to describe dwarven politics, it would be *terrifying*. He didn't think anyone but the sturdiest of dwarves could partake in it and survive.

Victria proved him so very wrong.

Perhaps it was because she didn't drink as often as dwarves did, but she was already smashed by the time Ronorim was just starting to feel his drink. Thuradin remembered the King's eyes change from amusement to horror as the alcohol took hold of the viatari and turned her into a monster.

Before the transformation, things had been going smoothly. Ronorim was already on his fifth pint and Victria had just filled her third. The two laughed at each other as they both realized they were tipsy. Then, Victria downed her third. Her head drooped as if she had fallen asleep in her chair. Ronorim chuckled some more and suggested they continue this another day when her head popped straight back up. A malevolent glint shone in her eyes as she refilled her stein.

After that, the meeting was controlled entirely by Victria. She raved and laughed maniacally as she suggested conditions and requirements that could be added to the treaty. The instant Ronorim disagreed or said he couldn't allow what she suggested, she would lean across the table, bare her fangs viciously, and threaten to "suck his life out," only to fall back into her chair and fall victim to a fit of high-pitched giggling.

The first few times this happened, Ronorim laughed along nervously, thinking it was a joke. Now he shrunk back into his chair every time she gave the threat. Not too long ago, she had lunged at him with her fangs bared, looking as if she might truly take his life energies. Only the quick actions of Natiari and Tessa, who intercepted Victria's lunge and tackled her to the ground, had saved the dwarven King.

Now they stood behind her with a hand on each of her shoulders and looks of bewilderment on their faces. It was clear they had never seen her behave so wildly before and didn't know what to do to snap her out of her drunken stupor. Their only option was to restrain her.

Thuradin could only watch Ronorim flinch and shrink away every time he was addressed by the crazed viatari. By the time negotiations were over, Ronorim was a mental mess and Victria was passed out.

The commander of the royal guard walked over to the table and picked up the several sheets of paper that were the unofficial alliance between the dwarves and the viatari—Ronorim had promised to place the royal seal on it later before being escorted back to his own room by several guards just as shaken as he was. Thuradin read through the papers and was surprised by how beneficial it was for the dwarves, despite Victria dominating the negotiations.

With this treaty, trade would be established between the two races, which would help solve the food shortage problem the dwarves had been facing for the past several centuries. The dwarves would be allowed to set up colonies in the outside world if they chose to, so long as they stayed near the mountains. They wouldn't be allowed to send up their own soldiers to protect the colonies, though—the viatari didn't want any complications coming out of that—so the colonies were to be under the supervision and protection of the nearby viatari, though this was subject to change.

There were other items as well, such as giving the viatari some cannons to add to the defenses of Aleganthia and the dwarves receiving aid from the viatari in return when it came time to set up farming facilities in the outside world. For the most part, the document was a military alliance. The viatari would come to the aid of the dwarves should they call for it, and the dwarves would do the same for the viatari.

Thuradin glanced up to see Natiari and Tessa dragging away their unconscious friend. He grimaced sympathetically as he thought of how her head would feel in the morning.

He looked through the papers one last time and handed them off to a nearby royal guard, telling him to place it in a secure location. The guard nodded and rushed out of the room.

Thuradin was alone now. Everyone else had already filed out and gone to bed—the negotiations had lasted well into the night. He sighed heavily as he made his way back to his room. He looked forward to sleeping in his own bed again after so long without it. But as thoughts of what he would have to do in the morning entered his head, he began to feel anxious.

He could think of no way around it. Now that he was back in Tinas Gran he would have to face Bronn Lightninghammer tomorrow and tell him about his failure to protect Threnn, Murtosh, and Agrethar.

Bronn lived in a part of Tinas Gran close to the training grounds—large arenas, each with a pit in the middle where several wooden dummies stood. The stone buildings were meant for dwarves to practice their skills in fighting, and often the sound of wood smacking against shield or flesh could be heard coming from within the open doors. Bronn was often found here, sparring with the wooden dummies as the gears within them spun, allowing the wooden limbs to come to life and attack whoever was within range. It was here that Bronn would take his apprentices to teach them strategy and fighting techniques. It was in these training grounds that Thuradin would have to share the terrible news.

Bronn was unaware of anyone watching him as he stepped just out of range of a dummy's arms while it swung around in a dangerous arc. Thuradin watched the older dwarf battle the wooden machine for several minutes, trying to think of how in the world he was going to get through this. What would he say?

As Bronn deflected a blow with his shield and brought his rounded hammer crashing into the dummy's side, he turned and saw Thuradin for the first time. For a moment, the two dwarves just stared at each other.

"Thuradin!" Bronn said, a soft grin spreading across his

face. "Ye're back! That means, then, ye found him?"

Thuradin nodded. "Aye. He was in Dun'Burell waiting for us, but we had ta wait for months for the tunnel ta be cleared out before we could travel back home."

"I'm sure ye did," Bronn said, his face darkening momentarily. "That blasted Dunkell did everything he could ta slow down the clean up. We were starting ta wonder if it would ever get finished."

Bronn walked over to Thuradin and clapped him on the shoulder.

"I'm glad ta see that ye're back, though, and that the saphyrium helm is back on yer head."

Thuradin nodded his thanks as he took off his helm and stared into the blue sapphire at the center. The moment was coming. How was he going to tell him?

Bronn cleared his throat. "I'm assuming my boys are back then?"

There it was.

Thuradin looked up from his helm and into the older dwarf's eyes and was surprised to see the raw sadness and anger within. Bronn already knew.

"They're—" Thuradin's mind was numb. "That's what I came ta speak with ye about. . . ."

Thuradin told him everything that had happened. He told him about their encounters with the humans, the darimun, and the Creature. He told him about the viatari and their quest to stop the Creature from starting another war. He told him about the humans who ambushed them and how Agrethar fell to a poisoned arrow. He told him how he had managed to find a cave for the young dwarf to die in before he was entombed.

His mind was a numb blank as he told Bronn about

Inadarim and how he and his companions had scaled its central mountain to the top and found the artifact, the Creature's dwelling place, and then how Dragos' betrayal had resulted in the deaths of Threnn and Murtosh. As an afterthought, he even told him about how he had gone into the artifact after Dragos and had witnessed the terrible demise of the young viatari.

Bronn listened to all of this with the same unchanging expression. Thuradin wanted the old dwarf to show his anger, to yell at him, maybe even bash his head in with that rounded hammer he gripped with a white-knuckled fist. Bronn had just lost everything again, and it was all his fault.

But when he had finished recounting his tale, nothing happened. There was no vengeful strike made against him, no angry words. Bronn only thanked him for telling him about the fates of his apprentices before turning away and resuming his battle with the wooden dummies.

Thuradin watched for a few more minutes before exiting the training ground. As he walked away, he heard the sound of splintering wood growing faster and louder.

The soldiers from Kul'Kriegar Ronorim had called for arrived within the week. Their camp, set just outside Tinas Gran, could be seen extending all the way to the tunnel to Dun'Burell. Apparently, the viceroy of Kul'Kriegar, a dwarf by the name of Dranthal, had sent every soldier he had to offer. The prospect of finishing off the burrowers once and for all was a good one.

Thuradin looked out of the small window in his room. He saw legions of dwarves marching out of the armories all over the city, all of them on their way to join up with the Kul'Kriegarans.

Ronorim hadn't been idle for the past week. He had called up, prepared, and even managed to put in a little training for Tinas Gran's own soldiers. He was taking half of them on the campaign, no small number, including Thuradin and the royal guards. With all the soldiers of Kul'Kriegar and half of Tinas Gran combined, it was one of the largest dwarven armies ever raised. Already the infantry alone amounted to several thousand.

They were set to leave soon. Thuradin began the long process of putting on his armor. Layers of plate armor, secured by thick, leather straps, went over his arms, legs, and torso. After securely strapping his large spaulders onto his shoulders, he moved to his last piece, the saphyrium helm.

He should have felt happy, content at least, that he had managed to do almost everything he had set out to do. He had found his King. He had kept most of his companions alive. He had reclaimed his saphyrium helm. He had even helped the viatari with their own quest. He should have felt accomplished, but instead, he felt like something was wrong, like something terrible was going to happen. And soon.

He shook his head. It would do no good to be distracted like this when it came time for battle.

Patting himself down, he checked to make sure his armor was on properly, that no single part was too loose or too tight. After packing a few personal items into a small bag to take with him, he left his room, and then the palace. He weaved through the crowd of war-ready dwarves as he headed for the rally point Ronorim had set the day before.

Upon arriving, he saw the King already seated on his ram, rearing to go. Stürn was mounted next to him, and behind them, also mounted, were the viatari and then the royal guards. Thuradin saluted hastily as he approached Ronorim, then turned to Victria.

"Ye're coming with us?"

Victria nodded. "We decided—" Natiari and Tessa leered accusingly at her. "Well . . . *I* decided, seeing how we're now allies, to help the dwarves with their campaign."

"And them?" Thuradin said, indicating the other two viatari, neither of whom looked pleased with the current situation.

"We'd rather not be part of this," Natiari said. "Felix only told us to form an alliance with your people, nothing else."

"But," Tessa continued, "as we said when we joined you in Aleganthia, we cannot let Victria go through with this alone. Despite our protests, she will not turn away from this course of action, so we must go with her."

"And there you have it," Victria shrugged.

"Thuradin—"

Thuradin turned to face Ronorim, this time giving a proper salute.

"If ye would mount, please. I'd like us ta get going as soon as we can. It's going ta be a long march with such a large force."

The dwarven commander nodded and mounted at once.

"Did ye see how many we have?" Ronorim said proudly as they began riding toward the tunnel to Dun'Burell. Soon it wasn't just them; the entire army moved out behind them. Thousands of armored boots struck the stone floor repeatedly and in unison as they marched. The sound was deafening and constant. Thuradin thought he could hear war drums coming from somewhere behind him, setting the pace with a slow, steady *Boom!. . . Boom!. . . Boom!. . .*

"Aye, several thousand infantry, and I thought I saw some cavalry too?"

"Aye, ye did," the King said, nodding happily. "Five hundred battle rams, fully armored, with the best fighters riding them."

Thuradin turned in his saddle to try and see these mounted warriors, but he couldn't make out much detail over the sea of helmeted faces.

"How are Ayrie and Borim doing?" he asked, giving up on his search for the cavalry. He hadn't heard from either of them since the night the alliance was negotiated, and that had slightly worried him. Stürn was constantly by Ronorim's side, so he hadn't needed to worry about the Enurg'en.

"They're both fine," Ronorim replied. "Haven't they told ye? I made them both officers. They have their own dwarves ta worry about now."

Thuradin turned once more in his saddle to see if he could spot some hint of his two friends, but once again the sea of faces proved too formidable a force to penetrate. No single dwarf could be identified in that mass. He faced forward again, deciding he would find them later, when they arrived to Dun'Burell, and rode for a time in silence.

The march took several days to complete.

It was a slow, serious process. There was hardly any time for idle conversation. Everyone seemed to realize that the upcoming battle would require everything they had, all their focus, all their strength. The next few days would determine whether they continued to live in fear of the burrowers.

They arrived at Dun'Burell. The cavern was filled with much more smoke that the last time Thuradin had been there. It looked like there had been a significant battle near the tunnel on the opposite end of the cavern. He recognized it as the one that connected the burrowers' caverns to their own. A burrower invasion must have been thwarted recently, and it didn't look like it had been an easy job.

The army marched directly to Kul'Burell and set up camp just outside its walls. The city was emptier than it used to be, but the dwarves who were still there worked tirelessly. A fire seemed to spring into their eyes as they saw the large number of reinforcements arriving.

Ronorim dismounted just outside the city gates. "I'm going ta speak with Baleth ta explain what I have in mind. Since he's the viceroy of this city, he should know what he will be leading his soldiers inta. Will ye come along?"

Thuradin shook his head. "No, I think I'm going ta look around, see if I can find Ayrie and Borim."

The King nodded, then trudged off into the city followed closely by Stürn and some of the royal guards.

Thuradin dismounted and started weaving his way through the mass of dwarven warriors who had started setting up camp. He would stop every now and then to check up on a few he recognized and hadn't seen since he had gone into the outside world, but he soon stopped doing that. It wasn't encouraging to be greeted constantly with: "Thuradin! I thought ye were dead!" or "I was sure ye were a goner!"

Finally, after what seemed like hours of searching, he found the two dwarves he was looking for.

Ayrie and Borim stood in front of a small crowd of soldiers, waving their arms around every so often. From the looks of it, he guessed they were recounting their adventures in the outside world. He could see the crowd looking at his two friends in awe, no doubt imagining the journey to be even more dangerous and gruesome than it actually was, as if the reality wasn't bad enough already.

As soon as they were finished with their story, the crowd

dispersed and began retelling it to other dwarves. They waved their arms around even more dramatically than his two friends had. Thuradin frowned. It wouldn't do to have hugely exaggerated legends about him and his companions popping up all over the Dwarven Kingdom. But he would have to deal with that later.

Ayrie and Borim had noticed him and were waiting for him to approach. He looked into their eyes, trying to detect . . . he didn't know what. He couldn't place why he felt compelled to seek them out and now that he had, he had no idea exactly what he wanted to say to them. It felt like his mind had simply stopped working.

Ayrie and Borim glanced at each other uncertainly, then walked over to where he was.

"Are ye alright, Thuradin?" Borim asked. "Ye don't look so good."

Thuradin shook his head. A cold shock coursed through him. It felt like a hand was clawing its way through his body. It wrapped itself around his heart in a vice-like grip. His insides felt like ice. He staggered.

Luckily, Ayrie and Borim caught him before he could hit the ground. They sat him down against a boulder and took off his helmet so he could breathe easier. Many of those around them noticed the fall and stared openly, a few with concern but many more curious. They began to gravitate toward him.

"Borim!" Ayrie hissed.

"On it."

Borim stood up and herded the curious dwarves away from the scene. It wouldn't be good for morale if the army saw the commander of the royal guard in such a state of distress.

"Alright lads," he said. "Show's over! Go back ta packing up the camp ye just set, I'm sure we'll be leaving soon!"

The dwarves did as they were told, albeit grudgingly. Several of them cast one last glance at Thuradin, who now leaned against the boulder with his head cradled in his hands. It wasn't a good image for them to leave with, but there was nothing more Borim could do. He could only hope those particular dwarves didn't have big mouths.

Thuradin took a shaky breath. "I thank ye."

"What happened?" Ayrie asked curiously. "One second ye were walking over ta us and the next ye turn as white as Borim's beard!"

"Oye!" Borim said. "My beard isn't *that* white!"

Thuradin shook his head. The cold shocks had never been as bad as the one he had just experienced. He felt utterly drained and wished he could dig a hole next to the boulder he sat against and lay there for the remainder of his life. The fact that the shocks were getting stronger couldn't be a good sign, but he couldn't tell Ayrie or Borim about them; otherwise, he would also have to tell them about the curse.

"I don't know," he said finally. "I've been having these sporadic fits ever since my encounter with the Creature—but this is the first time it's caused me to collapse."

"Since yer encounter with the Creature?" Borim repeated with mild alarm. "Have ye tried talking ta the viatari about it? They might know what's happening."

Thuradin was shaking his head before Borim even finished his suggestion.

"I cannae tell them."

He wanted to explain why he couldn't, but he managed to hold his tongue at the last second. He had already divulged more than he thought he would to them, but only *he* had to know about the curse. And that's the way he wanted it to stay.

Ayrie opened her mouth, no doubt to ask why, but then a horn sounded from inside Kul'Burell. There was a resounding cheer from the army as a thick column of armored dwarves marched out of the city gates. It appeared the dwarves of Kul'Burell were joining the final campaign. They would have their revenge.

"Go back ta yer legions," Thuradin said as he lifted himself up. His legs still felt weak, but the cold shock had passed. He was no longer in danger of collapsing. Ayrie and Borim looked ready to protest, but he raised a hand before they could utter a word.

"I'm fine. Go on, now. We'll discuss this another time."

The two dwarves hesitated, then nodded and began to walk away.

Thuradin rushed off back to the city gates. Some agreement had just been made between Ronorim and Baleth—that was what the horn sounding off had to mean—and he wanted to know the details.

He arrived just as Baleth left Ronorim's side to join his own dwarves, a look of satisfaction on his face.

"What's happened?"

Ronorim's eyes lit up as he saw Thuradin. "Ah, Thuradin, ye missed it! Baleth has committed all of Kul'Burell's forces. The city is being emptied!"

"All?" Thuradin repeated.

"Aye, all of them. *And* we have new weapons ta kill the burrowers with," Ronorim turned and called for someone to bring *it* to him. Thuradin had no idea what *it* was, but whatever *it* was made the King excited. Thuradin thought he even appeared a little crazed.

You will be allowed to continue your foolish quest to find your genocidal King.

Stop it, he thought, shaking his head. He didn't know if it was from memory or if he had actually heard the Creature's voice just now, but either way, he didn't want to have to think about it; he couldn't afford to show signs of weakness.

He heard a deep, raspy chuckle. . . .

He did everything he could to try and get the voice out of his head: emptying his mind, thinking happy thoughts, remembering old jokes, everything, and after a while, it faded away. Ronorim didn't seem to have noticed anything unusual, though. The King continued to look at him excitedly as a large slab of rock with a medium-sized, cylindrical piece of iron attached on top was rolled toward them by several dwarves.

"What—How—?"

"Incredible, isn't it?" Ronorim said with a small grin. "Mobile cannons. The first of their kind. They don't pack as much firepower as the larger cannons here, but they make up for that with their mobility."

"How does it move?" Thuradin asked. He had to admit he was impressed by the new invention. He had never thought it would be possible to make artillery mobile.

One of the engineers stepped forward. "We cut out four holes on the underside of this stone slab where we put in steel spheres so the cannon can be rolled ta wherever it needs ta go. They won't break under the weight, and they can be easily held in place by setting heavy stones around the slab so it doesn't go rolling away after every shot."

"Aye, with this," Ronorim continued, patting the cannon affectionately, "we have a guaranteed victory. Ye know as well as I do how the burrowers cannae stand up against cannon fire. Ah, this campaign will go along smoother than even I imagined."

Suddenly, the dreamy expression that had been on the King's face melted away and grew stern.

"Though, I must tell ye, Thuradin, not all goes as planned. Baleth tells me my brother never arrived to Kul'Burell. In fact, he hasn't been seen anywhere in the cavern. I had planned on having him join us for this campaign so he could see firsthand the terrible nature of our enemy. But now I'm left wondering where the fool has run off to. . . ."

As quickly as the change in mood came, it left. A quick shake of the head and a reassuring pat on Thuradin's shoulder and the King was back to his cheery self, not a hint of anything amiss on his face.

A few more explanations were given on how the cannon worked. Thuradin was even shown a demonstration. The cannon's firepower was certainly lesser than the fixed artillery located all over Dun'Burell, but it was still effective. He watched as a stalagmite toppled over, crashing to the ground after only two shots.

There were a total of ten mobile cannons and once they were ready to move, Ronorim called for the march to continue. The army cheered loudly as their King led them toward the burrowers' tunnel. But the eagerness soon faded as they marched through the desolate wasteland of Dun'Burell.

They passed many destroyed outposts. Several of the fortifications were in ruins. They even saw a few stone dwarves who had died in some past skirmish and hadn't been retrieved quickly enough before entombment.

The signs of battle made the army nervous and restless. Thuradin was also nervous, but for a different reason. He had a strong premonition again that something awful was about to happen. Perhaps the burrowers were waiting for them in ambush, waiting to massacre the largest dwarven army ever raised. Perhaps not. He turned in his saddle and saw Victria riding a short distance behind him. He hadn't seen her during their stop in Kul'Burell, and he wondered where she and the other viatari had gone.

Victria's expression wasn't comforting. It was one of uncertainty, rather than the mischievous yet confident mien she usually had. He found he also felt uncertain about the upcoming battle, but he didn't think that was what was worrying the viatari.

The air around them grew tense as they approached the gaping tunnel. There were no torches set inside it like in the dwarven ones, so the dwarves had to light their own and carry them if they wanted to see.

Several warriors hesitated before entering the chasm, but whether by their own will or by their comrades' shoving, they all eventually went inside. The sound of the war drums continued its slow, steady cadence and only grew louder as the sound reverberated off the stone walls: *Boom . . . Boom . . . Boom . . .*

No one mentioned it, but everyone knew, even the viatari: they weren't in the Dwarven Kingdom anymore. They were in enemy territory. Burrower territory.

Boom . . . Boom . . . Boom . . .

CHAPTER TWENTY-SEVEN

They set up camp deep inside the tunnel. Days of marching had passed with no end in sight. Some began to think it would never end. In order to try and stop the uneasiness spreading among the troops, Ronorim stopped their march and told everyone to rest while scouts were sent ahead of them. The scouts were only to come back once they found an exit.

So far, several hours had passed and none had returned.

Thuradin sat stiffly on his bedroll, staring at the lamp hanging in the center of his tent. He'd had a lot of time to think about what had happened in Kul'Burell. There must have been a reason why the cold shocks had suddenly become stronger, and he had a hunch it was related to the current campaign against the burrowers. Perhaps, he thought sardonically, the time for his curse to take effect was quickly approaching.

He hoped he was wrong because, if he was not, he would not be the only one affected. There were too many dwarves nearby, as well as his King and the viatari. He feared the curse might spread to them.

He thought back to what the Creature had said: *You will*

be seen as a traitor to your kind.

He thought about what he could possibly do that might make him a traitor, but nothing came to mind. That was still a mystery, but he was sure he could never do anything to betray his own kin. He always endeavored to make the right decision.

You will realize what I say about the burrowers is true, and you will try to wash away your guilt by bringing peace between your two races. . . .

Thuradin knew the Creature believed the burrowers to be as civilized and intelligent as the dwarves, but he still couldn't grasp the concept. However, if the time for his curse to come to pass truly was approaching, then he figured he would grasp the concept soon enough, if it was really there. Even if the Creature turned out to be right about the burrowers, though, he had no idea how he would even attempt to bring peace between the two races, even if he wanted to.

Your guilt will only increase the more you try to right your wrong.

Thuradin shook his head, frustrated. He didn't understand what the Creature meant and he was starting to not give a damn. He was a dwarf! The only thing he had to understand was that he had to fight the burrowers for his King, and should he die, he would forever be entombed within the mountains. If the Creature had wanted to scare him with his little curse, he should have cursed him in a more straightforward manner, rather than with all these riddles.

The sound of approaching footsteps brought Thuradin away from his moody thoughts. He looked up and saw Victria standing at the entrance to his tent.

"Can I come in? We need to talk."

Thuradin nodded. He bit his tongue hard to keep himself from grinning as Victria entered in an uncomfortable crouch and pulled up a chair opposite him. The tent was medium sized by dwarven standards, but even that was much too small for a viatari.

Victria gave him a look. Apparently, biting his tongue wasn't working too well.

"So," Thuradin began. "What is it—"

"The burrowers," Victria said curtly. "I don't think they're the evil savages your King makes them out to be."

"What do ye—"

"I know it isn't my place," Victria interrupted. "I don't live in these mountains. I don't know what dealing with them on a daily basis is like. After fighting them for so long, the dwarves may think they know their enemy well enough to know that they truly are savages. But what if you are all wrong? What if they are not as bad as you all think they are? I feel uneasy when I think we may be slaughtering an entire race based on a false idea."

"What makes ye think—"

"We saw them," she interrupted again, much to Thuradin's annoyance. "When we stopped at Kul'Burell, Natiari, Tessa, and I decided to explore the area. At first we just wanted to ride around the gigantic stalagmites nearby, but then we wanted to see more of the cannons we only glimpsed the last time we were there. There were so many battles before that we could never really make time to see them. We rode all over the cavern, and while we were nearing one of the cannons situated near this tunnel, we came across a group of burrowers."

She hesitated.

"I'll admit, they're certainly not the most beautiful

creatures in this world, as Ronorim constantly tells me. But as they noticed us and we noticed them, I didn't see how they could be categorized as savages. It looked like they had just been in battle. Several of them carried their wounded in their arms, even the ones who were wounded themselves. When they saw us, they looked just as surprised as we were. But even when Natiari and Tessa moved toward them threateningly, they didn't become some raging, bloodthirsty pack of animals. They cowered, and, well, when I looked into their eyes . . . Do you know what I saw?"

Thuradin didn't answer. He listened intently as Victria told her story, the grin on his face long gone.

"I saw fear, of course. But what was more shocking to me was the sadness. It's the same sadness you see in those who are unjustly persecuted. My people had the same look when we were fighting the Creature a thousand years ago. Many of us *still* have that look because of the way humans hunt us down like monsters today."

Thuradin nodded slowly. He had noticed the haunting sadness she described when he first encountered the viatari. It had been an especially strong feature in Felix's eyes.

"They looked so pitiful," Victria continued. "So I told Natiari and Tessa to stand down. We stood like that, staring at each other for several minutes, before the burrowers seemed to realize they had been spared. One of them, who I assumed to be the leader, stepped up and—"

"Ye let them go?"

The words exploded out of Thuradin's mouth. He hadn't meant for them to come out with such force, but the thought of burrowers being allowed to return to where they came from after battling and killing dwarves was outrageous. What if they returned with a larger force? What if they told their burrower friends a large army of dwarves was marching into their territory and set up an ambush? Several more disaster scenarios ran through his head before he realized Victria had gone silent.

"Yes, I let them go," she said, frowning. "They were no threat, and it was obvious they had lost their will to fight. They didn't even have weapons."

She shook her head.

"My point, Thuradin, is that they didn't look like the battle-crazed killers you and your King have described to me. They looked more like a defeated, broken race. So I will say it again, this campaign against the burrowers makes me feel uneasy. The Creature believed we were guilty of wanting to commit genocide. I don't want to prove him right."

Thuradin remembered telling everyone about the Creature's motives after he returned from the depths of the artifact. Everyone had looked insulted when they learned the Creature had accused *them* of wanting to commit genocide.

"I understand how ye're feeling," he said, recovering from his outburst. "What the Creature said about the burrowers still lingers in my mind as well. But I *know* they aren't our equals. They *are* savages. This should nae be likened ta genocide.

"I don't know what ta think about yer story. I cannae tell ye what happened in Dun'Burell didn't happen, of course—I wasn't there—but ye shouldn't fool yerself inta thinking these things are nice, innocent victims. Believe me, they're nothing but a plague. And like any plague, they must be wiped out so we may end our own suffering."

Victria studied him for several minutes. He hoped he looked as confident as he sounded, because he wasn't sure what to believe in either. But if it was to protect the honor of the dwarves, until there was proof otherwise, he was willing to affirm that the burrowers were savages and nothing more, even if he doubted his own words.

Finally, she lowered her gaze and nodded. "I believe you. That is why I am still here. I just hope you're not wrong."

"What about Natiari and Tessa?" Thuradin asked. "What do they think?"

"They have been against this campaign since the beginning, but as they said when we left Tinas Gran, they remain for my sake. They won't leave me to face a trial of this magnitude alone, and I can't blame them. If our roles were reversed, I would stay with them, too"

Thuradin nodded. He had figured as much. He was about to comment on her bond with the other two viatari when the horns sounded from the center of camp.

"What is it?" Victria asked, slightly startled. "Are we under attack?"

"No," Thuradin shook his head, poking it outside his tent's flap. "I think the scouts have returned. Let's go."

They made their way through the stirring camp as dwarves popped out of their tents to see what was going on. Thuradin's guess proved to be correct. As they neared the King's tent, they could see several dwarves already breaking up camp.

They found the central command tent and, upon entering, saw Ronorim talking with three scouts. Ronorim watched them enter and called them to his side.

"These lads tell me we'll start ta see the end of the tunnel after a few more hours of marching."

"We'll *see* the end of the tunnel?" Thuradin asked, confused. He had assumed that everywhere they went from now on would be pitch-black, since there was no dwarven lighting system installed.

"Aye," Ronorim confirmed. "Apparently, the connecting cavern is blazing with light. We won't have ta be in darkness for much longer."

"What's in the next cavern?"

The King shrugged. "No idea. The scouts didn't actually check ta see what we'll be facing, but that's no matter. However, we'll need ta extinguish our torches as soon as we see the exit so we can keep the element of surprise. Pass the word around, would ye?"

Thuradin nodded, saluted, then exited. Victria followed close behind.

It took the dwarves a little over one hour before light could be seen coming from the end of the tunnel instead of the several the scouts had claimed. It seemed to Thuradin that in their excitement, the scouts had performed their jobs poorly. The command to extinguish all flames was given. The dwarves marched on with no light save for the one source in front of them. Thuradin couldn't see very well, but he could feel the excitement and the eagerness of those behind him. They sensed a battle was imminent, and he didn't think they were wrong.

As they neared the tunnel exit, Ronorim called for them to halt and went on with only a few others, including Stürn, Thuradin, and the viatari. They dismounted and carefully crept their way forward until they could see every square foot of the cavern they were about to enter.

Thuradin wondered why the floor looked so far away, then realized with a gasp that they were about fifty feet above it. The tunnel ended in a steep drop-off. He briefly wondered how they were going to get thousands of dwarves down there in one piece. There was a slight slant to the wall under them. They *might* be able to climb down, but that would be too slow. He hoped Ronorim wasn't planning anything too crazy.

The cavern was immense. It even gave Dun'Burell a run for its money in size. Huge stalactites hung down from the ceiling, sometimes alone, sometimes in vast clusters. Another large tunnel could be seen at the far end of the cavern, though this one was at floor-level. Bonfires blazed across the cavern floor, giving the area light and heat. Around each of these fires stood or sat a large number of burrowers. Small, stone structures were also scattered across the cavern floor, mostly around the fires. Thuradin thought they looked like small huts.

He soon realized that was exactly what they were, and then he knew what he was looking at. It was a burrower camp. Never had he thought such a thing could be possible. He had always believed the burrowers incapable of organizing themselves to such a capacity. They should have just been a mindless horde.

Doubt crept into his mind once again. If the burrowers were organized enough to create such a sprawling camp, they could indeed be considered civilized. After all, if they had a camp like this, it wouldn't be too strange to think they might also have a city. And if they had a large, organized city, his life-long perception of the burrowers being lesser than his own kind would have to be questioned.

He glanced at Victria and knew instantly she was thinking the same thing. For her, this was further proof that what she had been told about the burrowers by Ronorim was either an intentional lie or a misconstrued idea.

Thuradin wondered if he should voice his thoughts to Ronorim, but the King had already returned to his army with the news. He had no choice but to follow and stay silent.

"I know what it looks like," he whispered to Victria as they all remounted. "But there's nothing we can do about it right now. I say go along with whatever happens for now and we'll figure out what's going on later."

Victria nodded, though she didn't look too happy about the situation.

"MY FRIENDS!"

They both jumped as Ronorim suddenly began shouting a rousing speech to his warriors. The King's voice boomed through the tunnel and traveled all the way to the army's rear as the sound bounced off the walls. The dwarves looked just as surprised. They stood uncertainly as their King delivered line after inspiring line. No matter how electrifying it was, however, they did not cheer. They still had enough sense to recognize that cheering at the top of their lungs would immediately draw the burrowers to their location.

The speech ended almost as abruptly as it had started, and Ronorim turned to lead everyone to the tunnel exit. Thuradin rode up next to him.

"Are ye insane?" he said. "What happened ta the element of surprise?"

"Pah!" Ronorim replied jovially. "I doubt those cretins heard me. They were probably too loud talking amongst themselves in their own brutish tongue. Don't worry; we still have surprise on our side. Look!"

They stood at the edge of the exit again. The camp of burrowers hadn't stirred a bit, even with Ronorim's shouting. Everything remained just as it had been.

Thuradin shrugged. "That was still reckless," he said. "Now, I don't suppose ye have a way of getting us all down ta the cavern floor safely, do ye?"

Ronorim grinned. "Everyone, follow my lead!"

Thuradin watched in disbelief as the King dismounted and jumped off the edge of the drop-off. He slid down the slope, his armor acting as a sled, which allowed him to slide down the rocky slope and protect his body from the rough surface at the same time. His mount loyally followed him, though it had a much easier time running down the slope.

The other dwarves began sliding down in the same manner without so much as a second thought. As soon as they hit the ground, they took off running toward the burrower camp, their war cries ringing throughout the cavern.

Those who were riding rams only had to hold on tight as their mounts did all the work by jumping from rock to rock or running down at top speed as Ronorim's mount had. Once all the rams reached the bottom, they gathered together and charged the burrowers as well, sending several of them flying as they lowered their horned heads and crashed into them.

The viatari abandoned their mounts and jumped off the edge completely, landing the fifty-foot drop without any difficulty.

"Of course," Thuradin muttered before he, too, urged his mount down the slope. As soon as he reached the floor, he drew his twin axes and unleashed his own war cry as his ram continued running and crashed into the first burrower it crossed paths with, sending it into one of the bonfires.

By the time the burrowers realized they were under attack, it was already too late. The dwarves smashed into them like a battering ram. They hacked and slashed and pummeled, killing any burrowers they could lay their hands on. They attacked with such speed and ferocity that the burrowers were forced to fight individually. They had no time to gather themselves up for a cohesive defense.

The burrowers now wore pieces of armor along with their loincloths and carried better, stronger weapons—a result, no doubt, of Dunkell's trade deal—but that didn't seem to matter. The dwarves slaughtered them as if they wore no armor and carried no weapons at all.

Thuradin soon forgot the doubts he had been harboring as he joined the battle.

The burrowers were fearsome. Their eyes looked wild and their blue-gray skin emphasized it. As soon as the first one lunged at him with a spear, Thuradin's battle instincts took over, and he killed without a second thought.

He urged his mount through cluster after cluster of burrowers, embedding his axes into their heads while his ram sent several flying to their deaths with its horned head. They tried to attack him with large clubs and spears, but he deflected them easily from where he sat.

Eventually, they began directing their attacks at his ram. Their clubs battered his mount's legs, shattering them while they shoved their spears deep through the beast's torso. Thuradin jumped and rolled away before he was trapped under the slain beast. He looked at his mount sadly, and with a soft bleat the ram breathed its last.

Anger burned through him. He shifted his attention to the group of burrowers responsible and tore through them with his axes, yelling profanities as he did.

He continued like this, whirling through groups of burrowers, swinging his axes in deadly arcs for what felt like hours. He dodged or parried every attack that came at him.

He twirled and spun and rolled as he moved among the burrower ranks, searching for his next kill. None could touch the dwarf with the saphyrium helm. But no matter how many he killed, there were always more to take their place.

Soon, Thuradin's arms grew heavy, and it took an enormous amount of will to hold onto both of his axes and continue swinging. His legs felt like they might buckle at any moment. His thoughts turned sluggish, and, had it not been for his thick armor, he would have suffered several serious wounds already as the burrowers began to get through his defenses. Thuradin shook his head to try and bring himself together. He had to regain some of his energy. He couldn't fight alone like this forever.

He joined the nearest legion of dwarves and began fighting alongside them in formation. He even led them when their officer's head was split open by a burrower's club. Fighting with a legion, he found enough respite to look around his surroundings—or at least what he could see through the thick clouds of smoke caused by the toppled bonfires.

He saw Ronorim fighting alone. The King spun in a continuous circle with his two-handed axe held in front of him, chopping in half any burrower foolish enough to attack him. The royal guards were close by, ready to swarm around their King the instant it looked like he might be overwhelmed.

Most of the dwarves Thuradin saw fought in typical wedge formation, similar to what he had used against the humans when they had ambushed the viatari. He occasionally spotted an Enurg'en standing securely behind a dwarven line, healing them as they fought the ferocious burrowers—but they couldn't heal everyone.

Several dwarves fell to the ground, bloodied, where they remained unmoving. Many who fought alone were surrounded by swarms of burrowers, who would swing their axes and clubs and swords at the dwarf until they were in pieces. Thuradin saw many instances of burrowers who had gathered enough numbers to charge straight into one of the wedge formations. The weight of their combined numbers was often enough to cause the wedge to crumble, and the dwarves were quickly overwhelmed.

As for the viatari, they moved all over the battlefield. They would appear behind a burrower, kill it, then suddenly appear behind another ten feet away. Thuradin had never seen them fight in a pitched battle before, and he was impressed by how quickly they managed to move from target to target despite the limited moving space. They were lethal, and certainly a boon to the dwarves as they utilized their aggressive speed and strength to save several dwarven wedge formations from being overwhelmed.

The burrowers seemed to think so as well. They began forming into close groups of twos and threes. The viatari paid no attention to this at first and continued to fight in their normal pattern. But now, as soon as they appeared behind one of the burrowers and killed it, the others would try to inflict any damage they could.

Their strategy had some effect.

One burrower cut deep into Natiari's thigh with an axe before she ripped off its head and moved on to her next target. Tessa was stabbed in the back with a spear when she appeared behind a small group of them. She killed all of the ones near her in a wild flurry of movement before pulling it out and jumping back behind dwarven lines to recuperate. He didn't see Victria actually receive any wounds, but the few times he did see her, she was covered in dried blood in some places while she bled profusely from others.

Almost as soon as they were wounded, the viatari's wounds would begin to heal, but that didn't seem to be helping them enough as the battle wore on. They moved on from target to target too quickly and received wounds faster than their regenerative abilities could heal because of it.

Thuradin saw Tessa collapse after being dealt a skull-crushing blow to the head with a hammer. The burrowers responsible approached her unmoving body warily, as if they expected her to rise up suddenly and lunge at them. Thuradin knew that wouldn't happen. Tessa had been dealt one major wound too many. A pool of blood seeped around her head, soaking the cavern floor.

He was just about to charge to her defense when the burrowers began falling limply to the floor. After all of them had been dealt with, Victria and Natiari dragged their sister away from the battle.

Thuradin didn't feel particularly fond of Tessa; she'd always intimidated him, sometimes more so than Dragos had, but he had never disliked her. He felt the rage inside him boil up even more as he looked around the battlefield. There were hundreds of dead burrowers, but mixed in with those corpses were many dwarves. Even as he looked around, he could see some of the slain already beginning to entomb.

He didn't remember much after that. All he could recall was that his vision turned red and that he foolishly charged against a large mass of burrowers by himself. The next thing he knew, they were running for the tunnel at the far end of the cavern.

"After them!" he heard Ronorim yelling at the top of his

lungs. "Slay them all!"

Thuradin was tempted to join in as the dwarves chased the fleeing burrowers, but he controlled himself. First, he wanted to see how the viatari were doing. He hadn't seen them since Tessa was dragged off the battlefield.

He ran around, asking anyone he saw if they had seen the viatari. Most had not, but eventually he found one dwarf who pointed him in the right direction.

After running almost the entire length of the cavern, he finally found them. The three viatari were all sitting, leaning against the same large boulder and drinking what he assumed to be water. Victria raised her hand in greeting when she noticed him.

Thuradin eyed the patches of dried blood everywhere on her body and her hand pressing firmly against her stomach where a dark red stain was slowly spreading. He reached into one of his bags and pulled out bandages to dress the wound, despite knowing that the wound would eventually heal itself.

"Stabbed by a dagger," she said as he approached, wincing slightly. "I'm fine, though. It'll take more than this to kill me."

The other two viatari nodded in agreement.

Thuradin was glad to see that they were alright. Even Tessa was back to her normal, sulky self.

"I guess we're winning, then," Victria noted, nodding her head in the direction of the dwarves, the majority of whom had already entered the next tunnel.

"Aye," Thuradin said. He finished dressing the wound. "Ronorim isn't going ta stop chasing the burrowers until all of them are slain. But he's no fool. He knows there's something at the other end of the tunnel, and he suspects there will be more of them. I heard one of the officers talking. Ronorim has ordered the artillery ta set up on that ledge over there."

He pointed to a slightly elevated ridge in the middle of the cavern. It would be a perfect place for the cannons since they would have a clear shot at the tunnel entrance.

"He plans on flushing them out of their hiding place, bringing them back here, and then finishing them off with the cannons."

Victria nodded, but it was clear her mind was elsewhere.

"You know," she said. "Even while fighting them just now, I could only see the fear and sadness in their eyes."

Thuradin knew what she was talking about, but at the same time he did not. He hadn't seen anything that might make him second-guess what he had done in the heat of battle, but he had seen something . . . different.

"But this time," she continued, "it looked to me like those feelings were intensified. I got the sense they didn't want us to go through that tunnel. It makes me wonder what we'll find on the other side."

She looked on at the delve far ahead of them. A few stragglers had yet to go through it, but soon enough they too would pass through to join their comrades in this last push to eradicate their ancient enemy.

"Aye," Thuradin said after some time. "I suppose we'll find that out soon enough."

CHAPTER TWENTY-EIGHT

As soon as the viatari were well enough to move, Thuradin led them to the tunnel that would take them deeper into burrower territory. Compared to the last one, the trip through was much shorter, and before an hour had even passed, they were on the other side.

They arrived to find the dwarven army holding their position, large shields locked together forming a wall of iron. There were no sounds of weapons clashing, no cries of the slain or wounded. There was only one voice yelling near the front of the dwarven host. Thuradin pushed his way through the crowd, trying to make his way to the front.

He had seen a lot in the past several months, and lately he had begun to think nothing could surprise him anymore. As soon as he reached the front lines, however, he made a note to himself to never make that assumption again.

In front of him, only about one hundred yards away, stood the largest burrower army he had ever seen. What he saw now made what the dwarves had fought in the previous cavern look like a small raiding party—which, he realized belatedly, it probably had been. Looking around, he saw the dwarves were outnumbered at least three to one.

But the large burrower army wasn't what surprised Thuradin most.

As his gaze passed over the first rank of burrowers, he noticed their leader standing a few feet in front of the rest. He wore full dwarven plate armor, which Thuradin had never seen a burrower do before, and was slightly shorter than the rest of them. It took a few moments, but he soon realized their leader was actually a dwarf.

Shock outweighed his rage. How could any dwarf betray the Dwarven Kingdom by joining the enemy outright?

"Wait," Victria said when she saw the dwarf opposing them. "Isn't that Dunkell?"

Thuradin looked again, and the color drained from his face. Victria was right. He now recognized the armor, the weapon, even the way the dwarf held himself. The one leading the burrowers against Ronorim was indeed Dunkell.

Now he understood why the King hadn't been able to find his brother in Kul'Burell. After being exiled, the banished prince must have traveled directly to the burrowers to warn them of the coming attack. He also understood now why the attack had been stopped. He imagined what must have gone through Ronorim's head as he emerged from the tunnel only to find his brother leading the enemy against him. The shock alone would have been enough for him to stop in his tracks, just so his mind could have some time to process what was happening. Thuradin didn't have long to imagine what he would do in the King's place. Ronorim's shouting was growing impossible to ignore.

"—what ye think! If our father were here ta see ye now, he'd be just as ashamed as I am. How could ye do this ta yer own people?"

"And what have I done ta my own people that is so evil,

brother?" Dunkell shouted back. "All I've tried ta do is open their eyes so they can see the burrowers for who they truly are. Behind us is their city, a city full of their own families. How can ye justify the slaughtering of so many when they're no different from us?'

"Pah!" Ronorim spat on the floor in disgust. "Look at them! They're disgusting creatures that have been harassing us for centuries! What say ye, dwarves?"

The dwarven host stomped the ground in unison with a thunderous *Smack!*

The arguing continued for several more minutes before Thuradin decided he could no longer listen. This back-and-forth bickering must have been going on for a while. He didn't know how those around him could deal with this madness, but he would not be one of them.

A sudden thought popped into his head. Dunkell had said the burrower city was nearby. From where he was he couldn't see any signs of it, but maybe if he moved to higher ground. . . .

"Follow me," he whispered to Victria.

As discreetly as he could, he made his way through the ranks with the viatari following close behind until he was at the far end of the left flank.

"Why are we here?" Victria asked in a low voice.

Thuradin took off his saphyrium helm and wiped the sweat from his brow.

"This makes escaping the battle easier."

"Escape?" Natiari hissed. "Why are we escaping?"

Thuradin locked his gaze onto Victria, who nodded in agreement. "I still don't know what ta think about the burrowers, but there's one thing I do know, and that's that this battle isn't one we should be involving ourselves in.

There's a high cliff we can watch the battle from, unnoticed. I saw it on the way in." He pointed out the cliff in question. It was a little farther to their left but not too far in front of them and it looked like there was a small trail leading to the top. "Ye're welcome ta follow me if ye wish, but if ye'd rather do battle, then by all means—"

"We're coming with you," Victria said. She looked back at her companions, who shrugged.

"Very well," the dwarf said. "Then, listen closely. Once everyone charges, run with them. When ye draw level with the cliff, split off from the host and head ta the top. I don't think anyone will notice our absence. They'll be too busy fighting."

"What exactly are we going to do once we're all gathered there?" Tessa asked.

Thuradin shrugged, shoving the saphyrium helm back onto his head. "I don't know yet," he replied honestly. "Perhaps we'll figure it out when we get there."

He didn't know how long they had to wait before the battle started. For all he knew, the royal brothers might bicker for the rest of the day, which he hoped was not the case, but there was nothing anyone could do to speed up the process. They just had to be patient and wait.

An hour passed. Then two. Then, when the third hour approached, a horn sounded within the dwarven ranks, followed by several more horns. Within seconds, thousands of dwarves unleashed their war cries. Thuradin was tempted to join in, the rush of the charge nearly taking his senses from him, but he resisted. He ran with the army for only a short time before ripping himself away and sprinting as fast as he could toward the cliff. He ran up the steep trail at full speed until he reached the top.

Ducking down, he crept slowly toward the edge of the precipice to scan the cavern floor but found no signs of Victria or the other viatari. He frowned. The battle raged fiercely below him. It was possible they had gotten sucked into it—

"You kept us waiting."

Thuradin scrambled to his feet and turned to see the viatari staring at him with amused expressions on their faces.

"How did ye—"

"You should know by now the viatari have always been faster than your kind," Natiari scoffed.

"I didn't even—"

"See us?" Tessa smirked. "We know. It was fairly amusing watching you scramble around as if you were the first to arrive."

Thuradin looked to Victria, hoping she would rein in her companions. That hope quickly died when he saw the huge grin on her face.

"There are more important issues ta focus on right now," he said gruffly, trying to draw the attention away from himself. "If ye don't mind."

He took back his position at the edge of the cliff and was soon joined by the three viatari. They watched the events unfold below them.

No one seemed to be winning the battle. In some areas, it looked like the dwarves had the advantage and were pushing the burrowers back. In others, it looked like the burrowers were close to overwhelming the invaders.

The burrowers fought with a fury and skill Thuradin had never seen before. They must know this is their final battle, he thought, a battle to decide their fate. If they were truly fighting for their home, as Dunkel claimed, they would not be defeated so easily.

There were a few times when Thuradin recognized Ronorim in his shining, red armor, fighting off hordes of burrowers. At one point the King started attacking another dwarf, who he quickly realized was Dunkell. The two fought ferociously, eventually creating their own circle to fight in as their flailing weapons killed or scared off all other nearby combatants.

Thuradin couldn't take his eyes away from the private duel. It was too fascinating. Ronorim had the advantage with his two-handed battle axe, but Dunkell still managed to parry or avoid each heavy swing the King made against him, though he couldn't land any blows either, since he could never stay past Ronorim's defenses long enough to strike him. He always had to jump back before his brother's next swing. For as long as Thuradin could remember, there had been bets placed on whether Ronorim or Dunkell would come out the victor if the two ever dueled each other. He had bet on the King, and now he would get to see if his bet paid off. But just when it looked like the private battle might be tipping in the King's favor—Dunkell had made the mistake of trying to grab for the King's axe but had instead slipped and fallen—Victria nudged him on the shoulder.

"Thuradin, look."

He followed her gaze past the lines of burrowers and saw a cluster of large rocks in the distance. He was about to ask what was so important about them when he noticed lights flickering within and around the rocks. It was then he realized the structures were not rocks at all, but buildings, and the lights were coming from torches or braziers.

They were not impressive. The tallest one, he guessed, was about two stories high. The majority of the buildings were simple stone huts. What was unique about these clusters, however, was that they were set up in a grid plan, very much like dwarven cities. Squinting his eyes, he could even make out small figures crowding in what appeared to be narrow streets.

It was a city, and Thuradin guessed the figures he saw were normal, everyday burrowers. There were probably families, elders, even children within. He could imagine them now, cowering in fear as they watched the battle that would decide their fate taking place just outside their doorstep.

He didn't know how he had missed it. All thoughts of the petty duel between Ronorim and Dunkell disappeared. The images of the helpless burrowers the Creature had shown him months ago flashed through his head, and another cold shock coursed through his body. He now understood. The burrowers weren't the barbarians the dwarves thought they were. They were no more uncivilized than the viatari—or humans, for that matter. What the Creature had said about the dwarves wanting to commit genocide was correct.

And with that realization came the first pangs of guilt.

He remembered the hundreds of times he had fought and killed the burrowers. He had seen them as nothing more than animals then, their unnerving, beady eyes, their throaty language, their cries of anguish every time one of their own fell. He had never thought of any of it at the time. Now the guilt overwhelmed him as he shifted his gaze back to the battle and saw the difference. He didn't see the bloodlust so often associated with the burrowers. The only thing he saw was their grim determination to defend their home.

"They don't look like savages to me," Victria said.

"No," Thuradin agreed. "They don't." He shook his head. "We must do something ta stop this. We cannae let my people win this battle."

You will try to wash away your guilt.

The time for the Creature's curse to come to pass was here, and Thuradin was beginning to think there was nothing he could do to stop it. If what the Creature had told him was true, something he was about to do would make his fellow dwarves brand him as a traitor.

We might be slaughtering an entire race based on a false idea.

The words Victria had said to him only hours before the battle rang through his head, and he realized what was more important. There was no time to worry about the curse right now. He had to do what he felt was right. And for the moment, that meant making sure the battle ended without a dwarven victory.

The dwarves below them were still blind to the burrowers' true nature. The easiest plan, though perhaps not the most efficient one and the one least likely to succeed, would be to explain to all of them that they were wrong and that they should retreat back to dwarven lands. Somehow, he didn't see that scenario playing out too well in the middle of a battle, and chances were high that if Thuradin tried to do such a thing, he would be labeled as insane, perhaps even as a burrower-sympathizer, which could be worse.

Besides, the guilt the knowledge brought with it ate away at him like acid. He couldn't inflict the same painful shame on his own kind. He would have to find another way, without letting his fellow dwarves know of their terrible crime. He would have to take matters into his own hands and stop a battle single-handedly, before too many more died.

"Do you think they can win?" Victria asked as Thuradin tried to think of a plan.

The dwarven commander scanned the battle once again before answering.

"No," he said. "It doesn't look like we have ta worry too much about that. There are just too many burrowers. Eventually, the dwarven host is going ta retreat in a panic."

"So then what do we do?"

"We do what anyone does ta children who fight. We separate them. Completely."

"And how do we do that?" Tessa asked, her voice indicating she didn't believe such a thing could be done here.

"Don't worry," he said, flashing her a bleak smile. "I've got a plan."

"This plan is crazy!" Tessa exclaimed for the fifth time as the four of them ran through the tunnel back to the previous cavern.

Thuradin ignored her. This was the only thing he could think of, so he had to stick with it.

"She has a point," Victria said. "Have you thought this through, Thuradin? This plan could trap or kill a lot of dwarves back there."

"It's the only one I have," Thuradin retorted. "We just have ta time everything perfectly so that our forces are already retreating by the time we've finished setting everything up."

They continued on in silence.

Soon they left the darkness of the tunnel behind as they entered the cavern where, only a few hours ago, the initial attack had taken place. They quickly located their targets and began making their way toward the cannons set up on the ridge ahead of them.

The plan was simple enough, but it required perfection in several areas for it to be carried out with the best results. Thuradin intended to force the tunnel they had just exited to cave in, and he was going to do it with the bags of dynath used by the army's cannons.

He had noticed there were several long cracks visible on the walls and ceiling of the tunnel entrance and exit, and he was sure they ran along its entire length. The tunnel was weak. He just had to place the bags of dynath in strategic locations, connect a few bags with a fuse, set off the fuse, run for his life, and let the following chain reaction do its work. Simple.

The hard part would be getting those bags of dynath. Cannoneers didn't just hand them out to anyone who asked. They would have to take the bags by trickery or by force. Thuradin hoped they didn't have to use force, but he told the viatari they could incapacitate the dwarves in whatever way they deemed fit if their first attempt to acquire the bags didn't work.

Another complication to the plan would be timing. Thuradin had to make sure he didn't set off the fuse too early, or he would trap his fellow dwarves on the burrower side of the tunnel, which would be the same as killing them. He had to make sure all of them escaped the burrowers' cavern before setting the fuse, but even that precaution still contained a chance that some would be killed by him.

He also had to make sure he didn't blow the fuse too late, or burrowers would also stream through, and if they did, they would surely die, something he now wanted to avoid. His entire life he had wanted nothing more than to end the very thought of burrowers existing. Now he wanted to make sure he could save as many of them and his fellow dwarves as he could at the same time.

As Thuradin and the viatari reached the top of the ridge, they saw the dwarven cannoneers, and instead of keeping watch over the burrower tunnel as they were supposed to, they were dancing with steins of what could only be ale in their hands. They were drunk. Thuradin couldn't really blame them. Their job was to sit there with nothing to do while the rest of their fellows spent hours fighting the burrowers. They had to find *some* way to entertain themselves.

"How did they bring so much ale with them?" Victria asked. She looked like she was going to be sick. Thuradin guessed she still hadn't gotten over the night of drinking she had experienced while negotiating terms for the alliance with Ronorim.

"It's nae uncommon for there ta be lots of ale wherever the army goes," he replied, patting the viatari's arm sympathetically. "I'll go talk ta them."

He marched up to the dancing dwarves and barked for them to stand at attention. Several were already too far gone to listen to him. One of them lay face-down on the ground, snoring away in a pool of his own drool and vomit.

A few recognized Thuradin's saphyrium helm, though, and they helped form the cannoneers into a sloppy line. Forgetting they had pints of ale in their hands, they tried to salute, only to splash the rest of their steins' contents onto their armor. The heavy scent of alcohol reached Thuradin as the brown, frothy liquid dripped down the dwarven plate and onto the floor.

"Soldiers," Thuradin began, trying to keep the distaste out of his voice. "Ye play a very important role in the battle that is taking place in the next cavern."

A few of the dwarves giggled and hiccupped and clapped each other's backs at the prospect of being important.

"The King has ordered us," he continued, pointing out the viatari, "ta bring all the dynath ye have ta the front."

It was a ridiculous request, and Thuradin knew it. He was hoping, however, that the cannoneers were too drunk to realize it. Unfortunately, some of them were not as intoxicated as they looked.

"Why would he want that?" one of them asked. "How are we going ta fire our cannons without dynath?"

Thuradin couldn't think of a good lie to tell. He decided the best thing he could do for now was to tell part of the truth and hope the cannoneers would just accept it.

"He plans on caving in the tunnel," Thuradin said. "We have ta line the walls with the stuff so it all collapses on the burrowers and kills them once and for all."

Some of the dwarves frowned and glanced at each other, the uncertainty evident in their eyes.

"Check with the King himself if ye don't believe me!" Thuradin shouted angrily. He hadn't wanted to make that particular bluff, but he didn't know what else to say. The plan would work much better if Ronorim didn't know about it. No doubt, the minute the King heard what he was planning, he would abandon the battle and immediately come running to stop it.

One of the cannoneers stepped forward. "I'll go check on it."

Thuradin glared at him, silently willing for the dwarf to just believe his story, but he knew it was over. It was time for their backup plan.

"Very well, then," he said curtly. "Go on. But know ye're wasting valuable time and dwarven lives by nae listening ta me."

The cannoneer hustled off toward the tunnel, quickly disappearing into its dark mouth. Thuradin walked back to the viatari and signaled for them to take action. The dwarves behind him lost interest and returned to their drinking and dancing.

The viatari walked calmly toward the cannoneers, who didn't seem to notice their presence. Then, almost as fast as Thuradin could blink, they attacked.

The cannoneers didn't put up much resistance and were easy to incapacitate since they were on the verge of passing out anyway. After only a few seconds, all of them had been dealt with.

Thuradin raced over to the crates and opened them, revealing sacks upon sacks of dynath. There were also several crates full of thick coils of fuse. He stacked two crates of fuse on top of a crate of dynath, lifted them, and ran as quickly as he could toward the tunnel entrance.

"Just grab the crates with dynath in them," he said to the viatari as he passed them. "I should have enough fuse already. And make sure ye *don't* drop them!"

His breaths came in ragged gasps as he reached the bottom of the ridge and started racing toward the mouth of the tunnel. He had been running all day, as far as he could tell, and now he was doing that with seventy or so pounds of extra weight.

He remembered chuckling several months ago over the idea of him getting too old for this sort of thing. He wasn't chuckling now. He was definitely too old for this.

Thuradin gently lowered the crates in front of the tunnel entrance and grimaced. It took him longer than he would have liked to bring the supplies from the cannons to the tunnel, and he didn't have a lot of time to waste.

The tunnel wasn't a long one, but it would still take much more than one crate of dynath for him to cave it all in. He estimated he would need about nine more in order to have enough, but even with all three viatari's help, he feared it would still take too long to move everything.

Just then, he felt a rush of wind as the viatari zipped past him, each with two crates of dynath. They set them down gently next to him and ran off to get more, moving faster than his eyes could follow.

Thuradin shook his head and whistled, impressed. He kept forgetting about the viatari's extraordinary speed and strength. Now he only needed three more, which would arrive soon enough.

He sat down on one of the wooden crates, hoping to rest a little with the brief spare time he had. He looked toward the cannons, expecting the viatari to materialize in front of him any minute now like they always did. . . .

He blinked.

The viatari stood in front of him, looking down at him, staring.

"Nice nap?" Victria asked.

Had he fallen asleep? For how long? It certainly didn't feel like he had rested. His body remained sore and his bones ached from the strains of the day.

"Sorry," Thuradin mumbled, lifting himself up from the crate. "Long day."

Victria nodded solemnly, but when the dwarf looked into her eyes, he got the feeling she was teasing him. He shook his head.

Looking around, Thuradin noticed he had much more than just ten crates of dynath around him. It looked like the viatari had brought the artillery's entire supply. It was much more than he needed, but he wondered if maybe this was for the best. A little extra dynath never hurt anyone.

CHAPTER TWENTY-NINE

As they moved the crates of dynath farther inside the tunnel, Natiari told Thuradin that he had been sleeping so deeply when they found him, they thought he had died and turned to stone. Thuradin thought she was exaggerating, but when Victria told him how long he had been asleep, he cursed himself. They had already been low on time. Now he wasn't sure if they could even set everything up before word reached the King.

They moved ten crates of dynath, along with the two crates of fuse, and placed them in the center of the tunnel. They worked in darkness now. Thuradin could hardly see, but he could feel his way around the tunnel without too much difficulty. He assumed, by the lack of complaints, that the viatari were doing the same.

"Right," he said. "We need ta cover as much of the tunnel walls as possible with dynath."

He opened all the crates. There were at least fifty small sacks within each one. He figured so long as a few were well placed in the right cracks and in an appropriate proximity from the other sacks, there would be more than enough explosive force to bring the tunnel down.

"Victria, go back ta where we entered the tunnel. Natiari, go on ta the other end. Start placing yer lot of sacks about ten feet away from each other in any cracks along the wall that ye think might be weak. By the time ye run out, ye should be back here with me. Tessa, go with Natiari and keep an eye out for any signs of trouble coming our way."

They all nodded and ran off to do their jobs.

Now Thuradin was alone. He felt another cold shock taking effect, but he shook it off before it could take hold of him. He had a job to do, not to mention the most complicated one. He didn't have time to be weak.

His job was to set up the dynath in the middle of the tunnel in such a way that when he lit the fuse, he would have plenty of time to run out of the blast zone. The sacks of dynath also had to be set up so when they exploded, they would be powerful enough to cause the rest of the tunnel to weaken. That way, the smaller sacks the viatari were setting up would be just enough to cause their individual sections to collapse.

Thuradin decided the best set up would be to line the circumference of the tunnel with the explosive material and then place the rest of it wherever he thought it might do the most damage.

The tunnel was riddled with cracks, most of them easily holding three or four dynath sacks. He carried as many as he could fit in his arms and searched all over the stone wall. Sometimes he could just walk up to it, find a suitable crack, and place a few sacks in there. Other times, especially when he began working on the ceiling, he had to climb, hanging precariously from shallow footholds.

Thuradin forced himself to keep going and not stop and rest. When doubt crept into his head, he would think of the burrower city, of all the innocents who were standing in the streets, fearful of his kind. The thought gave him new energy, and he returned to his work with fire in his heart.

Setting up the dynath in a dark tunnel was no easy task, even for Thuradin. There were several instances where he accidentally dropped a sack and flinched as it hit the floor. Luckily, it looked like dynath required more of an impact than just being dropped to explode.

Once he finished setting up the explosives, he began working on the fuses. He connected as many bags as he could in several different areas, then connected those fuses with other nearby lines, then those fuses with others until he was left with a single fuse—the one that would start and end everything.

By this time, Victria had returned with a few extra sacks of dynath, which Thuradin used to add a little extra punch to his set up. She reported no incidents during her set up and then moved to help him where she could. Natiari came back with the same report. Thuradin wished he could check on how they set up their sacks, just to make sure they were right, but he didn't have time. Everything had to be perfect if the plan was to work or it would all be pointless. He would have to trust that their setup allowed for a proper chain reaction

"How much longer until we're done?" Victria asked.

"A little more. . . ." Thuradin said, fiddling with the fuse. "Bah! It isn't long enough. I need another crate."

"I'l go—"

Before Victria could finish her offer, Tessa came into view. The tunnel was still dark, but Thuradin's eyes had adjusted enough for him to see the stream of blood flowing down her leg and the dwarven spear that had caused it. He grimaced as she continued walking as if the spear wasn't causing any discomfort or pain, even though half of it stuck out of one side of her leg and the rest stuck out the other.

"Yer leg," he said, finally. "What happened?"

Tessa looked down and broke off one end, pulling out the other with ease, barely wincing. The wound healed quickly, and soon it was gone. The bleeding stopped.

"Your King is on his way," she said calmly. "He's bringing a lot of dwarves with him; I think they're your royal guards. I might have recognized Stürn as well."

Thuradin cursed. He didn't want to have to fight the dwarves he had led for so long, many of whom were his friends.

"All of them?"

"It looks like it," the viatari replied. "So, what do we do now? The army hasn't started its retreat yet. In fact, they looked to be winning the battle last I saw. And Ronorim is coming with at least one hundred heavily-armed and well-trained dwarves to see what we're up to."

"Are you saying we should light the fuse now?" Victria asked softly. "All the dwarves on the other side would die!"

"So we should die instead?" Tessa retorted, still calm. "Once Ronorim discovers our plan, and he will, he will try to kill us all."

"We should light it," Natiari agreed. "I'm sorry, Victria, but even we can't fend off that many dwarves for too long."

"Even if I wanted ta light it now," Thuradin said before Victria could argue. "I have no way of doing it. We didn't bring a fire with us."

"There were torches placed around the cannons in the previous cavern," Tessa pointed out. "I can go get one."

Before anyone could argue, she ran past them at full

speed and was gone.

Thuradin's stomach tightened. He hoped that with Tessa's extraordinary speed, she would be able to bring back a torch before Ronorim arrived. He didn't like the idea of having to bury thousands of dwarves on the other side of the tunnel, but it was starting to look like there were no other options.

His hopes of Tessa returning quickly died, though, as soon as footsteps were heard coming from the burrower side of the tunnel. Ronorim came into view, followed by the royal guards—many of whom carried torches—and Stürn. Next to him stood the cannoneer who hadn't believed Thuradin's orders were legitimate.

There was silence for a moment as Ronorim looked around suspiciously, first at Thuradin, then at the two remaining viatari.

"What are ye doing here, Thuradin?" he said, his voice low and dangerous. "Why aren't ye fighting with the rest of us? Why did ye try ta deceive the artillery inta giving ye their dynath?"

Thuradin took a deep breath. He felt as if he were standing at the edge of a cliff and the next words that came out of his mouth would determine whether he would be allowed to stay on the edge for a little longer or be pushed off. He knew no matter what lie or excuse he came up with, it wouldn't hold for long. Ronorim most likely already had his suspicions as to what was going on but wanted him to say it out loud, to prove his treachery beyond a doubt. Once the truth was out, the King would try to kill him and the viatari, just as Tessa had said. Even their past friendship wouldn't be enough to save him from that.

This standoff couldn't end so quickly, though. He had to

buy time for Tessa so she could return with the torch. He couldn't think about what might happen after that. He had to focus on the current goal: buying time.

He laughed.

Everyone looked at him as if he had gone mad. Thuradin was confused too. He had no idea what had prompted him to start laughing, but he decided to go with it. He was going to let instinct take over. His laughter slowly died away to a softer, confused chuckle, as if he had expected everyone else to join in.

"Ronorim," he said. "Ye're joking, aren't ye? I wasn't trying ta deceive the artillery. I was carrying out yer orders!"

"I know ye're lying," Ronorim growled. "I never gave ye such an order."

"Nae directly," Thuradin agreed. "Someone relayed those orders ta me in the middle of the battle. I had no reason ta mistrust his words, so I rushed off ta carry them out." He shrugged nonchalantly as if to say, *what else would I do?*

Ronorim's anger was replaced with genuine confusion.

"I never gave such an order. . . ." he said again. "Who told ye I gave that order? And why are the viatari here?" he added, suspicion creeping back into his voice.

"The viatari possess the ability ta move at incredible speeds. I wanted ta carry out yer orders as quickly as I could, so I had them carry me back ta cut the travel time in half."

Thuradin spoke the lie before he could stop himself. He bit back a groan as he realized he had already dug himself into a deep hole. It was only a matter of time before he was caught in his lies.

Ronorim realized the mistake as well. "Ye needed *two* of them ta take ye here? That seems a bit excessive for those who possess both extraordinary speed *and* strength."

Thuradin wracked his brain for anything that could get him out of the hole. Fortunately, he thought of the perfect excuse. Unfortunately, the cannoneer spoke first.

"My King," the dwarf said, eyeing Thuradin and the viatari with even more suspicion than Ronorim was. "They were supposed ta wait with the others for my return. Isn't it a bit odd that, instead of waiting by the cannons, we find them here in the middle of the tunnel?"

Thuradin willed for Tessa to hurry up with the torch. He couldn't buy any more time. There was nothing more he could say that could possibly pull Ronorim back to their side. He stayed silent and watched Ronorim's eyes narrow as he looked around at his surroundings for the first time. The King's eyes wandered over to Thuradin's hand, and his face went slack as he saw the fuse.

"Aikrig," the King said in a low voice, almost inaudible.

"Yes?" The cannoneer stood at attention and saluted.

"I want ye ta go back ta the army and tell them that I am ordering a full retreat. Tell them ta get out of there as fast as they possibly can. I don't know what will be the end result of this mess, but tell them if they value their lives, they won't stop running until they're back in Dun'Burell."

Aikrig seemed to understand that something was wrong. He ran off as fast as his short legs would carry him and disappeared into the darkness without question.

"So," Ronorim said through clenched teeth, barely able to control his rage. "Ye would betray yer own kind. Just like my brother."

You will be seen as a traitor to your kind.

Thuradin shuddered. Was this what the Creature had foreseen?

"Ronorim," he said with as much sincerity as he could

put into his voice. "The burrowers aren't what we thought they were. They aren't savages that need ta be exterminated. They're the same as ye and me. Dunkell was right; I saw their city during the battle. They have their own families, their own children. They deserve ta live as much as we do. They were only defending their home from us."

"Yer sounding just like Dunkell did before the battle," Ronorim said, spitting the name as if it were poison. "I sent that traitorous brother of mine ta Dun'Burell so he might come ta understand what it was like ta face them day after day, and what does he do instead? He joins them and leads them against me! He betrayed me *just* as ye have!"

Thuradin knew it would be impossible to change Ronorim's mind; the young King was too set in his ways. He had hoped instead to get Ronorim ranting about his brother in a last-ditch attempt to buy more time, and it looked like his efforts had bought him a few more minutes as the King went on about the burrowers and his brother's betrayal. He decided now would be the best time to think of a way to escape. But nothing immediately feasible came to mind.

"I thought I knew ye, Thuradin. I thought we were the same. We were friends for such a long time. How could ye betray yer fellow dwarves like this? How could ye betray *me*?"

Ronorim's rant was over. Thuradin glanced behind him and felt a mountain of relief as he saw Tessa running toward them with a lit torch in her hand.

"I'm nae betraying ye or our people," he said, staring into Ronorim's wild eyes. "I'm trying ta save us. I'm trying ta bring peace between the burrowers and ourselves by destroying this tunnel so that our two races are separated. That way, we don't have ta live with the shame that yer actions would force upon us."

Ronorim bared his teeth when he noticed Tessa with the torch.

"I see ye've chosen yer path then," he said. "As King of the Dwarven Kingdom, and all the dwarves in its domain, it is my duty ta stop anyone who would dare carry out treacherous plots ta harm their fellow dwarves. As for the viatari, ye're no longer welcome anywhere in the Dwarven Kingdom. Yer kind will regret the day they made the dwarves their enemy."

Ronorim motioned for the royal guards to attack, which they did without hesitation. Thuradin was no longer their commander; though he still wore the saphyrium helm, he was already a traitor in their eyes.

"Defend the fuse at all cost," Thuradin commanded as he took the torch from Tessa.

The viatari leaped into action. They attacked Stürn first so he couldn't heal the royal guards with his powers. The Enurg'en dodged the first two attacks that came at him, but he couldn't fend off the three viatari at once and he fell back against the tunnel wall, unconscious. They turned their attention to the other dwarves. Royal guards went flying as the viatari unleashed a flurry of kicks and punches and occasional slashes with their slender dirks.

A few royal guards attacked Thuradin, but even with just one of his axes, he was able to fend them off with relative ease. After he defeated the first three guards, none of the others tried to attack him. They were more intent on defeating the viatari, who continued to send their fellows flying into the cavern walls or deep into the tunnel's depths.

The viatari were good fighters, but there were simply too many dwarves. Gashes, slashes, and a few stab wounds pocketed their bodies as they dodged one attack only to receive another. As the battle raged on, their wounds began to take their toll. Their movements slowed, and they dodged fewer and fewer attacks. Thuradin worried they might reach the point where they died from receiving too many fatal wounds.

He was especially worried about Victria. She hesitated every time before lashing out at a dwarf. This meant she received more wounds than her companions, as the dwarves took the opportunity to swing their weapons freely at her. He saw scrapes along her legs, gashes in her side gushing out blood, and her left arm was twisted in an unnatural angle.

Thuradin was tempted to jump in and help them, even if it meant abandoning the fuse, but before he could take action, Ronorim attacked him.

The dwarven King swung his two-handed axe like it was a toy as he brought it down with a thud against the tunnel floor, mere inches away from slicing Thuradin in half. The axe bit into the stone and stuck there for a few seconds as the King struggled to pull it out. Thuradin kept moving around, trying to stay out of reach of the heavy weapon. He didn't have the viatari's regenerative abilities. If he got hit directly by it even once, he would die.

Ronorim continued to swing his axe in a haphazard manner. He was in an uncontrollable rage. He yelled incomprehensible curses at the top of his lungs. It took everything in him for Thuradin to keep his composure and continue avoiding the King's attacks.

As they fought, streams of dwarves began emerging from the darkness and ran past the fight. The army had disengaged the burrowers and was now in retreat.

"I hope ye're happy," Ronorim snarled. "Ye cost me my

victory!"

That's when Thuradin made his mistake. Instead of dodging like he had been doing, he brought his small one-handed axe up to parry the next attack. His weapon flew out of his hand as the overbearing weight of the double-bladed axe made contact with it, and it landed with a clatter on the floor. He felt his armor then his skin rip apart as Ronorim's axe sliced through his spaulders and dug into his shoulder. Crying out, he fell to his knees. His arm went limp. It wasn't a fatal wound—Thuradin's weapon had managed to absorb most of the weight in Ronorim's strike—but just the shock of getting hit made it seem worse than it was.

Thuradin looked up in a daze as Ronorim raised his axe one more time for the finishing blow. He saw the viatari were still desperately fighting, but soon they too would be overwhelmed. Many of the dwarves who had been retreating stopped to join in the fight against the viatari. Many more were already on the floor. Whether they were dead or unconscious, he couldn't tell.

He closed his eyes, waiting for the death blow, the feeling of the sharp axe tearing through his body, leaving him a mangled mess.

But it never came.

Opening his eyes, he saw Ronorim slumped to the floor, unconscious. Above him stood Dunkell Ironaxe, the prince who was exiled, the prince who was a traitor, the prince who had just saved his life.

"Wha-?" Thuradin managed to say before being roughly lifted to his feet. Dunkell's eyes were sad but determined. There was an unusual fire in them he had never seen before.

"Are ye alright, lad?"

Thuradin nodded weakly. His shoulder ached painfully,

and he could feel blood trickle down his arm, but he was sure it could be healed. Once everything was checked out, Dunkell turned his attention to the dwarves fighting the viatari. "Dwarves! Stop yer fighting this instant. Get out of these tunnels or ye'll be crushed by the rocks!"

The dwarven soldiers stood still for a moment as they weighed their options. Finally, their fear of death outweighed their fear of disobeying Ronorim. They disengaged and ran for their lives. The viatari slumped to the ground together, exhausted, and closed their eyes as they concentrated on healing themselves.

"Ye all should leave this tunnel as well," Dunkell said. "It's going ta get messy here soon."

Thuradin turned his gaze to the prince and saw the fuse in his hands.

"Give that ta me," he said. "Ye don't need ta do this. Let me finish what I started."

"It's my brother who made this mess in the first place," Dunkell retorted. "I should be the one who puts an end ta it."

"I can't let ye do that," Thuradin said firmly. "If ye do this, how will the dwarves see ye? They will never see ye as their King. The Dwarven Kingdom will fall inta chaos, and civil war will break out. We cannae let that happen. Let me do it."

"They'll brand ye a traitor."

"Aye. But someone has ta do it, and it might as well be me. There's no place in Tinas Gran's palace for old commanders like me anymore, anyway."

Dunkell nodded his head slowly, though he didn't seem too happy about it.

"Very well, then," he said, as he handed the fuse over to

Thuradin. "I don't like it, but it doesn't look like anything is going ta stop ye, and I'd rather nae fight ye."

He moved over to Ronorim's limp body and plucked the crown off his head.

"I think this belongs ta me now. Farewell, brother."

Thuradin bowed deeply. He had been wrong about the prince. Dunkell was no traitor to the dwarves; he truly cared for his people. He had only wanted to protect their honor, to establish peace with the burrowers, rather than continuing an endless war.

Dunkell saluted in response and with one final nod, turned and ran for the tunnel exit.

Thuradin turned to the viatari. "Ye should go too."

"You're not staying here alone," Victria said.

"Yes, I am."

She opened her mouth to argue, but Tessa put her hand on her shoulder. They stared into each other's eyes for the longest time before Victria finally gave in.

"Fine," she sighed. "But you are not dying here like this. I will drag you out of here myself if I have to."

Thuradin grinned at the thought, which seemed to be enough of an answer for her.

The viatari stood and began limping away. Thuradin watched them go with a mixture of sadness and relief. He didn't want to endanger them with the plan *he* had thought up. At the same time, he didn't want to deal with this situation alone. But he had to. It was his duty.

He waited.

He had to make sure everyone was out of the tunnel before he lit the fuse. He didn't want to cause the deaths of his own people if he could avoid it. But it had been a while since he last saw a dwarf pass him. He thought perhaps it was safe to assume that all the survivors had escaped. The viatari, even with their injuries, should have exited the tunnel by now.

Looking around, he spotted the axe he had used to deflect Ronorim's last attack. He walked over to the weapon and retrieved it, hooking it back onto his belt so that he wouldn't lose it when he made his own escape.

It was time. He raised the torch and was about to light the fuse when he heard a sound coming from his right. He looked over to see Ronorim trying to get up. The King was already on his knees. Thuradin thought he looked like a beggar. Their eyes met.

There was a pleading madness in those eyes. They begged for him to stop what he was doing. They only wanted to safeguard the dwarves from burrower invasions, but they seemed unwilling to accept the fact that Thuradin was trying to do the same thing.

"Please, . . ." Ronorim croaked. "Don't."

The fuse lit with a *Fwoosh!*

The last thing Thuradin saw before running for his life was Ronorim still on his knees, his head bowed in defeat.

He ran as fast as his tired feet would carry him. Once the explosions started, though, they seemed to forget their exhaustion.

Thuradin heard the first sack of dynath explode, mixed in with what he thought sounded like an angry howl. It was tremendously loud. The tunnel shook furiously, making him lose his balance and fall. He lifted himself up as the explosions continued and kept running.

The setup had worked perfectly. As he ran, he could hear the tunnel collapse behind him as the chain reaction did its work. The explosions caused by the dynath the viatari had set up weren't as loud as Thuradin's, but they were enough to convince him that he had to run faster.

He picked up his pace, but there was no use. The explosions were catching up him. He could feel the heat on his back. Soon they would be right on top of him. Large chunks of rock fell from the ceiling and smashed onto the floor, shattering into smaller shards. One hit Thuradin perfectly on the head.

Spots filled his vision as he ran. *No,* he thought, *I won't die here!*

He put every ounce of energy and strength he had left into running, but he could feel himself begin to slip away into unconsciousness. He wondered, as he continued stumbling about, what would happen first: would he lose consciousness, or would he be crushed by the falling rocks?

He continued on for a few more steps, but he knew there was no point. He felt the last vestiges of energy leave him as the rocks continued to fall and the explosions continued to go off.

Just as he was about to allow himself to collapse and succumb to the rocks, he felt someone lift him. Wind rushed past his face as whatever carried him moved quickly through the tunnel. He tried to open his eyes to see who it was that had saved him, but he couldn't see anything except spots and stars.

He tried to concentrate and put the rest of his will-power into clearing his vision, even if it was just for a second. When they disappeared, he wasn't surprised to see the sharp, red eyes or the flowing, silver hair. Who else could it have been?

The last thing he remembered before blacking out was Victria's battered, determined, face as she weaved her way through the falling rocks. He slipped into unconsciousness. The Creature's laughter echoed in his head.

CHAPTER THIRTY

For the first few moments after he opened his eyes, Thuradin couldn't tell where he was. He thought for a second that he was in an infirmary, but when he looked around, he couldn't see anyone except Victria, and she didn't look injured. He noticed he was wrapped in bandages, mostly around his head and shoulder where Ronorim had sunk his axe.

Ronorim.

Had he really killed Ronorim? He tried to remember what had possessed him to do such a thing. He remembered seeing the burrowers cowering in their city. He remembered their desperate struggle against the dwarves for their right to exist. A wave of guilt washed over him. He wanted to sink into his bed and die.

"Nice nap?" Victria asked. There was no masking the sadness in her voice. Thuradin wondered if perhaps she felt the same wave of guilt he did.

He tried to grin, but his face, along with everything else, hurt too much. "How long?"

"A week," she said softly. "We're in Tinas Gran, in one of the palace rooms."

Thuradin tried to nod but quickly abandoned the effort

when his shoulder started to burn. He turned his head from side to side to take in his surroundings and gasped when he noticed his saphyrium helm on the stand next to him.

It was in a ruinous state. Dents and cracks riddled the once-smooth helmet. Worst of all, the central gem was missing. The sapphire that made the saphyrium helm *the* saphyrium helm was gone—probably buried in the tunnel.

He turned away. He couldn't bear to look at it any longer. It reminded him too much of his past, a much simpler time, a time without the viatari or quests or the Creature or darimun or curses. And like his saphyrium helm, there would be no recovering it.

The door to the room opened, and Dunkell strode in, followed by two royal guards. Thuradin noticed the prince now wore the royal crown he had plucked off Ronorim before escaping. There was a tired look in his eyes, but his composure and posture radiated nothing but confidence.

"How are ye?" the new King asked quietly.

"Considering everything that's happened," Thuradin grimaced, glancing at the two guards behind Dunkell. "I've been better."

Dunkell nodded. The royal guards glared at Thuradin and Victria with murderous eyes, but their threatening countenance faded slightly when Victria met their gazes and bared her fangs at them.

The King brought over a chair and sat next to Thuradin. "Ye've been gone for a week," he said. "I need ta tell ye everything I can before *they* come barging in ta take ye away."

"They?"

"Don't interrupt. Just listen."

Some of the news Dunkell told him was good, and the

dwarven commander was happy to hear it. But not all of it was good.

Dun'Burell was now a stable dwarven realm. There had been no sightings of any burrowers anywhere since the tunnel caved in. For the first time, the dwarves in Dun'Burell knew peace. They would be able to live normal, civilian lives without worry from now on.

Dunkell had succeeded Ronorim as King of the Dwarven Kingdom. The ceremony had taken place a few days ago, as soon as everyone had returned from the failed campaign. There had been no three days of mourning for Ronorim, as tradition demanded, because his body was too deep in the collapsed tunnel to retrieve. The Enurg'en who had crowned Dunkell was a dwarf by the name of Balig Forcewielder, Stürn's younger brother.

Stürn.

Stürn was in the tunnel with Ronorim when it collapsed and was presumed dead. Victria looked miserable when she heard this news. Thuradin guessed she felt his death was her fault since he had been one of the first dwarves the viatari had incapacitated.

Ayrie survived the battle against the burrowers, but she had come out of it changed. Instead of the calm, calculating dwarf she had been, she became crazed and murderous the moment she heard about Thuradin's betrayal. She had tried to attack Dunkell, refusing to accept him as her King. Several of the royal guards who had survived the battle with the viatari fell under her spear as they tried to protect him. Now she was being held in one of the most isolated dwarven prisons deep under the mountains.

Borim also survived, but barely. He had been severely injured during the battle—Dunkell wouldn't elaborate on the details—and was now being treated in one of the many infirmaries in the city, but the situation didn't look very promising. He still didn't know about Thuradin's betrayal.

The worst news was surprisingly the least shocking.

Thuradin was to stand trial for his actions against the dwarves during the battle. His fate would be decided by the Council of Judges after hearing his testimony and the testimony of several other dwarves who claimed to have witnessed his actions.

It wasn't surprising to learn that he was viewed as a traitor by every dwarf in the Kingdom; after all, the Creature had promised this would happen. Word had spread quickly on how he had murdered Ronorim, and the stories had grown more exaggerated to the point where Thuradin had apparently beheaded the King and raised his head in triumph in front of a ring of burrowers.

"When will it be?" Thuradin asked after Dunkell had finished talking.

"In a few days. They want ye well rested before the trial."

"How considerate."

Dunkell pursed his lips. "Because I'm the King, I know what ye're being charged for before anyone else. Do ye want me ta tell ye?"

"Why not?" Thuradin said, shrugging, and then regretted the movement as pain flared in his injured shoulder.

There were a lot of charges, many of which he thought the prosecutors had pulled out of thin air. But when Dunkell said he was being charged for the murders of Ronorim and the many dwarves who were buried along with him, he flinched. He hadn't thought of his actions as murder, but that was exactly what they were.

Ronorim had been incapacitated, helpless. The dwarves

around him, who the viatari rendered unconscious, had been in the same condition, as were any who may have still been running through the tunnel when it collapsed. It was murder. He had murdered them all.

Thuradin was so distraught by this realization he didn't even hear the rest of the charges. Not that they mattered. The only important ones against him were the two he had just heard. Dunkell stopped speaking but kept his mouth open as if he wanted to say more, yet nothing else came out.

"That is all."

"I see," Thuradin said, still shaken by his realization. It was all he could say.

Dunkell turned to the royal guards. "Leave us."

The guards shot one last accusing glance at Thuradin before leaving the room. Thuradin noticed they left the door slightly ajar, no doubt with the intention of eavesdropping on whatever was going to be said next. Dunkell must have realized this too because he barely spoke above a whisper.

"Thuradin, what ye did back at the tunnel, I know how difficult it was. No one thinks so, but yer actions saved our race from committing a shameful act. So first, I want ta thank ye for doing what had ta be done."

Thuradin tried to tell the King he didn't need to thank him but Dunkell held up a hand; he wouldn't be interrupted.

"I also want ta thank ye for stopping me from doing it. Ye were right back there. If I had done it, the Dwarven Kingdom would have fallen inta chaos afterward. Everyone would think I had done it just ta get the throne."

He sighed, and the next words he spoke were so low in volume Thuradin had to lean in closer to hear them.

"If I could pardon ye for yer actions, I would. But my

hands are tied. Everyone wants the trial ta end in blood, and if I do anything ta try and stop it, my head will be put on a pike right next ta yers, and that would serve no purpose. I have ta let things take their course, but I've told the Council of Judges ta consider sparing yer life in light of yer past services ta the Dwarven Kingdom."

Thuradin nodded. He understood everything better than Dunkell seemed to think he did. He had killed the King, and so he, in turn, must be killed. Most likely, the trial would be just for show. The list of charges against him was evidence of this. He knew that, even despite Dunkell's plea for clemency, he would most likely be executed in the most brutal manner. He didn't expect any real justice to come from it.

Still, he was grateful Dunkell had at least tried to influence the Council to spare him, despite the huge risk he took in doing so.

The topic of conversation eventually turned away from the upcoming trial, and the two dwarves began to share stories. Thuradin talked about the challenges he had to go through during his quest in the outside world. Dunkell talked about how he had gone to the burrowers' city to warn them of the coming dwarven invasion and helped them prepare their defenses. Both dwarves avoided the topic of Ronorim.

Dunkell was just starting to give details about the burrowers' city and what life was like there when the two royal guards reentered the room and stated grimly that there were important affairs waiting for the King's attention. Dunkell left his chair grudgingly, gave one last nod in Thuradin's direction, and left with the royal guards.

Now only Victria, who had sat in her chair silently the

entire time, was there to keep him company. The two shared some small talk. They tried to stay on light topics, but Thuradin could tell the viatari's thoughts were elsewhere.

"Why are ye here?" he asked suddenly.

"What do you mean?" Victria said, taken aback by the question.

"Why are ye still in the Dwarven Kingdom? Why haven't ye returned ta Aleganthia yet?"

"Don't misunderstand," he added quickly when he saw her eyes fill with hurt. "I'm nae trying ta chase ye out of here, I'm just curious. Is there a reason?"

"Yes, actually," Victria said slowly, as if thinking how she should best explain her presence. "I stayed because I was worried about you."

"Worried about me?"

"Is it surprising?" she said with a shrug. "We *are* friends, after all. It would be stranger, I think, after everything we have been through, if I just left you to struggle through your troubles by yourself."

Thuradin thought on that for a moment. He hadn't thought about it before, but he quickly realized he *did* see Victria as a friend. They had looked out for each other in the outside world as well as within the mountains. He always felt relaxed when he was in her presence, something he didn't feel around the other viatari, even Felix. They were friends, and friends didn't abandon each other in their darkest times.

"What about Tessa and Natiari?" he asked.

Victria laughed softly. "Oh, they left a few days ago once they decided I no longer needed their protection. Plus, they needed to report to Felix what happened here. We've been gone for months, after all."

After that, the conversation continued to change from one small topic to another. They didn't really care what they talked about, so long as it distracted them from the memories of recent events and thoughts of the upcoming trial.

At one point during a conversation about food, Thuradin asked Victria what was going to happen to the alliance she had made with Ronorim.

"The alliance is still valid," she said, grinning with relief. "Not many dwarves know the viatari were involved in Ronorim's death since most of the ones who did were buried along with him. Dunkell placed the royal seal on the document a couple days ago."

They continued talking for a couple more hours, but eventually even Victria had to leave. She got up, keeping her gaze on Thuradin as she walked toward the door. He hadn't thought of the upcoming trial the entire time she was in the room, but now that he watched her leave with eyes full of worry, as if this might be the last time she saw him, he felt his stomach tighten.

He forced himself to relax. He didn't deserve to be nervous. He knew he deserved whatever sentence he received from the Council of Judges.

When the door to his room closed, he lay down on his bed and closed his eyes. He doubted he would be allowed to leave the room while he waited for his trial to come, so he decided to sleep the days away. That way, at least, time would seem to go by faster.

The day of the trial started with one of the royal guards waking Thuradin up with a gauntleted fist. He was then taken, wearing nothing but a gray robe the guards had given him and chains clamped around his wrists and ankles, to the

Hall of Judgment.

Now he stood in the center of the Hall. He was in the middle of a ring of bright torches. The glare from the flames made it impossible for him to make out any of the judges on the lower tier of seats. As for the judges, he knew they saw him perfectly.

Thuradin looked around, trying to catch a glimpse of at least some of the dwarves in the circular room. Because of the flames from the torches, though, he could only see those few sitting on the highest level of the tiered, stone seats.

He saw Dunkell sitting on his throne, far above the line of judges on the first tier. He thought he saw Victria sitting nearby. Her arms were placed on her lap with poise, but he noticed her start to fidget as time passed. He saw a few more familiar faces in the upper tiers, many of whom he had thought of as friends. He wondered how many of them still saw him as such.

A deep, gruff voice penetrated the low mutterings of the spectators. "The trial of Thuradin Stonebeard will now begin."

"Ye are hereby accused of the following crimes," proclaimed a voice on Thuradin's left, the herald, who then went on to give a list of mostly nonsensical charges. It wasn't until the voice started to near the end of the list that Thuradin began to pay closer attention.

"—the murder of King Ronorim Ironaxe, the murder of an estimated three hundred and sixty dwarves during the Battle of the Tunnels, and the hiring of the assassin responsible for the murder of King Thelm Ironaxe. What say ye ta these charges?" the herald demanded.

For a moment, Thuradin forgot how to speak. He was being accused of hiring the assassin who killed Thelm? He was sure Dunkell hadn't mentioned that particular charge earlier. He shifted his gaze to where the King sat. He couldn't see clearly because of the flames, but he thought he saw Dunkell shift uncomfortably in his chair.

As if it weren't bad enough he had killed Ronorim and almost four hundred dwarves, he had to be charged with killing Thelm now, too?

"What say ye ta these charges?" the herald repeated impatiently.

"I say I am innocent of all charges except the murder of Ronorim and the three hundred and sixty dwarves."

Murmuring could be heard from the assembled dwarves. Thuradin didn't care what they thought. He wouldn't be dishonored further with these false, ridiculous charges.

"Very well," said the deep, gruff voice from somewhere in front of him. "Give us yer testimony."

Thuradin started from the very beginning, the day Ronorim was crowned King. He told them about everything that happened to him during his quest to find the lost King, both in the outside world and in Dun'Burell. He talked about Dunkell's apparent betrayal and of his banishment. He recounted every single detail he could remember about what happened during the final moments before the last battle with the burrowers.

Again, the only piece of information he withheld was the curse the Creature had bestowed upon him. He still didn't feel like he should share it with anyone, even if his life depended on it. Even if he had mentioned it, he doubted anyone would believe him after everything else he had just told them. They would only see the curse as a poor attempt to justify his actions.

So instead, Thuradin explained what he had seen during the final battle with the burrowers. How their city had been filled with innocents. He explained his belief that they weren't so different from the dwarves and that they had only fought so aggressively in order to defend their home from invasion.

Scoffs and grumbling echoed throughout the hall as he said this. No one believed him, not that Thuradin had expected them to. Even with Dunkell as their King, the majority of dwarves still believed the burrowers were nothing more than savages who needed to be wiped out.

He finished giving his testimony and stood silently as he waited for the judges to continue with the proceedings.

There was a pause, then, "We now call for any witnesses of the actions of Thuradin Stonebeard ta please come forward and give their testimony."

Many dwarves volunteered to be witnesses, and Thuradin could do nothing but listen, often in disbelief, as they created fantastical stories of him summoning and controlling hordes of burrowers to steal fruit from the markets, vandalizing the many banks across Tinas Gran, and doing several other things he wasn't guilty of.

One of the witnesses was Aikrig, the cannoneer who had foiled Thuradin's original attempt to take the dynath from the artillery. The young dwarf talked about how Thuradin had been acting like a psychotic burrower-sympathizer ever since his return from the outside world. He mentioned the ridiculous lies the dwarven commander had told to try and trick the cannoneers into giving him their crates of dynath. Finally, he mentioned that Thuradin was the one who had attacked Ronorim first after Ronorim had tried to barter a deal. Out of all the dwarves who had survived the cave-in, Thuradin thought, why him?

All in all, Aikrig's testimony gave everyone in the Hall of

Judgment the exact image they wanted to see Thuradin as: an insane traitor.

The final witness called up to give testimony was Dunkell. The King left his chair and made his way down to stand before the judges. Thuradin wondered what he was going to say. He didn't care if it was bad; everyone else's testimonies had already ensured he would be put to death. He just wanted to hear what would be said.

He lost sight of Dunkell as the King walked across the other side of the torches' glare, but he heard his calm voice perfectly.

"I don't deny that what Thuradin Stonebeard has done must be punished," he began, "but I think many of us are forgetting the many centuries of service he has given to the Dwarven Kingdom. He served us first as a regular soldier and later as the commander of the royal guard. He was the bearer of the saphyrium helm. Aye, he killed my brother, but that doesn't automatically erase every action he has ever performed in the service of our Kingdom. Before ye judge and sentence him, Council, I urge ye once again ta remember Thuradin for the dwarf he was, an honorable warrior, instead of just thinking of the one mistake he made which he believed was for the greater good."

Dunkell returned to his seat in silence. The crowd of spectators was stunned. Not a single dwarf turned to his neighbor to discuss what had just been said. Everyone seemed to remember, even if just for a moment, the admiration they'd had for the dwarf Thuradin had been.

He dared not hope, but he wondered if Dunkell had just saved his life with his testimony.

"The Council will now meet privately ta discuss what Thuradin Stonebeard's sentence will be," announced the deep, gruff voice.

Thuradin was left standing in the center of the ring of torches. He didn't know how long he would have to wait, but not even ten minutes passed before the herald on his left piped up in his ringing voice.

"Has the Council decided?"

"We have," several dwarves said at once.

"What is the sentence of Thuradin Stonebeard?" the herald asked.

It was the deep, gruff voice Thuradin had been hearing that answered. "We, The Council of Judges, find Thuradin Stonebeard guilty of all charges except the hiring of the assassin who murdered King Thelm Ironaxe. We hereby strip him of his title as commander of the royal guard and sentence him inta exile. He shall never again be allowed ta set foot within any part of the Dwarven Kingdom. Should he do so, his life will be forfeited immediately. He has a week ta leave our borders. That is all."

Thuradin was in shock. He heard dwarves getting up all around him and moving about, but he hardly registered it. He felt a mixture of relief and tremendous sadness. He may have been allowed to continue living, but after the next seven days, he would never again be allowed to set foot within the mountains he had called home for his entire life. For him, it was as good as sentencing him to death. The Thuradin who was born here, raised here, fought for everything within the mountains here would no longer exist. That Thuradin would die the minute he stepped out of the mountains. What type of dwarf he would turn into now that he had no home, he had no idea. The future was nothing but a sea of uncertainty now.

The torches were put out, and a couple of royal guards

grabbed him by the arms and led him out of the Hall of Judgment and back to his room. He collapsed onto the bed and, within minutes, was already falling asleep. The trial had exhausted him more than he cared to admit.

As Thuradin drifted off, his thoughts returned to what he was going to do now that he had no home. Should he become a wanderer, wandering the lands outside until the day he died? He didn't like the idea, but that seemed to be his only choice.

You will never find peace in those mountains you call home.

The Creature's curse was fulfilled. Thuradin supposed he never had a chance of stopping it. But, he thought suddenly, maybe the curse was not yet *completely* fulfilled. He remembered the last line of the curse.

By the end of this, you will wish I had decided to kill you.

To stop the Creature, he had ended up having to kill his King, one of his closest friends. He had managed to bring peace between the dwarves and burrowers by separating them, but in doing so, he had lost his reputation and his home. Everyone thought he was a traitor and despised him. He had lost everything.

Despite all that, though, he still didn't wish the Creature had killed him in the artifact. He had lost a lot in the months since his encounter with the strange being, but at least he had managed to prevent one part of the curse from coming to pass. He didn't give in to despair. He did not wish for death.

Three days passed, and Thuradin remained in the Dwarven Kingdom.

Dunkell dropped by his room every once in a while to

remind the exiled dwarf that he should leave soon if he didn't want to be executed, much to Thuradin's annoyance. Victria also remained in the Dwarven Kingdom and dropped by often to talk to him and see how he was doing. He appreciated her visits, but he wondered why she hadn't left for Aleganthia yet, now that the trial was over, and decided he would ask her about it.

The night of the third day, she dropped by once again, and the two shared a meal together and discussed their future plans.

"Where are you going to go?" she asked as she watched the dwarf before her shovel more food onto his plate, which consisted of steamed mushrooms, grilled ram meat, and a few rare pieces of fruit.

Thuradin shrugged, more concerned with his food than with anything else. "I don't know. I was thinking I would just become a wanderer."

"A wanderer?"

"Aye, a wanderer. One who wanders. I'll just wander across the land until I die."

"Well, that's a happy thought," Victria muttered as she bit into one of the rats she had brought for herself and started consuming its life-energies.

"What else am I supposed ta do?" Thuradin demanded. He had thought long and hard over his future but he could think of no alternative, and he doubted Victria could either.

"Well. . . ."

The dwarf stopped eating and looked up at the viatari, wondering what she was about to suggest. She stared back at him with such intensity he thought she might be preparing to attack him.

"I want to help you," she finally said. "So, if you want—if

you think it's a good idea—perhaps you could come back with me to Aleganthia and live there. Aleganthia can become your new home."

She went back to sucking out the life-energies that remained in her rat with a slight frown on her face. Thuradin stared at her with a mixture of hope and surprise.

He was surprised the viatari would offer, on behalf of her entire race, to take in an exiled dwarf. If her offer was genuine, and he could think of no reason why it wouldn't be, he would be able to remain relatively close to the mountains. He would never be able to set foot within them again, but at least he could see them whenever he wanted. Plus, he would have somewhere to stay permanently.

On the other hand, if he took on the life of a wanderer, he would travel through strange lands with unknown dangers for the rest of his life. He would never know what it was to rest again. He would never know peace. And he would be alone.

"That sounds like a fine idea," he finally said.

Victria looked up, the frown vanishing from her face.

"Then we leave tomorrow!" she said, startling Thuradin with her enthusiasm. "Trust me, I know how hard it is to lose your home. I know . . . but I promise you, in time, you will consider Aleganthia your home just as you once considered this place your home."

Thuradin frowned slightly. He might have decided to try living in Aleganthia, but he doubted he would consider it his home, as Victria seemed to think. If there was one thing he knew with absolute confidence, it was that he would always consider the Dwarven Kingdom his only home.

They left early the next day.

Thuradin said his goodbyes to Dunkell, the only dwarf who didn't think he was a traitor, and followed Victria out of Tinas Gran. Borim was still in critical condition, but it looked like he would survive his wounds. Unfortunately, he was still unreachable. Thuradin wouldn't be able to say goodbye to him.

The two travelers rode through the tunnels on their mounts at a fast pace and soon found themselves standing outside the ancient dwarven gates Thuradin had exited several months ago when he first began his quest to find Ronorim.

He sighed. He wanted to stop thinking about the late King, but every time he tried, he could think of nothing *but* him.

They made their way down the mountain with very little difficulty. They had only one encounter with a small pack of grattles. The beasts came hissing at them, thinking they had just cornered an easy meal. Victria dealt with them quickly and ruthlessly, slaying half the pack with her bare hands within seconds. She allowed only a few of them to flee with their lives. Thuradin didn't even need to draw his axes.

As soon as they reached the base of the mountain, they steered their mounts southward, toward Aleganthia.

Thuradin didn't want to turn back. He had promised himself he wouldn't do so. He didn't want to confirm the fact that he was truly banished from his own home. But the temptation was too great. He turned in his saddle and looked up to the spot where they had exited. He narrowed his eyes and thought he could just make out the ancient gate at the mountain's midsection.

The gates were shut.

He faced forward. That was it, then. He was officially exiled from the Dwarven Kingdom.

They had wasted no time in closing the gates to show their unwillingness to welcome him back. He knew it was coming, but still, he felt discouraged that this was his fate. He may be living with the viatari now in Aleganthia, but doubts still pervaded the dwarf's mind. What would happen next? He felt another one of the Creature's cold shocks try to take hold of him like a hand slowly creeping its way to his heart.

He looked around at his surroundings and let everything he saw and felt fill him. The trees were a beautiful mixture of reds, yellows, and browns. The sky was a vibrant blue. The wind, crisp and fresh, held within it a heavy scent of dry wood and old leaves. The sun glowed warmly as it slowly sank toward the horizon. His ram bleated softly, affectionately, as he ran his hand along its shaggy neck. And as he saw all this and listened to the sound of hooves crunching leaves underfoot mix in with birdsong from overhead, the cold hand retreated.

Thank you for reading this book, dear reader! As an indie author, I appreciate each and every one of you for supporting me. The best way to support an indie author, aside from buying and reading their book, is by leaving a review on Amazon and/or Goodreads! If you liked this book, I would appreciate it so much if you took the time to do so. Thanks!

THE ADVENTURE CONTINUES. . .

With Daniel Fansler's second book in the
Chronicles of the First Gods, *Lifting the Siege*…

LIFTING THE SIEGE

Much to Thuradin's annoyance, nothing ever seemed to happen in Zane. The only thing he had witnessed that had been of any interest was a fist fight in the town's market. And disappointingly, it had been stopped too soon by the town's guards and the violators led away.

It was the day after this, while Thuradin was trying to replay the short seconds of the fight in his head and nibbling on a stale piece of bread, that Natiari nudged him.

"Look."

She passed him the spyglass she had been looking through for the past few hours, her short, braided hair bouncing off her shoulders as she pointed to the town's center where a group of figures stood.

As the dwarf looked through the spyglass, the figures took shape. Three of them were clearly human, their rough, weathered features a stark difference to the viatari or even the dwarves. In front of the humans, however, were four cloaked strangers, all of whom were hunched over. They didn't look like any humans he had ever seen.

"What are they?" he asked.

"Keep looking," was all Natiari said.

And so he did, and the longer he did, the more his suspicions grew as to what the figures could be. His fears were confirmed when one of their hoods slipped off due to a sudden gust of wind.

"Burrowers. . . ." he said, shocked.

There was no mistaking the egg-shaped head, the impossibly wrinkled face. He felt Natiari nod next to him as Aniria, the skin around her eyes crinkling from an eager grin, snatched the spyglass from Thuradin's grasp so she could see herself.

"Burrowers." Natiari repeated.

"Wow, those are some ugly—aw, he's already pulled up his cloak!" Aniria muttered, the spyglass jammed against her eye.

"But, that's nae possible!" Thuradin protested. "The burrowers—I trapped them inside their own caverns. The only access they had ta the outside world was through the dwarven tunnels and they can't access them now. Ye were there, ye know this."

Natiari nodded again. She had indeed been involved with the final dwarven conflict against the burrowers along with Victria and another viatari named Tessa Shadoweaver. In fact, she had even helped him do it.

"I remember," she said. "But that doesn't change what we are seeing right now. Besides, these may not be the same burrowers. Look at them again. They seem different from the ones we fought in the Dwarven Kingdom."

Thuradin took back the spyglass from Aniria, whose eyes shone excitedly, and looked at the distant figures again.

Natiari was right, he had to admit. The burrowers he was looking at right now were distinctly different from the ones he had fought all his life. The only ones he had ever known were only slightly taller than a dwarf, due to their hunched backs. These also had hunched backs, but they were at least a foot taller than the tallest human. Their skin looked dark purple rather than the blue-gray he was accustomed to seeing. Thuradin even thought he caught glimpses of sophisticated armor and weapons under the cloaks they wore.

"Do ye think there's a separate burrower civilization that lives out here in the north instead of in the mountains?" Thuradin asked as he passed the spyglass back to Natiari.

"I can't say for sure, but it looks to be the case."

Thuradin didn't like what this could mean for the future. Centuries of fighting between dwarves and burrowers had only recently come to a halt, but if the dwarves, who were now venturing to the outside world more often these days, came into contact with these outside burrowers, old hatreds might reignite. A new war could start, and this time it wouldn't be kept isolated within the Silent Mountains. Thuradin had no doubt that humans and viatari would get involved, and he was certain their involvement would only make matters worse. Much worse.

"My people must never learn of these burrowers," Thuradin said, running his hands through the unbraided parts of his beard. "The consequences if they knew—"

"—would be catastrophic," Natiari finished, her gaze flicking over to Thuradin for a second. "I know, but there is no way to keep such a secret. If they do roam freely outside of the mountains, the dwarves will eventually run into them. We can only hope Dunkell will have gained enough popular support by then and that his ideas are widely accepted by your kind. Otherwise. . . ."

Silence feel between them. Neither one seemed to want to voice just how much death and chaos such a war between all the races might bring.

About the Author

Daniel Fansler has known he's wanted to be a writer since he was thirteen. His debut novel, The Lost King, was written and the world and peoples of Azar born during his senior year in high school. He graduated from Stephen F. Austin State University with a BFA in Creative Writing, which helped him hone his book into what it is today. He lives in Fort Worth with his wife and his cat, Fluffykins.